BOOMER1

DANIEL TORDAY

BOOMER1

ST. MARTIN'S PRESS
NEW YORK

BOOMER1. Copyright © 2018 by Daniel Torday. All rights reserved. Printed in the United States of America. For information, address St. Martin's Press, 175 Fifth Avenue, New York, N.Y. 10010.

www.stmartins.com

Library of Congress Cataloging-in-Publication Data

Names: Torday, Daniel, author.
Title: Boomer1 : a novel / Daniel Torday.
Description: First edition. | New York : St. Martin's Press, 2018.
Identifiers: LCCN 2018018748| ISBN 9781250191793 (hardcover) |
    ISBN 9781250191809 (ebook)
Subjects: | BISAC: FICTION / Literary.
Classification: LCC PS3620.O58747 B66 2018 | DDC 813/.6—dc23
LC record available at https://lccn.loc.gov/2018018748

Our books may be purchased in bulk for promotional, educational, or business use. Please contact your local bookseller or the Macmillan Corporate and Premium Sales Department at 1-800-221-7945, extension 5442, or by email at MacmillanSpecialMarkets@macmillan.com.

First Edition: September 2018

10 9 8 7 6 5 4 3 2 1

For Erin, Generation X; and Abigail and Delia,
giving hope for whatever's next

It is reported that Caesar, when he first heard Brutus speak in public, said to his friends, "I know not what this young man intends, but, whatever he intends, he intends it vehemently."

—PLUTARCH'S *Lives*

He was one of those ideal Russian beings who can suddenly be so struck by some strong idea that it seems to crush them then and there, sometimes even forever.

—DOSTOEVSKY, *Demons*

Let the age and wars of other nations be chanted and their eras and characters be illustrated and that finish the verse. Not so the great psalm of the republic. Here the theme is creative and has vista. Here comes one among the wellbeloved stonecutters and plans with decision and science and sees the solid and beautiful forms of the future where there are now no solid forms.

—WALT WHITMAN, 1855 PREFACE
TO *Leaves of Grass*

BOOK ONE

Book One

PART ONE
CASSIE

CHAPTER ONE

CLAIRE STANKOWITCZ CHANGED HER NAME to Cassie Black at the beginning of her first year of college. It was the best decision she'd ever made. The most decisive she'd ever been, too. It wasn't that she didn't love her mom and dad—they'd been models of parental exceptionalism since she was a kid, allowing her all the freedoms a child, a teenager, could hope for. But upon her arrival at the Wellesley campus after a two-hour flight from central Ohio, what Cassie needed was a clear-cut, empirically observable change. Her parents didn't object. They got a hotel room in Back Bay, a couple blocks from Comm Ave., and the Wednesday before the first day of classes her freshman year they dropped her off at a Boston courthouse, where she legally changed her name. It seemed perfect to Cassie that she would share a last name with the lead singer of the Pixies in the town where the Pixies had grown their legend two decades earlier.

By the time she was a sophomore, Cassie's response to her new name had grown reflexive. She'd picked up the bass and joined a punk band—well, a post-punk band. Though she'd played violin in school bands since she was six, and though some part of her musical mind would always love playing bluegrass and old-time fiddle, holding a big black Epiphone bass down somewhere below her waist, thumping it with a .50mm black pick while glaring into the middle distance behind the crowd, was the look and the sound she wanted *now*. By the time she was a senior, the U.S. had been in Afghanistan for three years, and her bandmates made a plan to move to Greenpoint, Brooklyn. A group of

alums from the class of 2002 had rented a two-story row house on Eagle Street, and rooms were renting there for six hundred dollars a
month, about half of what Cassie had heard it might cost to live in
Brooklyn. They'd named themselves the Pollys (their lead singer Natalia's early desire to have them be called either the Rape Me's or the
Box-Shaped Hearts was slammed shut the moment she spoke them
into her P-58) and within their first month in the city they had a gig at
a house party in Williamsburg. It wasn't the Williamsburg they'd
pictured—every block closer to the Bedford L was more perfectly renovated, chrome-and-glass façades and Mercedes GLK SUVs double-parked
outside of Planet Thailand—but their part of the mega-neighborhood
Greenpoint and Williamsburg and Bushwick combined to make was
ugly enough in winter, devoid of trees, children, and available parking.
Cassie watched old Polish women in their babushkas push their black
wire carts home from the Pathmark and felt she'd arrived.

That first gig was on the eleventh floor of an iconic building on Kent
Ave. The place was pre-cancerous with artists' lofts. It was owned by a
group of Hasids who rented the basement to a matzoh company that
baked the cracker tar-black to be sold for Seders around the city. A
couple years after the Pollys' first gig the building would catch fire
from those Orthodox bakers and burn, only to be rebuilt to spec within
a year. Now it was still standing. Cassie and her bandmates plugged in
at the back of a wide-open loft, 1,200 square feet of mostly unfurnished
urban mixed-use space, at its back a wall made of windows. Out across
the bottom of the East River stood the buildings of the financial district like some static play being eternally staged. Maybe fifty bespecta-
cled recent college grads milled around drinking Pabst Blue Ribbon
from the can and Miller High Life from the bottle.

The Pollys played their set loud, closed with their blazing-fast punk
version of Ralph Stanley's "Pretty Polly"—if Kurt Cobain could cover
Lead Belly, they could cover the Clinch Mountain Boys—and then a
traditional bluegrass band set up to play next. How would anyone even
hear them with the instant tinnitus in their ears? Cassie wondered. By
the time the second band got their radio mic set up and huddled around
it, bass far to the back and guitar, mandolin, banjo, and fiddle crouched

near the mic, her ears had stopped ringing. The band was good. Unlike the banjo-fronted Ralph Stanley setup, now the mandolin player functioned as the lead instrument—he picked out sloppy lines, but he sang high and hard like a girl, and Cassie found herself paying more attention than she'd expected. There was a certain poetry to the fact that they did their own version of "Pretty Polly" themselves, a wink right back at the Pollys, making the old sound new sound old. After the gig ended the mandolin player came over to her while she was packing up her bass.

"You guys slayed tonight," he said. He was probably five or six years older than she was. Cassie could see where his hair was thinning around his widow's peak, light trickling its way through to his white scalp, though what hair he had still was longish. He was wearing a kelly green T-shirt that said GETTIN' LUCKY IN KENTUCKY. Part of Cassie couldn't help but wonder if he was making fun of her own home in the Midwest wearing it. "Probably should've opened for you instead of the other way around. I doubt anyone could even hear us after your amps."

"They're not our amps," Cassie said. Then she went over to find the rest of the Pollys. She'd been sleeping with Natalia for a month now, and the last thing that relationship needed—that the band needed—was for their lead singer to think she was flirting with a bluegrass-mandolin-playing, ironic-thrift-shop-T-shirted twenty-something-year-old boy.

The best thing that came of that first Williamsburg gig was that the younger sister of the guy who booked shows for CBGB was there. She e-mailed Natalia, who did all the booking for the band, to tell her that she thought her brother would like them. Did they have a CD? They didn't, but they'd made a MySpace page where you could stream two tracks they'd recorded on Cassie's iMac back at Wellesley. Natalia sent a link. Before they knew it, they had a gig in Manhattan. It was three months away, but it was a gig. It didn't make Cassie's day job feel a whole lot better. Really it was a night job, working as a cocktail waitress at the bar in the basement of the Chelsea Hotel. She only had to work three nights a week and she made more than enough to pay rent—bottle service meant sometimes a group of Russian oligarchs' kids might drop two grand in a night, three even, might leave a half-full bottle on the table on their way to Scores. The tip, if they were drunk enough on Grey Goose shots, could be two, three hundred bucks. It was exhausting work. It took Cassie a day to sleep off the nights. That left her the equivalent of a long weekend every week to rehearse, read, just walk around Manhattan and Brooklyn.

The night of their CBGB show Cassie was nervous, but not as nervous as she suspected. This was CBGB! Television had played here, Talking Heads and Big Star and Patti Smith. It was like she was walking between the silent ghosts of still-living Alex Chilton and David Byrne as she made her way to the space backstage. Sure, there was an ATM up front now, and next door they'd opened CB's Gallery, where keening acoustic guitarists could sit on stools and whisper-sing Elliott Smith covers into a mic like they'd been booked at the Living Room. But this was at least a version of living out her dreams. There were four bands on that night. The Pollys were second. They stood in front of the stage and watched as a six-foot-eight bundle of gangly limbs flailed around and screamed into the mic like he was the embodied ghost of Ian Curtis. They were just about to head backstage when someone pushed her shoulder.

"You're gonna kill tonight," the guy said. She knew him but it took her a second to place how. Her brain just began to formulate an image of a mandolin before her when he said, "Mandolinist. From the Willow Gardens." Cassie did remember him, but she continued just to kind of scowl at him. "The bluegrass band from that Billyburg loft party this summer."

"Right," Cassie said. She gave a look around her—she was still with Natalia, though outside of band practice they hadn't seen each other much the past month, and she didn't want this to look bad. But the rest of the band had already headed backstage. "Right, the Willow Gardens. Terrible fucking name."

"That's the hardest thing," he said. "Coming up with a good name. My name's Mark, by the way. Which would also be a terrible band name: The Mark."

"The Mark By the Way would be worse," Cassie said.

"Yeah. Sucks trying to come up with a band name. We had friends who performed for a year as Hard Raisin' before they realized it sounded like they were named after a hard raisin." She didn't say anything. "Yours is damn good, though. Name. Your band name. That was always one of my favorite Nirvana songs."

Cassie was surprised to learn that this bluegrasser even knew about Kurt Cobain, but she supposed being a bit older, they must have been big when he was in high school. She couldn't keep eye contact, so she looked down to where she could see he was clasping his hands together. They were very nice hands. She could see where they had a light covering of blond hairs. They looked soft, but she could see as his left hand worked its fingertips over his right that they were calloused from fretting his mandolin. Cassie had always been attracted to hands. She looked up. She asked Mark what he was doing here.

"The Willow Gardens are playing next door at CB's Gallery in like an hour."

"Oh, right, next door," Cassie said. "Of course."

"You know the 'BG' in CBGB does mean 'bluegrass,'" Mark said. "It's not that weird we're playing here." Cassie figured he must have noted the sour look on her face, which come to think of it she wasn't doing much to hide.

"Anyway," he said. "Saw your guys' name up on the ad in *The Village Voice* and thought I'd drop by to say hi. So. Hi." He turned to leave. For a second she felt bad for having given him a hard time about the band name. She hadn't slept with a man in a couple years, more, so maybe Natalia wouldn't assume anything even if she saw them.

"You know, I used to play fiddle," she said. All at once she could see something brand new in this guy's face, a dimple that appeared in the lower right corner of his mouth and a tautness that developed at the corners of his eyes—he started to ask all kinds of questions about where she was from, what brought her here, telling her that fiddlers could make good money in bluegrass bands in the city playing weddings and brunches, and it was feeling comfortable, less like he was trying to pick her up than that he was trying to be her friend, when she saw Natalia was standing next to the stage watching them talk.

"Shit," Cassie said. "Shit shit fuck. Shit." She walked away without saying good-bye.

The Pollys played their gig and they were good, the best they'd ever been, but they were second billing at CBGB, so maybe forty people were there, bobbing heads a bit in the beer-rimed room. Even Mark turned tail and headed out before they finished, whether because he needed to get next door for his show or because he'd grown bored of the music, she couldn't tell. They didn't get another invite to play, but more problematic, what Cassie thought was a good gig, full of energy, Natalia thought was something different.

"The fuck were you talking to before we played," Natalia said. She was five foot four, with a thin, tight black faux-hawk and a smattering of freckles on her Cremona-colored cheeks. Cassie told her that it was the mandolin player from the band that they opened for in Williamsburg.

"The Pussy Willows?" Natalia said.

"Willow Gardens," Cassie said. "C'mon, they were—" Before she started to defend them only a couple hours after telling their lead singer and mandolin player to his face how bad she thought the name was, she stopped herself. But she didn't stop the inevitable. Natalia felt the show had been a debacle. She grew convinced it was Cassie's fault. In the coming months a sense that something was off grew among the Pollys. Natalia kept stopping mid-song at band practices. Cassie was dropping the beat, she said. She stopped so many times their drummer stopped one time herself—"*Someone's* dropping the beat," she said, "and I'm not saying who it is. But. It's not me. I don't think the Yeah Yeah Yeahs got to where they are because someone couldn't keep time."

So one afternoon the day after she made almost six hundred bucks on bottle service, Cassie came to band practice to find that no one else was taking their instruments out. No mics were plugged in. They were just sitting.

"Listen," Natalia said. "This one's a little tough, but we met this chick after a show at Mercury Lounge. This—this bassist. From another band. But now the band's breaking up."

"She used to sit in with Liz Phair," their drummer said.

"You met another fucking bassist?" Cassie said. "What does that even mean. We were in Early Modernist Poetry together freshman year. Who cares you met a bassist?"

"Liz fucking Phair," the drummer said. "She has Kim Gordon's cell number," she said. "They text."

So Cassie was out of the band she'd founded. Not only that—all at once she wasn't sleeping with Natalia anymore. The house on Eagle Street seemed newly an impossibility. She found a room posted on Craigslist just a couple blocks away and sent an e-mail. It was a room in a house with a bunch of dudes, but Cassie wanted out yesterday. She was gone within a week. Not one member of the Pollys was home the afternoon she moved. She made twelve trips from Eagle Street a block south to her new apartment, hunched over as she lugged her books in one of those black wire carts the old Polish women used to lug groceries around the neighborhood. She passed twelve old Polish women in their babushkas on her way. Suddenly they didn't look so much like what she *wanted* to be as they looked like, well, what she was *becoming*.

Had become.

CHAPTER TWO

THE FIRST WEEKEND in her new place Cassie found she'd lost a shift at the Chelsea Hotel—there was a private party, the people were bringing their own catering service. She asked Curtis, her new housemate, what was happening in the apartment that night. "We're having kind of a big party," he said. "There's a band playing." Cassie considered just holing up in her new room and reading the Jeanette Winterson she'd found earlier that week at Housing Works, but she couldn't concentrate. By ten there must have been fifty people in the apartment. She heard someone picking a banjo. She came out into the main space. She didn't recognize one face. Where for the past seven years at every party she went to there were, like cairns appearing on a long hike, the faces of Natalia and Svetlana and all the friends who'd come to every Pollys show, now she was on a barren granite rock with no sign to confirm she was headed any direction but lost. She needed something to drink.

She was about to return to her room when she looked up and there, standing by the refrigerator with a Pabst Blue Ribbon trucker's cap and a Miller High Life bottle in his hand, was Mark. The mandolin player from the Pussy Willows. The Willow Gardens.

"What on earth are you doing?" he said when she walked up.

"I live here," she said. "What the fuck are *you* doing here?"

"My buddies from Colgate are your roommates, I guess," he said. "And the Willow Gardens are playing here tonight." So Cassie settled in and listened while Mark's band played. They were better than last time. Without a radio mic to huddle around—the room was small enough they needed no amplification, they sang loud and played their instruments as loud as they could be played—they were far more natural. The three-part harmonies they sang were balanced, sharp, like one big chord projecting out into the room on each chorus. Cassie had always liked the idea of a chord, three notes struck together to make a single sound. Mark's mandolin playing was far more refined than the last time she saw them, tight and loud and precise, jumping the one like Bill Monroe.

As the Willow Gardens came to the end of their set, Mark said, yelling as loud as he sang, "We're gonna get a special friend to come up and play one with us here tonight." He let his mandolin fall by his side. He grabbed the fiddle and bow out of his fiddler's hand. "The killer bassist from one of my favorite new bands, the Pollys, is here tonight." Mark was looking right at Cassie. It felt as if he'd just asked her to marry him in front of the whole party. "Well, come on up, friend!" he said, in an Appalachian accent he'd never before used. Cassie tried not to, but now everyone around her had taken a step back, and it was as if a whole bucket of pig's blood might be dropped on her head if she didn't move from where she was standing. Or it was weirdly like being called out by her father—knowing she didn't want to do what he said, but knowing she would have to. By the time she got to the front of the room, the guitarist was capoing his guitar to the second fret.

"What the fuck," she said as quietly as she could.

"Nothing the fuck," Mark said. "You said you could play. So let's get you playing. 'Pretty Polly' work for you? Like the way David Grisman does it, straightforward in A."

Before she could pick up the bow, the guitarist had started the song, and the bass was thumping, and the truth was that Cassie had gone with her father—her conservative father, who lectured her on how sex was an act with a purpose God intended to take place between a man and a woman for the express intent of procreation, any pleasure was an ancillary—to the Mohican Bluegrass Festival in central Ohio every summer since she was three. She couldn't *not* play the melody to that song when a band was playing. All at once it was as if she'd changed her name back, as if she was Claire Stankowitcz again, her name less rock and roll but her hands far more adept at their instrument. And here was the thing for Claire/Cassie: it was the freest she'd felt in years. Ever. Though she felt timid for the first bar or two, soon she tore into each fiddle break the band gave her, and the small crowd in the teeming apartment roared. She stayed up there for five more songs, then finished playing and shotgunned six Pabst Blue Ribbons with Mark in the kitchen of her new apartment, just a block and a half from the Eagle Street place, and at a little past five in the morning, as the thin Greenpoint sun was starting to wriggle its wretched bony fingers into her new apartment, she took a man back with her to bed for the first time since her sophomore year of college. His hands were just what she'd hoped they might be when she saw them in CBGB—the soft hands of a man who'd not worked with them, but not too soft, rough and hard at the fingertips from his calluses. Her and Mark's expressed intent was not procreation—Jesus, she hoped it wasn't and wouldn't ever be, and for certain little was expressed other than the need for a condom— but for the first time in years, whatever anxiety she felt, thinking of her father's imperious face, was gone. Cassie fell into a drunken state that passed for sleep with a strange jittery calm. For now.

CHAPTER THREE

A YEAR INTO LIVING with him in her new apartment, the only thing that changed for Cassie was everything. Mark got her a job as a fact-checker at *US Weekly,* a magazine she hated more than she hated the Republican Party—more than the very notion of political parties, even. Natalia had called it "United States Weekly" with as much disdain for the "US" as the "us." But now here she was, making eighteen dollars an hour calling Hollywood publicists to make sure they'd spelled Tom Cruise's name right in galley pages (one time they actually somehow *hadn't* spelled it right, but that was beside the point). On weekends she and Mark spent their afternoons walking deep into Prospect Park, instruments in tow, where they would head into the woods or over to the duck pond and play some new fiddle tune together. Mark had quit his own magazine job and was working on a Ph.D. at CUNY now, and so he had all the time in the world—to worry about what was ahead. The world wasn't conforming to his ideas of what it should be.

"I mean it's impossible to find a full-time teaching job," he'd say. "Quentin himself said that after four years on the market, he just decided to go back to his magazine job—but it was gone. Some twenty-two-year-old was doing it, and making a grand a year for each year he'd been alive. There was one disciple of some *New Yorker* staff writer who's been at the magazine since like the fifties, who got a replacement gig at Wesleyan last year, teaching a full load for the year, and that's best-case scenario. Maybe one class at Sarah Lawrence making seven grand if things go well. Meanwhile, some eighty-three-year-old professor still won't retire." At times it seemed like he was thinking about it even when they were singing—she'd be blaring a high tenor over his lead on "You Won't Be Satisfied That Way," and she could see in his eyes all he was thinking about was the English tenure-track jobs wiki and the tenured faculty, already past retirement age, who would be interviewing him if he ever got far enough to be interviewed. The pallor of his face grew more and more like the color of pulped paper.

It did not seem healthy.

At the same time, it felt almost as if there was a groundswell rising, people decrying baby boomers in louder ways every day, just like Mark, articles in the *Times* and the *WSJ*. Some small pockets of protest had arisen on college campuses. It wasn't enough and it wasn't fast enough for Mark. Nothing was ever fast enough for Mark—progress, his own place in the academic world, her solos on Jimmy Martin songs, her orgasms. His face was a pallid mandala of impatience. His whole world was one homogenous inert rush.

He did encounter a shadow of hope one day the second winter they were together. Mark had been working on his dissertation, and around the same time he started writing about the influence of nineteenth-century American writers on Emma Goldman, there was a prominent reissue of Goldman's early essays. Mark had always been drawn, intellectually, to the strident tone Goldman took on, her anarchism was secondary, tertiary—Mark cared about language, and he loved hers, the forcefulness of her tone. For years he'd tried to get the editors of the magazine where he worked to send him to Marxism conferences to see what Goldman's influence was now. But it just wasn't clear what the story was—there were no assassination-of-McKinley reenactors, no Goldmanists in small cells across the country. After years of failing to figure out how, now he would get to write about Goldman. He'd loved Thoreau and Emerson and Whitman. Mark had sent an e-mail to the editor of the most prominent hipster intellectual journal in the country, *The Unified Theory*, and the editor was somehow interested. They wondered if he might want to write ten thousand words on Goldman and the great nineteenth-century Americans. Six writers whose work had appeared in *The Unified Theory* in the past four years had appeared in *The New Yorker* sometime soon after. The editors were all recent graduates of Ivy League Ph.D. programs in English and Cultural Studies, but they'd gotten the approval of some of their former professors, baby boomers whose word carried a different kind of cultural capital and whose blurbs appeared on the magazine's covers as if it were a debut novel instead of an intellectual quarterly.

For the next six months that was all Mark did with his free time—work on this piece on the prophetic voice in Thoreau, Emerson, and Emma Goldman. Cassie had been making good money on the side playing Sunday brunches with the Willow Gardens. Suddenly Mark wanted the Willow Gardens to go on hiatus for the year. It was not a good situation for her, but at the same time there was a thin pink hue to his cheeks for the first time in months. Cassie asked him if he couldn't do both—play music and write this banal essay no one would ever read (she elided the words "banal" and "no one would ever read" when she said it). He said he couldn't do both (Mark never elided anything when he said anything). Cassie asked him how he might feel if he was denied the opportunity to have sex with her during the hiatus.

Mark paused. He looked at her.

"I don't see how that's relevant," he said. "Fucking and art. They are entirely separate."

Cassie agreed.

For a month and then for another month the Willow Gardens didn't play gigs, Mark and Cassie didn't so much as kiss, and Mark's skin began to look increasingly wan again on the few walks they took in Prospect Park. The only benefit to her from sleeping with a man for the first time since she was an undergraduate was the low-level anxiety over her father it alleviated, that subconscious sense that he might approve that their being together at least *could* lead to procreation if she would one day allow it. But now they weren't having sex, which couldn't lead to procreation, either. At least if she was with a woman, she would be not procreating while experiencing pleasure.

"Listen," Cassie said. "I know it hasn't been a great period for you, but I care about you. I'm a little worried."

"What about?" he said. He was not making eye contact. He kept looking at something behind her or next to her, or at her elbow.

"About you, shithead," Cassie said. "You're gonna make me say it out loud? I'm a little worried about you."

"I'm a little worried, too," Mark said. "About me. But I gotta get this draft knocked out."

"I don't care about your draft anymore, Mark," Cassie said. "I don't know if I ever did. I don't know how much longer I can do this." She heard a cardinal call out its sharp chirp somewhere in the oaks over their heads. When she was a kid her father had one of those little red wood-and-iron bird-call makers and the one birdsong he'd taught her to recognize was the cardinal's. Maybe that's what he'd been looking at instead of her eyes. Three kids rode by on longboards, and once they passed and she could see their faces, Cassie realized they weren't kids but grown men with beards and more likely than not wives, jobs, kids, 401(k)s, 403(b)s. Was maturity immutable? Like energy, a property finite and calculable in the universe? Grown adults acting like kids. She wondered if it was because they wanted to, or because the baby boomers kept their death grip on all the jobs and possessions they had to maintain their adolescence until adulthood was relinquished to them by the previous generations. She wondered if she thought that because she thought that, or if she thought that because Mark had said it so many times it had become reflexive for her to think it, too.

Now for the first time in months Mark looked at her.

"Shit," he said. "It's gotten that far?"

She didn't say it hadn't.

The next weekend, rather than heading down to Prospect Park, Mark told Cassie he wanted to take her on a trip to Midtown. They never went into Manhattan on weekends—Manhattan was where young Brooklynites went to work on weekdays. It was not where they spent their free time. Brooklyn was where they rested, played, drank hoppy IPAs. But on this Sunday they rode the train up to Midtown, and after they got off at Times Square, Mark walked her over to Forty-eighth Street. She was so quietly pleased to see him doing something other than moping, she didn't yet ask what they were doing there. On occasion they ironically went to the Carnegie Deli for an ironic Reuben. Perhaps they would do so today.

For one whole block every storefront displayed every kind of jewel and precious metal you could imagine. Emeralds, rubies, but mostly diamonds. Diamonds, diamonds, diamonds. Princess cut, perfect cut, colored and uncolored and VV-2, I-1, every way of evaluating stones was used there. Cassie knew you weren't supposed to buy blood diamonds, that DeBeers and the others had ravaged South Africa and Zimbabwe (her college anthro professor had still called it Rhodesia) for them, but now they'd walked down a short flight of four steps somewhere in the middle of the Diamond District—every storefront looked the same to her, the way when you were walking through Prague at some point you realized every store selling amber jewelry was selling the same amber jewelry. Across from them was a Hasid with a wide, black-brimmed hat. Cassie was so disoriented it took her a minute to understand he was waiting for an answer to something he'd said. He was asking them questions about how they felt about white gold.

"One can have a feeling about white gold?" Cassie said. "Like a pre-established feeling? Or one that develops from long experience?"

The Hasid just stared at her for a moment. She didn't like being stared at and she didn't understand why she and Mark hadn't talked about this first.

"A woman makes her choice between white gold and platinum," he said.

She looked from him to Mark, who sat next to her, at the very front of his chair, both feet propped up on their toes, looking at her. "Or titanium. If you prefer."

"What the fuck's the difference, even?" Cassie asked.

"Gold is softer," the Hasid said. His teeth were the yellow of a buttered-popcorn Jelly Belly jelly bean. He'd bared them. He bit into the strip of white gold in his hands. He passed it to Mark, whose fingers slipped over the saliva left there. "See?" the dealer said. "Little marks. Not to worry—that one needs to be melted down for solder at this point. But you pick. Titanium is so hard even a saw can't cut it. Which means it is beautiful and strong but can pose a problem."

"A problem?" Mark said. It was the first question he'd asked since they started talking. He'd been leaving as much space for Cassie to talk as possible. She could tell.

"Say a couple got in a car accident—let it not be so, Ha'shem, but it does happen, everything and anything can happen—and they can't cut the ring off. Instead they have to cut the finger off. Very unlikely. But that's why sometimes a woman will opt against it."

Cassie hadn't given a single thought to the difference between hardness in metals, let alone being in a couple that rode in cars long enough to chance getting in an accident that might require digital amputation. She'd been living in New York without a car for long enough that when she visited her folks at home in Ohio, driving felt like a novelty, like playing at taxi driver. Next she might pretend to be a fireman, she'd think as she passed back down beneath the gargantuan leaves of the oaks lining State Route 36, not far from their house. Next a schoolteacher. Ichthyologist. Philatelist. Limo driver. Maybe her parents' friends could afford to pay her to drive them around, invest in her rare stamps. Fish research.

Mark walked Cassie across to the downtown side of Forty-seventh Street, where there was a bazaar of gems—she didn't even realize when they were in with the Hasid that he was there only to show them settings, that looking at the stones themselves happened in a different market. A woman in her forties, with straw-like hair and a scalp-line that could only be made by a wig, pulled out a tray with maybe three dozen diamonds. She asked Cassie which she liked best. Cassie had to say something, anything—the only thing she wanted less than being here was to make a scene at that moment and draw attention to herself and to Mark—so she pointed to an elongated stone, shaped like the eye of Sauron in the *Lord of the Rings* movies, because it seemed to throw light back up at her like a star.

"That's the one?" the wigged woman said.

"Well, we're looking," Mark said. He kept not saying much, as if to protect himself from having to admit he'd thought this was a good idea, that it would please her somehow. Cassie hadn't said anything yet. This was the first time she understood his intentions.

She said, "We haven't even discussed it," and looked at Mark, hard. "Like, ever." He looked angry. But also a little confused.

"Well, what did you think we were coming to Forty-seventh Street for?" Cassie said nothing. "Well, you never know," Mark said.

"For now I sure do," Cassie said. She saw how hurt he appeared and she said, "I mean, I think. Assume." The woman in the wig stared down at her fingers. Clearly this wasn't a new thing to her, a couple fighting while shopping for rings.

"Perhaps you'd like to consider an emerald instead? For the time being?"

Cassie thought that while she had no interest in an emerald it was at least more likely to be something she'd accept.

Mark turned to the woman.

"You could e-mail me prices later," he said.

As they were leaving Cassie saw that the booth next to it had little white tags attached to the tray each diamond sat on—a perfect-cut like the one they'd seen was labeled $12,988. They could pay rent for six months for what one of these diamonds cost.

On the subway ride home, Cassie sat staring across the way to an advertisement from the Department of Homeland Security: "If You See Something Say Something," which had been as ubiquitous as the "Dan Smith Will Teach You Guitar" flyers posted to every bulletin board in every sandwich shop near her office in Midtown during that period. She was more likely to pay Dan Smith to teach her guitar than to say something about something she'd seen. What she'd seen this afternoon was delusion from Mark on a scale so immense she didn't know what to say. She had to say something. The whole thing was so surprising it was as if she hadn't had time to comment. The obvious thing to say was: *I don't want a ring because I don't want to marry you. Marry anyone.* At one point she almost did say just that, but when she looked at him, ready to speak, his face had color in it again, and he smiled at her and she just looked back down at the copy of *MOJO* magazine she'd brought with her as if not seeing or saying anything, at the same time.

When they got back to their place she let Mark kiss her neck, let

him get her near to the point of orgasm and quickly well past it himself. Then, while he kissed her neck, she brought herself around, too.
Then they lay there. Three mosquitoes bobbed by the bed as Mark and
Cassie lay naked and lightly covered in grime from a Saturday afternoon in Midtown.

"So did you get a sense of which ring you liked best?"

"It wasn't like buying a ring," Cassie said. He asked her what she
meant. "It was like building an avatar—this setting, this kind of stone,
this color, this metal. Maybe the diamond could help the woman pick
out a new hair color. Wasn't there a time when you could just walk into
a store and give them an ungodly sum and you were paying *them* to
figure out what the fuck you wanted?"

Neither of them said anything for quite some time. Mark had his
arm draped across his eyes. Cassie watched as one of the mosquitoes
landed on his forearm, placed its spindly legs on his skin, dipped
its needle, and withdrew what it needed to make eggs. Somewhere on
his skin the tiniest oil rig dipped and slurred, blood coagulated and
sucked up into its parasite. As it withdrew she saw him jerk a bit. He
took his arm from his eyes and started scratching. A not-small part of
her felt joy watching him injured by the female of a species.

"You don't seem all that psyched about it," Mark said. She wasn't
going to say anything. She thought about how this was by far the longest they'd gone without talking about Emma Goldman in one full year.

"Regardless of how I feel about the insane ambushy trip you just
took me on, without asking if I wanted it or even telling me where we
were going—where is that kind of money going to come from, Mark?
I don't get it. It takes six months of fact-checking for me to make that
kind of money."

"I'll find a way," he said. "That's what I do. I find a way." He allowed
himself not to respond to the first part of her questioning. Cassie didn't
raise it again, either.

CHAPTER FOUR

IN THE MONTHS TO COME Cassie understood that not only did she not want Mark Brumfeld spending more than ten thousand dollars on a ring for her, she didn't want him spending that much money on anything, or spending another cent on her. One night a couple weeks after their trip to the Diamond District, Natalia texted. "The Pollys plying Mrcry Lng then aftr to sn cty. come?" Every month or so she would hear from Natalia, a text here or there, asking her to come see the old band play. For a couple of years now it seemed like the last thing in the world she'd do. She even thought of writing her ex-bandmate and ex-girlfriend back to say, "Y th fuck wld I wnt 2 do tht." But she was ready for a night away from literary talk, away from titanium rings and various cuts of diamonds. So while she didn't have it in her to go see her old band play with their new bassist, she headed up to the bar for drinks after. It was nearly midnight by the time she arrived. She'd taken four shots of rye whiskey and had a Brooklyn Lager at home before she got there.

Far to the back of Sin City, all her old bandmates were bellied up to the bar. There were four or five other girls standing beside them. It was unclear to Cassie who was part of the crew and who wasn't. But Natalia caught her eye before she even had a chance to figure out who she should say hi to.

"Well, Jesus Christ if it isn't Cassie Black," she said. She was far enough into her night that her gaze kept falling down to Cassie's elbow, then back up to her face, like she was looking her up and down. "The fuck're you doing here?"

"I figured the time had come, I might as well see what you were up to." Her shoes stuck to the floor. Natalia put an arm around her like they'd never broken up. It felt like returning to her parents' country home in the Wisconsin dells: not just nostalgia for what she'd been missing—though there was that, too—but something new, a new experience that was also every bit as good as she remembered it. A bartender who couldn't have been a day older than Cassie was when she first arrived in the city stood on the bar and poured cans of Budweiser down the front of her shirt. She was wearing a blue tank top that said PBR across the front. Cassie couldn't tell if it stood for Pabst Blue Ribbon or Pro Bull Riding. Natalia kept coming up from behind and snaking her hands up right onto Cassie's breasts. Cassie remembered what those tobacco sunburst hands could do, their brown cuticles so distinct from the pale hands Mark had been touching her with since they got together.

By three A.M. they were back at Natalia's place. She lived in a one-bedroom at the corner of Second and Second, in an apartment her parents had bought as an investment. She'd grown up on the Upper West Side and the New York Cassie and the rest of their Wellesley alum friends were inhabiting would always feel like Natalia's New York, not theirs—both to them and, clearly, to Natalia. Now, here in her apartment, with her arms squeezed around her ex-girlfriend, Cassie felt like time had passed in the tiny observable increments by which Natalia's middle had expanded—it wasn't anything you would notice looking at her in clothes. But when she wrapped her arms around Natalia, Cassie found they didn't fit as neatly as they once had. She was like a balloon with two more breaths breathed into it. Like herself, only now a little more of it. In the morning Cassie's head felt like her brain was a terrible fit for the size of her skull.

"Morning, darlin'," Natalia said. She was wearing the same GETTIN' LUCKY IN KENTUCKY T-shirt Mark had been wearing the night she'd met up with him again in her new apartment. Natalia had slept in it. Cassie couldn't have told her so if she wanted to.

She didn't want to.

"Coincidence of all fucking coincidences you were there last night," Natalia said. "What were you doing at Sin City, anyway?"

"Uh, you texted, yet again, and I decided to go with it. Bored."

"No, I didn't," Natalia said. She'd pushed herself up so that her back was against the crumbling plaster wall next to her bed. The hair in her faux-hawk was mussed against her head.

"Didn't what," Cassie said.

"Didn't fucking text you," Natalia said. "Okay, I'm a little freaked out." She grabbed her phone from her bedside table. It was a little slate-gray Nokia you could slide open to reveal the world's tiniest QWERTY keyboard. "Oh, fuck," she said. "Your number is attached to some old messages I always used to send to Deron. How fucking long have you been getting texts from me?"

Cassie considered lying. But what good would lying do at this point? She was in bed naked with her ex-girlfriend. She said it had been al-most two years. Maybe once a month or so. Natalia had begun to develop light crow's-feet around her eyes. They wrinkled just the slightest bit. A small dimple drew in at the side of her mouth. She looked like she might get truly angry, but then her whole face settled like the topwaters of a man-made pond after a cannonball. "Well, I'm glad I have been. I'm glad you're here. It's like a meet-cute, but in real life, so I guess just a meeting of people, that is also cute. Kind of thing." Cassie wasn't so glad she was there, but she kissed Natalia on the forehead.

"If you're going to text me again," she said, "text just me."

On the 5 train back to her place Cassie thanked the fucking Lord that she knew Mark wouldn't be home, that he'd be out at the coffee shop working on his Goldman essay. Still. Again. But when she got back he was sitting in the kitchen nook.

"Morning morning," he said.

"Listen, before you say anything—"

"No, before *you* say anything," Mark said. "I know I've been crazy. I get it, I truly honestly get it. I was depressed, I wasn't paying attention. *Faites attention!* I know I must've been a nightmare. But it's gonna get better, I swear. First, because this." He was holding a stack of maybe

forty pages of paper between thumb and forefinger. "I finished and
e-mailed the Goldman piece off today. Should hear back soon. But I've
also been realizing—so I got us a couple Willow Garden gigs. A brunch
at a Bobby Flay place up in Midtown that pays, like, crazy money.
Like you-won't-believe-it-if-I-tell-you money. And you're never gonna
fucking believe this—we're gonna headline 9-C finally."

It was the best gig they'd ever had, and while Cassie knew while
they were talking that she wasn't in love with Mark one iota—even his
hands just looked aspic and grimy to her all of a sudden—in the midst
of the ambient guilt of the infidelity she'd just walked home from, she
said, "Great, great, great, that's just great," and went into their bedroom
to sleep off the pleasures of a night with Natalia.

THE FOLLOWING MONTHS moved with the lugubrious pace of waiting for a dial-up connection to get on AOL. Cassie got more fact-
checking for *US Weekly*, and a couple other celebrity rags even started
e-mailing when they had extra work. She got so much work she was
able to give up some shifts at the bar, and to pass work off to Mark, who
was going to run out of funding from his Ph.D. program that summer,
even if he still bought people drinks and used his MasterCard to keep
a bar tab open. The Willow Gardens started getting more gigs—they
opened for Old Crow Medicine Show at Irving Plaza, recorded the
background music for a documentary that was later shelved by PBS.
Mark's Emma Goldman/Thoreau/Emerson piece was accepted by *TUT*.
For a period after the piece came in galley pages, he seemed happy.
The issue arrived and Cassie would come into the bathroom and find
the journal on the back of the toilet, spine cracked to the middle of the
piece. Sometimes she would come home and find Mark lying on the
couch, looking at the contributors' notes page of the journal—they
only allowed contributors a single line of bio. Mark's said, "Mark Brumfeld is a writer living in Brooklyn," which seemed to Cassie a tautology,
or at least a solecism. But six months after the piece ran he'd still never
had even an e-mail from a single reader, and the next issue came out
and there wasn't a single letter to the editor about it. The publisher of

the new Goldman book did not get in touch to thank him. That fall his attempt to go on the academic job market was a near total failure. He had one Skype interview. It didn't go well. He was so stressed during that period he couldn't have had sex if he'd tried.

He hadn't tried.

Not that it mattered to Cassie. She was going to see Natalia's shows again, and found herself at the place on Second and Second almost every week when the Pollys weren't touring. Some nights she went home with Natalia, some nights she didn't, and the uncertainty of it was just the antidote she needed to the stagnation with Mark. During a period when the old band was on the road, for what she figured was no reason other than that she was around more, Mark asked Cassie if she wanted to get dinner.

"Who's paying for a night out?" Cassie said.

"Let's just go. To Superfine. We haven't been there in ages." They walked the long way from their place to DUMBO, and down to Front Street. The Willow Gardens had played a Sunday Bluegrass brunch there every weekend for two years, until they gave it up so Mark could finish his essay. The whole neighborhood was unrecognizable from when they'd first started playing there. For years it had been broken façades and empty storefronts, twelve-story apartment buildings inhabited by squatters and rats. Or just rats. Now they passed a Pinkberry and a West Elm and some huge new bookstore with plate-glass windows and concrete and they were in front of the restaurant before Cassie realized where they were. Inside was all exposed brick and huge oaken joists running the length of the ceiling. The owner of the place came up to greet them.

"Saved you guys your favorite, right next to the stage," Jenna said. She had a long, forced smile on her face. Cassie couldn't for the life of her understand why. They'd left Jenna in the lurch after Mark decided to cancel their last gig on only two days' notice so he could get started on his essay. He'd told Cassie she never even e-mailed him back. Now here she was pulling out a chair for him, and bringing over huevos and Bloody Marys for them both before they'd even had a chance to start looking at the menu. There was a duo onstage, just a mandolin and banjo player playing clawhammer versions of Radiohead songs. Cassie recognized the melody of "Exit Music (For a Film)" just as soon as they started playing.

"I know you probably thought it wasn't on my mind anymore," Mark said. "And I know you expressed ambivalence. Confused. I know. But I think the reality will bring it home for you. And the thing is, I just needed time to get the details together. I mean, it takes more than you might think to put in an order, and get all the specs right, and before I had to take care of selling stock and all—complicated." Cassie hadn't the slightest idea what the fuck he was talking about. "But here," he said.

He pulled a black felt box out of his jeans pocket and put it on the table in front of her.

Probably Cassie should have understood by that point she was being proposed to. But the banjo player kept popping his high G string next to her when it should've been pegged to his fretboard, and the jalepeño-ey smell of the huevos was pervading the space all around them, and so it wasn't until he'd opened the box that Cassie saw Mark was putting a diamond ring in front of her. It was everything she wouldn't have picked. There was a huge stone in the middle, perfect cut. It must have been two, two and a half carats, and a kind of sickly sepia color, like she was looking at it in a 1920s photograph—or better yet like she was looking *through* it at the table, which was sent back to another epoch, much like her sex life had been as a result of her father's retrograde gaze. She could see from the harsh shine on its setting that the band was titanium. Cassie pictured herself hanging half out of the passenger-side window of a Honda Odyssey, somewhere halfway between New York and Philadelphia, on the New Jersey Hellacious Turnpike, her finger swelling, EMTs getting ready to amputate right then and there—"Take the finger off," they'd say, "and if that won't work, just cut from the elbow."

"This really isn't—" Cassie said.

"I know we haven't talked about it since we went up to Forty-seventh Street that day, but like I say, it took me a little while to get things together." He wasn't quite smiling. He was saying a lot of words in a moment that even in the best case was meant to speak for itself. This was not the best case. She could see sweat on his forehead, a little color back in his cheeks for the first time in ages.

"Where on earth did you have money for that?" Cassie said. She was speaking against her own better judgment, but it was all she could do.

"My grandmother bought me Disney stock every year for my birthday since I was a kid. I forgot about it. Then I got to telling Julia about our visit to the Diamond District and she got all excited about the idea, and she reminded me. Then it took some time to get the certificates from down in Baltimore, and go to the bank to get it sold and—well, but wait. Who cares. I'm asking if you'll marry me."

Cassie looked at him with his aspic hands on the table and that huge diamond in front of him. It could have paid for another eight months' rent for them both (and *would* pay for another year's rent for him one day) and the mandolin player onstage kept haphazardly hitting his open G string while he was trying to play the melody of a song from *Kid A* he'd transposed into B-flat minor. It was literally the worst note you could play against the melody. She could see Jenna watching from behind the maître d's station. She'd always had a little thing for Jenna but had never been able to pursue it because she was with Natalia, then Mark, and now Natalia *and* Mark, and Jesus fucking Christ if she didn't just get up from the table, walk out onto Front Street and over to the huge green park that had been built there in the past year, an immense refurbished merry-go-round at its back next to the river. She walked all the way down to the water, where she looked out across the river to where the brown, flat, windowless façade of the AT&T building was staring blankly back at her, evincing not one iota of whatever emotion was buried beneath. She took the A train to Natalia's place, where she could crash for a couple nights while the Pollys were on tour in the Midwest. No matter how she tried, she could not get herself to picture the look on Mark's face as he sat jilted and alone at that table in Superfine. In fact, as seemed to be the case whenever she wasn't in love with someone, or was, for that matter, she couldn't get herself to picture what he looked like at all.

CHAPTER FIVE

IN THE MONTHS THAT FOLLOWED, Cassie saw Mark only at the Willow Gardens practices, where he didn't mention her having jilted him and she didn't say a thing, either. She wondered at first if everyone knew and was just trying to play it cool. After a couple of weeks it became clear no one knew but the two of them—and, she guessed, Jenna, who they wouldn't see unless they went to Superfine again. They had a wedding gig to play up in Connecticut, so they needed to learn a whole slew of new songs. Months passed during which Mark didn't say anything and she didn't say anything until the summer came back around with its blazing heat seeping into the city's asphalt, which seemed to retain daytime heat like the memory of recent scorn, and convection-heated subway stations. One afternoon Mark texted her to see if she'd have lunch with him. It was Brooklyn, so instead they had brunch, they met early, which seemed the safest way. They met at Tom's Diner— Mark had moved to a place on Adelphi, above a coffee shop that had opened there just the week before he moved in, but people were hanging out in Crown Heights now, so he was, too. She still wondered where he'd gotten the money to live alone.

"So listen, I have to tell you something," Mark said after they'd sopped up all the excess hollandaise from their eggs Benedict.

"Me too," Cassie said. She could see in the light that flickered in his watery eyes that he wanted to go first, but she went first instead. "I know I shouldn't have just cut out like that, but I just wasn't ready to talk marriage and I never had been. I never even *could* talk about it. I mean even that first time you took me to the Diamond District, I was like in shock—we hadn't even discussed it. I mean I guess I should've said something, but with you all into it how could I? I just couldn't. Didn't. I don't know how we got our signals crossed so bad—"

"Well, you did go on that trip up to the Diamond District to look at stones with me," he said. "I'm not sure how mixed a message it could've been. Least not on my end. I thought it was a romantic surprise, not some shock. But that's not why I wanted to meet."

Cassie dragged one last piece of English muffin across the viscous yolk-and-hollandaise mess on her plate. She didn't have the energy to argue, to say she didn't even know they were going to the Diamond District that day, and by the time she realized what they were doing, there was no way to tell him.

"I'm moving back home to my parents' place," he said.

She was shocked.

"After you just moved?" she said. He told her that he'd used the money from selling her ring back after she'd stormed out. Blew $2,500 of it on a broker's fee. Then he'd received a bill from the IRS for the sale of all that Disney stock—apparently you were supposed to calculate the difference between the basis points on the stock from its purchase date against the historical value—or was it the current value?—"Jesus, fuck," Mark said, "I still don't even get it—but I owe the IRS thousands of bucks I don't have, and you can't just sit on it like you can a credit card." He was out of money, out of prospects, there was nothing left in magazines these days, and the chance to go back on the academic job market and maybe by some deus ex machina be saved was still months away. He figured a move down to Baltimore, where it was cheaper and where he would reassess, would do him some good. Also his parents said he had to. He could get some shit job and figure out what was next.

So Mark left the city. It was as if Cassie were allowed to romp as free as the mind of god. For the first time in years she could go out with Natalia when the Pollys were back in town and not worry about one of Mark's friends seeing them, or running into him at a bar. She went down to Superfine one night and after closing just went ahead and told

Jenna she'd always wanted to fuck her. She did. She even picked up her Epiphone again—one of the bands Natalia was touring with needed a bassist to fill in on a leg of a Midwestern seven-city tour, and while Cassie didn't get the gig, it was only because the band's regular bassist ended up being able to make it after all. Mark would still be coming up to the city every month or so for gigs with the Willow Gardens, but it was as if Cassie was a fourteenth-century bound Chinese foot who had suddenly been set free of her binding. She only hoped the damage the years of constriction had done to her wasn't irreparable.

CHAPTER SIX

AROUND THAT SAME TIME, mid-summer, Cassie came to Natalia's place one night to find that Deron was over. He was six foot five with a single tight dreadlock down his back and *Steal Your Face* tattooed on the inside of his wrist. Deron had been Mark's editor on the Emma Goldman piece. Deron and Natalia were crouched over his MacBook Air. On the screen in front of them some guy was ranting and rambling, loud but controlled—she heard him punctuate each thing he said by repeating, "Boom boom." She saw a trickle of blood running down the side of his face and then all at once she realized it was Mark Brumfeld himself, hair wild and eyes all red.

This was the only time his own face would appear on-screen, before he got smart and started wearing a mask for his transmissions and took the video down. After not having seen him in person for more than a month, seeing him on-screen like this, it was as if Cassie was able to take him in for the first time in years. He was only six years older than her, but they were the six years that appeared to serve as a caesura between early adulthood and the beginning of middle age. He looked like the deity had puffed one breath too many into his baggy face. He was losing enough hair now you might properly call him more bald than balding—hairlessness having become a state of being, not a mode of becoming. But more than that, he looked so, so angry, a rictus of angst twisting his appearance.

"The fuck are you watching?" Cassie said. She waited for Natalia to light into the insanity of her former fiancé and current bandmate, head Pussy Willow, but Natalia had a kind of sanguine glow in her cheeks. Her eyes were wide.

"You won't believe it, but Mark's kind of fucking awesome—in a batshit crazy kind of way," Natalia said.

"Kind of," Cassie said.

"Not Mark," Deron said. "Isaac Abramson. Everyone I know's watching these YouTube videos he made." She was waiting for him to crack a smile, to start making fun of Mark, or her, or Mark and her, but instead he just brushed past her and headed out into the rollicking summer heat. Natalia paused the video and there Mark sat on the screen, suspended in a state of all-encompassing static anger. Below his face a number very close to ten thousand signaled the quantity of times the video had been viewed. Cassie could see that another browser window was open behind it, where Natalia had shared the video on Facebook, and behind that, another window open with her Tumblr, and the paused image imbedded there, too.

When she got back to her apartment that night, Cassie watched the four videos Mark had posted. In the second half of the one she'd already seen, and in the next three, Mark was wearing a mask, his voice obscured. With him disguised they were oddly more affecting— something about them seemed almost like satire, but once you started listening it was hard to stop. At this point more than twenty thousand other views had been added to the latter videos. Cassie closed the window where she'd been watching Mark on YouTube and clicked over to her own Instagram, where as she scrolled down it seemed as if half the people she knew—people who didn't know Mark—had shared one of his videos. He seemed so sure of what he was saying about the need for millennials to get jobs and the need for baby boomers to retire from theirs, and the truth was that just about everyone she knew needed a job, and just about everyone she knew's parents were in their late sixties or early seventies and still working, and rational or not, it tapped an anger hiding somewhere deep inside her she didn't know was there.

She didn't say anything to Mark about having seen him on YouTube when he came up to the city next. Their gig at the Lakeside Lounge was on a Thursday night at the end of July. They played and she asked Mark if he wanted to stick around the city for a night or two—there was going to be a *The Unified Theory* issue release party that Friday night. Everyone in the literary world showed up at those parties. The full press of the crowd comprised mainly hipsters, grad students, and hangers-on, more creatively curated facial hair than you might find in an HBO series set in the early 1910s, but by the end of the night at least one junior literary editor from *The New Yorker* would come and be swarmed/not-swarmed by writers who hoped one day to write for her. Mark tried to play it cool but it was clear he wanted to go, and he said, yeah, sure, of course he'd come. They met up for soup dumplings and sweet buns at Joe's Shanghai and then walked through the thick mellow stench of hot fish blood, and up to a door on Doyers Street, right in the middle of Chinatown. Mark pushed the buzzer next to a piece of duct tape that had been pasted up there and had the magazine's initials scratched into it. Nothing happened. Cassie was already on her phone.

"Yeah, we're down here, come get us," Cassie said into her cell. Then she looked at Mark. "You have to call to get them to let you in. Buzzer doesn't work." They stood waiting while Mark told her about his day-to-day in Baltimore. He wasn't doing much other than preparing his Boomer Missives. That was how he said it, "Boomer Missives," as if you could hear the capitals when they were spoken, as if she should know that's what he was doing. Something in the way he played it cool, telling her and not telling her about it, she could just tell that he wanted her to be watching. He flirted with her now less like her ex-boyfriend and bandmate than like a toddler, punching the girl he liked most in the pre-K class. He told her he'd gotten a job at a coffee shop near the Barnes & Noble in the shopping center where he'd worked at a TCBY as a teenager. Living in New York, the idea of each detail he provided was so foreign and loathsome to her Cassie couldn't even take it in: feckless shopping center, feckless chain bookstore, feckless chain fro-yo shop awful awful awful. Probably they piped in Elton John and Celine Dion over the speakers.

Deron came down and opened the door for them. He had his

dreadlock wrapped up around his head like he'd started wearing a turban made of his own hair.

"Cassie," he said, though he seemed only to be looking at Mark. They came in through the door and under his breath she heard Deron say, "Boom boom," then smile. She'd never once seen Deron smile. Mark looked up at him like he'd seen an old friend or an old bully, but Deron said nothing further, pretended like it had never happened, returned to his characteristic scowl, and they went up into the party. The building where *TUT* had its office was mainly studio apartments, but on the fourth floor they had rented a huge suite with a couple of rooms with nubby old couches. There was a keg in the corner and some red Solo cups. People stood in groups of four or five. Cassie didn't see anyone she knew but it felt like people were looking at them.

Deron left them. Mark went off to pour a couple of PBRs from the keg in the corner. She saw Deron walk up to him and whisper in his ear, and then the two of them walked off to the room next door. Cassie didn't have her beer yet, and she didn't have anyone to talk to. She followed them. Against her better judgment, here she was following Mark Brumfeld around.

In the next room over, Mark was now sitting on a couch. Deron and a woman she'd never seen before were sitting on metal folding chairs across from him. There was a Che Guevara sticker on the back of the seat the woman was sitting in. Their conversation was hushed and yet animated. Mark looked up and saw that she'd joined them. The woman and Deron were both looking at her like she'd interrupted.

"What's so important that you couldn't bring me my fucking drink?" Cassie said. Mark apologized, and she saw how full of new energy he was and she couldn't believe it but honestly, she felt a little jealous. Of the attention he was getting, of the jolt Mark was getting from all this. Mark kept talking. This was Deron, he said, the editor who'd worked on his Emma Goldman piece—she said she knew him, of course, she was the one who'd introduced *them* to each other to begin with—and one of his co-editors, who had a first-name/last-name name, Regan or Jordan, Cassie couldn't bring herself to care or remember which. Okay, fine, Regan.

"Well, I work for a start-up but mainly I'm the editor of *Czolgosz Quarterly*," the woman said. She was maybe five feet tall, with a sandy brown faux-hawk. Why was it that all the women Cassie met these days had faux-hawks? She was wearing a *TUT* T-shirt and dark black eyeliner. "You might have read it." Cassie said she hadn't. "We disseminated some good information and planning for some protests but the organization never coalesced around a single personality, a single articulable goal."

Regan/Jordan asked who she was and Cassie and Mark looked at each other. Mark told her they played in a band together. Cassie checked facts at some magazine, he said. Regan/Jordan's countenance remained entirely flat. Not a muscle in her face moved. "Okay, this is all beside the point. Look, as I was saying to Isaac, the first thing he needs to do is take down these first four posts. Like, yesterday. Erase the footprint. Does she know about your posts?"

Mark looked at Cassie, who took a second to decide how to answer. Before she could, Deron said that she did. Regan/Jordan's face stayed placid. Then Mark said that if Deron said she did, then she did. The woman assented.

"And as I was saying," Mark said, "that seems crazy. The third missive has ninety thousand hits already. It's all over social media—*and* I'm wearing a mask in it. People are starting to watch. It's taken me like two months to build even this momentum. Momentum which is probably just luck. Why would I stop the momentum now?"

"That's exactly *why* they need to come down. Later on you'll get your viewers back on track. I mean you've got your foot in the chat rooms and those trolls can make things spread like crazy. Easily enough done. Right now you need to scrub all your activity on the surface web and to move all of this over to the Deep Web. No passwords, no IP addresses that your log-ins could be traceable to, nothing on the surface web at all. It could already be too late, but if you're planning to continue, you need to be smarter about it."

Cassie looked at Mark and Deron, expecting to see them laugh at Regan/Jordan's having just said "the Deep Web" aloud as if they were in a Philip K. Dick novel, or something William Gibson had imagined, but they both were listening intently and in earnest. R/J went into a disquisition on the Deep Web. Cassie was even more surprised to find what she was saying was fascinating. Some people called it the Dark Web, or the Deep Web, R/J said. But whatever name you gave it, this other Internet was the place Mark needed to be posting his videos. Getting onto it was simple enough: you just downloaded an application called TOR, which stood for The Onion Router. By clicking on an icon, you would go to a whole different version of the Internet. This other web wasn't searchable on Google, and it wasn't traceable, either. For a period R/J started talking about encryption tools and overseas IP routing, and during all this technical talk Cassie glazed over—could they possibly care about this programmer lingo? Listening to it made her feel like she would never want to have sex with anyone ever again in her long Luddite life.

But Mark seemed to be listening more closely now, and there was something attractive in how attentive he appeared. Deron was just nodding, his turban of hair bounding atop his head. Cassie wondered if Mark wanted to sleep with R/J, or if he was serious about this conversation. From the look on his face, it seemed like some complicated mix of the two. Or uncomplicated. Either way she felt ready to move on. So while Mark learned what he needed to know about a new untraceable web footprint and erasing the details of his current Internet usage, which details these boys were lost in and which sounded like the least revolutionary thing she'd heard in years—Che and Fidel and Raul debating the intricacies of telex messages—Cassie went off to find herself another drink.

Out in the magazine's narrow offices, twenty-somethings packed the space. Talk was of books and employment, of the long-term solvency of entitlement programs and revolution. Cassie moved in and out of conversations where people were talking about the jobs they didn't have and the jobs they didn't think they'd get. One of the first things she'd noticed when she moved to New York was that unlike in other places, the first thing people asked you was what you did. Among friends her age the answer was "unemployed." But she had no one even to ask at that moment. She was still for all intents and purposes alone.

For a period she listened as a kid with a thick Nigerian accent gave a long synopsis of both his reading of Thomas Piketty and his minute critiques of Thomas Piketty and his critiques of Paul Krugman's critiques of Thomas Piketty's critiques of Keynes. Then someone broke in to discuss the latest Houellebecq, which they said wasn't as good as the second Houellebecq, or as *The Possibility of an Island*, which interested her—she hadn't yet read him, but at least they were talking about fiction. When Mark came back into the main space, it seemed like people all around the room were looking at him.

"Seems you've got some fans," Cassie said. "Who would've thought a move to Baltimore would be so fruitful for you, Mark."

"Isaac," he said. She asked him if he was serious. "As I'll ever be. That shit Regan"—so it was Regan for sure then—"was talking in there just blew my mind. I've got some serious work to do at home. Time for me to get going."

There was a new look in Mark's eyes, a color to his face she'd never before seen. For the first time in years Cassie found she wanted to know what he was thinking, rather than to be told, crimson and clover, over and over, every last thought in his thought-tormented head. For the first time *ever* she almost wondered if she should have wanted to marry him, but let the thought pass. He started in on the same talk she'd seen on his YouTube postings, and Cassie was shocked to find herself listening. Soon, instead of going into their deep vocal critique of diluted Keynesian economics and its effect on the current administration, post-morteming once again the effects of the bank bailouts and too big to fail, a half-dozen other people were listening to Mark.

Isaac.

Whatever.

Maybe it was time for them both to clean up their web footprints. Because the talk in the offices of *TUT*, out in the open, wasn't about the minutiae of cleaning up web footprints. It was about the damage that the baby boomers had done to the job prospects of every person in their generation. It was about an organization she'd never heard of, called Silence, of FOCO cells that had begun to crop up, young people talking about how to release the palsied prehensile claw of the baby boomers from the scarce resources in this country, around the globe. At first Mark was talking and people were listening, but at some point Deron returned to the room, and it was like a strong breeze had blown at the back of each blade of grass in there, pushing them from their leaning toward Mark to their natural leaning toward Deron. Cassie couldn't believe it as she watched him do it, but Deron stood up on an actual literal soapbox as he started talking.

"So listen up," Deron said. "We're here to celebrate the launch of issue thirty-three of *TUT,* 'Pretirement,' an issue that wouldn't have come together without the hard work of many of the people in this room. We're especially excited about Grayson's profile of academic union organization in the Midwest, and about Blythe's piece on homegrown terrorism in Finland, which has been getting tons of traffic." There was a smattering of applause. Deron went on to talk about the various NPR shows that would be interviewing writers from the issue, a panel they'd be hosting at the New School later in the month, and Cassie was glad to be listening to just one speaker, all the attention of the whole crowd focused on one leader, rather than the splintered, directionless conversation that had begun to make her head hurt in the previous couple hours. Maybe this was what Regan had meant about coalescing around a single personality. Maybe not. Cassie had had a lot to drink.

When the crowd thinned out around two A.M., Mark and Cassie found a cab out on Canal Street. Mark stared out to the east as they went over the Manhattan Bridge. To the right of their window they looked off to the scattered lights of DUMBO, and beyond that Flatbush, where new towers loomed skeletal in the late-night sodium light. As they reached the other side of the bridge they passed a clock tower that had for years been dark but was now converted into an apartment Cassie had read in *New York* magazine had recently sold for eight figures. The lights were on. Purple neon glowed cool against the East River, stretching miles in either direction past the bridge. Cassie could see maybe a half-dozen people dancing inside the apartment, from that distance in a kind of barely-slow-motion.

"We're headed right over Superfine, right now," Mark said.

"Are you gonna tell me what on earth you talked with Reagordan and Deron about all that time?"

"I'll tell you all about all of it. All in due time."

"Look, I'm not after a fucking Zen koan. I want to know what they were talking about."

"I told them about the Boomer Missives I'm planning to record once I clean up my surface web postings, and they had ideas."

"Ideas," Cassie said.

"Whatever's next," Mark said. "New missives, new ideas. Next up for Isaac Abramson, just as soon as he gets set up on the Deep Web."

Cassie couldn't tell how serious Mark was, but he looked the happiest he'd been in years. His skin looked healthy and fresh, his eyes somehow open just a bit wider, and she was too drunk to do much more than stare out her window at Flatbush Avenue as they roared past the Barclays Center and straight up the middle of freshly urbanly renewed Brooklyn.

PART TWO

MARK

CHAPTER SEVEN

MARK BRUMFELD WAS THIRTY-ONE YEARS old when he changed his name to Isaac Abramson online. A decade had passed since the attacks on the World Trade Center towers. For five years he worked as an editorial assistant at a glossy magazine in Midtown Manhattan. His goals in his twenties were noble: He wanted to write stories that would in some way better the world. He wanted to edit stories that would unearth corruption, grant clarity to the bleary discourse he often found in the glossies, speak the various truths to the various powers he imagined it was journalism's job to speak. He wanted to publish short stories people would love the way they once loved Salinger, Cheever, Hemingway, or Fitzgerald. He wanted to publish exposés and political tracts that had the power of *Mother Earth*, of *The New Yorker* in the thirties, *The Kenyon Review* in the forties, and *Commentary* in the sixties. He wanted to find, make, be imbued with, and propagate love. He wanted to marry a strong-minded woman and have strong-minded children and lead a strong-minded life.

He wanted a lot of things, mostly things he'd never have no matter how hard he tried.

The day he'd arrived at the magazine, summer 2001, they did still run ten-thousand-word features on stories like the hijacking of Egypt-Air Flight 648, profiles of presidents and rock stars, interrogations of the work of quantum physicists and maximalist sculptors. But within a couple of years, it felt to Mark at least that they mostly ran photographs of celebrities and advice on how to wear a pocket square. It was not clear how this was going to better the world or propagate love or change much of anything, but at least it was work in a noble profession, while everyone he'd grown up with wanted to become investment bankers or corporate lawyers. Mark Brumfeld did not know how to dress, and he couldn't care less about discovering how to do so. He still wanted to fall in love, to be loved, but he did not believe proper pocket square use would have much influence.

For the first two years he was working at the magazine, Mark had a single idea he wanted to write about. It wasn't so much an idea as the germ of an idea. He'd read a lot of Emma Goldman in a college course called "John Brown and His Inheritors," and he thought there was a story in *her* inheritors—in whatever modern-day anarchists and extremist socialists were up to in New York, or in Pittsburgh, in Osawatomie. He went into the office of his boss, an articles editor at the magazine, to talk about it a couple months after he was first hired.

"I see why that might interest you," Mark's boss said. His name was Glen. He was five foot five with a strip of bald pate that ran overtop his head like a skunk's stripe, tufts of hair standing out from the sides of his head like moss on the side of a boulder. Mark would later come to understand that such a tepid response was a de facto rejection of his pitch, but early on—and still charged with the energy of his college professors, who did their best to encourage all his intellectual endeavors and larks—Mark took this as a reason to look into it. The next time he longed to come by Glen's office, he started to walk in but saw that his boss was in the middle of a game of computer solitaire. Mark wasn't experienced or mature enough yet to laugh it off, so when Glen Open-Apple-Q'ed right out of it and said, "What can I do for you," Mark just said, "Oh, nothing, nothing, don't worry about it."

Two weeks later Mark came back into Glen's office, this time having asked him in the morning if he had a few minutes around lunchtime. "So here's what I'm thinking," Mark said. "Emma Goldman and Alexander Berkman used to hang out down in the East Village, in a place called the Sachs's Café. What if I were to spend some time down there, just checking it out? Seeing what it's like down there?"

Glen never spoke immediately after being spoken to. He worked his jaw so it looked like a small rodent was trying to find a way out underneath his ruddy face skin, looked Mark in the eyes. It lent him an enormous power, this control of silence. Behind him was a wall of plate-glass windows, and light struck into the space, reflected off the glass of a building across Fifty-fifth Street from them. If you listened you could hear the traffic on Eighth Avenue speeding uptown.

"Um, well, is there anything happening down there?" Glen said.

Mark tried out Glen's power move and didn't say anything for a moment. It was a moment of pure pain—the anticipation, the quiet of it, not knowing what his boss was thinking.

Before Mark could say anything else, Glen said, "Yeah, that's not gonna work for me." He didn't say anything further. Mark asked why not. "I mean, I think you've kind of got it backwards here. You don't want to come up with an idea and then go searching for a story to tell it. You need to *find* the story. I mean, if there was a terrorist cell somewhere in Lower Manhattan? If there were anarchists actively reviving the spirit of Goldman and Berkman? Sure. That'd be a story. I mean, even if there were anarchy reenactors like Civil War reenactors . . . I dunno . . . acting out McKinley's assassination in Buffalo or something, sure. That could be a story, maybe. But you'd have to find it."

Mark slinked out of Glen's office. For the next six months his disappointment about the meeting shifted from active to reactive. At first he kept wondering: So what if there was a McKinley reenactment group in Buffalo? Could he cover that? This was in the days before Google, when maybe you could ask Jeeves something and maybe he'd tell you, but your job as a reporter was to get on the phone, or get out in the field, and try to find stories like the one he was looking for. Anarchists or anarchist reenactors weren't just going to find him.

But the thing is, he *wasn't* a reporter. He was an editor, and his job was to edit. So now as he edited pieces on celebrities and suits, he found himself imagining that meeting with Glen again, first with all the things he could've said: "Well, could the magazine pay for me to go to Buffalo and check it out?" or "You know, I'm a good writer, you've seen my sentences, I know I can make it work." But soon enough it was another kind of rejoinder until he kept picturing Glen saying, "Um, that's not gonna work for me," and then Mark himself standing up and saying, "Yeah, well, you know what? Now *I* don't work for you," and slamming the door behind him. If he couldn't write about those anarchists and their inheritors, that was fine. But he didn't know what was ahead for him.

What was ahead for the city, and the country, was also unclear in those moments, and it only got muddier. Two months after the magazine where he worked was the only one of the nineteen owned by a single corporation to report on 9/11 immediately after the attacks, the corporation's CEO called a surprise meeting of the magazine's entire editorial staff. Mark assumed that since they were the only magazine to have covered the events in real time—for the first time in the magazine's history they literally stopped the presses, taking a week to produce a new cover and two five-thousand-word features, with extensive sidebars, on the event—he was coming to praise them in person. Instead he spent twenty minutes telling them of the changes to come.

"I know in the past you have edited lengthy features. I'm here to tell you the days of the ten-thousand-word feature are over," he said. "Advertising dollars will dry up, editorial pages with them. The World Trade Center towers are gone. We don't want to see magazines go, too. Changes are coming. Big, big changes."

Within two months, three of his favorite colleagues had been laid off. Though he'd managed to keep his job, it wasn't clear what his job was anymore.

His next logical move was to apply to Ph.D. programs in English literature. If he couldn't change the world by editing the articles it needed, if he couldn't do the writing he wanted for a glossy magazine, he could do it one student at a time, one paper at a time. Though he hadn't shown that much promise as an undergrad, he was accepted into a prominent program in Manhattan. He did not have to move. He would be able to make money freelance fact-checking for the glossy magazine where he'd worked ("beer money," Glen had called it when he offered, though Mark replaced "beer" with "rent" when he explained it to his anxious mother, Julia, who never quite seemed to comprehend what it was Mark wanted from life). He spent two years doing course work, three years researching and writing a dissertation on postwar suburban fiction, his focus on Roth, Bellow, Richard Yates, and DeLillo—he might have liked to write about Emma Goldman but the primary research felt way too dry when he looked into it and it would've meant learning Russian—and then for two years he applied for jobs to become a full-time faculty member at universities across the U.S.

He did not get one job.

He did not get any jobs.

He continued to play in a band and to check facts for a magazine, but he did so a little despondent, a little sad, a little heavily medicated. Occasionally he was able to teach a class to freshmen, but those classes for an entire semester barely paid his rent for a month and a half. It was not a career path, and Mark had the idea that he should be a tenure-track professor. It was noble—and all but unattainable. Around that time he fell in love, but in the end, as with all the relationships that preceded it, it didn't work out—and while that failure would come to feel like everything later, consuming him, at the minute he was making decisions about what to do next, it hardly felt like a factor in his life. He managed to write a long piece for a respectable intellectual magazine, on Emma Goldman of all subjects, but to his surprise it didn't get him anywhere. It didn't pay anything. His expense account at the magazine had once covered for a year his take-home for two months. He made a series of bad decisions in love and in money and his continuing in New York became untenable. He wasn't following love—if anything, he was moving fast from it. From love, money, anything keeping him in New York. His parents would no longer help keep him afloat.

So one day in the early spring of 2010 he told his bandmates he would be giving up the apartment he'd just paid a large broker's fee to let. At the moment he had in his possession: $29,492 in debt spread across three major credit cards; a $5,000 invoice from the IRS for a tax bill from the sale of stocks; a closet full of clothes he'd bought at Century 21 more than ten years earlier, a location which now existed in most memories only in photos of the dust from World Trade Center Two covering all its merchandise; and no real prospects for long-term employment, in New York City or elsewhere. His one chance at love had failed, and he couldn't even bring himself to think about it. He would miss playing tennis on the well-kept courts in Fort Greene Park. He would find something to do next.

First he would move back to his parents' house outside of Baltimore.

CHAPTER EIGHT

WHEN HE WAS ASKED BY REPORTERS, by friends, by his mother in the years after the Boomer Boomers became the most infamous domestic revolutionary group in the country in four decades, what had set him on his path—an inciting incident, people wanted an inciting incident, so he gave them not one but two—Brumfeld did not think of the day he left the New York borough where he'd lived since the month after he graduated from a prestigious liberal arts college in Maine. He did not attribute his actions to his failures in love or money, which explanations interviewers were most likely trying to elicit. He didn't think about Cassie and her jilting him, or the lack of response to his Emma Goldman piece in *The Unified Theory*. He did not even think of the day Glen had shot down his best idea for a feature for the magazine, no matter how influential that rejection had been on him. Instead, two stories would come to Isaac Abramson's mind:

The first was of a pickup basketball game.

This was an unlikely occurrence. The summer after Brumfeld was forced to give up his apartment and move into the basement in the suburban Baltimore house where he'd grown up, he was idle. He hadn't maintained relationships with his high school friends, most of whom had stayed in the area, or perhaps moved down to D.C., while he was in New York. His close female friends were now married, and in their mid-thirties their husbands frowned upon their keeping up with a thirty-year-old unemployed bachelor. He hadn't even accepted Facebook friend requests from his high school friends, had lost touch with them when he moved to New York and kept it that way. On occasion he was able to take the Bolt Bus back up to the city and play a gig with the bluegrass band he'd played in in his decade in New York. But without work, without a solid income, travel grew expensive and doing so meant seeing Cassie, which bore its own pain—while she might not have factored into his decision-making while he was leaving, after just days in his parents' house, alone with little more than self-harm to keep him occupied, he was consumed by how much he missed her. So rather than just sitting around pining for—or worse, e-mailing—his ex, on Mondays, Wednesdays, and Fridays, he went to the same JCC where he'd played pick-up basketball as a kid. One afternoon in mid-June, a month after he'd moved back into his parents' basement, his thoughts on the America he lived in in 2010 changed.

There was a break between games. The men Brumfeld played with were in their mid- to late fifties. Brumfeld had been plagued with an eidetic memory. He remembered every face he saw, and every face on the court. The tall hirsute Sephardic man who set up in the middle of the lane every trip down, who missed every baby-hook he attempted, who on defense was a single lethal elbow seeking a hack-worthy face, was Jaime Silver. The point guard who ran his mouth the whole time he ran the ball up the court was Stan Finkel—Mark's own freshman Social Studies teacher.

He'd hated Mr. Finkel, who wore TJ Maxx blue blazers in the classroom and burgundy Members Only jackets out of it, who had once accused him of cheating on pop quizzes (he *had* been cheating, but that didn't change the fact that he hated being accused of it), whose balding pattern matched to the follicle the balding pattern on Glen's head.

On that water break, Finkel was talking to Silver courtside. Mark kept to himself. In the first month or so he picked up his iPhone and looked at what the editors of *The New York Times* selected to tell him about what was happening in the world. But his subscription had run out. While he could read his parents' paper copy in the mornings, he had access to only ten articles a month for free. It occurred to him that the word *news* was a plural noun: more than one new. A multiplicity of new things. Ten things that were new, then a paywall, was not quite what people meant by "news." So, undistracted by the screen before him, he sat and listened instead:

"I made almost forty thousand just this past *week* on the stuff," Finkel was saying. Silver was hirsute and swarthy and his Latino first name rhymed with "buy me." He nodded and yessed as Finkel spoke. "They call it hydraulic fracturing. The tree huggers hate it and, sure, if I think about it or talk to my kids about it, I hate it, too. But it's not like I'm the one doing the whatever they call it—fracking. Frucking. I just invest in the sand they use. I'm telling you—forty thou, this week alone. I won't tell you how much I've made this year. I don't like to talk money, kind of thing. Indiscreet. I'm taking Val to Positano next month, if that tells you."

Brumfeld in his entire decade in New York had gotten out of the city maybe twice a year. A couple times he had taken Cassie to a B&B, but she seemed to prefer being in town and had gigs most weekends. By the end of their relationship he wouldn't even have thought of trying to take a vacation with her. Mostly he went home to see his parents with the hope of returning with a check in hand to help out with rent.

"Amazing," Silver said. "You'll have to put me in touch with your broker."

"Broker? Shit, I just read about it and do it myself on eTrade. Sometimes I e-mail with an old friend who knows about it. I just see what they say in *Bloomberg News* and then go for what's hitting, kind of thing. And then—Positano."

Silver was looking down at his hands. Mark could see him racking up the eTrades, and their proceeds, and the coastal Italian vacations all those proceeds could afford him, in his big Sephardic elbow of a head. Brumfeld didn't say anything, but his face must have betrayed what he was thinking—Finkel looked at him again this time and said, "What?"

Being spoken to sent a charge through Brumfeld's body. He looked away. It had been weeks since he'd talked to anyone other than his mother. After years in a magazine office Brumfeld had learned about the social constraints of hierarchy—the kind of free conversation a group of editorial assistants might have, and how it would shift if an assistant editor joined in, or how it would stiffen if the editor-in-chief came around: all eye-tightening smiles and reflexive nodding. This had softened for him in his time as a grad student, but when he was with a mentor it was mentorial, another kind of power. This was Stan Finkel. His high school Social Studies teacher, he of liberal politics and Members Only jackets, who had driven the same Volvo 940 that Mark himself had driven over to this game, borrowed from his parents.

"Oh, I know what you're thinking," Finkel said. He looked at Mark and then looked back at Silver. "You know what he's thinking, too, Jaime. I see it on my kids' faces. I don't need it on the basketball court. I'm retired, I'm living a life I never led when I was working. I planned to collect my couple thousand a month from Social Security and live quietly, kind of thing. A timeshare in Boca Raton. But here we are."

"Here you fucking are," Mark said.

He didn't mean to say it. He wouldn't have talked this way to Glen, or to any of the critics and writers he studied with in grad school. But some combination of the shock at news of Finkel's small retirement fortune, and of Mark's hearing about fracking, had put words in his mouth. Now that he was talking, what was he going to do?

"Sorry—here you *frucking* are," Mark said.

"Who are you?" Finkel said. He was well under six feet tall, with soddy patches of brown hair on either side of his head. On Finkel it looked like capitulation to death two decades early, like wearing sweatpants outside the house (which incidentally the magazine where Mark used to work had just declared a trend). Mark remembered the antagonistic tone Finkel had taken when he'd called young Mark into his office to accuse him of cheating. He heard it again now, shimmering with the thin glowing filament of memory.

"Mark Brumfeld," Mark said. "I was in your ninth-grade Social Studies class." He couldn't help himself: "Kind of thing."

"Not what I meant. I mean, who are you to talk to me? We're having a private conversation. You millennials with those computers in your pockets, zapping radiation into your nutsacks, noses pressed to your screens—you think you can just blurt out whatever comes to your mind."

"Felt like an awfully public conversation to me," Mark said. "No one wants to hear about your money. Just sitting around in public bragging about destroying the environment. I remember you as a teacher. As a man who wouldn't have made financial gains off destroying the water supply in West Virginia or Pennsylvania. Making it so rural people's water could be set on fire just by lighting a match, like we were returning to life under the fucking robber barons."

"Take care of yourself."

"I am taking care of myself. And more than myself," Brumfeld said. "It's you who only takes care of yourself, your whole generation just doing just that. Taking care of yourselves."

When he said it Finkel took a step closer to him.

The way he told it later, something shifted in that moment. It was like a fourth wall had broken down. Mark Brumfeld eight years earlier had assigned and edited an eight-thousand-word feature on the first companies to begin fracking. Even then, almost a decade earlier, they'd been predicting that the environmental costs of fracking would far outweigh the financial benefits. At the time the last fiduciary benefit Mark suspected that evil would bring was vacations in Positano for the very man who'd taught him Social Studies. Back then there was a distance a teacher kept from his students, the way a thirty-five-foot barrier was maintained between pro-lifers and women entering Massachusetts abortion clinics.

Now that distance had been closed.

"I said take care of yourself," Finkel said. Mark had been in two bar fights in his years in the city, had been mugged three times on the Myrtle Avenue side of Fort Greene Park in the first two years he had lived there. But now he just said, "You're not worth it," and walked to the water fountain. The whole time he was drinking it was as if something in him had been fractured, some new energy loosed, a new anger that had been hidden in the shale of his veins but now was being released all at once, valuable and voluble and volatile. Rage hidden and kept discreet within the sedimentary walls of his own adult civility was rising to the surface, raw power ready to be burned for fuel.

By the time he got back to the court, the rest of the players were ready to run one more full. First time down on defense, Finkel passed the ball to Silver on the wing. Mark was defending the post. Each bump of each body in the lane was like the blast of chemical-saturated water opening crude in the bedrock of his arteries, combustible chemical-suffused water swelling all around him. The anger that had been building up in him each night he'd gone to sleep in his childhood bed, in his childhood basement, two hundred miles from Cassie and broken up with her, alone, felt ready to burst. When Finkel cut for the basket Mark was there. Instead of jumping to block the shot, he kept down on the floor and undercut his former Social Studies teacher, whose legs went out from under him. Finkel's body rolled across Mark's back until he flipped over one full turn, slammed to the floor hard on his lower back, then popped right back up.

"What the fuck was that?" Finkel said.

Mark swung.

He got one good hook into the side of Stan Finkel's head before bright lights flashed in front of Mark's eyes. Silver jumped between the two, and he threw an elbow for good measure. It caught Brumfeld above the eye. Mark put his hand to his face to see that a sticky sluice of blood was trickling down his cheekbone. It left him dazed, the space above his eye feeling like it was swelling big as the Ohio River in early spring rains. He saw Silver standing in a capoeira stance, one foot back and arms moving in strange dancelike arabesques until the older man saw that Mark meant his friend no further harm.

Silver ran to pick Finkel up. Mark felt the slow trickle of blood now reaching his stippled chin like water seeping out of a haystack. With it seeped the slightest ease to his angst. His eye was throbbing with each beat of his throbbing heart. At that moment a world opened up in Mark's head. He was already more Abramson than Brumfeld.

He left the JCC. He got into his parents' sea-green 1993 Volvo 940 and drove the roads outside of Baltimore he had once driven daily to clear his head and smoke pot without being caught. A sharp pain in his fist surged along with the pain in his eye with each hydraulic pulse of his heart. For the first time in a year, maybe more, he felt not pain, not embarrassment, not self-loathing. The fear fell away like shale from a hydraulic-blasted mountainside.

He felt pure, crude, previously untapped freedom. Resist much, obey little—Whitman had been telling him just that since he first read the opening section of *Leaves of Grass,* and it felt for the first time in his life like he'd heeded the call.

There were four dozen reasons he'd heard for the economic downturn, for the paucity of jobs available in the two years since the Great Recession had started. Trillions of dollars were headed to pay for the two Forever Wars that had been ongoing his entire adult life. There were credit default swaps and collateralized debt obligations; there were soon to be eight billion people on Earth; global ecological catastrophe was so much a foregone conclusion that half the serious novels and television series people watched or read were about what life would be like after it hit. Part of him suspected those entertainments let people continue at their environment-destroying behavior, allowing them to think, Well, if *Mad Max* or *The Walking Dead* is ahead for us, we're fucked anyway, so why not keep tearing through these Keurig individual espresso pods, washing our faces with micro-bead-filled face washes, trash-filled oceans be damned? But on that ride up Falls Road, through Pikesville, and off farther into the dense deciduous-covered roads, it occurred to Mark that there was a clearer reason for it all—for his high school Social Studies teacher now to be enjoying unprecedented leisure and return on his investments only twenty months since the financial sector had imploded so badly the likelihood of Mark's ever getting a real job was nothing more than a distant dream:

It was the baby boomers.

It had always been and was always going to be the baby boomers.

It grew so clear to Mark as the flow of blood slowed on his face, drying and caking against the tissue he found in the cracked plastic slot in his driver's side door. It was the baby boomers who had what he wanted, who in their geologic later years had petrified until they were protecting all the natural resources, who had what his friends and his colleagues and his fellow alumni and all those twenty-year-olds and thirty-year-olds and even some forty-year-olds in all the bars in Fort Greene and Bushwick and Williamsburg, in Oakland and Berkeley and

Petaluma, in Crown Heights and Prospect Heights and Pacific Heights and Ditmas Park, wanted.

It was the baby boomers.

It was time for someone to do something about it.

So while it felt like a kind of cliché—while becoming any kind of cliché was all he'd been trying to avoid since he was old enough to understand what a cliché was—Mark slammed on the brakes. He did not look in the rearview mirror. He was lucky no one had been behind him. It took a nine-point turn to reverse direction on that narrow suburban street. As he sped back to his parents' basement, he began to craft his initial diatribe. By the time he opened his three-year-old black MacBook, he was gravid with complaint, gibbous with jeremiad. He'd bought the laptop just months before the first one with a built-in camera had been introduced, so he set up the iSight next to it, pointed it at his face. He'd worked on some Internet shorts for the university admissions office once he finished his course work, so he knew a little about production on the fly.

In the background, just over his shoulder, was a poster from the first Grateful Dead show he'd attended, RFK Stadium 1994, almost two decades earlier. It was a huge portrait of Jerry's face. He thought about taking it down but decided he liked the irony of it in the background, so he turned it upside down, like declaring war while flying the enemy's flag. On the laptop screen in front of him he could see the sweat-soaked hair plastered to his forehead. The blood on his right cheek appeared on the right side of the screen. It had dried in a tacky trail on his face, and his right eye was puffy like a boxer's in a late round. He didn't stop to take a shower, didn't wipe any more of the blood from his face, or the wet hair from his forehead. He didn't take the time to have a look at how you upload a video onto YouTube, not a part of the production process he'd engaged in in the past, though he had a user ID and a password (ID: BlackPeter3@yahoo.com; psswd: mightaswellmightaswell). When he left for college Mark had never even sent an e-mail. He brought with him the magenta-and-white iMac his parents had bought for themselves, good baby boomers that they were, but never learned how to use, and passed along to him. He left college and took his first job working as an intern at that glossy magazine, where he worked off and on for the next decade, having sent perhaps a hundred e-mails in his lifetime. Now here he was a decade later, sitting in front of an iSight camera, in front of a Mac laptop.

He hit Record.

"This is the first Boomer Missive. Today is June 12, 2010. Earlier this morning I hit a baby boomer in the face. He hit me back. Now I will hit back again. I will hit back harder. We will all hit back.

"Resist much, obey little.

"Propaganda by the deed.

"Boom boom."

CHAPTER NINE

THE SECOND ANSWER Mark gave for what set him on his path was an image that lodged in his mind and later drove him to reinvent himself online as Isaac Abramson, and it was even more tangential on the face of it than the basketball game incident. It took place in the performance space in the Union Square Barnes & Noble a year before Mark Brumfeld left his apartment in Brooklyn for his parents' basement. He'd come to see one of his former professors, an essayist of some renown who'd never sold many books, read from a new collection of essays, which would be well reviewed and revered and sell fewer than a thousand copies. A thousand objects passed his gaze that night but only one stuck with him. He had arrived an hour early so he could get a seat toward the front. He sat with the professor's book, reading an essay he'd earlier read when it had appeared in a respected literary journal with a circulation of under ten thousand. He was deeply involved in the reading when a voice broke his concentration.

"Are you enjoying it?" the woman said.

Mark looked up, prepared to be annoyed. But he recognized the face. It was the professor's wife. The professor had held his Baldwin/Didion/ Himself seminar at his home. She'd been in the parlor room of their spacious prewar four-story brownstone on Joralemon Street in Brooklyn Heights at each class meeting. At the time, Brumfeld hadn't thought about the fact that this poor-selling but prestigious essayist professor lived in what must be a $4 million brownstone, and provided for his wife whatever she needed. He didn't recognize the deep narcissism in the professor choosing to include his own work alongside the two greatest essayists of his generation. Mark didn't think about it now, either.

"Yes, of course I know you. You had us over."

"He's my husband."

"He was my professor. Baldwin/Didion/X used to meet at your place. You made that zucchini bread."

"Ah, my zucchini bread," X's wife said. "You know those zucchinis come straight from our garden. X built the raised beds himself."

Mark didn't say it, but he knew, he did know, he couldn't not have known that the zucchini had come from their garden. He knew X had built the raised beds himself. When the seven graduate students had come to his brownstone for the first meeting of Baldwin/Didion/X, X himself had taken them on a tour of the garden. It was the first week of September, the first clear, dry week since the oppression of New York summer humidity, one that would always remind Mark of that thin-aired morning in September the year he'd moved to New York when the planes flew into the buildings and he and his reporter and editor colleagues had all run downtown into the gray silty mass, and now they sat out back, ate zucchini bread, drank the Duvals and Leffes and Westmalle Trappists X offered. The placidity, the quiet amid the din of the city—at that moment Mark didn't say to himself, One day I could have this. He didn't know that he would later understand, There will never under any circumstance be a day when I can have any of this or the peace and love it would provide. He had just been happy to share in the generosity X had shown him.

That's not what struck Brumfeld as X's wife talked with him about the particulars of X's new book, where his publisher would send him on a reading tour, how even though they don't send authors on tour anymore they would do so for X since they'd done so for all of his books, or where X and his wife would vacation after that book tour was finished. All he could see, all he could think about, was the immense princess-cut diamond on X's wife's left ring finger. It threw off more brightness than the sodium lights over the Fort Greene tennis courts after dark, the fluorescence of the Barnes & Noble's reading space some-how transformed and minimized to that single diaphanous sparkle.

It must have been a VVS-1 or a VVS-2, five or even six carats, worth as much as the down payment for the apartment Mark had once shared with five late-twenty-and-early-thirty-year-olds in Fort Greene. Brumfeld knew something about diamonds—his mother's closest friend was an Israeli dealer in colored diamonds in Midtown. She'd walked him through the process when he'd planned to propose to his ex-girlfriend Cassie—he'd gone to her with it in mind to get Cassie an emerald or a ruby, thinking a diamond might be too bourgeoisie for her punk tastes, but his mother's friend had convinced him it was a diamond or nothing. That's how people proposed when they proposed. Men did not propose with emeralds, punk bassist girlfriend or otherwise. That was not, his mother's friend assured him, a thing. Mark would never know how much of a role that particular mistake played in his breakup with Cassie, but like an object approaching the speed of light, it grew larger the more time passed. He'd spent months figuring out how he would afford a diamond and then months more with his mother's friend trying to pick out the right-colored diamond for Cassie, only to have her stand up and walk away and never come back after he offered it to her. He now assumed he'd read all the signs wrong, he'd been impatient and he'd forced it. But that didn't make the jilting any less painful. Jilting was jilting, and the pain of it was permanent and as inescapable as the time-and-space-warping gravitational pull of a black hole. He couldn't stop looking at her left hand. The voices around them, the book in his hands with its deckle-edged pages and rubberized matte dust jacket all faded. A single thought stuck in Brumfeld's mind:

How did a professor whose books of literary essays were read only by a small cabal of serious readers ever afford such a ring? He did not think about the brownstone then, about the homegrown zucchinis in the home-baked zucchini bread or the La Cornue oven in which it was baked. He did not think about the eighteen-dollars-a-six-pack Belgian abbey tripel he'd drunk in X's garden. He just saw that ring, watched it flash light at him from wherever X's wife's hand moved while they talked. Maybe it was even that diaphanous sparkle that had been loosed in Mark's mind when he heard Finkel talking about his fracking wealth on the court months later.

Boom boom.

Later that night when Brumfeld took the L train across the river into Williamsburg for his gig, his whole head was still filled with the light from that ring. What could have afforded these literary people such leisure? Had they received huge sums of money through trust funds? Lived other lives as financiers, surgeons, corporate lawyers? It occurred to him then, not in the same fullness it would later:

They were baby boomers.

They had and they had and they had, as if that was the very condition of their own existence—having, owning, getting, living out Bellow's I want, I want, I want—while he and his generation had not. They, too, wanted plenty, but they did not have.

Brumfeld walked the ten blocks from the train to Pete's Candy Store, where his band would be playing that night. He stashed his mandolin case in a corner when he arrived. He downed four Maker's-and-sodas. While they played their traditional bluegrass music and some covers of well-known country songs for the couple dozen people there that night—that was enough of an audience to fill the small space in the old-time performance area Pete's provided—he kept picturing that diamond. "Picturing" wasn't quite right, as it wasn't the image of the diamond itself as much as the flashing glint of light it threw off. His head was filled with light. While they were playing, Cassie—his exgirlfriend, his ex-almost-fiancée, who had taken so easily to life without him he somehow felt fine about it when he wasn't around her, then felt it eat at him the further and longer they were apart—would step up to the mic to take a solo after he finished singing the chorus of "Mama Tried" or "Knoxville Girl," and he would look at her, thinking, Maybe if I'd been born in the fifties, this would all have been easier. Any fifties, that is. He looked out at the twenty-year-olds and the thirty-year-olds in their H + M shirts, their thrift-shop jeans, and he thought, Maybe if we'd all been born to our parents' generation, we would be in a different situation now. Maybe we'd all be going abroad on paid book tours, buying our wives precious diamonds and ovens worth more than a new car, working the jobs he'd always dreamed of. By the time the show ended he was a little drunk and a lot tired. He and Cassie sat down at the bar together. It had been more than six months since they'd broken up. Playing in a band was fine. Cassie had long since realized she didn't want to be with him, refused his proposal. Mark had long since come to terms with it, because he had to.

"What was on your mind that whole show, Mark?" Cassie said. She wasn't looking at him. They were belly up to the bar.

"I'll have a Maker's and soda," he said to the bartender.

"You didn't take one single break with any energy behind it. It was like I could feel the black hole across the stage when you were singing. We all noticed."

What was there for Brumfeld to say? There was no way to tell the story without telling her what they'd tacitly promised never to talk about again, not in front of people at a bar—how he'd spent a half-dozen afternoons on Forty-seventh Street, walking in and out of the Hasids' shops with his mother's friend, looking at settings, looking at diamonds, before spending the ten thousand dollars he'd discovered he had access to on a ring for her, though she'd shown no perceivable signs she was interested in getting married to him, or to anyone.

"Just tired," Mark said. "But you were amazing on your fiddle breaks all night. Killer double stops on 'Wheel Hoss.'" Cassie blushed. No one didn't like being flattered—compliment a clam effectively enough and it'll give up its pearl. It was one of the best things Mark had learned as an editor, and used as an editor, though it felt inappropriate to use it in his personal life. He'd always believed the line between professional and private life was impermeable. Work was work and life was life, and unless protest and revolt were to take over your life, it was ever important to set up and keep up a line between the two. And now that he and Cassie were only bandmates, working together, he was uncomfortable crossing the divide.

"Thanks, Mark," Cassie said. "That makes me feel good." He saw a light in her eyes he hadn't seen in months, if ever. It was like the light sparkling from a diamond.

It would be a year before the diamond returned fully to mind.

CHAPTER TEN

BACK IN HIS PARENTS' BASEMENT IN BALTIMORE, Mark hit the space bar on his laptop keyboard. He transferred the video file he'd just recorded over to iMovie. He began editing. He left it mostly raw, left in a long silence a little more than halfway through. He slash-cut between each thing he'd said so that while it took him almost ten minutes to speak all those words on-screen, the video he created went for just over four. He had almost spliced it all together when he realized he'd forgotten the most important part. So while he'd need more material for the second missive, which he hoped to record in just a couple of days, and while he still needed to sign in to YouTube so he could post the video he'd made, he put the iSight back up, and he spoke for a couple minutes more, until he'd said all there was to say that first day.

Mark stood up from his desk aflame, crude oil fractured free from shale and lit by a spark, immiscible and joyous for the first cathartic time since the day he cowered home from New York City, in more debt than he could think about. He took a shower. While he showered he sang a baby boomer anthem to himself, a famous Buffalo Springfield song. He got out of the shower and dried off. He looked on the computer. It was like he'd been given a present, like the feeling of the first night of Hanukkah. The video was still there. He came back to his computer once more and spliced his speech about the Akedah into what was there before. He went to YouTube and uploaded it. He watched. Under the video it just said the number "one."

One hit.

Him.

He was the first to watch it, to watch his own screed on-screen. He hit Command-Q and closed the browser on his computer.

Then he walked upstairs and said hello to Julia, who made him a pastrami on rye with deli mustard, the same sandwich she'd made him every lunch throughout high school.

PART THREE
JULIA

CHAPTER ELEVEN

JULIA BRUMFELD WAS NOT BORN JULIA BRUMFELD, just like the vast majority of the women of her generation were not born with the last names they carried for the entirety of their adult lives. She was born Julia Sidler and she would always be Julia Brumfeld née Sidler, whether people thought of her that way or not, a secularized Jewish girl growing up in a theologically stringent Orthodox household in the westernmost neighborhoods of Philadelphia in the fifties and sixties, daughter of a WWII veteran and, in the years ahead, an alumna of the finest Friends schools in the area, product of the spoils of the biggest war of the century, which in turn bought an education with the people who invented conflict resolution and peace. When she was asked what struck her most in the days after her son Mark became one of the most notorious revolutionaries in the U.S. since Weatherman filled the thoughts, hopes, and fears of her friends at Syracuse when she was still an undergrad over the broken course of almost six years, what struck her most about those days he was broadcasting his revolutionary views from her suburban Baltimore basement—which she'd spent weeks emptying of her vintage instruments to make room for him in what had once been his bedroom—without her knowledge, making her a pariah until the end of her own days, Julia Brumfeld did not answer. She knew her rights. She had not enjoyed the days of officials from the FBI coming to her house to ask questions, their guns and badges left carefully innocuous on the seats of their unmarked black sedans parked curbside outside her house. But she was savvy enough to know that she should not say much. It took all the forbearance she had not to discuss it, not to express anger at their presence—or, frankly, at Mark's—but she did not divulge information or bear emotion. She'd hidden enough of her own secrets from him over the years. It seemed only natural once it came to pass that he'd been expert in hiding his.

For two frantic weeks before Mark returned to their basement, months before she even had an inkling that her son had the slightest interest in anything revolutionary, Julia spent her days clearing the guest room on their second floor of everything but its guest bed in order to make room for her fiddles, her father's old Martin D-45, mandolins, and mandolas, and her record collection. For almost a decade now since her son had moved out to attend college in rural Maine, and then on to New York City, where he'd tried and now failed to make it as a journalist and then an academic and then a musician and a writer, her husband had kept her happy by buying for her and allowing her to buy the expensive vintage instruments, whose value had skyrocketed in the past decade. Between the return of the popularity of bluegrass music in the days after the planes flew into the buildings—there was a sense of a return to things most identifiably American, to all things Americana in those Patriot Act–infused days—and the fact that Japanese collectors had taken to buying old mandolins and arch-top guitars to frame and hang on their walls, vintage instruments were as valuable as they had ever been. And so it was both a boon for Julia, who still picked her fiddle up from time to time to keep herself happy and who had learned to play mandolin and guitar over the years of teaching and playing but would never have let Mark bring these expensive old mandolins to the beery bars where he played (she'd seen the beer stains *inside* his own F-5)—and for Cal, who had grown convinced that buying a ten-thousand-dollar mandolin that would in five years be worth eighteen was a surprisingly safe investment.

But then Mark announced he'd be returning, tail tucked, to Baltimore. In two weeks. And so for two weeks it was all Julia gave her time over to, clearing out the basement of its instruments and records and high-backed, armless chairs where she would go down to play, so that now she could clear out a second-floor guest room and move them up, one by one in their expensive hard-shelled Calton cases and stands and set them all up in a guest room where guests couldn't stay in comfort without the imposition of music, music, music. All because when a son returned, tail tucked, to the house where he grew up, he expected to return to the room where he'd grown up. And when he was going to high school Mark had convinced his parents to let him move down to the basement for privacy—a word they understood later to mean "smoke pot without getting caught." And of course it was more complicated than that—for as she opened up each case Julia found that now that she was playing her instruments less, they were all badly in need of work. She had seven fiddles and really only played the one she'd had since she was a teenager, and as she opened each Calton case—each forest-green and Cadillac-red case with its humidity control and bulletproof back, making them the choice for traveling artists and sedentary rich ones like her, both—she found that bows' hair had grown slack and tangled, that bridges needed resetting, that cracks on soundboards and fretboards of mandolins were in need of work, new work, old work. Work. Fixing up. So she took them two by two and three by three to the best luthier in the area, out in Owings Mills, and on the way there her nose was filled with varnish, with the particulate of years and decades of old rosin, with the smells that once covered her hands and her skin and filled her head with music, light, and memory.

It was memory now and it would become memory different in the months to come when her son returned and made her a pariah. If she was being honest, if she was to divulge the emotional reality of her memory in therapy, say—a thing she'd surely never do in the days after Mark's actions—there were two images that overtook her preconscious mind. They were images that had always been not far from the surface, flashes of memory's lightning that, she came to realize, had struck her throughout her life in times of crisis, and had struck her while she was cleaning out the basement. This was the way the mind handled crisis as far as Julia could tell. There was the immediate physical response, a wetness at the underarms, weird shots of spidery tingle in the hands and at the back of her neck. Sometimes there was a sour taste at the edges of her tongue. But the main response was one of reflexive memory: an image

flashed, then another. These images came unbidden and remained un-
parsed and arrived without order, and perhaps in drunken conversation
with Mark's father she would begin to divulge them one day. But such
a day had not yet arrived after more than three decades of marriage.
Instead she was stuck experiencing those two images over and over,
each time she opened a fiddle case to find a bow's hair had grown
slack, and later when she saw her son's name on a network news report
that flattened his story into something people had decided to compare
unfavorably with radical Islamist terrorism and call "generational domestic terrorism," dangerous, single-faceted; every time a letter came
via registered mail with a new summons or clarification of charges or
lawyers' fees, every time later when she went into the city and on the
ride out Falls Road, she found that an unmarked black sedan seemed
to have been following her, fifty yards back, since she got on Park
Heights Ave. Through it all the two images were the same, one seemingly
innocuous, one whose odious severity was undeniable and not subject
to interpretation:

The first image was of her bubbe, Bertha, ironing tinfoil. That was
how she remembered her grandmother. Her zayde, Herschel, was a
foreman at a shoe factory in the northwest of the city. He walked the
three blocks every day to the small factory to oversee the production of
those shoes. Her mother worked nearby, worked all the time since her
father's mind had fallen apart, his business with it. Most afternoons
when she was a child Julia would go to her bubbe's row house in East
Mt. Airy, where she would help her at her chores. So that was the image: Bubbe Bertha ironing tinfoil. Tinfoil was a different proposition
in those days, a robust product, thick and substantial and suggesting a
certain possibility of reuse, a sheet of thin metal used sparingly if at all.
When she was a kid it had only existed on the market for less than a
decade, was still a kind of novelty, to wax paper what two generations
later the iPod was to the Walkman. What struck Julia if she thought
back on those days was that her family wasn't well-to-do but they
weren't yet hard up, and what brought her loving bubbe with her an-
kles covered in raised purple veins that looked like they spelled out in
sanguinated Arabic some indecipherable verse from the Koran and

whose flowered candlewick dresses hung off her like the skin off an ancient Congolese elephant to reuse this tinfoil with such ardor was an atavistic need of a generation prior. Bubbe Bertha was only a decade removed from the worst of those years between the Depression and the War, when even to have a luxury like tinfoil, when it came on the market, was more than most had. It made sense she would be plagued still by whatever fear of penury surrounded everyone for decades—until long after the war ended. But the next war was over, the U.S. had won, and all that was coming back from across the Atlantic was good news, good cheer, and pounds, lire, marks, drachmas, forints, francs, all the sovereign money that would buy U.S. goods and services and make their lives here in the westernmost neighborhoods of Philadelphia easier for decades to come, bringing prosperity, relative ease, and unlimited options to the next generation. It was the beginning of a period, an era, that appeared then to have no limit.

If she was even more honest, Julia Brumfeld would admit no scrim or interpretation so full and knowable came to her in those days after her son came to incite violence against his own government, against the country her father had lost his sanity fighting for. It was simply the image: an old steam-powered iron sweeping again and again over a piece of tinfoil on a countertop. Out of the top of the triangular white iron, translucent clouds of evaporating water would puff like the spume of a whale, huffing out sound like something live and breathing. If Julia got too close, Bubbe would stick her substantial knee out, shift her weight, and direct her granddaughter away. Julia had no idea how old she herself had been at the time—five?—eight?—could she have been as old as ten or eleven even, moving toward her early teens, that period they now so facilely called the "tweens" in young girls, as if to diminish the fact that one wrong move could lead them to progeny of their own?—only that she was there, that she had no real purpose but to watch Bubbe at her ironing. The crink, crink, crink of the iron passing over foil, each of the myriad wrinkles finding its half-indelible pattern turned flat, turned back to the foil that might cover a glass container of lard-soaked Brussels's sprouts, a dozen chicken livers, whatever found its way to the Frigidaire or the pantry in the days ahead.

And again the more she was honest about what she had seen in those days, the more Julia would admit there was no context, there was no knowledge, there was no *world* or abstraction these images carried. There wasn't a narrative. She could not have recounted that image, could not have told a story about it, because there was no story to be told—narration implied causation, one thing leading to another in a knowable way. She did not know what having remembered this image caused. It could not be divided, splintered, or repelled.

She did not remember at the time how the light looked filtering slowly into that kitchen on East Sedgwick Street, east of Germantown Avenue, though when she tried to think of how that kitchen looked, she realized most memories were not of the kitchen itself, but of a picture she'd seen of the kitchen in her later years. She did not know how much of this was how *her* mind worked, and how much of it was simply how *the* mind worked: there were memories of events, events both traumatic and mundane, meaningful or seemingly without meaning. And then there was the recounting of those events, the keepsakes we looked at again and again which became their own memory. She knew that she did not suffer from what the new generation seemed at every turn to want to call PTSD. PTSD suggested to her that trauma was singular and finite, an event that took place like the snapping of a picture, then ended. There was nothing "post" about what she was suffering. There was no single event that had transpired, then ended. It occurred to Julia Brumfeld almost daily that PTSD must be the most egregiously mis- and over-used medical term in the history of American popular culture. There were soldiers in VA hospitals all over the country who actually suffered from it; most likely her own father suffered from something very much like it long before the term was coined in the very city where they lived. But she herself suffered and suffered and suffered from something that was neither post- nor trauma, not finite nor ended. She suffered from an eternal and eternally recurring present. She suffered while she cleaned out her basement in advance of her son moving back in; she suffered while the smells of the luthier in Owings Mills where she brought her favorite fiddle to get set up filled her nose. She suffered in the months when after her son was arrested she couldn't bring herself to leave the house to do anything other than shop for groceries—an activity during which she suffered even more. She recognized that perhaps the greatest misunderstanding her son's generation had of the world was the misguided belief that an event transpired—traumatic or mundane, painful or mundane—and then ended in an ineradicable clean way, like a television show or a YouTube clip that began when called forth by the pressing of a right-pointing isosceles triangle, could be skipped by that triangle paired, replayed by a click on an arrow manipulated into a spiral, moved in a direction left or right: to the left, back in time; to the right, forward. This belief wasn't religious but it was a belief system like any other—and perhaps more erroneous than most, cloistered and credulous. Had any generation in the history of the world been so duped about the nature of time, been rendered so complacent by the appearance of control over perception? Facts so easily undermined: That an event could take place in the time it took for it to be viewed as a video. That the reproduction of the event could be recounted in the same span it took for the event to take place. Julia knew that time was not finite in such a way, that it wasn't finite at all—there were no beginnings and endings and then retrospective suffering. There was time experienced in a single eternal present of being, being, being, being, being. Julia didn't know what memory was or why images flashed at her amid this eternal present, but she knew those images themselves were not finished. They existed and persisted in her mind, neither to be overcome nor forgotten.

What Julia did know was that this image of Bubbe Bertha ironing tinfoil returned to her at the oddest times, unpredictable and unpredicated, strangely if only momentarily debilitating. In the summer months after Mark first returned home, moving into the basement of the house where he had been so peacefully raised after she had long ago abandoned dreams of stardom or even modest success as a musician, that period after she'd given over every waking moment for two weeks clearing her instruments out for him to be able to sleep there, with a low-grade ringing in her right ear that she refused to allow her physician to diagnose as tinnitus or to correct when her hearing loss became something more, where Julia and Cal had poured every ounce of effort they had into reading Dr. Spock, into listening to their son's hopeless violin practice and driving him to his hopeless baseball practice and his desire to take on a dying profession at which he'd never showed any real promise, when the torrential downpours of a Baltimore summer would bring along their inevitable electrical storms and ozone waft, it would come to her: The glint of light off a single piece of tinfoil. The puff of vapor jumped and spewed from the top of a white and bronze iron. A puff that never started and never ended but simply was. Was, was, was. Her bubbe's varicose-veined hand pushing back and forth, back and forth, the slight smack of iron against tin on the countertop.

What could she have told Cal she was experiencing, even if he asked? Could she say something like, "Oh, I think I've got that PTSD everyone is always talking about"—and not in the least mean it? At best you experienced what you experienced and then called it a flash, or a migraine. At best people would leave you alone to your indefinable indiscriminate inscrutable suffering. On any of countless nights when he came back from the hospital, from one of his endless shifts on the OB ward where he was bringing into the world the next generation of sentient memory-making eternally present beings, what they would call the latter stages of the millennial generation in the media in the decades ahead, lay back and said, "Any new revelations about what pushed the kid?" what would she have said? "Cal, Bubbe used to iron tinfoil in our kitchen so we could reuse it"? Or better, "I'm not sure my mind thinks Bubbe has ever *stopped* at her ironing"? This was less a conversational non sequitur than an ontological non sequitur, like seeing a duckbill platypus in its natural habitat, then applying for some kind of gene therapy that might allow one to have a beak grown from her face in the months ahead.

Julia kept it to herself.

CHAPTER TWELVE

THE SECOND IMAGE THAT CONTINUED to return to Julia Brumfeld in the months and years after Mark's troubles—it was a kind of flattening to call them troubles—was an image she'd pushed from her mind for so many years she didn't know if what bothered her more was seeing it, or the futile and exhausting energy she'd put in to expunge it from her memory. It, too, was a simple visual image, but one that bore identifiable antecedents: bright white subway tile, a fluorescent-lit floor. On the tile, three stark streaks of red blood. The tile was white. The blood was red—when Julia allowed herself to think about it in words, it felt flat, meaningless, almost a cliché—oh, beautiful, you've described tile as being white, blood as being red, how evocative! Original! It could not be evoked and it could not be displaced, though it appeared as she cleaned out the basement, and again as she sat in her house in the days after Mark's arrest. Words flattened the image, distorted and falsified it. It didn't need words. Julia had long since accepted the clichés in her life. When she was seventeen it was as if her only goal in her life was to avoid becoming a cliché. She ran thousands of miles from her parents at great expense to her future selves to try to outpace becoming one. But after having Mark her life was a long, slow evolution of accepting and then walking inside well-worn paths and making them her own. That was parenthood itself when you viewed parenthood as an effect on the parent, not a responsibility to the child: living inside existing clichés, but lending them nuance. There was joy in it. Julia felt it every day until it was stolen from her by her own son, the responsibility for

whose actions it was anyone's but her own, a theft that began the day
Mark announced he was moving home from Brooklyn and was confirmed the day she learned of his actions in that very basement she had
spent weeks cleaning out for him.

Images on the other hand were each their own, original and unique
like DNA, and the image was image—incontrovertible, irreducible, and
tangible as the tile in her own kitchen a hundred and fifty miles south
of its referent. When she imagined herself speaking it, saying words
like "tile" and "white" and "subway" and "blood" to anyone—to her
beloved son, because Mark was still her beloved son even if she couldn't
bring herself to visit him for months after the attack or fully understand the charges against him, and no matter how her feeling for him
might shift in response to his actions she would never stop loving him;
to her husband, who would recommend to her a good therapist she
would never assent to see and wouldn't be able to hear, having rehearsed
the narrative surrounding the images themselves enough times that he
could no longer look at them with any semblance of objectivity; to a
therapist, who would analyze the unanalyzable—it was somehow more
painful than the image itself. As if that was possible.

But that was the image: white subway tile, clean taupe caulking between each, fluorescent lighting, three long, thin splatters of red blood.
It wasn't that Julia could not have provided the data points, the useless
facts she had sought through officious Dewey decimals or asked obso-
lescent Jeeves or looked up on facile capacious Google in the years after
those images returned. She was six years old. That's how old the memory was: she was sixty-seven now, she was six then, do the arithmetic.
A memory older than many of her friends. A memory older than the
federal agents pursuing her son, knocking politely on her door, trailing
surreptitiously her car. Almost a year prior she had come home from
school to find no one at her house. A neighbor came by to say her mother
and father were out, they would be back—one of her parents would be
back, someone would be back. But that wasn't accurate. Her father
wouldn't be back for years, if ever. Instead he was sent to the state
mental institution, known at the time in the official register as the Lunatic Hospital and in their neighborhood as the Nuthouse or the Loo-

neybin, and though she couldn't remember much of the long ride out Germantown Avenue until it became Germantown Pike, far past the western boundary of the city and into the city's western suburbs into Montgomery County, past the low pastoral hills of the Erdenheim Farms and into the semi-urban realms of Norristown and Conshohocken— though she couldn't remember walking into the immense brick edifice, or what she and her mother talked about or what music was playing in the background or what a squirrel looked like scaling the corrugated bark of a tree outside her window when they stopped at a stoplight at the intersection of Bells Mills Road, or what it felt like, or what its conse- quences meant when she would be raised without all the real spoils from the war, a war that had flattened her father to a mental patient and narrowed her access to all the spoils coming home so that only after she married Cal and got Mark off to college could she afford these instruments she was now being forced to move out of their au- tonomous space in the basement so Mark could return home—she had just a flash of white subway tile and the three thin lines of blood on it.

If she was pushed, sure—sure she could picture the brick façade, the entry wing jutting out like the snout of some great rust-red brown bear, but memory was as much the result of looking at photographs over the years since as walking in—of plugging it into Wikipedia to see it and just as quickly selecting "QUIT" on the draw-down at the top of the screen, fumbling with the mouse to make it go away though she knew it would never end, as if a memory could be quitted like the screen on a computer desktop—it was so immense she wondered if that was a perspective she'd seen it from as a child. So instead it was just: white tile, three lines of flung red. It was not a memory she would have cho- sen to recover or would have chosen to discuss. But in the months after her son was placed under arrest by federal officers, it began to return to her in flashes of pure image so that at times only a healthy 2 mg dose of Xanax, its acerbic bite dissolving under her tongue, or if things were really dire chewed and chalky in the pouch of her inner cheek and then feeling as it flowed sweetly into her veins relieving her of her burden, could save her from it as some inescapable, enduring present.

CHAPTER THIRTEEN

AND IT'S NOT THAT THERE WEREN'T MEMORIES of her father that pleased Julia from that period in her life. Those returned, too, as she took each fiddle in its case, each valuable mandolin Cal had let her buy though she could barely play it now, up to the cleared-out guest room. As a musician, so many of those memories were aural, came to her as the sounds twanging and warbling from their radio on weekends. Julia's father was pious in shul and as secular as they came outside of it. Soon after his return from service and starting in business with his high school friend Fyodor Semyonich, Julia's father had used what spoils they'd accrued after the war and bought a house more than ten blocks from her bubbe in Mt. Airy, his west of The Avenue, on Pelham Street. There on Sunday evenings her father would tune their old radio to the *Grand Ole Opry*. It was among her first memories, crossed with the vertiginous sounds of Hebrew on Saturday mornings, listening later in the weekend to the warp and wobble of Bill Monroe's mandolin, to the schticky humor of Grandpa Jones, to the tough low growl of Jimmy Martin as he tore into "You Don't Know My Mind." It was how she'd learned to play fiddle, in fact—trying to play over her father picking his Martin D-45 worked after a fashion; by the time she could saw out a tune he was institutionalized, and in playing over the professionals there was a limitless sense of forgiveness, a sense every sour note or dropped beat was swallowed by that great brown box, incorporated into the tight performances being broadcast from a thousand miles south in Nashville. It was the only place her father seemed at peace in the times he did come home—guitar in his hand, tune in his throat. In retrospect was there a frown that came to her mother's face when he was there and the radio was on and the King of Bluegrass sang his lyrics, when he sang "I'm lonesome all the time"? Memory had already skewed any hope Julia might have had for interpretation. She remembered they would turn the radio off and her father would play a couple of bars of taters on his pick-worn guitar, and she'd rub the thin amber of her rosin across her bow hair, kicking up a rarefied dust in the air around it, and she'd try to squeak out the melody of "Jerusalem Ridge" or "Whiskey Before Breakfast" or "The New Five Cents." The titles made Julia almost wish there was a song called "The Fresh Ironed Tin Foil." It might have seemed odd to their neighbors, she supposed, this family of Jews playing old-time American music on their long front porch in one of the westernmost neighborhoods of stolidly Northeastern northwest Philadelphia. But her father loved Woody Guthrie and Dave Van Ronk and her mother might have liked to have *been* Maybelle Carter minus the raised-top Gibson guitar, and anyway the Sidlers had been in this country since the Civil War, Jews who'd known what it was like to vote for Lincoln and read Thoreau, Whitman, Emerson, Dickinson in the pages of *The Atlantic Monthly* as it came to their front doorsteps, even if they wouldn't be able to attend Yale or Princeton for half a century.

By the time she was ready to finish high school, Julia Sidler was a strong enough fiddler to sit in on gigs with her father's friends from time to time, burly Jews who'd learned to play guitars and banjos like they were goyische and who welcomed her presence as a reminder of the old friend they were missing. She'd tried to get up a bluegrass band or two, but when she was a freshman no one at her Quaker Friends school seemed to want to play in that traditional idiom anymore. In the coffee houses in Center City it was just a guy with a guitar, Bob Dylan–style, mangling the classics into some new singer-songwriter message of political and social polemicism. Her first boyfriend had written twelve different versions of "The Lonesome Death of Hattie Carol," each its own didactic attempt to make rhymes out of local crimes and half of them still containing variations on the line "and emptied the ashtrays on a whole other level," a line which, indivisible as shorn memory, could not be improved upon ("and emptied the trash cans on a whole nother level"; "and cleaned out the gutters on a whole other level"; "and washed off her art smock on a whole other level"—each worse than the one before).

By the time Julia was ready to head for her first semester at Syracuse University, Dylan had already been proclaimed Judas in London's Royal Albert Hall, and he had Al Kooper's frenetic, jittery, raucous basslines running through his new songs, and a handful of freshmen in her central New York dorm owned tweed Fender tube amps, Strats and Telecaster Thinlines of varying pastel colors, and wah-wah pedals, trying to burn out chords and puff out shaky joints of seed-popping weed. That first semester and a half had gone fine for Julia, carrying over from her solid Quaker education at the Friends school she'd attended against her bubbe's protestations, the best school in the neighborhood, but here in college she just couldn't seem to find the right musicians, no matter how much she liked reading the history of art and Shakespeare and Plato and going to parties and hootenannies out in the barns of rural Dewitt. Her mother had set her up to wait tables at an Italian restaurant down on South Street starting in mid-May after that first year so she could earn some pocket money.

Then halfway through her first spring semester she met Willie Schtodt. These were memories that arrived now because she'd willed them, allowed them as she rosined up her bows and looked at those old instruments in the guest room of her and Cal's home. Willie lived in the dorm next to hers and kept to himself, though from time to time she would see him out behind the Hall of Languages, strumming a cheap dreadnaught knockoff of her father's D-45, which to this day she still owned and had set up with a new nut, new strings, before Mark returned home. She'd watched all year as Willie's hair grew wavy, then curly, a wispy beard mossing his lower jaw. But after holing up in the northeast cold all winter—it wasn't unheard of for a half-foot of snow to fall off the lake the second week in April—one day late that month the sun came out. It blazed so hot after almost seven months of gelid winter it was like an outright assault on every sense. Girls walked from the Bird Library up to the quad in halter tops. One time she saw a girl from her pre-law class wearing no top at all, just her breasts taut on her chest covered in paint like a pre-modern Scotsman marked for battle. And sitting with his back against his dorm there was Willie Schtodt, a new ersatz Gibson Hummingbird pressed to his shirtless, hairless chest, a rudimentary attempt at a bird on its burgundy pick guard, singing Jimmy Martin tunes, one after the other, affecting Jimmy's rasp and growl. He'd been holed up all winter like some snowbound Robert Johnson, learning bluegrass tunes at his own lake-effect-blizzard-imposed crossroads. They didn't even make eye contact. She ran back to her dorm and grabbed her fiddle. Before she knew it, they'd jumped into his MG-B and were headed across the country to San Francisco. His friends phoned to say they'd rented a place in the Inner Richmond, and against every objection her mother—her mother who'd been reduced to visiting her father in the State Lunatic Home on weeknights and weekends, who'd managed to send her to schools that allowed her scholarships to get to university in the first place—treading those very blood-strewn white tiles Julia couldn't strike from her memory more than fifty years later—she left all but her fiddle and the clothes she could fit in her backpack at a friend's house off Westcott Street and headed for the opposite coast, taking advantage of a freedom that felt earned and necessary and all but inevitable.

What she found there was nothing like the idyll Willie Schtodt had promised with his energetic renditions of "Sophronie" still ringing in his throat and the mushrooms his friends had picked off the manure dropped by some cows in a farm east of campus in Skaneateles looping gossamer threads through his brain. The three-room apartment his friends were all—all!—to share wasn't in the Inner Richmond after all, but in the Mission, a dingy old Victorian at Dolores and Twenty-second, where kids slept on flattened dirty cardboard in the cool misty San Francisco evenings and begged beers and joints from all the new heads headed in from the same coast they'd themselves just fled. There were good parts to the first weeks there—the Dead played a free show in Golden Gate Park and Julia got almost far enough to the front to see Bob Weir in his ripped jean shorts barking about empty spaces and someone named Cowboy Neil driving the Further bus and taking the band through the entire twenty-two sententious minutes of "The Other One"—but after she came home to find one of Willie's friends, a high school kid from suburban Boston, pumping naked atop his girlfriend on what she'd understood to be her and Willie's bed, Julia resolved to head back to Philly however she could, as soon as she could catch a ride.

Willie begged her to come to a party with him that weekend. "Fine enough if you wanna head back to Momma," he'd said, "but at least have some fun before you take off for the straights back East, you're out with the heads now." He sounded to her even then like someone reading lines from a poorly written screenplay about the era, hippie language loose in his mouth like ill-fitting dentures. Whatever authenticity Willie had evinced when he sang like Red Allen was absent when he tried to talk like a character in an Antonioni movie. So she was ready to leave but Willie convinced Julia to go out for one last night with him and his friends. There was a big old Victorian on Haight Street where some friend of a friend of a friend of Owsley Stanley had dosed the entire bowl of lemonade with some of Bear's own acid, at least they all said, and it was as if the top of Julia's head had been blown off for the next two days. They all brought their instruments with them, carrying them all the way from the Mission up the hills to the Haight. Where in the past she might have waited for Willie to pull out his ersatz Hummingbird and start a jam, and then lug out her fiddle and play quietly so no one would take too much notice, now Julia had her fiddle in her hands at all times. All in one epic night she became that Girl with the Fiddle. The Fiddle Girl. TFG. Tiff. It had been the only comfort to her that first night with Bear's lemonade—she could feel her jaw tightening half an hour after her first thimble-full of the stuff, could see that somewhere at the seared edges of the visible world the corners were turning up just the slightest bit, like the corners of a photograph touched on all sides by fire.

Hallucinating wasn't like the scenes she'd seen in *Dumbo* as a kid at the Sedgwick Theater on Germantown Ave.—no elephants exuding bubbles and turning colors. It bore no resemblance at all to the paisley-and-purple-swirled posters her kid would hang in his room thirty years later, lit by cheesy black light. It was more like the whole world lost its purchase on her mind—she understood later it was the other way around, but that was how it felt—and in that new state she might imagine something awful. Her back ached and her stomach felt like it had contracted into a gravity-sucking black hole somewhere at the immediate center of her body, and for what felt like hours or weeks she couldn't stand up. If she stayed perfectly still this would all at some point pass. But when it started to feel bad, like it might never end—and she understood then that nothing ever ended, it only repeated on some eternally recurring imagistic loop—if she dragged her bow across the fat G string of the fiddle she'd been playing since before her father was institutionalized, since before she had ever seen red blood on the white subway tiles that she pushed, pushed, pushed away lest it shift her trip to some whole new horror, taking over the beauty of hallucination with the ballast of memory, if she felt her right thumb against the cool ebony of the frog of her bow, things settled. The prodding of her fingertips against catgut felt right, cool and solid in the hot, vacillating world. The edges of the world still flitted up and sizzled, but now they turned toward her, everyone turned toward her while she scratched out "Wheel Hoss" on just the G and D strings of her instrument—then turned back to what they were doing. The morning a week later when some acquaintance of Willie's came by their Dolores Street apartment asking after Tiff—okay, TFG—okay fine, The Fiddle Girl—she couldn't even remember having played with his band. But what she'd done had impressed him.

"We've got a show down in Noe Valley later this week," the guy said. He had huge muttonchops like some kind of deep-forest insect larvae had grown homeostatic inside his cheeks, and the spice of his unwashed armpits seemed to enter her and Willie's room before he did. She looked at Willie. They'd been going so hard since that party they'd never even acknowledged she hadn't yet returned to Philly as she planned. She was still here. She didn't appear to be going anywhere anytime soon. The muttonchopped guy said his name was TR. He was the bassist she'd played with the other night at the party. She didn't remember playing with a bassist at the party.

"But listen," he said, "I'm shit on that old double bass and I know it, tears holes in my fingers, had blisters like water balloons after that night, I'm a professional on the electric, you'll see, you'll see, I promise you'll see." He did after all have his fingers wrapped in duct tape. He mentioned for the third time since his odor had preceded him into the room how much he loved her fiddling. "And then our manager talked to Bill Graham about a gig backing Spencer Willmont at the Fillmore next month."

This was a whole new thing now. This was something more than TR's BO entering into their place. Spencer Willmont had been a student at Yale before he dropped out to start a band out here playing what he called "Transparent Eyeball Folk." They made a record in Bakersfield that came out Julia's junior year of high school, and in addition to the pile of old Decca records her father had left her, it was the only thing she'd listened to for months her senior year. What had drawn her in, of course, was their version of Bill Monroe's "Blue Moon of Kentucky"—what Elvis had done at Sun Records to slow that song down and make it a pure country hit, Spencer Willmont had blown up the way Bear's acid had blown the top off Julia's head. It was listening to Spencer Willmont that had led her to the Grateful Dead in the first place, and in turn to an education in a whole area she never would have encountered. In their wide-ranging covers it was as if they were her own personal jukebox. She knew when she heard them cover Hank Williams or Marty Robbins what she was listening to—but when Pigpen sang Elmore James, or when Jerry found his way all the way to Sam Cooke, she found herself tracking those records down at a shop in Old City, where worlds of music now became familiar and new all at once.

But Spencer Willmont, who hewed closer to the originals than any of those more hard-core rock-and-rollers, bringing space and edge to the Louvin Brothers or Delmore Brothers songs he covered, made a sound that felt like it had come out of her and found its way into his mouth. It was pure American music, America distilled as it was in "Young Goodman Brown," as distilled as it was in the em dashes of Dickinson or the varieties of William James's religious experience.

Listening to him was like reading a line of Melville that reached out across the decades and thousands of miles and layers of stilted language to speak back to her what was in her own chest. Jerry Garcia himself had even played pedal steel—her father called it "the electric table"—on Spencer's first record. And here she was, in the Mission, bridging those miles and languages right back, being asked to gig with Spence Willmont himself. It was like traveling to the Temple Mount only to discover the plan was to eat shawarma and tahini with King David.

Julia actively avoided making eye contact with Willie.

She said she'd come sit in on some sessions with them, when and where.

The minute TR left the room—he didn't take his spicy odor with him, but left it in the room for days after his departure, where it settled in like a new roommate, reminding her and Willie what had been proffered—while continuing to avoid eye contact she told Willie she wouldn't do it. She didn't need it.

"I mean, Fillmore West? I'm not good enough to play Fillmore West. It could be the biggest opportunity for the biggest embarrassment of my whole life. It's an opportunity to fail on a bigger scale than anyone we know has ever had an opportunity to fail before. It could be like failing myself and all of America all at once. It could come to define me." Willie didn't say anything. "Or it could come to make me. Who knows. It's just so risky."

Willie put a shirt on for the first time since they'd arrived in San Francisco almost a month earlier. He found the roach of an old joint in an ashtray and emptied it on a whole other level. "I mean, I've never even played my violin through an amp before, let alone played one onstage in front of three thousand people."

"Bill Graham has roadies at the Fillmore to set up a fiddle player," Willie said. "He could make your grandmother's matzoh ball soup sound hip on that stage."

Now they did make eye contact for the first time since TR had left his pheromones behind. It was like the edges of her world were searing again, only this time not from a hallucination but from tangible jeal-

ousy and confusion in the man—well, boy—who'd brought her west in
the first place.

Willie left their apartment and didn't come back for days. Julia
wouldn't have known he'd come back at all if it weren't for the fact that
three days after he walked out, a lid of weed was gone from their top
drawer, and only the two of them had keys. She found herself thinking
about something other than Willie Schtodt for the first time in a
month. The next night, she went to the address TR had left for her. For
the first hour after her arrival, no one said a word to Julia. She was
The Fiddle Girl and she found that what had made her comfortable
when she was tripping her eyelashes off at a party was the same salve
in any social situation—she clamped down on her fiddle with her chin
and sawed out a line of "Soldier's Joy." It was only notes to them, but in
her head she blurted out the lyrics her father used to belt in his mock-
drunkenest blurt when he'd come back to join them on their Mt. Airy
porch: "Well, it's twenty-five cents for the morphine, and it's fifteen
cents for the beer, it's twenty-five cents for the morphine, won't you get
me out of here!"

Spence's new band was to practice in this huge empty house in
Pacific Heights, in a part of the city Julia hadn't even imagined existed
after three weeks of the trek up and down hills from the Mission to the
Haight. Long, open streets were lined with pastel-painted Victorians—
but these Victorians reminded her more of the subdued ones she'd seen
back in Westcott, her favorite neighborhood in Syracuse, more than the
rococo flourishes and bright solid colors of the Haight. These were
buildings that had gone up since the fire of 1904, that had been around
when Emma Goldman came here speechifying, that had been standing when the U.S. joined the war effort twenty years earlier and that
were now better-up-kept, flourishing in the dollars flowing back across
the Atlantic after V-J Day. San Francisco may have gone from haven to
hellion in the last couple years, tens of thousands of kids flocking to a
city that would never be able to hold even a million people total, bur-
bling over into the outskirts of its Bay Area neighbors, but they were
still flush with the ease of the two decades since their parents freed the
world's wealth for them, cashing in on the last breath of the breadth of

resources all those European colonialists had been collecting from Africa and Asia for almost a century, freed to grow their hair and minds and drop out. Did any of these musicians give a thought to it then, in their lysergic smudge, as notes flew improvised from the instruments their parents had bought them? Julia sure didn't, not then at any rate. Not until she was back on the East Coast with that same fiddle she would one day come to move to a second-floor guest room so her son could move back into the basement, anyway. Living in the moment afforded a freedom from memory but it demanded a freedom from thought as the price. Thought was not a primary mode of currency for anyone in those moments. It was in fact the one time in her life when Julia could live mostly free of thought, free of that thought-tormented age she would later live in, free of perseveration guilt and overweening memory. Free.

The newly formed Cherub Band rehearsed inside a house that must have been three, four thousand square feet, not an inch of it furnished—no rug touched its floors, not a chair to be sat in. The only way to sit was backed up against a wall or in the ample space of the house's uterine bay windows. It was like playing music inside the body of a giant flat-backed violin, part of some acoustic infinite regress, San Francisco as imagined by M. C. Escher. In a room at the back of the house a guitarist in a raggedy poncho picked out the opening lick to Johnny Cash's "Folsom Prison Blues" over and over and over and over, never looking up, bum bum bam-bum, bah bum bah-ah bum. Years later when Julia read Joan Didion for the first time she found the famous passages in "The White Album" about Didion's going to visit the Doors both familiar and off-putting—of course the rest of the band had waited hours for Jim Morrison to show up for recording sessions! You didn't become a rock star so you could arrive at rehearsal on time. You didn't become a rock musician so you could drive straight to the hospital to give birth. You became a rock musician exactly so you *could* take a detour to eat some Chinese food on the way to giving birth to your first kid. It wasn't a cleverly-if-cynically-observed ancillary. It was the thing itself.

An hour after she arrived and just after she was herself considering leaving—she hadn't learned the lessons yet that Didion herself hadn't learned—TR came in, with Spencer behind him. TR's muttonchops had taken on a whole new dimension, and the body odor now carried a sense of peculiar familiarity. It was its own kind of image, never as strong as the visual images Julia kept of her grandmother and her tinfoil or her white tile with its lines of blood, but the evocation of a different kind of memory nonetheless: sense memory. That smell. She would smell it on her own son when he got old enough to perspire but hadn't yet discovered deodorant and again when he returned from his interminable games of pick-up basketball when he came home in his thirties. Spencer Willmont himself was a whole other variety of human. He was maybe six foot three, six foot four, and while in photographs she'd only ever seen him in the most audacious of his intensely American Nudie Suits, that first time she saw him in person in their Pacific Heights rehearsal space he was wearing a dun brown suede serape with beaded tassels hanging down off his thin, flat, hairless chest. An acoustic guitar was slung across his back even as he walked in through the door. His gait was reserved, genteel even, as if he was preparing to lecture to them from Wheelock's Latin, not play his spaced-out American music. Before anyone said a word to him he flipped it around his body and across his chest and started pounding on an E chord with the flat pick in his right hand. For the first time since the first time she'd drunk Bear's acid, Julia stopped sawing on her fiddle. She'd never heard anyone play Bill Monroe's "Sitting Alone in the Moonlight" in E before, a key that would make playing it cleanly next to impossible on the mandolin or fiddle, and it took her a second to consider how she'd move from the E a step back to the E-flat that defined its changes before she realized everyone was looking at her. Well, not everyone—Spence wasn't looking at her, but somehow the rest of the band knew he wanted her to kick it off on fiddle without his even having to. She hadn't played a note yet. TR was thumping an open E string on his bass and staring at her. She could see the collective hairs of his left muttonchop writhing under the clenching of his jaw. But while it felt like they'd been staring at her for seventeen days, it hadn't even been two bars yet, and no one had spoken or would speak, and Julia hit the

first note of the melody as if she'd been waiting to voice it with the
conviction of her own syncopation, hopping in on the shimmering slip
between an E and an E-flat, jumping back and then away from that
blue note in the melody, and it was clear now she knew what she was
doing, that she was a fiddler with the solid up-the-middle chops of
Kenny Baker and the blue notes thrown in like she was Vassar Clem-
ents or Stéphane Grappelli, she was the right choice. She saw Spencer
look up at TR and TR look down at his fingers and everyone else look
down at their toes, bangs willowing into their faces, a coy smile playing across Spence's lips as he stood in the half-light filtering in through
the bay windows behind him.

CHAPTER FOURTEEN

THREE WEEKS LATER JULIA was taking that same solo onstage at the Fillmore. Back in her and Cal's home in suburban Baltimore, the only evidence of her ever having done so was the fiddle itself. There was no iconic photo of Julia onstage to hang in their basement and she didn't know if she would've wanted it hung if there was one—not a nanosecond of image that was meant somehow to capture what it was like, the thirteen milliseconds of an infinite and infinitely life-defining night. No one but her, Julia, knew what it was like—she was emperor of her memory palace and not even her son or husband was invited to join her. Moving her old fiddle from basement to guest room along with all her vintage instruments was enough for her now. She remembered as she carted that fiddle up two flights of stairs now how she rode up Market to the venue in an old Volvo station wagon with TR behind the wheel and she and Spencer in the backseat together. No one sat shotgun—Spence put the jacket from his Nudie Suit up there like it was another member of the band, which in a very real way it was. It was more identifiably a part of Spencer Willmont's act than she would ever be and it had been with him longer, too. This was his Captain America suit—he'd met with Nudie Cohn himself after he saw *Easy Rider* for the first time (he saw it more than a dozen, he said) and told him he wanted his closet stocked with jackets and pants like Peter Fonda and Jack Nicholson wore in the movie. He had a real and easy friendship with Nudie, who'd come to the States just before the war from Ukraine with his real name—Nuta Kotlyarenko—still emblazoned on his papers and who by two years after the war was already putting together some of the loudest embroidered rhinestone-laden suits ever to come into shimmering existence in the American South, just another immigrant whose audacious original aesthetic was straight up the middle of what we come to think of as our country. He was working on a Captain America Chevy convertible for Spence to drive around in.

"There's a kind of sartorial self-mythologizing that's maybe my favorite part of all of this," Spencer said as they climbed their way up Market Street. He said "all" like it was the tool. Despite his light Southern drawl, he spoke in grammatical, specific sentences like he was, after all, teaching Julia Latin now that he spoke to her at all. Awl. "One puts on a suit and puts on a show and the rest just goes."

"Why would you leave your opportunity at good schooling after coming out here?" he'd asked Julia after their second rehearsal. She'd just looked at him and said, "Why did you?" And he broke out in a big smile and said, "Touché, sweetie, touché."

Now in the car the awning of the Fillmore jutted out from the building up before them. Maybe three thousand kids filled the sidewalk and poured down into the street in front of them, maybe four—Spence was big, but this crowd was there to see the Dead, who they would be opening for. Julia would be lying if she said she didn't wonder who was paying for all those suits and cars, and it wasn't until she'd gotten free of those days of her late teens that she read about Spencer—about how his father had been a war profiteer in Raleigh, North Carolina, who'd helped lead the way for the arming of the USAF as they joined up with the Brits and Canucks as they began bombing Nazi Germany in 1944. His parents had sent Spence north to attend Yale, hoping a dose of Northeastern snow might help wet him down, but Spencer Willmont burned hot as a white phosphorus incendiary, and Julia should have realized he would stay in one place for about as long.

Tonight on the ride Spencer was the stiffest she'd yet seen him. "How do you feel the Cherub Band has developed," Spencer said, but it was clear he was seeking no answer, just looking out into the crowd. Then his arm was around her, pulling her across his lap to look at a whole slew of bell-bottomed kids waiting to get into the Fillmore. "Just get a couple drinks in you and I know you'll be fine," Spencer said, and as ever when he said "you," he always meant "me."

Backstage she watched as Spencer had a drink and then another and this was how he transformed, how his shoulders dropped and a spliff hit his lips and suddenly five minutes till showtime and it was like the Nudie Suit was wearing him. The band was called out by its full name for the first time onstage there when Bill Graham announced them.

"Ladies and gentlemen, we have a special treat here at the Fillmore West," Graham said, his thick Slavic lips and basso-deep voice carrying up to the second deck of the Carousel Ballroom. Julia could only see the shimmer of his thick brown hair under the sodium lights, and she was clutching the frog of her bow like she might choke it to death, like the abalone-inlaid ebony might give way beneath her clutch, all those kids in their nimbus of smoke writhing out there before them. Spence had his Captain America–jacketed back to the audience like he was Miles Davis, hitting a tater over and over, sliding up the D string of his nacre-crackling D-45, and he turned his Elvis head over to Julia, gave her a nod, his transformation complete, and she started tatering a G on her fiddle, too.

"On behalf of the band, it is my distinct pleasure to welcome to the Fillmore stage for the first time, Mr. Spencer Willmont and his Band of Cherubs." TR thumped hard on the G on his bass and Spence spun around, Nudie Suit jacket sparkling like a dwarf star in the Fillmore lights overhead, the Dead's huge tube amps blaring acoustic instruments at a level that might never be replicated in human history as he sang high and hard the opening lyrics to the Louvin Brothers' "You're Running Wild," a song he'd adapted as if it was his own. They played one long, cosmic, spaced-out set, forty-five minutes to the bounding heads out across the ballroom as they were picked out like individual motes by the lights above. They were opening for Moby Grape, who were opening for the Dead, who were the main act for the night, but Julia never even said hello to that other Spence, the Grape's lead singer, as by now she could do nothing but look at Spencer Willmont.

After the set he hadn't said much more to her than, "Nice solo on that last one," but she knew all his covers and all his own songs from listening to his record, and he had her singing tenor harmonies over him on half their set. She'd heard that Dylan rehearsed and recorded this way, too—just some charts up on a stand someone else had drawn up, one sketched-out run-through of each song on a guitar or piano so the musicians had an idea of what he was after, and the band was expected to get in there and sing and play as tight as a polished group. She was happy to do it all on the fiddle but she truly didn't know if she had the vocals to go there, too—there was no hiding behind a flat note three steps above a singer like Spence, no matter how blazing stoned they or their crowd were. You could make your voice all forceful and strident like Joan Baez or Donna Jean Godchaux, who had sung a couple steps above Dylan and Elvis, or you could get right in there and hit the note like you were doing a session in Motown. But song after song, rehearsal after rehearsal at that big, empty, echoey house in Pacific Heights, she nailed it. So while Spence seemed a lot more interested in the spliff he and Skip Spence were sharing in their backstage room there, Julia sat back and just continued to saw out double stops on her fiddle while all the rest jabbered and sang a chorus or two. At one point she felt certain Jerry was looking over at her, his big black beard roiling in the half-lights backstage like some wiry hirsute sea, but he was wearing a big old pair of aviators and there was no real way to know if he was looking at her without being able to see his eyes. He didn't say a word to her. For years later it was the story she *didn't* tell anyone because what story was there to tell? What was the beginning, what the middle, and how could there ever be an end? What was the story? Once when she'd almost become a famous musician she'd almost talked to Jerry Garcia after a show but in the end she was too shy so she didn't? It was like another image in and of itself, a nanosecond and an eternity, an event never begun and never finished and nothing to tell. It was like she'd have to take a story all the way back to the day of her birth to try to track what story she'd be telling—I was born and I played music and then I didn't and then I spent weeks cleaning out my basement so my one-day-to-be-a-domestic-terrorist son could move back, the end.

Before she knew it, Julia was calling her mother back in Philly to let her know she was going to be on the road all summer. In a phone booth outside of the one-ish-plus-star hotel where they were staying, she dumped dime after dime into the slim slot and pulled the slick plastic of the receiver close to her face. She didn't even ask how her father was doing because she didn't know what she would say if she learned the answer, any answer. The Cherubs were planning to hop on a bus and travel the southwest route, through New Mexico and Texas and across to Tennessee and North Carolina, playing shows at night and performing on radio stations in the afternoons, supporting Spencer Willmont in all his Nudie Suited peregrinations. She never even said a proper good-bye to Willie Schtodt—the afternoon she came back to their apartment he was still gone, though there was a fresh seed-and-stemmy quarter of weed in their top drawer, and she only saw his high school Bostonian friend, the same friend she'd walked in on with his girlfriend that week they first arrived on the West Coast. Looking at him now, it was like a year had passed instead of a month. She could hardly even remember the kid she'd been when she first got there.

"Going somewhere, sweetheart?" the kid said when she walked in. He was wearing a shirt for the first time she'd seen, but no pants, just a loose pair of tightie whities that hung around his hips like pachyderm skin. He looked like a boy, like a child, like some kid calling her sweetheart without knowing any better he was about to be grounded.

"I'm going everywhere, Yank," she said, already out the door. "I'm going fucking everywhere."

CHAPTER FIFTEEN

IT WAS LATE ONE NIGHT all the way across the country, in their only gig at the Fillmore East, of all places, that Spencer Willmont let them all know of his change of plans. He'd been absent at rehearsals in hotel rooms all the way across the country. He'd missed two radio shows in the past week, one in Columbus, Ohio, and the next in Morgantown, West Virginia—at each the whole band had showed up in the studio and waited around for hours for him to arrive before the DJs had to tell them they could perform with him or without him and regardless of their talents together they had to admit they couldn't go on without him—they were a totalitarian nation absent the Great Leader.

"I know we have all these shows scheduled," Spence said to TR. Julia was sitting on the sidelines, as ever, not saying anything. "But they're recording in the South of France and they need my vocals." Though she didn't know it, the winter before she started playing with them, Spencer had opened for the Violent Blossoms, and the Blossoms had just rented out a whole house east of Grenoble to record what they were certain would be their groundbreaking, big-sound record. Whoever could afford to pay for travel out there would have a place to sleep and they could come play on the next record and who knew what else after? Who knew. Julia thought that between that night and when he left Spence would come to her room, as he had been doing for the past two months, after every show. That night, she didn't see him at all. After the show he didn't stick around backstage. He didn't come to her. The next afternoon she saw TR in the lobby. Somehow she knew just from looking at TR's sycophantic face Spence was already gone. The heat of the summer day blazed in Midtown Manhattan. Julia took an hour to walk from the Plaza up Fifth Avenue, toward the Met. She decided to go into the museum. Somewhere in the statuary, amid the white Roman alabasters of kings and generals, Julia slumped onto the floor and cried for almost half an hour before a guard came along to tell her she had to go.

She had to go.

Julia couldn't even bring herself to find the rest of the band in the big apartment down on Houston and Attorney Street where they'd holed up before the show they were supposed to play at the Fillmore East. Spencer Willmont was on a plane for the Alps to the far east of the French countryside, headed for some little town called Bourg d'Oisans, where he would go record with the loudest, most flamboyant rock band any of them had ever heard. A decade later the Rolling Stones wouldn't even be old yet, but the Blossoms would be all but forgotten, one record reissued by Rhino Discs in the eighties to modest sales, a vinyl copy of which Julia also moved up to the guest room. The Cherubs were to scatter to the winds. With some luck Spence hadn't known about a couple thousand dollars TR had socked away knowing that a day like this would come for the band. When Julia snuck in later that day to grab her stuff and find some cheap way back to her parents' house in Mt. Airy—she had nine dollars and thirty-seven cents in her pocket, which on the day her son moved back into her house four decades later would buy her a copy of *The New Yorker* or a cup of coffee but not both—the rest of the band was sleeping off the damage they'd done the night before, but TR was up scrambling eggs in the kitchenette in the place.

"Want some?" he said. "Got some of that good chorizo from the market down on Second Ave. It's spicy. Spicy might be just the thing right now. Burn your mouth like the memory of fire."

"What the fuck kind of person," Julia said. She was standing with her back pressed to the cold plaster wall next to the range TR cooked on. There was a high-pitched ringing in her ears from all the shows they'd played in the last month, a literal sound in her head that would never subside. Like the tinfoil and images of her father, it wasn't a memory, it wasn't over, it would never end. She didn't even know what she was wearing—a pair of bell-bottoms she'd never seen before, a thin halter top though it was November, and a big old Sherpa sheepskin coat that might have been Spence's, or might have been someone else Spence had slept with's. She tried to picture herself party to the thousand-year-old statues she'd just been crying amid at the Metropolitan Museum of Art in Manhattan, stone and silence—what was it that Rilke had called music, the breathing of statues, the quiet of images—what someone would have seen if they'd seen her then, but she couldn't get above it. The sharp smell of Mexican sausage leaking out into sizzling eggs brought her right back.

"So here's the thing," TR said. "I socked a whole bunch of money away knowing this was going to happen. I mean . . . not *knowing* knowing, but you know—knowing. Knowing character is destiny, that kind of knowledge." Without taking his hand off the spatula or his eyes away from the eggs on the stovetop, TR reached into a brown paper bag on the counter. "Your share," he said.

TR pulled out a thin stack of bills. It had a rubber band around it, which made the edges curl up. He handed it to her. In Julia's fingers it was hard to describe how thin it felt, like the absence of substance you felt when you had filo dough in your mouth. Her hand told her she was holding a paltry sum and TR could see it in her face.

"Count it," he said. It was two thousand dollars. It was hard to believe that two thousand dollars, enough to live on for months, as debt enough to break you, amounted to so insignificant a stack of hundreds. It was the objective correlative of that whole period—enough to live on but in your hand so thin you almost couldn't feel it. "He's in a little town called Bourg d'Oisans. It's easy to find. France is lousy with expats these days. You can get there no problem. I'll write it all down for you if you decide you wanna go. You could. Easily. Or you could keep that and start what comes next here in the States. Free of Spence. Character, destiny. The good ol' United States aren't going anywhere anytime soon. The Cherubs, they dead."

Julia took the bills and shoved them into her pocket, their fibrous paper crumpling against her hand. She went back to her room. She had a decision to make, should I stay or should I go. For years she'd wanted change and now she was the agent of her own change. It occurred to her as she sat in that room that she never had made a decision of this size before. Never actively made it, anyway. She bolted her father's hospital after seeing that blood on the floor. She left her home in Philadelphia for Syracuse University because she was accepted to Syracuse University with a scholarship and that was what she should do. Even the thin wild mercury decision to head west to the coast with Willie, then back plinko-circuitiously across the country east with Spencer's band, had felt less like decisions than non-decisions: If Spencer Willmont asked you to join his band, you joined his band! If Willie Schtodt asked you to travel to San Francisco, you traveled to San Francisco. Now she had a choice to make, to head back home to the land she knew, or to thrust east across the ocean, back to the very country where her father had left his sanity behind him, along with any real prospects of his family's happiness, and of course she should've known then she couldn't and wouldn't do it.

Of course, she knew even then she'd one day end up being the kind of Julia Sidler or Julia Steinberg or Julia Goldfarb or Julia Feinberg or Julia Steinsteenowitzowitzsky who would spend weeks cleaning out a basement of all her expensive vintage instruments she and her husband could now afford so that her thirty-year-old son could move back in to live with her, but first this, for the space of those moments in that life in those nanoseconds not captured on film and not able to be captured on film or video or selfie or even in words or images, she could imagine it, it was possible, it was present and it was real and it was who she was—is—would forever and always not be.

BOOK TWO

BOOMER MISSIVE #1

"BOOM BOOM," ISAAC ABRAMSON SAID. He was sitting in front of the iSight in his parents' basement, Jerry Garcia's upside-down face over his left shoulder. It was late afternoon at the end of June.

"Today I punched a baby boomer in the face," Abramson said. "Today he punched back." Abramson motioned to his eye, touched his face. He felt the blood tacky against his finger. "Tomorrow he won't. This is the first Boomer Missive. Today I will lay out what there is to lay out when we think about the baby boomers, as Boomer Boomers, in the years ahead. There will be much more to say in the days ahead. Today I want to do two things, having already punched a baby boomer. I want to tell you a story, and I want you to think about just where you fit in that story yourself. Here's the story I want to tell you:

"Sixty years ago your grandparents went across an ocean to the continent of Europe to reap the material benefits of a singularly promising business opportunity. There was a war going on overseas. Your grandparents, not your parents, they helped. They helped us all. They had the noble intentions, the greatest generation's greatest generational intentions, the ones you've heard about your whole life. They were liberators, they were the deus ex machina Europe needed. They liberated untold treasure. It wasn't their fault—there it was before them, so they collected it up and brought it home. They came back with this treasure. Unfathomable treasure. Maybe even enough to send you to college, to buy you expensive sneakers when you were a kid. But your parents,

who did not help and did not themselves even plunder that treasure—
they grew up with more and more and more and more. They were not
liberators. They were not the purveyors nor the architects nor the exec-
utors of the noble task nor the players in the great game. They were the
recipients of the spoils, and they basked in it. They received the signi-
fier but not the sign, they were the first generation to have fall in their lap
all the lucre without exerting one iota of the toil. This was not their
fault, nor was it their responsibility—just as it was not your fault, nor
your responsibility, when it fell a generation further, to you, when there
was no more draft and no active war to join even if you wanted to.
When you were too young to know. Some of it they may have given on
to you in part. My parents, for an example, gave me a lot. They sent me
to college. When I was a kid they bought me expensive Air Jordans
and, later, Reebok Pumps. David Robinson's Reebok Pumps. They live
in big houses, our parents, the baby boomers. My parents, for example,
allowed me to have a room in the basement of one of those houses.
They cleaned out the basement for me, my old room, so I could move
back in. Here I am, sitting in that house.

"Here I am.

"But now they are old. And we are young. And our grandparents are
passing on. But our parents, they still have all that treasure their parents brought back from Europe. They live in big houses. They own the
goods that all that resplendent treasure afforded them. They own tall,
well-appointed brownstones in big cities. They have jobs. They own
mansions and more mcmansions and mcbrownstones and mctwobed-
rooms. They have jobs.

"They have *the* jobs.

"They have *all* the jobs.

"They were meant to retire at the age of sixty-five, these parents of
ours. They grew up amid a world in which they made a promise, signed
an unwritten social compact: you worked until you were sixty-five and
then you stepped aside. But not these baby boomers. That was the
promise that was promised them—but more important, that was
the promise that was promised us. And they have not retired. They have
not. They have not."

Abramson put his finger to his face again. He could feel it was flushed. For a couple of minutes he did not look at himself on-screen, but now he could see his red, red face. He barely recognized himself with his bulging eye, sweat-plastered hair—what remained of it—all over his forehead. He thought to pause the video, but he decided he would leave that long pause in. You could always edit later. Always. Then he continued.

"Now I want to tell you another story. A different story. I bet it's not totally different from your story. It's a story of failure. It's the story of my own failure.

"I, Isaac Abramson, am a failure. An abject, complete, massive, total failure.

"I graduated from a very good liberal arts college with a degree in English. I graduated cum laude. No one told me how little it would matter. The day I walked onstage to be handed a diploma, September 11 hadn't yet happened. No one would even have imagined it could happen. The tech boom was still a boom boom. I did the things I was supposed to do. I wrote good papers, I drank first bad beer, then good beer. Then bourbon, then scotch. I watched as the kids who graduated before me left for San Francisco and made money in Internet start-ups. Bought homes in Palo Alto, on the Russian River, in Sausalito. I watched that all go away. But I didn't want that anyway. I wasn't ever going to be in on the ground floor of Yahoo! or Google—I never thought Ask Jeeves was all that bad a site. Jeeves gave, I took. I had a MySpace account, wrote Friendster testimonials. I never once chatted in a chat room. I didn't know what the eye and em in IM stood for. That was fine for me. I wasn't greedy. I didn't want a new-economy job. I wanted an old-economy job.

"I wanted a job.

"I want a job.

"I wasn't a failure at first! I went to New York City, where I got a decent job. I lived there for ten years—ten years! one decade!—and I never once lived in an apartment alone. I had that job and then magazines went into the ground. Old media started to die. They didn't publish words anymore. They created content instead of publishing journalism. So I went back to graduate school. It was like a job. I read books and prepared to be an educator.

"Then I finished.

"Then there were no jobs.

"Then I accrued debt and I could no longer afford to live on my own. Now I'm back in my parents' basement.

"Does this sound familiar to you? Perhaps this doesn't sound familiar and if it doesn't, click away. Stop listening. Go stream some pilfered free music.

"But if it does sound familiar:

"Do you know who still had the jobs? I think you know who still had the jobs. I tried to get a job but I could not. I tried and tried. Then my money ran out. I could not find a job.

"This spring, I moved back into my parents' house. They gave me the room I grew up in. The basement room. They did not give me a car. They let me drive the same beat-up old Volvo they let me drive in high school. Today I live in a basement. My father is sixty-nine years old, and he has not yet retired from his job. It will disappear so that his hospital can pay for benefits so that its employees can pay taxes. My mother is sixty-eight years old, and she is, again, a stay-at-home mom today. Only now I'm who she stays at home with.

"Again.

"I am infantilized.

"Again.

"Now I want you to do one more thing. If you have no job, I want you to look at the basement where you live right now. Is it a basement like my basement? Does it make you happy, this basement? Does it smell musty? Does it contain the same couch on which you kissed your first girl when you were in the eighth grade?

"But that's not who I want to talk to right now. Instead, if you *do* have a job, I want to talk to you. I want you to do something different:

"If you do have a job, I want you to pull out your latest paystub. Or to pull it up online. Do you see the line that says 'Social Security Tax'? I want you to see how much money you pay every month so the baby boomers can live off Social Security. And I want you to know one thing: You will never see a cent of that money. You will *never* receive Social Security. You will never have a retirement. You will never have your parents' jobs, because those jobs will not exist. And you are paying not for you, but for them. You are *not* paying so that when you are sixty-five, you will receive security in the form of money. You are paying for them, now. You are paying so that they will be able to live well now, now that they are retired. But they are old and you are young and this is America, land of the young and home of the young, and when the system is broken you fix the system. Think about that until my next missive. Think about how this might look if it were different. Think this: Social Insecurity.

"*Social* Insecurity.

"Social *Insecurity*.

"Social In*security*.

"Resist much, obey little.

"Propaganda by the deed.

"Boom boom."

PART FOUR

CASSIE

CHAPTER SIXTEEN

THERE WERE TWO CENTRAL DEVELOPMENTS in Cassie's life in the months after Mark Brumfeld left for his parents' basement in the small city two hundred miles south of Brooklyn where he'd grown up. Neither was in any way expected, though both came to make her unexpectedly happy. The first was to solidify a job she'd never have wanted in the past. In early July she received a cryptic e-mail from someone at a news website that was looking to do, they said, something different from most news websites. They wanted to develop a well-funded, robust, and meticulous fact-checking department. On the face of it, the e-mail itself sounded almost farcical. The second paragraph started with perhaps the worst adverb known to man, the word *thusly*. Cassie intensely hated the use of adverbs, and she *really* hated the use of a pretentious one like *thusly*.

"Thusly," the second paragraph of this e-mail read, "upon seeking out an established and impressive researcher with extensive experience working in traditional print media settings who might bring an established skill set to our vertically integrated content-driven media organization, we have received your name as an apt candidate to take over and build a fact-checking division for RAZORWIRE. If working for a company such as ours, in which you could be entering on the ground floor of a start-up which has received major resources from a Silicon Valley VC firm, angel investors who can make the kind of resources available that traditional print media is no longer able to undertake, myself and my colleagues request that you send along a resumé and a letter of intense by week's end."

After reading the message a third time—oh, that neologistic solecistic use of the word *myself* almost literally turned sour in her ear, never mind the never-before-coined-but-surprisingly-awesome phrase "letter of intense"—Cassie felt the e-mail itself was far more in need of a copyedit than of fact-checking. It was dictively devoid of checkable facts.

But Cassie also felt she couldn't afford not to send along her materials and see what would come of it, if only to make it to an interview round in which she could discover who had sent this e-mail so full of empty palaver, the written equivalent of particleboard. No sooner had she sent her resumé than she had an e-mail back from RazorWire's director of HR, setting up an in-office, in-person interview for the following Monday. There had been no street address in the signature of the initial e-mail, but now she was provided with an address for her interview. A quick double-check on Google Maps confirmed what Cassie suspected: RazorWire had offices in an outrageous location. On her favorite block in the whole city, no less, on Mott Street near Elizabeth, just below Houston. While it was not a feeling she wanted to have, she now found herself curious about going into Manhattan for this interview.

She may just want this job.

It was, after all, the kind of job every liberal arts school senior with a degree in the humanities was in some way yearning for at that exact moment. Was she skeptical of the inept e-mail writer himself, of websites with West Coast VC funds and angel investors and editors who rather than thinking of magazines and newspapers as magazines and newspapers thought of them as "traditional print media"? She was. Was she into the idea of having a job that would take her to an office only three blocks from the Angelika, where she could watch the best indie films on the planet on a lunch break and be back to work without missing much? She was. She was that, too.

Cassie spent the weekend drinking with Natalia, who was around town for the first time that month, just off a long Southern tour. Their relationship had settled into a familiar but confusing condition of being at once routine and undefined. If Natalia was in town she texted Cassie, had her come over to her apartment or met up with her at one of their SoHo fixtures, Tom and Jerry's or Botanica. There was no question whether Cassie would come back with Natalia and sleep in her bed afterwards. Once she had even come back to Natalia's and, finding her whatever-Natalia-was-to-her already passed out by the time she got to her bed, curled up into the fetal position in the space left on her twin mattress and slept there, no sex, just actual sleep.

At the same time, any markers of a real relationship were conspicuously absent. They did not go on dates. They did not go out to dinner. Ever. There had been no conversation about how a night like the one in which Cassie slept over would proceed. There was, above all, a chasm instead of a space in which any conversation of the future might take place. They lived together in a kind of Heiddegerian phenomenological relationship present, in which only the present moment of drinking or playing music or fucking existed, an immediate *Dasein* of mutually undecided and uncommented-upon cathexis, Eros and lust. Cassie had read enough in her 200-level existentialism class to understand that much. She'd read enough to identify a sense of "thrownness" in her current situation, but perhaps not enough to understand what it signified.

What she did not know how to handle was the broader feeling of sadness and confusion that descended upon her as soon as she left Natalia's apartment. Or sobered up. Or tried to have sex with Natalia sober, which had only happened once, to genitally arid and generally stultifying effect.

So Cassie made her way into the city for her interview at RazorWire. The N train was densely packed with morning riders—it had been long enough since Cassie had ridden the subway on a weekday morning that she'd forgotten what a packed train looked like. She let the first train pass down the tunnel, it was so writhing with the press of morning passengers. But when the next train seemed to have an identical press of American Apparel T-shirts, handlebar mustaches, manbuns, cut-off corduroy shorts, and Warby Parker eyewear, she decided she had no choice but to get on, or arrive at her interview late. Two stops down the tracks she noticed the next car over appeared to be empty, so while she did not like passing between cars while the train was moving, she pushed her way through the press of morning bodies until she got to the end of her car, passed through the terrifying space between them, and found herself in a car bearing only three other passengers.

As soon as she heard the sliding subway car door click behind her she realized she'd made an enormous mistake. There was no air-conditioning in this car. Of course that was why it was empty. She could feel the sweat rise on her brow, a trickle of perspiration sliding down into her lower back, within seconds of stepping on. Worse was the smell. At the middle of the car, by the doors closest to her, was a shiny pile of what appeared to be still-warm human feces. She looked at the three other riders on that car and saw that all three were home-less, one of them now staring at the sweat on her brow and, she thought, imagining the sweat sliding from her lower back to, well, lower than that, and she turned to get back into the car she'd come from, but it was now somehow even more packed with Warby Parker American Apparel manbun facial hair and cutoffs and what choice did she have but to stay on this mobile underground clogged toilet until the train stopped? One of the homeless men on the car took out a cigarette and lit it and smoked the whole way into Manhattan. At least the smoke smell covered some of the shit smell.

By the time Cassie arrived at the RazorWire offices on Mott, it was already 10:17 A.M., and she was covered in a perspiration cycle that wouldn't give up as she walked into the lobby. There was no doorman, only a bank of elevators with a set of buzzers, one of which read "RazorWire" in a font she'd never before seen. There was something suspicious about the fact that the name above the company's was writ-ten in pencil and said "Schlict/Dick," and that the one below it was a fortune cookie fortune: "Not all opportunities knock," followed by a B&W smiley face. But the elevator doors opened before she could in-terrogate it further.

Cassie's mood lifted when the elevator doors again opened. She stepped out of the car into a wall of air-conditioned air. She was stand-ing in a loft of maybe ten, maybe twelve thousand square feet, and it was as if she'd come into some filmmaker's idealized sense of what a successful start-up office might look like. Above her head was the sinewy thick wood of centuries-old exposed joists, fastened to iron T-bars by bolts the size of one of her ulnae. The open floor plan included a copse of desks with nothing but laptops, some open and some shut like lady's slippers in an early-spring field, and along a far wall a glass encasement for a single office with a desk in it. Between the desks and the office was a long, thin, rectangular depression, dropping maybe four inches below the level of the floor. It was filled with sand. Two men about her age were standing in the pit. She watched as one lifted his hand and flipped his fingers effetely back toward his face, did it again and again, then transferred some kind of heavy-looking red orb into the hand from his other and let it fly until it stuck in the sand twenty feet in front of him.

"Bocce." It took Cassie a second to realize someone was standing next to her, speaking. "It's a bocce court. The only one in any office in Manhattan. We got the same people who put one in at Union Hall in Park Slope to do it. Someone knew someone there. It was tough to decide between it and shuffleboard, but I decided shuffleboard seemed less retro, more geriatric." The guy standing next to Cassie was maybe six inches shorter than she was, with a thick black beard, wiry and slick against his face, and a neck tattoo crawling up near his chin—on the left side of his neck in gothic lettering it read "BOY" and on the right side in the same lettering she could read only "NNY." "And I'm guessing you're Cassandra."

"Cassie," Cassie said. "Black. Cassieblack. Sorry. It's hotter than . . . well, whatever is a thing which is very, very hot . . . out there . . . and I had a bad subway ride up. There was shit, like, actual human shit and no AC and—well. Smoking. And. But here I am. I am here." The tattooed beard announced himself as Danny (not Granny, as Cassie had been glibly imagining) and said that she'd be interviewing with someone from Native Content and did she want a kombucha or aloe water? They had mango or loganberry if she wanted one. She said she did not. Danny opened the door to the glassed-off office in the rear of the place and a wall of even cooler air-conditioned air hit Cassie. Frigid. Sustaining for a polar bear atop a globally warming ice floe. Though it did not seem as if it would be possible just ten minutes earlier, Cassie was freezing. She could feel her metabolism, cellular production, her own thought process slow. It was as if an environment had been created in which a group of young people would be cryogenically kept twenty-six years old for the rest of their existences on Earth, staving off the ultimate horror of ever reaching their aging baby boomer parents' age. Individual beads of sweat picked themselves out on Cassie's upper arms and shot needles of biting cold into her skin. No sooner than she had felt it, the door to the office opened again and in walked her person from HR, author of the e-mail that had thusly brought her here. He was also six inches shorter than Cassie, but he did not have a beard or tattoos suggesting his name—or melanin, by all appearances. He was albino, his skin pale save where, across his broad nose, a smattering of orange freckles stood out in the artificial air. He had another splotch of orange freckles around his mouth that obscured where his lips were.

"So you must be Cassandra," he said. He sat down behind the desk, which was a repurposed, unfinished, rough-hewn oak door, with the blunt edges of rusty nails sticking out in arbitrary directions. It looked like someone had made a desk out of a planed horizontal telephone pole, and it was unclear how one could write on a desk with so uneven a surface and with so many asymmetrical protuberances, but the only evidence of an attempt to do so was a pad of neon-pink Post-its sitting beside a chrome laptop and a huge flat screen in front of it, the shiny newness of all of it making it appear to be only seldom used.

"Just Cassie," Cassie said. "Cassie Black. That's the full name. And you are?"

"Oh, sorry, how rude of me," he said. "Mario Wilson. I'm the director of the newly formed Native Content Division here. Well, newly form-ing. Currently amidst formation. I'm the one who sent you the note last week after you were recommended so highly."

"But you have the only office in the place?" Cassie said. It occurred to her that there was no attendant whir or rattle of air-conditioners to accompany the reverse-entropic cold of the office she was in. It was as if the cold was extended by the air of the room itself. It was so cold the only smell in the place was a whiff like snowballs each time Cassie breathed in.

"Oh, myself and my colleagues share this office when outsiders come in," Mario said. "Or potential future insiders or whatev." Cassie looked at him, deciding whether or not to ask how it was possible that they'd reverse-engineered the summer heat but couldn't afford to have separate offices for each staff member. She decided to keep her mouth shut. Increasingly she wanted a share in it. "Whatever. So you know why we've brought you in for."

"Not exactly," Cassie said, swallowing whole the circumlocutory way Mario spoke. It was all she could do not to correct him. Maybe she should be looking for a job at a copyediting desk somewhere—old media concept!—after all. But the truth was there were so many solecisms, so many grammatical and usage errors in the way he spoke, she didn't know where she'd begin in correcting him. "I mean, I got your e-mail and I've looked at your site before and all. Read a couple of funny lists you've published. But beyond your stated desire for a fact-checking division I don't know anything about the job."

"Well, things move fast here," Mario said. He had both his elbows on his desk now—not *his* desk, after all, he would say if he said it, but the desk he was sitting behind—and Cassie could see where the texture of the wood was digging deep red creases into the taut skin on his forearms. It did not look comfortable. She may even have detected a grimace on his face, but his posture was set for this part of the interview and he wasn't going to move it. "And the position has transmogrified a little even from the period when I first wrote you."

"Less than a week ago," Cassie said.

"Right. We toyed with our motto being 'Moving at the Speed of the Internet.' But that seemed too old-school. You know, having a motto. At all. We're a nimble, kinetic, rapidly transforming media landscape, right? RazorWire has now been in talks to move to the forefront of native content production in the new media landscape. Do you know what native content is?"

Cassie said she knew what "native" meant, and she did understand how the new media culture currently defined the word *content*—but, no, she didn't know what native content was, exactly.

"Native content is the current best shot journalism has of surviving in a sustainable financial model. Companies and advertisers will approach us with the desire for us to create native content for a specific product or campaign, or for their company or industry in specific. Our editorial department then creates, crafts, hones that content, and we package it on the site alongside trad content. It is designated as such, with some small but clearly identifiable design element to make sure the reader can distinguish between traditional story content, and native content." Cassie sat there looking at him. "Here, let me literally explain with an example. Literally, say HBO is putting out a show about bluegrass music."

"HBO is putting out a show about bluegrass music."

"What?"

"You said to literally say it."

He just looked at her. "Hah, okay," he said.

"I'm literally a bluegrass fiddler myself," Cassie said, trying to right the ship. She found herself at once skeptical and more interested than she'd been since they started talking, which seemed evidence of a certain benefit of the service itself.

"I know," Mario said. "It was on your resumé under 'other skills.' That's literally—that's why I used it as a example." Cassie felt heat come to her cheeks, her throat constricting, and was brought back to herself only by his use of the article "a" when he should've said "an." "So we might send a music reporter to do a piece on the bluegrass scene in Lower Manhattan, or a profile of the Station Inn in Nashville, or the Cantab Lounge in Boston, or a long profile of Chris Thile if he's attached to the project and how could he not be these days, he's such a rock star."

Cassie said that he was a long way from a rock star, given that he didn't play rock music.

"Bluegrass star," Mario said. "You know what I mean."

Cassie said she did.

"But that's it. That's the future. It's the future of where things are headed, and we want to know if you want to be a part of the future."

"Well, who wouldn't want to be a part of the future," Cassie said, while thinking, Unless I was actually to die of the cold in this office right now, I'm more or less certain I will have no choice but to be part of the future. "But honestly, isn't what you're describing just an advertorial? They always made advertorials in the past. Advertorial. Worst compound word ever?" She looked at Mario, who now just looked back at her. "But there you have it."

"The advertorial is a thing of the past," Mario said. "Very much an old-media concept. Our goal is to test out all kinds of new-media concepts to see if we can monetize them—and of course to use them to support the trad journalism and reporting we'll always continue to do. We'll do, say, this native content and use it to pay for arts coverage. We have a division that we haven't branded yet that will develop a kind of hybrid of political satire and reportage which appears as if it could gain serious traction on social media as we approach each upcoming election." Cassie asked him for an example of what he meant, if only to see if he'd again try for bluegrass. "Well, say, for example, Kanye ended up running for Senate—we might try to see if stories about his relationship with Kim, or about his childhood in Chicago, might gain traction, though they weren't true. We could let our readers come up with the concepts and then have our trad op-ed reporters write the pieces."

"So in this case what you're describing is crowd-sourced propaganda?"

Mario paused. "I'm not sure that's quite what we'd call it, but I like the way you think, Cassieblack. Moving straight to branding. I guess maybe . . . Open-source speculative journalism? Oh. That's actually kind of good." Though there was that pad of pink Post-its in front of him, Mario took out his iPhone and typed it in. "I could share credit for it with you if you joined us. When." Cassie held her face still, trying to keep her jaw from slamming against her chest. "Okay, fine, I'd give you all the credit. You drive tough deals. I'm liking you more by the minute."

For the first time since he began talking, he sat back in his chair. On his forearms, long red streaks had burrowed into his skin from his desktop, running lengthwise against the orange freckles up and down his arms. As inconspicuously as he could, Mario rubbed the tips of the fingers of his opposite hands along the painful-looking grooves. "But the main thing is that as you join us you need to stop thinking in terms of trad media and start thinking new media. The trad stuff was fine back whenever, in the Clinton Era or whatev—sorry, what-ev-er—but we're obvi moving in a new direction, new revenue streams, the places where journo and content and editorial will all be heading."

"And you want me to fact-check it," Cassie said.

"Join us as our director of research. That's right. I guess that part of it is trad, after all—a traditional research department. Like, our own snopes.org. Or factcheck.org, only without the dot org. Bringing a kind of retro feel to the way we do cutting-edge journalism. RazorWire thinks one of the best ways to solidify the native content model will be for us to be able to offer to partners that the work we do for them will undergo the same strict kind of overly meticulous, disproportionately funded scrutiny editorial always did in traditional media. So. Yes. You'd come in to head up an initiative to start a robust research department."

"Fact-check advertorials, and down the road, gussied-up propaganda."

"Come on with the title of director of the Research Department for RazorWire's new Native Content Division."

Cassie sat back in her own chair now. The way he stated and inflected it, it was entirely unclear if that last sentence was an interrogative or an imprecation. There was nothing in need of rubbing on her own forearms, and Mario wasn't going to lean forward again himself—he had to maintain some sense of self-preservation even while having his crack at interviewing someone in the big office with the big repurposed wood desk—and the two of them were suddenly sitting very far from each other. "You've come very highly recommended. I can honestly tell you without your having to walk out of here that folks want you in."

Cassie didn't say anything. An image flashed in her head again of the thousands of liberal arts school senior English majors who would view an offer like the one being presented to her as the goal. She was not savvy in these situations and honestly didn't want to be, but before she left her home in Ohio the summer before graduation, her father had given her one piece of business advice she had taken, and which helped: always leave as much dead space in conversation in a job interview as possible. Leave pauses, allow the interviewer to play his hand. "If you wait," Dad said, "just count to ten, or sing the chorus of a song you like in your head, you'll get two benefits: you won't say something untoward or overenthusiastic yourself, and you'll force the person opposite you to tell you what they want, even if they don't want to." Which is what happened now in a way that made her father look like a sage.

"Oh, and I'm sure you'll want to know what the compensation package looks like." Now Mario reached for the neon-pink Post-its on the desk. He pulled a Uni-Ball Vision from his pocket. He put the thin pad down on the desk and wrote something, and Cassie could see the Post-its bend and crinkle as he attempted to write. He picked it up, brought it very close to his face and looked at it, squinted a little, and handed it to Cassie. She couldn't tell what the last five numbers said, but there were six digits in the number, which made the salary at a minimum three times what she'd ever in her life earned in a year. It might have added up to more than she'd made, total, in her twenty-seven years on the planet. It was enough to consider overseeing crowd-sourced propaganda.

"Well, I will be very happy to take the night to think about it," Cassie said. She did not need the night to think about it—you'd have to be in possession of a trust fund or an M.D. or far more scrupulous scruples than Cassie possessed not to take a job in that office with that bocce court and that salary, whatever it was—but this was part of her father's advice, and she was decent at following rules when she needed to be. She stood and left the office and headed out to the broiling summer midmorning after having left it with Mario that he would message her with the offer package.

CHAPTER SEVENTEEN

OUT ON MOTT STREET the heat was no longer an issue. She was so frigidly recalibrated from the forty minutes she'd spent in the glass office within the RazorWire office within the building within SoHo within Manhattan that it seemed she might never perspire again. In addition to the elation she carried out of the office, she carried a realigned core temperature.

She swiped her phone and went to make a call to Natalia to tell her the news, to get a reality check on whether this was possibly a good thing, and if there was any reason for her not to take the job. When she unlocked her phone she saw a text had already come through from Mario. He had AirDropped the offer package onto her phone before she left the building, which was not a thing she knew how to do herself. She couldn't help but feel impressed by his technological acuity—no matter how great a Luddite a person was, Cassie had observed in her not quite thirty years on the planet, they couldn't help but be awed in the face of true technological aptitude. It was like seeing a staggering wave on an ocean beach: its enormity could only be comprehended when witnessed in person. She opened the file and the number she saw there was fifty grand a year *more* than she thought she'd been offered. The differential between offers itself, even after taxes, would have been the most she'd ever made in a year. While she didn't understand anything about vesting or what vesting was, short of being the word *investing* without the prefix *in*, it appeared she could also stand to make a large, large amount of money if she continued to work for RazorWire for more than a year.

Now she was ready to talk to Natalia, but before she could tap her finger on the green phone icon again—she had not taken a step further from the entrance to RazorWire, had stopped in her tracks as if the only thing that could exist in the phenomenological present was whatever information was brought to her on her phone—she heard someone say, "Cassie. Cassie Black." She looked up to see a face that was familiar, but which between the disorientation of leaving the building and the dislocation of stepping into the summer heat from the arctic air and looking up from her phone and trying to have any emotional understanding whatsoever of what it would mean to be a twenty-seven-year-old liberal arts school alumna working at an Internet content development company making six figures, was not placeable to her.

"Regan," the person said. "Remember? Regan, from that *Unified Theory* party earlier this summer." She was. She was the same Regan Cassie had met along with Mark and Mark's editor Deron when she brought him to that *TUT* party, who for a substantial part of the evening she'd been certain was named Jordan. Cassie still hadn't quite found the wherewithal to speak aloud that recognition, but neither was Regan the kind of person who would be willing to stop long enough to force her to acknowledge what they both clearly understood. "So you'll take the job."

"The job," Cassie said.

"The research director position at RazorWire." Regan was pointing back up at the building where Cassie had just finished her interview. "I was the one who recommended you. I'm director of content there." Cassie mentioned that Regan had said she worked for some socialist or anarchist journal when they met just months before. She must have left that job? "So you do remember me, then. Good. Oh, I still do the *Czolgosz* gig on the side when I have the time. But it's a labor of love. Working at RazorWire is a job. The minuscule amount of skillz that pay the not-so-minuscule billz. Obviously. You must have some bills. Seriously. We'd love to have you join."

Cassie fumbled her phone back into her pocket, and left her hand in there after, feeling for the first time some warmth return to her fingers.

"It's an opportunity," Cassie said.

"It is that," Regan said. "I went to bat for you for it in a major way. Don't fuck it up." She looked directly into Cassie's eyes, so directly Cassie felt compelled to look down at her own feet. By the time Cassie looked back up, which was not seconds later, Regan had already turned and walked into the building's tiny lobby and out of view. Cassie realized that she had now been standing more or less in the middle of the sidewalk on Mott Street for five solid minutes, and that if she was going to have any luck making her call to Natalia she would need more privacy. She walked up to Houston and back across town until, wending her way through the quaintest cobblestoned blocks in Lower Manhattan, she found the stairs up to Housing Works. She ordered a drip coffee, pulled a copy of Emerson's *Collected Writings* off the shelf, and called Natalia. She told her about the offer.

"Jesus, that's a lot of money," she said. "That's like, 'Go ahead and own your own Econoline van for tour' money. Of course you take it. And oh, man, will your Pussy Willow be miffed when he hears."

Cassie was off the call with Natalia and back to her coffee and looking around the wide-open space of the café in Housing Works before she took in what that last comment of Natalia's meant, what it would mean to tell Mark about this new gig. He'd been finished with magazines—a job he'd gotten her into in the first place, a job she'd never trained for, never wanted, and never sought herself—and finished with a New York he could no longer afford, while giving over his life to an attack on the impossibility of finding a job, and now here she was, still three years away from thirty and living in New York and about to draw a substantial salary for doing a job she wouldn't ever have wanted until it was offered to her. Which was one definition, she supposed, of work: doing something you don't want to do in exchange for money. That wasn't Mark's definition of work. It was something like the exact opposite of his idea of work. But it was just about everybody else's. She didn't realize it when she was in the RazorWire office, but it was Mark she was thinking of when she tried to imagine someone so scrupulous they wouldn't even consider taking a job like the one she was about to take. Mark's definition of work was more like: doing a thing you love so much, with such artful labor and natural talent, it doesn't matter how much you get paid for that work, or by whom. Or if you get paid at all, even. You'd do it anyway. That was surely not how she would view this RazorWire job, or how anyone there viewed it. And it occurred to her how many of her views of the world were her espousing Mark's views, or her father's—or Natalia's, for that matter.

She would have to take the job.

It didn't change her view of Mark's protest, his quixotic Boom Boom revolution—if anything, it only intensified her support of it—or of him, anyway—clarified the need and immediacy of the argument he wanted to make so publicly. Because who wouldn't want to live in a world where people were given an opportunity to do the thing they loved most, as opposed to *not* being invested in the work being a precondition of doing that work? Mark's Boom Boom fanaticism was about a certain kind of love, it occurred to her, and it was a variety of love she'd like to support. But it still didn't preclude her from taking this new job. If so arbitrary an offer could come to her, in an office chilled and bocce-courted or shuffle-boarded and populated by humans born after 1985, Isaac Abramson was more right than he even knew about how fucked the landscape had grown.

That still didn't mean Cassie was stupid enough to contact Mark about it, or about anything, until she had to. She understood that he still loved her, or lusted for her, or just wanted to be around her, and something about that sense of neediness pushed her away from him. The Willow Gardens didn't have any gigs lined up again until a possible spot opening for Punch Brothers at Mercury Lounge in early December—that one hadn't yet been confirmed, Natalia was helping out—and there wasn't much reason for Cassie to e-mail or call. And since he'd grown so obsessed with his Boomer Missives and whatever weird stuff he was up to surrounding them, he hadn't gotten in touch with her much, either. There was an irony in her ability to keep track of Mark by watching him on the Internet, now two levels removed, in time and in space, from him. It allowed her to feel as if they were in touch, knowing she could see him, and it allowed her to absolve herself of whatever implicit guilt she might feel in not getting in touch.

CHAPTER EIGHTEEN

HER FIRST MONTH WORKING AT RAZORWIRE, Cassie found herself acclimating to the office environment, a fact that was both true of all office experiences and one that was born of the relative lack of difficulty in her duties themselves. The Native Content Division of the company wasn't technically a "division"—it wasn't divided from anything physically, or conceptually for that matter. Cassie was assigned a long desk by a wall as far from the windows looking out on Mott Street as any in the office, and while her e-mail had the title "Director of Research, Native Content Division, RazorWirePublications" added to the automatic signature stamped at the bottom, there wasn't anything for her to direct. She did not have any subordinates. There was no budget to hire other fact-checkers, and so there was no one to oversee or whose work to coordinate. The work itself moved fast. Mario sent out an e-mail company-wide, telling all editors that each native content piece they worked up should be fed into a Google Doc, which Cassie would open, fact-check, and sign off on before it went live, by placing in caps her initials, CB, at the bottom.

For her first week at the company Cassie opened the file to look for pieces, but after four days of finding nothing there for her to work on—she read over a couple of listicles and caught spelling errors, the purview of a copy editor but there was no copy editor, and signed off on them, while it was unclear if she was even supposed to—she stopped checking so much. She went on iTunes and bought the new tUnE-yArDs record, listened to it three, four, sixteen times, while pounding out rhythms on her desk and watching from a distance as Regan played bocce with her coworkers. She left for long lunches, scouring her part of SoHo for the best cheap pho place. One afternoon she walked all the way down Mott to Chinatown, where the summer heat made fish blood smell like the city itself had vomited, pushed in by the press of tourists and workers out on lunch break. On the Tuesday of her fourth week, just as she was beginning to feel she had no real purpose at this office at all, she got an e-mail from regan@rw.com. The subject line was "bocce," and the content in the note (she'd begun in her head calling all written material she read for work "content," though if she'd realized she was doing so she might just spoon the frontal cortex of her brain out of her content-driven head through her content-driven nose in order to again feel emphasis-on-the-second-syllable content) just read, "Bocce. Ten minutes."

So the bocce-playing portion of Cassie's time at RazorWire began. There were only seventeen employees who came to the company's offices, as the vast majority of their content was provided by freelancers in Iowa or Boston or Qatar. Three of those on-site employees were Cassie, Regan, and Mario. So the three of them played a lot of bocce. Cassie was terrible. Both of her colleagues were seemingly ready to go pro. Mario had perfected the technique she'd witnessed on her first day before she knew it was him she was watching: ball in the hand, palm to the ground, flicking all five fingers toward the oak joists high above. The grace and ease of the subtle backspin it put on the ball allowed him to place a shot anywhere on the court, the ball sticking there without rolling forward or back after it landed. Regan, on the other hand, treated the game like she was a pro bowler with a pugilist's sense of decorum. She flung balls underhanded like a softball pitcher—and with a pitcher's natural sense of command. Every time Cassie felt she had a ball in position to score, even a ball touching the littler ball they were all aiming for (Regan told her it was called the pallino though Cassie didn't have the temerity to ask in person, e-mailed her from across the office to find out), Mario would come in and drop a ball closer, or also touching. Then Regan would strut up, fling her own ball down the middle, scattering everyone else's to the four winds and leaving her a winner. Cassie got better, grew closer to her colleagues, and she entered into a new relationship in the days that followed.

CHAPTER NINETEEN

BY THE TIME THE FIRST WAVE of Boomer Boomer videos calling for action against baby boomers across the country started to take over the news cycle in early fall, Cassie was afraid she was in love with Regan. This was the second major development in her world since Mark Brumfeld absconded for Baltimore, and it was somehow even less expected than her taking a job at RazorWire had been. She did hate Regan—Jordan—whatever she thought her name was—that first day they met at the *TUT* party. But as they stood down on Elizabeth Street smoking cigs (Regan called them cigs and though Cassie resisted at first, the two syllables saved did come to feel efficient in free-wheeling conversation), getting the stinkiest stink eye from all the healthy baby boomer Manhattanites and tourists passing them by, Cassie first came to find that she didn't, in fact, hate Regan. That was a start. Regan had a certainty to her that came off as abrasive at first, a way of speaking so quickly and with such precision that it appeared she was a complete know-it-all. But as they began to talk more, Cassie saw that (a) Regan might be on the spectrum, and (b) Regan did seem to know almost everything about everything, which didn't make her a know-it-all, but instead someone who did, in fact, know almost all. Of it. She was barely older than Cassie and yet she already had a Ph.D., had published multiple academic articles in major humanities journals, *and* now had a high-ranking job at one of the hottest start-ups in New York.

On their second cig break down on Elizabeth, Regan asked Cassie outright if she'd read any recent issues of *TUT*. The last two were the edition with Mark's Emma Goldman piece in it and the one after.

"I haven't." Cassie had no choice but to admit it.

"Why not?" Regan said. She didn't look at Cassie when she said it—she had her eye trained to the gray sidewalk that was growing grayer in the covering of her own cigarette ash. A woman in her mid-sixties walked by and looked at them and said, "You know you're not supposed to be smoking so close to that building," and Regan said, "Fuck off." Once the woman was out of sight so she wouldn't see them acquiesce, they moved a couple hundred feet down, to the edge of a park. Back when she was a senior in undergrad, every person Cassie knew smoked, at least before finals week. The school paper reported that 93 percent of seniors polled smoked at least five cigarettes a day. Now, only six years later, smoking in public was like masturbating in public, only with less pleasure.

"You still didn't answer me," Regan said. "The new one just came out. But why didn't you read *TUT* 34? At a minimum you must have had to read Isaac's piece after all he put into it."

"Mark," Cassie said, correcting her. Regan just looked at her. Part of Cassie wanted to say it was because she didn't fucking want to read a magazine with no pictures, with no celebrities, whose acronymic name sounded like an expression of parental disapproval. Tut. Tut, tut, tut. She'd heard they wanted to call the magazine *Les Mots Justes* but decided to rename it when they realized a lot of their friends thought they were saying Lame-o Juice. Lame-o Juice. But she didn't say that. She thought better than to. Instead she said, "I guess maybe because I was so invested in it, in what it meant to Mark—Isaac, whatev-er—that now that he's left the city, and it didn't do for him what he thought it might, it would be just painful to have to go back through it, good or bad. Reading it would be more like the emotional experience of reliving watching Mark work on it than it would be like reading an essay. Which I wouldn't want to do, either. And I really, really don't want to have to talk to him about it. Thusly . . ." Cassie finished talking and waited for Regan to lay into her, to tear down all the reasons this made her anti-feminist, anti-intellectual, the subordinate in this formerly central relationship in her life.

Instead she said, "That makes sense." That she said it while rolling another American Spirit with its dry, coarse tobacco, while not looking up at Cassie, and without evidence of any emotion on her face, was a good example of why Cassie thought maybe she was on the spectrum, if just barely. It occurred to her that anyone not affable and full of social graces was referred to as "on the spectrum," and that that could in and of itself be a signal that it wasn't quite true, that most people's grasp of what it would mean to be on the autism spectrum was probably pretty tenuous. Herself included. Honestly she had no real idea what it was even a spectrum of. But.

"I do think you should have a look at the new *Czolgosz* we just put out, regardless," Regan said. "I know it's not your aesthetic or political bent, but it's smart, I think. There's a long comparative history of John Brown's attacks in Osawatomie, and of Czolgosz himself, in there. All about how Brown was essentially the first American terrorist. His goals were pure: he was the strongest voice in favor of abolition and the only one doing anything, while Thoreau and Emerson and those lazy effete aesthetes just sat around Boston talking about it. But never mind Harper's Ferry. He killed twenty-three people in Kansas trying to make a statement against expanding slavery into the territories. Cut off people's hands while their wives and children sat inside waiting for him to bring them back. They had to hang him one way or another. But we should take him seriously in 2011."

Cassie didn't know anything about John Brown, other than that a song she'd played at bluegrass jams when she was a kid in Ohio was called "John Brown's Body." She didn't know the lyrics. She'd never heard of the other guy, and she said so. She took a long pull on the American Spirit Regan rolled her with expertise despite its harsh tobacco. Stuff like that had stirred some of the love she was feeling—she didn't have to ask. She just stood there on Elizabeth Street and talked and listened, and Regan took care of her nicotine needs without her even having to ask. She anticipated Cassie's need for a cig, where Natalia anticipated being gone on a West Coast tour for much of the fall.

"Leon Czolgosz was an anarchist who assassinated President McKinley. McKinley was on a whistle-stop tour. Czolgosz was pissed, had seen Emma Goldman speechifying and fell for her hook, line, and sinker, and McKinley was going to do away with the gold standard—it's a complicated macroeconomic problem with a complicated background, but it was a major issue of the day, like talking about Islamofascism or NATO or the future of the Middle East today.

"Anyway, Czolgosz walked up to McKinley while he was on a whistle-stop tour, in Buffalo, pulled out a pistol, and shot him in the gut."

For some reason the details, the names and references Regan was making, were sounding so familiar to Cassie. But she couldn't place where from, so she didn't say it. She could see Regan could see it on her face.

Regan said, "Hold on while I finish. So McKinley was dead in a day. Czolgosz they put to death by the end of the week as well—can you imagine a world in which a capital case could be decided in a matter of days? They put him in front of a shooting squad, then they dissolved his bones in acid so there would be no remains for the rest of the anarchists to fight over, be spurred on by Czolgosz." Regan took a long pull off her own cig. "You really didn't read Mark's piece on Emma Goldman? He was mentioned in there."

Cassie had to admit once again that she was so exhausted by the whole process with Mark and that piece that she'd never read it.

"Okay, but you're a bluegrass fiddler—you must have heard the song about him. There was a version on the Harry Smith anthology. Later I think Bill Monroe did it as 'The White House Blues.' It's an old folk song."

"Shit, yes, right," Cassie said. The sense of familiarity all came washing over her now, to the point that without even meaning to she sang a verse to Regan: "McKinley he holler, McKinley he moan, you gone and shot me with your Iver Johnson gun, you're bound to die, you're bound to die." Cassie blushed, realizing she'd just been standing on a street corner in SoHo on a work break singing bluegrass music rather loudly and authentically. Regan just smoked and didn't smile because she appeared to be incapable of smiling. Cassie hummed to herself, feeling some of her hiatus from music prickle on her skin—she'd barely touched her bass, let alone her fiddle, since taking the job at Razor-Wire. Regan was a fount of this stuff, knowledgeable about every aspect of American history, American folk music, posters, songs, and native religions.

"What's happening now with our very own home-grown anarchist?" Regan said. For the first time since they'd been out there, she looked around—it wasn't clear if she was looking off anyone who might complain about their smoking, or if she was protecting them from ears in the next part of their conversation.

"I don't think he's an anarchist," Cassie said. "Not avowedly, anyway." Neither acknowledged who they were talking about, just as neither of them acknowledged that after talking about the long essays she was going to publish in her journal, Regan would head back up to the RazorWire offices to edit a list called "Ten Amazing Things You Didn't Know about J. K. Rowling!" But they had both worked on an essay about protests that were popping up all over the country, the main demands made on baby boomers by the Boomer Boomers as well.

"Whatever outcome comes from these missives, from whatever's brewing, it's going to be anarchic. It might not be led overtly by an ideological principle of anarchy—there's an oxymoron for you—but he has to think that anarchy is the only viable end product of his ideology."

Cassie said she didn't have any idea of what the end product of any of his actions was at this point—it seemed like he was just a guy in his thirties without a job, living in his parents' basement, having found some direction for his energies for the first time since his fall from grace and forced good-bye-to-all-that. She didn't have the heart to say she hadn't been in touch with him in almost a month, that when he did write her it was becoming clearer and clearer that he still pined for her and even if he didn't say it outright, that she both didn't want to tell him about her new gig—which might send him further into his rage—and didn't want to tell him about Regan, whom she suspected he'd been attracted to and who she suspected she herself was now not only attracted to, but was starting to have feelings for in a deeper, more meaningful sense. So she just said:

"I honestly don't know. I guess I could ask him, or you could, but I honestly don't know."

"I'm not going to e-mail him, if that's what you mean," Regan said. "I don't even want contact with him on an IRC channel or anything. Not a good idea in any case. I'm trying hard to limit my online footprint these days." Then she didn't say anything. But there on the sidewalk in SoHo on a hot late-August afternoon she walked up to where Cassie was standing, put her hand on Cassie's face, smiled for the first time Cassie had ever seen, and said, "Can I kiss you," and when Cassie, amidst her surprise, said, "Yes," kissed her, and Cassie kissed back.

"I've been wanting to do that for a very, very long time. Since we first started coming out here for cigs. Or playing bocce. Or met each other." And though the last claim wasn't true for Cassie, the others were very, very true and so she said, "Me too," and they went back up into the RazorWire offices to fact-check and edit, respectively, lists that would, with any luck, go viral on the Internet.

CHAPTER TWENTY

IN THE WEEKS THAT FOLLOWED, Cassie and Regan began to have what looked far more like an overt relationship than anything you might have called her romantic involvement with Natalia. Or with Mark, for that matter. Cassie didn't hear from Regan for most of the weekend after they kissed until, on Sunday night, Regan texted her to say that she'd made a reservation at Prairie Fire, a haute cuisine restaurant on the third floor of the Time Warner/AOL Center, off Columbus Circle. The place was very far from either of them in Brooklyn, but it was an easy shot uptown from work on the R. It was implied they would simply leave work together after the day was done.

Dinner was the best meal Cassie had ever eaten, and she and Regan kissed on the train home, hands on each other's faces but little more, and up to Regan's door on Joralemon Street in Brooklyn Heights, where the ailanthus trees spilled green oval leaves on the ground like they were undressing, and when Regan didn't invite Cassie back up to her place, Cassie had no choice but to walk back to her own apartment, feeling jealous at the scantily clad trees the whole way back.

This was as markedly different from any relationship she'd ever experienced, and so wholly in contrast to her recent trysts with Natalia, that she came to feel even a little paranoid: Did Regan not want her up in her apartment? Was she, in her weird on-the-spectrum way, not interested in sex? But they did kiss, Regan had initiated it—at work, it occurred to Cassie, which was no small risk—and they did seem so into each other. In the days ahead Cassie tried not to pay too much attention to how it was developing, and the attention Regan gave her on the bocce court, at cigs on Elizabeth Street, and in the few editorial meetings RazorWire held—their twenty-six-year-old founder said he was constitutionally allergic to meetings, had instituted a rule that meetings could only be called on Tuesdays and Thursdays, anything else could be handled by e-mail—that whatever paranoia she felt was present only when she wasn't around Regan.

It was amid the strengthening of that relationship that on a Thursday morning in September, Regan called Cassie over to her computer.

"You'll want to see this," she texted her, though they were sitting only a hundred yards from each other in the frigid office.

Cassie came over to Regan's computer, where she saw that what she thought was one of Mark's videos was on, full-screen. He was in his David Crosby mask, imploring everyone who was watching to be a part of some new wave of action that sounded minor and overblown to her. Even amid all the evidence to the contrary, it remained hard for her to believe anyone would follow any of what Mark said into action, but why would anyone listen to anyone about anything? So.

"This looks like a Boomer Missive," he said. "But this is not a Boomer Missive. This looks like Isaac Abramson, Boomer1, but it is not Isaac Abramson, Boomer1. It is Boomer2. This is Boomer Action Number One. This country has lived long enough with the hegemony of the baby boomers and their profligacy. The time has come to start hitting back. We have shut down the American Association of Tired People. What will you do? We are Silence and we are myriad and we contain multitudes. Resist much, obey little. Propaganda by the deed. Boom boom." When Cassie heard the person behind the mask identify himself as Boomer2, she realized that at least one person who wasn't Mark Brumfeld was involved in the Boomer Boomers now. And he had posted a video calling for action to accompany the ideas Mark had put out there.

Regan asked her if she knew anything about Isaac's plans for the immediate future. Cassie said she hadn't been in touch with him in a month but that she would write him. So she went right back to her desk and e-mailed Mark, being careful not to say anything at all related in any way to the actions or the videos or the Boomers—or Regan or *TUT* or RazorWire, for that matter. She even used her personal e-mail address to write him.

It was a full day before she heard back—he said he missed her and when would he see her and also that he was sorry it took him so long to get back to her but that he rarely checked his surface web e-mail anymore, spent virtually all his virtual time on IRC chat rooms. She didn't know what IRC even meant—she had a college friend who worked for the International Relief Committee, but she was certain that's not what Mark was referring to, just like when people said WWF these days they meant World Wildlife Fund, not World Wrestling Federation, which her dad loved to watch when she was a kid on weekends on their local Ohio Fox station.

By the time she heard back from him it was all over the Internet, all over the news: baby boomer institutions across the country had received something called distributed denial-of-service attacks. Much as she had when she was first offered this job in Native Content, Cassie had to go to the Urban Dictionary website to discover what a distributed denial-of-service attack even was, that it was abbreviated DDoS, some of its history.

No sooner had Cassie closed the window on the Urban Dictionary entry than an e-mail came across her desk from Regan. She'd just assigned and gotten back already a list of the top ten DDoS attacks of all time—they'd only been happening for about five years so "all time" wasn't quite accurate, but Cassie couldn't think of a better phrase so she just left it—starting with a group called Anonymous's taking down the Church of Scientology website. The current attack on the AARP, which was the most conspicuous attack the Boomers had carried out, was number three. Though she'd been hired to work fact-checking native content pieces, they got so few through that now Cassie was doing research on any piece RazorWire ran that might get a large number of views—lists about celebrities and animals, the earliest attempts at the crowd-sourced propaganda Mario had suggested they might test out and which had failed. A savvier businessman might have negotiated for more compensation before taking that work on, but Cassie was neither savvy nor a businessman—in any sense of the word or its component parts—and she didn't care: she was bored, and fact-checking was what she should be doing if she was sitting in an office working as a fact-checker. The director of research. It took her much of the rest of the afternoon to fact-check the piece. By the time she got to number seven she e-mailed Regan to see if she wanted to take a bocce break but Regan just wrote back, "That DDoS piece ready to be posted yet?"

It wasn't. Cassie still had three more entries to go. She wrote back: "Just one entry away. Getting close." It was almost seven by the time Cassie felt solid on the piece, and by then Regan had to head out to a dinner with friends, so Cassie had to go home alone, where she streamed the night before's *The Daily Show* on her computer, drank a six-pack of Brooklyn Lager, and passed out on the couch. One of her roommates woke her after midnight and told her to go back into her room if she was going to pass out. The common space was not for passing out. That's what bedrooms were for.

The next week news of another huge round of DDoS attacks was all over the Internet—magazines, stores, baby boomer icons of all kinds were being hit. People were posting GIFs from the Boomer videos on Twitter and Facebook and asking excited exclamation-filled questions about what was up next. Cassie worked on no less than twenty-three separate RazorWire pieces related to DDoSing, to baby boomers and millennials and the differences in their taste (Take This Quiz: Are You a Millennial/Boomer Lover? Find Out!).

But half the pieces she worked on were just lists of quotations or GIFs from the Boomer Missives themselves. There was even a long think-piece from a disciple of Edward Said called "Generational vs. Religious Fundamentalist Terrorism," about the differences in the responses law enforcement made to these new attacks (the *Times* reported the FBI was investigating the AARP attack, an attack on the website for *Rolling Stone* magazine, and one on Eddie Bauer as well, and Cassie could only imagine how terrified Mark himself must be reading some of this). One RazorWire compilation of the best of the BB rants got almost two million hits in its first three days up on the site, the rants themselves re-edited with more effective slash-cutting, and when Cassie went back to look again at some of Mark's early videos, she couldn't believe how many hits they had. The first missive, the one he'd gone back and re-recorded with his David Crosby mask on so he could lay down his case against the baby boomers in its broadest form, was nearing nine million views. Cassie wasn't sure if she was more surprised to see that number, or to realize that of all the advice he could've gotten early on, her own now-girlfriend Regan's guidance on moving his whole operation to the Dark Web, and erasing his earlier footprint, was the best. If that video had contained Mark's unmasked face and undisguised voice, she could only imagine the scrutiny he'd be under right now.

And though it was far more a product of her new job than her own curiosity, Cassie found herself doing a fair amount of scrutinizing of those videos herself. The first thing that became clear was that in the world of trad media, these missives would never have gained traction. But here she was, working at a website of the kind that could help disseminate them far and wide. Where an anarchist like Emma Goldman might have had to travel to 120 cities in 180 days to rouse a movement— Cassie had finally read Mark's piece on Goldman, if only in case Regan asked again, and of course Regan hadn't asked again—now Mark could just record a video and suddenly he was in all the cities, all at once.

She looked and looked at those videos. Once she actually lined GIFs from the videos down a couple of screens for publication—online posting—whatev—she started noticing all kinds of inconsistencies between them. Sometimes the David Crosby mask seemed to have black hair, while in other videos it looked auburn. One had a blond (blonde?) ponytail peeking out the back. The upside-down Jerry poster over the speaker's shoulder was hung at all different angles. Vocoder or no vocoder, it was clear that pitch and timbre of the voices on those videos were quite different, missive to missive. Even just a couple dozen missives in it was becoming clear that there was no way Mark Brumfeld, or Isaac Abramson, or whatever he wanted to call himself now, was posting all these videos, and that had been the case since even before the guy on the first action had identified himself as Boomer2. Mark had spawned imitators or co-conspirators—it wasn't clear which—and apparently lots of them, others who'd take up the cause and were now posting their own missives under the auspices of what Mark had started. Maybe this was what he'd hoped, maybe it wasn't. What Mark had started was becoming a bona fide movement, one that would no longer be under his control. If Cassie could see that, she was sure he must know it by now, too.

CHAPTER TWENTY-ONE

A MONTH AFTER THEIR FIRST DATE THERE, Regan took Cassie out to dinner at Prairie Fire a second time. They left work together and again took the R uptown. Rather than taking the train across town, they got off at the southeast corner of the park. When they came up out of the subway station Cassie saw that across from FAO Schwarz there was a huge group of people standing or sitting, carrying signs and shouting slogans. As she and Regan started to walk west, she saw that on the signs were familiar slogans: "Boom Boom," and "Social Security Not Social Insecurity" and "Once We Have the Jobs, You Can Live in *Our* Fucken Basements," "Retirement or Retire the Mint" and "#Resist-MuchObeyLittle" and even "#RMOL." Every fifth person was wearing a David Crosby mask. A couple of what looked like teenagers carried a reproduction of Mark's Social Insecurity Card—in fact, six or seven of them were in the mix. Police kept a tense watch over their protest.

Every person in the crowd appeared to be under the age of thirty. Cassie asked Regan if she thought maybe they should go over and talk to them, but it was only fifteen minutes until their reservation at Prairie Fire, and it was a solid fifteen-minute walk to Columbus Circle, and just as they were talking a mounted police officer's horse reared up, spooked by the sound of a foghorn one of the protesters was blowing to get the rest of the group's attention. Holding a protest right next to where all the mounted police in the city went with their horses didn't seem like a good idea.

So Cassie and Regan walked on.

They walked past the Plaza, west on Fifty-seventh Street, until they arrived. When Cassie first came to the city to visit as a college student, this corner of Columbus Circle had been an open-air market where mostly West African men sold pirated CDs, T-shirts, and trinkets in front of a big old white building that looked like a huge church. The circle itself was just a round plateau of brown dirt with a statue of Columbus at its middle. Now the circle was filled with perfectly land-scaped flower beds, and the TimeWarner/AOL building was fifty-five stories of chrome and glass reflecting the verdure and stone of the south-west corner of Central Park.

In the restaurant they ate well, four courses and a wine pairing menu. They were seated next to a window looking out over the huge green scar at the center of the island. The sun was falling behind the build-ing, and heavy shadows cast out over the Sheep Meadow, where from this distance Cassie could make out groups of young people roving back into the mess of the city as the sun began to set. Inside, where they ate forty-to-sixty-dollar entrees, every other patron of the place was at least old enough to be Regan and Cassie's parents. The white-hairs largely ignored them, but there was a new sense of ambient anger coming off the two couples seated across the aisle from them—whether it was real or something she was causing herself to feel, Cassie felt it. Since the Boomer Missives had gained media attention, and then the huge outpouring of press over the first action had caught everyone's thoughts, Cassie felt certain that a new animosity had arisen when she found herself around people of her parents' generation here in the city—which wasn't all that often. All the bars they went to in Brook-lyn were diverse by every demographic metric except age. There was no bar in Fort Greene or Greenpoint or DUMBO where she would encounter a person older than, say, thirty-five. When she saw a sixty-year-old woman now, it was almost impossible to tell if the animosity she felt was coming from her, or if it was her perceiving it in the other and then feeling anger in response to the anger she was perceiving. What was certain was that her *own* anger was present, palpable—and if she was feeling it, many others of her generation were, too.

That was the trouble with the kind of generational strife the Boomer

Boomers were sowing: at some point animosity based in the broad strokes of identity simply pervaded, its origin obscured, only the intangible residue of its conflict remaining. Ideas obscured in favor of jagged emotion left in their wake. It was growing clearer and clearer that it wasn't simply Mark or his disciples who'd stoked that anger. Maybe they'd channeled it. But they were also speaking what so many were already feeling. And once that anger was on the surface it would be very, very hard to dispel. It was uncontrolled and uncontrollable, anxiety-inducing and pervasive.

Here in Prairie Fire, amid the $250 prix fixe menus and thousand-dollar bottles of wine, Cassie and Regan represented a kind of tiny ageist minority. Here she felt the conflict, and she felt more and more certain it went both ways the more she thought about it. She was being made uncomfortable and making people uncomfortable all at once. Its nexus was at the table behind them. The two couples there kept talking in low voices, looking at them, looking back.

"I kind of think they're talking about us," Cassie said. Regan was seated with her back to the couples. She didn't say anything then. But between courses the two of them went to use the bathroom together. Not long after they entered, the two women from the table behind them came in as well. The woman in a flowing maroon dress and salt-and-pepper hair cropped tight to her head stared right at Regan.

"What are you looking at?" Regan asked. Cassie would never have had the confidence to confront someone in a public restroom. She wasn't certain Regan would have done so two months ago herself. "You have a problem with two women in love sitting at dinner together?" She took Cassie's hand in hers and held it tight.

"No," the woman said. "Oh God, no! We started the equal rights movement, for Chrissake. But now that you've emoted at me, I do have to say we *have* been wondering what kids like you thought of your fellow millennials trying to threaten an entire generation in some Internet videos, causing all this mishigas."

"What do we think?" Regan said. She dropped Cassie's hand and turned toward the woman. "Boom fucking boom," she said. "That's what we think."

Then she turned and walked out of the bathroom, where the baby boomers still stood in stunned silence. It took a second for Cassie to wash her hands—ignoring the women—and head back to their table. Regan was already sitting.

"That was pretty—" Cassie said.

"Pretty what," Regan said. The light from the setting sun glared off the façades of buildings all around their window, glints flashing off the tower outside onto Regan's face. Though the glare must have been attacking her eyes, Regan did not lift a hand to protect herself.

"Pretty badass," Cassie said. "I think I love you."

Regan didn't bat an eye at the comment before she said, "I love you, too," and she didn't bat an eye at the more-than-eight-hundred-dollar check they received when they were done. She just took out a Visa with the RazorWire icon in the lower right-hand corner and made clear that it was on the company.

"We talked about that list about lists that I'm working on at some point, didn't we," Regan said.

Cassie said they did.

By the time they got up to leave, the table of baby boomers behind them had emptied, but now, whether it was true or not, Cassie felt as if all the fifty- and sixty-year-olds in the place were glaring at them as they walked out arm in arm. Aside from the multifarious varieties of sexism that pervaded the culture, and the looks she endured at college when she and Natalia first got together—she'd never dated a black girl in high school, though surely she would have, her father's weird conservatism wouldn't have stopped her—Cassie had never felt discriminated against. Not as a kid, not in school. And the mere fact of being questioned for her identity in those moments was both oppressive and invigorating. Later it would cause active paranoia, forcing her to expend energy she didn't want to expend, being in a constant state of angsty inner conflict. But as she walked out of that restaurant with a woman she loved, believing she'd been glared at for being born when she was born and having an assumed set of political opinions, having assumed a stance, she felt like a camera was tracking her, music playing to the rhythm of her steps, soundtrack of Rage Against the Machine or

T. Rex blaring in the background. While they walked Regan started telling her all about how *Czolgosz* and its staff had plans to partner with *TUT* and start a publication devoted to covering Boomer Boomers and their actions, and protests, and transcribing various of their missives, but at that point Cassie only heard the rampant edgy birdsong of love in Regan's voice. Even when Regan started talking about the boring specifics of all the actions the group was planning she couldn't help but smile smile smile.

CHAPTER TWENTY-TWO

CASSIE WAS IN THE MIDDLE of scrutinizing sixteen GIFs of Boomer Boomer protests for a piece RazorWire was to post as soon as she was finished with it, three weeks after the Boomers' initial call to action came, when she got a text from Regan, from across the office. "Need you over hr rt now," it read. Though she was pretty certain "rt" didn't mean Retweet, it wasn't entirely clear if "hr" meant "here," or "HR." Cassie got up and was stepping across the bocce court before she saw that two men in tight-fitting suits were standing on either side of Regan's desk.

"Hi, Cassie," Regan said. She had swiveled around in her chair, but stayed seated. "Cassie is our director of research for our Native Content Division, but she works on many of the pieces we post. This is agent— and agent—sorry, what did you say your names were again?" The tall twenty-something guy flanking her on her left reached out a hand.

"Agent Todd Flavius," he said. He had a startling shock of black hair, gelled straight back, and wore a brown gingham shirt underneath his navy blue suit. "We're just here from the FBI," he said. "Agents. FBI agents." Cassie half turned away from them without actually going anywhere. "Nothing to be alarmed about, sweetie. We're just looking into whatever can be looked into around the group that calls itself the Boomer Boomers. There were a series of threatening comments in the thread under one of your recent stories about the group, and we're doing a routine follow-up."

"Routine," Cassie said.

"Routine," said the other officer. He was old enough to be her father, with thinning yellow hair pushed back over his head in whatever the opposite of a comb-over might be called. Just, combed. "I'm Agent Miller." He flashed his badge.

"The routine," Cassie said. The first agent asked what she said, and she said, "Oh, just routine, as you said, only with a definite article in front of it. You know I think we could do well to head back to an office we use for these kinds of things. I mean not that we have federal officers here often enough to have it be a 'kind of thing.' I've only been working here for like a month. Or I guess five months. Time flies! Five months. But."

Regan said she agreed that using the shared conference office was a smart idea. She walked the three of them back to the glassed-off office where Cassie had interviewed for the job. There, with the door closed, the two agents asked Cassie a series of questions for almost twenty minutes: Had she herself received any direct threats? Did she receive any suspicious e-mail? Strange phone calls? Notice any faces recurring on her subway ride? Had she heard of a notorious hacker organization called Silence? Had anyone from Silence ever contacted her? Did the fact that the anniversary of September 11 was just around the corner come up in any communications she'd had with anyone she didn't know?

The whole time she just kept thinking: Mark Brumfeld, Mark Brumfeld, Mark Brumfeld, Mark Brumfeld, Mark Brumfeld, while actively thinking to herself, Whatever you do, don't say Mark, or Brumfeld, or Mark Brumfeld. For as long as she could remember she'd had a problem where when she knew she wasn't supposed to say something she'd find herself right on the cusp of saying it, aloud. Loudly. Shouting it, even. Like in the rare instance when she was around small children she found herself right on the verge of saying "fuck," or back in Ohio in synagogue with her parents, she had an almost Tourette's-like desire to shout out "kike" as loud as she could. When she was somewhere very high, she had a deep, giddy desire to jump. Not something she wanted to do, or would do—but it was still a conscious act of self-possession not to do it, the wrong thing, the damaging thing, the irrevocable thing being her reflexive response.

Somehow she kept answering no to the agents' questions now, and when they'd finally exhausted every possible way someone might contact her about watching a video on YouTube, tested every possibility that she'd heard of Silence though she hadn't, they said thank you and left their cards on the rough-hewn horizontal-telephone-pole door-desk she'd first interviewed on, and told her to call or e-mail if she thought of anything at all she might remember that she hadn't remembered here today at this interview.

"Well, or not interview," Agent Flavius said. "I don't want you thinking it's anything too formal. Conversation, more like."

She said she wasn't all that worried, but thanks, and then she said, "Thank you," all of which was an active way of not saying "Mark Brumfeld."

The agents seemed satisfied they'd asked her enough and scared her enough and they left. Cassie walked by Regan's desk and tried to get her attention, but Regan kept her eyes to her computer screen, and Cassie looked up to see that everyone was not looking at her all around the office, and no one was playing bocce, so Cassie went back to her computer. She was about to text Regan "cig" but she figured they needed to leave at least half an hour or something before talking to each other to make sure the agents had left, but when she looked down she saw that it was almost six P.M., time to leave for the day, so she pulled up the Comedy Central website to watch Jon Stewart's monologue—the opening of *The Daily Show* was the only good part, she never even made it through to the interviews—after which she figured enough time would have passed to go debrief about what-the-fuck-was-that-was-that-really-the-real-FBI with Regan. If Regan was still there.

She was barely even paying attention when the buffering finally finished and instead of the "advertising experience" that preceded watching the previous night's *Daily Show* on her computer, the site seemed to be playing another Boomer video. That didn't make sense. Maybe she had the wrong window open on her browser. So Cassie pressed Open-Apple-Q, opened up Firefox again, and went back on the Comedy Central site, brought up *The Daily Show*, hit refresh.

Now she had the volume up. She didn't even think to plug in her headphones but wished she had when loudly, in a vocoder-distorted voice, this person who wasn't Isaac but was again instead calling himself Boomer2 gave some whole spiel about how this was Boomer Action Two, Vandalize, and people should attack baby boomer icons all over the country in the coming days. He'd been talking for almost two minutes—advertising experiences on the Comedy Central website lasted thirty seconds, otherwise who on earth would sit through them—when a list of addresses started scrolling down the screen. Cassie noted the names Bob Weir, Oprah, Stevie Wonder, Philip Roth, and Magic Johnson before she hit Open-Apple-Q and cut it off again.

"Hey, what the fuck," Mario said. His voice almost made Cassie pee a little, she was so startled. She had no idea anyone was there. Mario and three engineers who sat in the bank of desks behind her were standing watching with her now. Cassie said sorry, she didn't realize they were all standing there, but before she could say anything more they were all scattering back to their desks to watch the new call to action themselves with their company-issued Beats Bluetooth headphones on. Before she could close the new window on her own desktop Regan was at her right shoulder, grabbing her to stand up.

"Let's get out of here," Regan said.

They walked out of the building and up to Houston and into a table at Botanica, which was empty for this hour, even for a weekday.

"What did they ask you?" Regan said.

"They wanted to know why I turned off this new Boomer video—"

"Not our coworkers, Cassie. The federal agents. What did the federal agents ask you."

"I guess what you might expect an FBI agent to ask you?" Cassie said. "I can only say that, having never been asked a thing by the FBI before. Or ever considered that as a possible outcome of any situation I've ever been in. I mean in college I guess I'd get so paranoid getting high sometimes I could kind of *think* maybe cops or feds or whatever were coming to get me, but they'd never been coming to try to bust me and my friends for smoking a spliff."

Regan stared at her.

"Oh. Sorry. I don't know. They wanted to know a lot of stuff about who might have contacted me related to the one piece we did on the DDoS attacks last month. I guess there were some nasty, threatening comments there. All very specific, about people I could have been in contact with. And they wanted to know if I'd heard of an organization called Silence but I hadn't—haven't—and I told them I haven't. Hadn't. I told them nothing. But Jesus fucking Christ—if they could have read my mind, they would be at Mark's house right now. Well, Mark's parents' house, I guess. Or at the house of every Mark Brumfeld in America, however many there may be. They can't read minds, right? Sometimes when I was high enough I thought people could read my mind but never any actual feds. Fed. Eral. Federal agents."

Regan just looked at her again. She went up to the bar and came back with two Maker's and sodas. The low thud of a track from the first Digable Planets record vibrated the seat of the bench where they sat. Underneath the smell of stale cigarette smoke was the strident ammoniac smell of urine emanating from the Botanica bathroom, which was nowhere near where they were sitting. Cassie took two sips of her whiskey drink, but it tasted like dish soap, so she put it back down.

She asked Regan if she thought they needed to do anything and Regan just said, "What would you do? Call a lawyer?" Neither of them had done anything illegal, she said. Neither of them had done anything, and Cassie hadn't even been in touch with Mark for weeks except for the one e-mail she'd sent him from her personal e-mail address, innocuous, so. Regan said that feebees came to talk to people all the time and didn't do anything more than just note it down. You were careful after, acted just as you would if you'd never been questioned.

"Feebees," Cassie said.

"Federal agents."

"You talk like you're experienced at being questioned by the FBI," Cassie said. "Feebees. Whatev."

"If the shoe fits," Regan said.

"If the foo shits," Cassie said. "Wait, what? The shoe that in this case would be fitting is your having been questioned by the F fucking B-I?"

"Not a regular occurrence. On two occasions, *Czolgosz* has run profiles about dissidents who have been deemed 'of interest.' Well, if I'm being honest one wasn't a profile, it was an essay, and I edited it, which meant a lot of contact with the writer. And the essay was advocating the violent overthrow of the Mubarak regime. Which did kind of come to pass not long after, but that made it the purview of the CIA, and the CIA did not come to question me. Well, except for one time when we did a piece on the Assad regime, but that was different. It's not as if these are regular occurrences. But the truth is that when you begin to speak truth to power, power often wants to come speak back. Often politely, dressed in a suit, and without much idea of what is being asked or what they're looking for or what they would do if they found it. It's called fishing, and it's not very effective. It shows they don't even know what they're looking for."

"Fish."

"Right."

Now it was Cassie's turn to sit and stare. Having interacted with two federal agents earlier that day was enough to make Cassie want to apply for a job at Goldman Sachs, teach elementary school back in Ohio, go to law school or something. Rock and roll was about as revolutionary as her endeavors had been in the past.

"It's not like you didn't think some of that kind of questioning was going to come down on Isaac, and you were close to marrying him."

"Mark."

"Mark."

"And Jesus, not close to marrying—he had a mistaken idea of our relationship, and I told you that in confidence, over some unconsciona-bly expensive branzino. And you know, none of Mark's plunge off the fucking deep end had happened before he left for Baltimore. The last I saw him, his main goals were finding a job as a boring academic at some small liberal arts school in the Midwest somewhere."

"Okay," Regan said. "But you've agreed with his stances on much of his approach to inter-generational conflict. You've been working on pieces about it. Now you've been questioned by the FBI. You've done nothing illegal, have no plans to do anything illegal, and will go back up to that office tomorrow morning, where you'll continue checking facts."

"Right, but—"

"This is still the United States of America, right?"

"Right, but—"

"And we're still protected by the First Amendment, protected by an inalienable right to a freedom of speech, a free press intended to keep those in power in check."

"Right, but—"

"Check those facts," Regan said. "The ones above. My words. All truth statements, yes?"

"Yes, but—"

"Once a piece is fact-checked, your responsibility is to post it on the Internet, a modern form of publication, and sit back and wait for Google Analytics to tell you how it's doing," Regan said. Then she put her hand on Cassie's face, the other on her thigh, and kissed her. "Now I think we should finish these drinks and get out of here."

They finished the drinks in front of them and then got one more drink, and then another, and then got out of there. The whiskey in her head, the experience of being with Regan, who was the most confident, most beautiful woman she'd ever spent time with, did somehow allow Cassie to forget, or at least stop obsessing over, the fact that earlier that day she'd been interviewed by feebees. FBI agents.

Regan paid for the drinks. They walked across town to a cheap sushi place on Sixth Street, and that night, for the first time in what was now clearly a real, full-on relationship, Regan invited Cassie back up to her place.

CHAPTER TWENTY-THREE

THERE WERE TWO THINGS REGAN wanted Cassie to do for her in the weeks after they consummated their relationship, and it grew clear that she was just as much in love with Cassie as Cassie was with her.

The first was officially to break things off with Natalia, once and for all. This was more easily requested, acquiesced to, and desired than it was executed. Natalia was still on tour, and wouldn't be back for another week. Cassie texted her, told her they needed to talk when she got back to town, and Natalia wrote back saying, "Ooh talk sounds fun you know how good I am @ talk talk talk talk," followed by the poop emoji.

In the week she waited to meet up with Natalia, Cassie found herself—while sitting in the RazorWire offices, glancing across the open floor plan at Regan, checking facts—giving some real thought for the first time to what she'd be losing. She'd been close to Natalia since they were eighteen years old, college undergrads. In some ways this would be the end of her last close friendship from that period. That mattered, but it mattered in concept, not in any observable way—there was a sense of freedom in disconnecting from someone who'd heard her pronounce the word job like it rhymed with slob in a religion classroom full of their peers, who'd seen her stumble over the cadences of Chaucer, watched her puke into the bushes outside a dorm for an hour at a sophomore Halloween party.

Her connection to Natalia's part of the music scene and of the Lower East Side scene Natalia had grown up in would be severed at that point,

and with Mark in Baltimore and the Willow Gardens on de facto in-
definite hiatus, her connection to music more broadly would be tenuous.
She didn't know many bands anymore, and every gig she'd had since
Mark left town had come through a recommendation from Natalia. But
the truth was she played probably a half-dozen gigs all summer, and
with the hours she was now putting in at RazorWire, she could barely
consider herself a musician anymore except in conversation, as a kind
of factoid about a former self, a chance to send a new acquaintance to
search YouTube for grainy video of an old show she'd played at Southpaw or 9C—which was a bigger deal, still, in principle than it was in
practice.

    For as long as she could remember Cassie had played music in some
all-encompassing capacity, from elementary school sessions with the
Suzuki method through her time in bands with Mark and Natalia.
She had a habit on the side of reading popular books on quantum physics.
When she first read about the ideas behind string theory it confirmed
something she'd always believed deep down, in some precognitive place
where ideas are still the stirrings of something ineffable. If the palpable
universe, if all that we considered to be solid matter, was in fact a series
of infinitesimal unobservable strings vibrating at differing frequencies,
Cassie figured that meant that playing music was speaking the tangible world back to itself. Music was the only nonrepresentative art form.
But where a novel, no matter how experimental, was meant to bring
across the visible palpable auditory world to its reader, or paint a new
window on the visible world as it was, music was music—until you
realized that all matter, no matter how solid it felt, contained and comprised its own literal music. So if you sang a note high and hard,
thumped out a bassline that vibrated with the low thump of a beating
heart, you were actually speaking to the physical world in its own language.

    Or that wasn't even quite accurate. Better yet, you were superseding
language itself, and attempting to mimic the very substance of the observable world. For that and for so many other reasons—reasons far
less high-minded, like the fact that Cassie enjoyed standing in front of
people and having them watch, liked going to bars where she was given

respect, bars that would give her all the free drinks she wanted even when she wasn't playing—the idea of giving up music as an active part of her life would have been hard to fathom even three months prior. It would be like going blind or deaf, like going to prison for the rest of her life, losing some huge tangible purchase on the known world. But now here she was, at a job that paid more than her father made in a year as a contractor in Central Ohio (it was not lost on Cassie that his job was to help build physical buildings, to erect campus buildings in Elyria, Ohio, where college students would pay exorbitant prices to stay in six-hundred-square-foot poorly insulated boxy spaces, and that he did not see the tangible world as made up of sub-molecular vibrating strings, but as pieces of lumber and steel that could be nailed and soldered together, and that he would have thought her making an intellectualized connection between quantum physics and music—and quantum physics itself, and music itself—to be a whole bunch of bunkum). And she was in love.

That was the main thing.

What was a greater expression of love than giving up the things that have interested you most in the past, ceding those interests to the things that will interest you in the future? It was the part of being in a real actual relationship, sustained over time and including dinner dates at which each party in the relationship was expected to talk, that Cassie found most challenging. She would have a solid thought on something, on anything—and in order to keep the peace, when she discovered that Regan's opinion was in direct opposition, she would have to cede to it, or figure out why she thought what she did in order to defend herself. Whether it was her own opposition to Zionism—Regan held conservative views on Israel and supported not only Netanyahu but the very idea of Settlements in the West Bank; or her own opprobrium of the Cure—Regan held sentimental views on New Wave music in general and Robert Smith in particular; or her own concerns over the politics of socialism—Regan held sanctimonious views on anything associated with the most basic tenets of communism, actively called herself a Fourierist, whatever that meant: Whichever of these kinds of arguments might arise in nightly or cigarette-rolling-on-the-street-daily or now-surprisingly-satisfying-postcoital conversation, Cassie found herself coming to a point of compromise in conversation so far from her previous stances that it appeared to be what it was. Locked in a new relationship, made happy by it and by her circumstances, Cassie was doing something she hadn't done since she'd arrived at college with a new name.

Cassie Black was changing.

So when Natalia returned from tour on the third Tuesday in September, Cassie showed up at her doorstep at the corner of East Second Street and Second Avenue. She rang the bell and Natalia buzzed her up. Cassie found the door cracked, and her old friend/lover still lying in bed, wearing the kelly green GETTIN' LUCKY IN KENTUCKY T-shirt Cassie had stolen from Mark years earlier, when they'd started dating. A waft of what smelled like the water in the abandoned quarry near Cassie's childhood home signaled that Natalia hadn't yet brushed her teeth. It was a little past noon.

"So," Natalia said. "New York is still here."

"Does not ever appear to be going anywhere, New York. Even if you— gasp!—go away from it for a period. You keep growing older, it stays the same age." Cassie did her best Matthew McConaughey. It wasn't very good. "So listen, we need to talk." Natalia said that she'd already said that in her text message. About talking. The one about talking. Ones.

"A couple of them, in fact," she said. "More than that—a few. A few text-based messages, about at some point in the future talking. And here we are now. In the future. The future is now."

Cassie explained to her that she'd found someone else. Well, not just found. She wanted to be with someone else. Was. Was with. In love with. Someone else. This time she was really, honestly in love. She thought. Love like she'd never felt before. "We like go out to dinner together," Cassie said. Natalia just looked at her. "Like, expensive dinners. We went to Nobu the other night. Like, the actual Nobu. And we work together. In an office. Romance, in an office. I'm like in a for-real actual office romance."

Natalia said, "Okay, that seems fine to me, whatever. Will you hold on a sec?" So while Cassie sat on the edge of a bed she'd slept in dozens of times before just having made the most self-expository confession of her young life, having confessed to the woman she'd been sleeping with off and on since college that she was for the first time in her life in a relationship, Natalia went into the apartment's lone bathroom and peed. Audible, straight-up-aggressive micturation. With the bathroom door wide open.

Cassie just sat there. Then Natalia brushed her teeth. Then she came back out, tackled Cassie onto the bed, and started kissing her neck, rubbing her between the legs. She did this little nipping thing where she got just a small piece of Cassie's skin between her front teeth and bit until it hurt.

"What the living fuck?" Cassie said. "Did you hear any of what I just told you. Confessed. Catholic-confession-style confessed to you."

Natalia let herself fall back on the bed next to her. She still had her hand on Cassie's thigh. On top of her bed was a stained white duvet with no cover covering it—she and Cassie had a long-standing plan to take the bus down to IKEA in New Jersey to buy one, but it had never materialized. Port Authority was just so awful neither of them wanted to go.

"And so in your version of this we don't even get to fool around any-more?" Natalia said.

"We do not."

"But we still get to play in bands together, trying to deal with the fact that we used to be together for years?"

"We do not. We do not do either of those things. We do not play in bands together specifically so that we might avoid such awkwardness. Awkwardnesses."

"And so who will you play music with, then, Cassie Black? I am, I must say, not to be a dick, your lone link to the downtown music scene at this point. I am the sole person who has gone to bat for you with a lot of bands that could have found much more talented bassists, and just did me a favor having you fill in. So you could still feel like you were a musician."

"That is mean," Cassie said.

"It was meant to be."

"Well, I'll figure it out. Myself. I will by myself figure it out. I've thought about it. Don't think I haven't."

"And now you're using double negatives?" Natalia said. "I don't know if I even know who you are anymore."

"You do not," Cassie said. "Single negative."

"Well then," Natalia said. She was sitting up now with her legs dangling off the edge of the bed. She was still sitting very close to Cassie, so she kind of hopped away a couple inches. "This *is* new, then, isn't it? I won't say I won't miss you."

"That, in turn, is one even more serious double negative."

"I won't not not say it isn't," Natalia said. "Quadruple negative, mother-fucker." She rolled over on her bed, now a couple of feet away from Cassie, picked up her iPhone, and started flipping through social media. Her thumb flipped upward on her phone, stopped. Flipped upward, stopped.

"So that's it?" Cassie said. "No further conversation? You're good with this?"

"That's it," Natalia said. There was no further conversation. She appeared to be good with it. But as Cassie was getting up to leave, Natalia said, "Bat-crazy shit with these Boomer Boomer terrorists and their making threats against all old people, right? I guess some shit like that was bound to happen sooner or later. But Jesus, the violence."

"I wouldn't call them terrorists," Cassie said. "More like what we used to call activists before everyone got crazy about radical Islamism. At best, tricksters. Did you know that back in the seventies there used to be like hundreds of bombings every month from domestic terrorists— in mailboxes, post offices, other places where there wasn't mail being delivered though I can't think of any right now?"

"I didn't," Natalia said. "But. I did know that every social movement in this country from Frederick Douglass to the Weathermen to Martin Luther King Jr. has been to defend the rights of people of color. Black people. All they wanted in the seventies was to be perceived as being friends with Panthers. Where the fuck are the Panthers Mark's sup-porting? This boom boom thing sure seems white as fuck."

Cassie didn't know what to say. She and Natalia hadn't talked about race since they were in college, where there was no trucking of dissent because there was no dissent. When they did, Cassie was always copacetic, always listened attentively and always agreed. Now here she was having just broken up with Natalia and she didn't know what to say. So she didn't say anything. She hadn't thought of Mark's activism on those terms—and she was reasonably certain he hadn't, either. She was quiet.

"Well, think about it," Natalia said. "At some point you might want to think about it. That and the fact that the whole thing seems awfully violent to me."

"The violence!" Cassie said. "Again bringing up the violence. Very unlike you to be against violence. You do after all have an anarchy sticker on the headstock of your Fender Jaguar."

"My Telly Thinline," Natalia said. "My Jaguar has a Che Guevara sticker on it." She said Jaguar the British way, elongating the "u" and enunciating the "a." "But yeah, I guess violence seems like a reasonable outcome until it becomes the actual, you know, outcome. At which point it just looks like a stupid horrifying outcome. And terrifying. Whether it's terroristic or not."

"Well, first of all, vandalism against a website is not violence. And by degree vandalism against a window barely is. And second of all, it's a natural consequence of years of subtler economic and structural acts of violence perpetrated by the baby boomers themselves," Cassie heard herself say. She felt back on surer footing and was talking reflexively. It was an almost verbatim quotation from something she'd heard Regan say, but it was consciously that. It was almost as if rather than saying the thing she wanted to be saying, she was attempting as accurately as possible to repeat a thing the person she loved had said. This again felt, in the moment, like the very definition of what it was to be in love.

"Easy there, Chomsky. I guess I'm just saying I wonder how far it'll all go. But then here we are, you breaking up with me, talking about being done playing bass, and that sure as shit is not an outcome I ever thought possible. Maybe you'll change your name back to Claire. Claire Stankowitcz, anarchist start-up list-making website fact-checking professional in actual love."

Natalia was the only person in New York who still knew Cassie's birth name. Cassie did not like hearing it. She turned and opened the door to the apartment.

"I'm just saying," Natalia said, and Cassie was already halfway out the door by the time her now ex-lover finished her sentence, giving her a chance to pretend as if she hadn't heard it, "seems like someone's bound to get seriously hurt, and shit to get really out of control."

Cassie said that she agreed, that it did, indeed, appear as if someone would get hurt. Was bound to. But by the time she said it, the door was closed behind her. It was as if she was saying it to no one but herself. She'd never know if Natalia even heard.

CHAPTER TWENTY-FOUR

THE SECOND REQUEST REGAN made was more or less the opposite of the one regarding Natalia, and it came as a surprise: she said that while it might not seem the most intuitive move after having been visited by the feebees, she thought Cassie should keep in contact with Mark Brumfeld. Cassie and Regan had just gone to a movie at the BAM Cinemas in Fort Greene. They went to a showing of the second *Godfather,* where they were annoyed when the person behind them talked through the first half hour of the movie until Cassie turned around to shush them and saw it was John Turturro sitting with his teenage son, explaining all the complicated relationships to him throughout the movie. When she turned back, instead of annoyed she was giddy with the iconic Brooklyn experience—"John fucking Turturro is behind us," she whispered to Regan.

"Fuck him and his baby boomer smug face," Regan said.

The giddiness Cassie felt turned to discomfort. She got up to use the bathroom and when she came back Regan wasn't sitting in their seats anymore—Cassie had to squint in the dark for three minutes of the Michael-Corleone-in-Sicily scene before she found her six rows closer to the screen. Afterward they went up to have dinner in the BAM Café. Corrugated tin covered the ceiling maybe twenty feet above their heads. They sat so that they both had a view out the three-story windows onto the fits and starts of traffic on Flatbush. In the cacophonous room they could barely hear each other, but it was one of Cassie's favorite spots in the whole city. It was one of those venues that made

Brooklyn seem superior to Manhattan, as if in the past decade something had flipped cultural currency from the island and down to the
western end of Long Island, where they now sat. Across the avenue the
sign on Junior's awning was the same neon orange it had always been,
touting the same cheesecake it had always touted. But BAM's façade
had just given up scaffolding it had carried for what felt like years, a
teenage mouth free of braces, and inside the café its patrons were all
newly chrome. Let the Manhattanite baby boomers who could afford
it have the Met, have the Frick, the Guggenheim, the Flatiron Building, Central Park. Cassie and Regan and their generation had BAM
Café, had Rumble Seat music, had the Barclays Center, the new water-
park in Prospect Park. They had the youth and they had the numbers.
They were ugly but they had the music.

At the back of the room a funk band played. It was rumored Vernon
Reid would join them on guitar by the end of the night. Cassie had
ordered locally sourced lamb shank, and Regan was eating pumpkin
risotto. They talked about a couple new attacks that were all over the
news that week: A Boomer Boomer had attempted yet another vandalism of Bob Weir's house, but this time the Marin County Police
Department was prepared. They'd set up an officer in an unmarked car
at the end of the block, and they caught the kid as he was taking a
baseball bat to the house's gate. Pictures surfaced on the Internet of his
blackened eyes, and he'd hired a lawyer, said they gave him a "rough
ride," leaving him unbuckled in the back of a paddy wagon as it bar-
reled down the tight esses of PCH. A new round of indignation had
gripped young people all over the country. The baby boomers were
fighting back, using their money and influence and their institutions to
allow the system to harm the bodies of millennials. Things were ramping
up. Regan said so, and Cassie agreed, and then they were quiet for a moment as the horn from the funk band blared in its Pee-Wee-Ellis-esque
solo so loud they couldn't hear each other. After their silence, Regan
asked Cassie if she'd given any thought to her suggestion about her
friendship with Mark.

"I don't care either way," Cassie said. "I just would have figured you'd
want me to stop being in touch with him."

Regan said that she could understand why she might figure that. But she knew how close the two of them were—"I have a fundamental belief regarding people who don't stay in touch with any of their exes," Regan said. "It strikes me as a kind of inherent character flaw."

Cassie asked what she meant.

"It seems to me that in most cases when a person is no longer in touch with their ex, it is for one of three reasons. The first kind: they have had a problematic breakup of a variety that doesn't allow them to be friends any longer. This can be a serious red flag—how are you to know the fault for said ugly breakup doesn't reside with your now-current partner? That it won't happen to you, down the road. In this case, I know you're still friends with Isaac. In fact you were with him when I met you, and it was one of the things that attracted me to you—knowing you were still friends with your ex. Walking into a party with your ex, allowing him to buy you a beer and listen to exposing information about his own clandestine political activities. It seemed to speak well to your character."

"Thanks," Cassie said. "I—"

"You're welcome. So that being the case, it strikes me that the latter two reasons why—sorry, reasons, 'why' is implied by 'reasons'—the latter two reasons a person may no longer be friends with their ex if they *were* friends with said ex after entering into a new relationship are both fraught. The first of these two new scenarios is that the new partner in the new relationship is too insecure to handle her new partner being friends with her ex. I am opposed to being that kind of partner. My biggest fear in life is of being insecure. My second biggest fear in life is of simply being *perceived* as being insecure. Which I suppose could be perceived as its own brand of insecurity, but I'm willing to accept that as inherent to the syllogism. Regardless: the point to this second reason is that I am expressing to you my full-throated approval of your continuing to be friends with Isaac here."

"Okay," Cassie said. "Mark. Noted. And the third thing."

"The third thing would be an inversion of the second: that *you* were not comfortable being friends with your ex because you were somehow insecure yourself that that friendship could intrude upon our own."

Cassie said that, oh, man, was that not a concern, and that there were plenty of things she was insecure about, uncertain about, but that was not one of them. No matter how hard Mark pushed or still cared for her. She was not interested. Like, that was the last last last thing Regan ever needed to worry about.

"Exactly," Regan said. "I believe you. And so I think you should remain friends with Mark, and even try to reestablish some of the connection to him you've lost. Set up a gig, go visit him, keep in touch." It was the first time Cassie had ever heard her new girlfriend call him by his real name without being cajoled into doing so, and she took it as the kind of extension of the olive branch it was meant to be. "I will also say that I like the idea of your staying in contact with Mark. It is amazing how effective the most recent calls to action have been. He's an impressive person. Plus, if he really does go and get himself into any real trouble it makes *more* sense to have an innocuous paper trail of your innocuous communications with him than to just go radio silent on him altogether."

Cassie wasn't sure she agreed with the amazingness that the last month's actions in the name of Boomer Boomers had accomplished, and Natalia had put new questions in her head that she might have liked to discuss with Regan now if it didn't seem hopelessly awkward to do so right after all Regan had just said about breakups. It seemed to her that in attacking baby boomer icons like Bob Weir, who had no real job to retire from in the first place, they were muddying their case— but this was one of those places where it wasn't certain how much it was worth arguing. The violence in response to the second Boomer Action call had ramped up in a manner even Mark Brumfeld himself could never have anticipated. Attacks on major visible venues across the country. Even if no one had been hurt, the vandalism was a serious ratcheting up of the possibilities of what people might do in the name of the Boomer Boomers. To what end or extent it was unclear.

It might not have been apparent to every person in the country yet, but to those who were inclined to watch it—to believe or follow it—it was pervasive. And Regan had made clear at every turn that she was ideologically aligned with it. And now this week, one of the videos had made the first call to execute the Boomers' ROWRY initiative. Boomer2 had declared that if baby boomers across the country didn't retire from their jobs—"retire or we'll retire you"—something serious would happen on March 15. It wasn't clear what was being threatened. It wasn't at all clear what connection Mark had to the threat. But this call to action had come with a threat of real violence that winter. It created a new round of jittery excitement. Even if nothing at all came of it, the coming three months of waiting to see what the Boomers had planned would be nervous ones.

"Okay," Cassie said.

"Okay," Regan said, but she did not have a mode in which she would admit she didn't quite understand what was being said to her, so Cassie said, "I'm okay with staying friends with Mark, of course. I love Mark, just not in the way Mark loved me. And if anything I'm a little concerned about him."

CHAPTER TWENTY-FIVE

SO FOR THE NEXT MONTH Cassie called and e-mailed Mark more, and while he didn't answer his phone often, when he did he sounded very much like his old self. Energized, even. He said he'd hooked back up with an old high school friend, Costco, who he'd told her about only in the broadest strokes, and just having someone down there in Baltimore with him was doing wonders. He conceded over the phone that he himself had not put out the ROWRY call, but it was the most revolutionary of any of the actions the Boomers had called for—and so far it had amounted to nothing other than ramping up anxieties.

Exactly zero baby boomer professionals had declared that they would be leaving their jobs as a result of the call. The sheer amount of time between the call for action and the threatened action made it feel futile. And like any futile threat, the back half of the proposition was growing more apparent as time passed, which was . . . how did these Boomer Boomers think they were going to "retire" someone? Was it an implicit threat of real violence? Was it suggested that someone might even get killed? Cassie didn't think so, and she was sure Mark didn't think so, either. But that didn't mean that they knew what any of the hundreds, or thousands, or who knew how many other Boomer Boomers, shooting their own incoherent missives and planning who knows what, were planning.

During that same period things were going about as well as could be hoped at RazorWire. Native content requests were coming in at a rate the editorial side at the site couldn't even handle, more than one a day,

and they paid better than the sales force at the company had anticipated. They'd added a new division that created short video clips,
pulled from existing content on YouTube, to complement much of the
written content they were creating—and it was a huge success. While
Cassie didn't want to learn how to use Adobe Premiere herself she figured out some of the basics and could help give at least a cursory copyedit to any text included over video. They were taking on freelancers at
rates that rivaled major magazines just to get folks on the pieces and
the videos. The work itself was less compromising than Cassie had
thought it might be—now that she was also fact-checking so many of
RazorWire's traditional pieces, the act of fact-checking a piece that
had been created to get people to watch a television show, or to buy a
new dietary supplement, or down the road to vote for a falsely impugned
candidate, was just another part of a workday.

It helped that Cassie herself never saw the design elements that the
company's designers created to barely distinguish the native content
from content content. Each morning she would open a new Google
Doc with a list—"Seventeen Great New Recipes that Use Splenda Instead of Sugar," or "Eight Grate New Emo Records Not Featuring Ben
Gibbard," "The Thirteen Most Heinous Hate Crimes of the Decade"—
and tackle them as she would any other piece she was doing research for.
She did a fair amount of communicating over e-mail with the pieces'
writers, but again there was no reason for her to think about whether
they'd been hired to write copy for regular content or native, given that
many of the same writers were doing both kinds of pieces now.

One afternoon after winter began to set in, as Cassie walked up Canal
Street from her N stop—she liked the long walk up to the RazorWire
office, it gave her time to decompress after the mass of morning subway
riders—she noticed something conspicuously lacking. It wasn't something she didn't see but something she didn't smell. It was cold enough
now that the fish waste on the Chinatown sidewalks no longer baked
its emetic waft with the heat of the morning.

She sat at her desk and found two unrelated documents. The first
was a Facebook message from Mark. He was not all that happy again,
he said. Even with Costco in town now he was a little lonely. A lot.

Lonely. He missed her. He'd been saying he missed her, but this was more explicit. He *really* missed her. He'd been thinking about her more since she came to town and . . . there was innuendo but that was it, he left it there.

She didn't know what to say back to him so she didn't reply. In fact she'd noticed that of late she did a lot less e-mailing, a lot less responding quickly—or at all—to messages she received over social media. It was as if in the past six months or so the sheer quantity of written messages she received in a week was insurmountable, and so in response people had collectively decided not to answer all messages. Texts— sure, she'd reply to texts. But not e-mail or FB Messenger.

The second document she found was a list in the RazorWire Google Docs folder entitled "Eleven Vulnerable Baby Boomer Venues." The piece was by one of their riskier writers, who had been covering the Boomer Boomers in their early days, and was getting tons of hits for pieces that seemed to cross a boundary from reporting *on* the movement, to advocating *for* it. In the past months he'd published a kind of data-dump of e-mails from Social Security officials, detailing the vulnerabilities to hackers of the organization's firewall that seemed to invite hackers to attack it. He'd made three lists of new baby boomer targets—Jeffrey Koons, Denzel Washington, Stephen King, Shel Silverstein's childhood home, and more—that hadn't yet been hit. His third list even included a target that only two days later was vandalized—Jim Davis's cartoon factory in Muncie, Indiana, where *Garfield* comic books were still manufactured. But they each had accrued hits into the hundreds of thousands, and it wasn't clear that there was any actual intent in their having been written, and they went viral, so legal let them keep posting.

Even with all that in mind this latest list felt like an escalation: it had specific addresses for a baker's dozen of government offices, national and local, that the Boomers might take next. It was one thing when private citizens were attacked, or when there was an almost tricksterish bent to the list-making and speculation: Was anyone really going to go after Neil Young's Northern California ranch? Cassie texted Regan to see if she wanted a cig. Regan texted back to say that she didn't have time to leave the office, had a couple deadlines she needed to hit by lunch, but why not bocce. Smoking had grown to be an even more fraught activity than it had been before—now every time they went out for a cig a baby boomer would attempt to serve as a kind of in loco parentis and tell them they should quit, to which Regan would say, "Who the fuck do you think you are to tell me anything," and launch into a diatribe about how it was the baby boomer generation that was the first and last in human history to smoke machine-produced cigarettes on such a prodigious level, and fuck them if they didn't think we could enjoy just a little of that experience ourselves on our own time and on our own dime. By the time her jeremiad had ended, the misguided boomer would be long gone down the street.

So they stayed inside among their fellow twenty-something-year-old colleagues and played bocce. They played to twenty-one, and within three minutes of starting their game, Regan was already up fourteen to three.

"I'm not sure about this latest list from Edmund Steiner," Cassie said. She bent down to pick up all three of her heavy balls and cradled them against her midriff. "It just seems so specific, going out with a list of the addresses of government agencies. I did a little poking around and in three instances, he's included addresses of D.C. offices that aren't publicly listed."

"Then he's doing a public service, don't you think?" Regan said. "More like traditional journalism if you ask me. Bringing information to readers they wouldn't already have."

"Under the auspices of advocating illegal attacks against them."

"Advocating? Absolutely not doing so. It is a satirical piece in the form of a list. A satirilisticle. Very much in keeping with the work we publish."

Regan reached back and bowled a green ball through the sand, through the mix of Cassie's balls. It hit the pallino and the two went spinning together against a wall. Two points.

"And what if one of those venues was hit?" Cassie said. "Would we have those FBI agents coming around my cubicle once again, asking questions?"

"Would it matter?" Regan said. "You would bear no culpability. The shadow of the First Amendment looms large over what we publish. There's always *Times v. Sullivan* in the background." She walked over to where all six of their balls were and picked her own up. It would be too heavy to bring Cassie's over for her, and Cassie knew it, but something about it still felt ungenerous. She came back to where Cassie was standing. "And aren't there venues on that list that maybe *should*, after all, be hit?"

Cassie didn't respond. She went to pick up her balls, brought them back, threw them as if it didn't matter. And it didn't. Regan won by fifteen points.

Back at her desk Cassie went through with the full fact check on the piece. Regan was right: there was nothing more controversial about that piece than any other they'd published. She went through and confirmed the addresses on each. Cassie finished checking the piece, got up from her cubicle, and with a force she'd almost never had in their now months of dating, she grabbed Regan and said, "I need a cig. Come roll me one." They walked out of their still-frigid office into the frigid streets below, two young people working together and in love.

BOOMER MISSIVE #3:

"TODAY AS I START OUT MY FIRST DAY as a Boomer Boomer, I will take on a new name. I was—I was. But now I am. I am. I am Isaac Abramson. Every day for the rest of my life, from this day forward, when a Boomer fist brought the word of the Lord to my face, I will be Isaac Abramson. God told Abram to go to the top of Mt. Moriah, to take Isaac there for the sacrifice. Abram did as He said. He would have done it. He would have picked up that knife and put it through his son's chest if at the last minute God hadn't said to stop, hadn't given him the lamb for the sacrifice in Isaac's place.

"We are all Isaac now. Sacrificial lambs every one of us, to the person. Your baby boomer parents are all Abraham, every one of them. Remember every day of your life that they aren't afraid to take you to the top of Mt. Moriah for sacrifice to keep their jobs. Their way of life. The knife they wield is the debt they've accrued, the seventeen trillion dollars in debt in the form of Social Security and in Medicare, another three trillion-plus still accruing from these wars they've gotten us into. We didn't vote for it. We weren't old enough.

"They did.

"We are all lying on the altar. But there is a difference: Isaac did not know what Abraham's intentions were. He had not heard the voice of the whirlwind in his ear.

"We have.

"I am the whirlwind.

"Hear me in your ear.

"We *have* heard the voice of the whirlwind. I will *be* the voice of the whirlwind. I will be the Behemoth, I will be the Leviathan, I will speak from your desktop in the words of a burning bush, in the sound of the flood and the force of the deluge. I will be Isaac Abramson, Isaac son of Abraham. Hear the whirlwind."

"Social Insecurity.
"I am Boomer1. We are all boomers now.
"Resist much, obey little.
"Propaganda by the deed.
"Boom boom."

PART FIVE
MARK

CHAPTER TWENTY-SIX

IT WAS AS IF THERE WERE three lives Mark Brumfeld, Isaac Abramson, Boomer1, was living, in the months after moving back into his parents' house in Baltimore. The first of these lives was lived online, and that life online was as fractured as his offline life was—between taping missives, engaging in IRC chats, and finding ways to allow his missives to reach as many viewers as possible. The second of his lives was lived in his parents' house almost as it was lived when he was a teenager—quietly, desolate, and with extreme reticence. The third life he lived was the one anyone could observe if they saw him outside his house, the life of a man dejected, living in his parents' basement, lovesick, yearning, and alone. In those early days it was the component of life that felt least in his control.

It was as if he were living three lives in this new existence in Baltimore, but for the first couple of weeks after uploading the initial video he'd made, Boomer Missive #1, Mark walked around like the world was being shown on a newly unveiled Apple Retina display, and as if there was just the one life: Life Online. Maybe this was what it was like for the callous shale gas purveyor, after years of studying petroleum geology, having discovered that no matter what wasn't working aboveground, the sand and rock beneath his feet were as valuable and procurable as oil was in Texas a century before, like the first Brit to bend down and in the soil outside Baghdad feel sticky crude so plentiful it was bubbling up out of the very sand. Natural resources so abundant and so near to hand one almost couldn't *help* but plunder them. Anger in the moment, newfound powers of manipulation and control accessible simply by logging on, met by people typing away all across the country, all across the globe.

He didn't want to go back to the JCC after his altercation with Finkel. For the next couple of weeks he drove over to the outdoor basketball courts at the middle school he'd attended before he was a teenager. It was hot and his eye was healing, the cut having sealed into a small, tight scab. Each afternoon for the rest of the month at four o'clock a foreboding swarm of gray-blue clouds crowded the hazy sky. An hour later thunder boomed in the distance. Then the skies opened. He sat in his parents' Volvo and waited for it to pass before hitting the courts. As the skies cleared he watched as first finches, then ravens, began to return from wherever they sought refuge from the rains, to forage for the easy kill of worms and insects and rodents doing the same. For the first time since he was a kid he had pulled down the Stone Tanach, the best English translation he knew of the Hebrew Bible. At his magazine job if someone alluded to the Bible, he was forced to use the New American Version their style guide required. Now he was reading the Stone Tanach, and taking it in. He was halfway through Exodus by the time his eye healed.

The response to Isaac's initial handful of missives was a jolt, but soon watching it grew stale. The jolt wasn't jolt enough. It did not bring even the same charge as hearing his bluegrass band applauded when they were onstage in front of three dozen people, and if he wasn't careful his thoughts would turn too far back to Cassie, to what he was missing in New York. It was just plain different to be alone, in a room, in front of a computer. It was controlled on his end and volatile and capricious on the other, and when the response wasn't enough, he found he needed more. He would e-mail Cassie from his Mark Brumfeld e-mail address—nominally to see if they had any more gigs, but he knew that in his heart what he wanted was to just hear anything from her, maybe even a sense that she wanted him to come visit—but beyond that he didn't talk to anyone much.

Midsummer he made a trip up to the city to see Cassie and to play a gig they'd already had on the books. The night before they went out to dinner and then went to a party for the magazine that had published his Emma Goldman essay. While what he most wanted was as much time alone with Cassie as she would grant him, Mark found the scene at this magazine party something else. He was shocked at the response he got there, not for any of the three lives he was now living but the single life he'd led before. People recognized him from the first missive, before he'd put on the Crosby mask. His editor, Deron Williamson, who had been aloof while they were working on the piece and had provided him only radio silence since, showed him a ton of attention. While he'd expected to spend all his time at the party with Cassie, Mark quickly forgot about her as he sat down with Deron and Regan Lightman, whose work on Foucault he'd read when he was in grad school though she was younger than him, and they talked about how best to push his missives out.

By some wild coincidence it turned out that Cassie saw his first missive along with them and all three knew he was Boomer1. But Regan seemed concerned by the idea that he could be identified if someone saw his face in that first missive. She showed him all the ways he could clean up his footprint, cloak his identity, and continue apace with his missives without fear of anyone but her, Deron, and Cassie knowing he, Mark Brumfeld, was Boomer1. When he went back out into the party Cassie showed him more attention than she had in ages—it was enough light and energy to carry him all the way back to Maryland. Mark returned from that trip to the city full of the verve that accompanies purpose: He took down Boomer Missive #1 and, filling himself with the same angry energy he'd been full of when he first recorded it—which was easily done, the feelings and thoughts he'd presented then having been kept inside for so long—he rerecorded it wearing a vocoder and David Crosby mask he found in his old closet. This new version was even more convincing, a second draft given time to percolate, imbued with energy and contained by inchoate command. After recording it Mark dove deep into the Dark Web, posting videos and chatting with people in IRC chat rooms with new resolve, new confidence. He discovered how to cloak his identity, how to communicate with people without their having any sense of who he was. He only posted under the screen name Boomer1, and never logged on to the web without first encrypting what he was doing using TOR.

He supposed this wasn't entirely unlike his experience of working for a traditional magazine—publishing pieces that were edited under his byline, e-mailing sources and publicists in the early days of the Internet, a faceless name behind an electronic message. But by degree, if not kind, this felt different, chatting anonymously on IRC channels, negotiating the world as Boomer1, which itself was an alias for Isaac Abramson, which itself was an alias, a nom de cyberguerre. It was what made it feel most as if the three lives he was living were separate: there was no Mark Brumfeld when he was chatting online. Isaac Abramson hadn't been jilted by Cassie Black. Isaac Abramson hadn't grown up in this suburban basement, didn't depend on his mother at the age of thirty to have a sandwich made for him at lunchtime. It was as if Mark Brumfeld wasn't even in the room during those times, as if he could feel however distantly what Edgar must've felt when he donned his Poor Tom disguise in *Lear*. There was a semblance of safety about it, and yet something that felt like a risk, the freedom that came from combining anonymity with purpose, to a whole greater than the sum of its parts.

Life went like this for the rest of that summer: chatting in chat rooms and posting Boomer Missives in the morning once Julia left the house to do whatever it was she did during the day, basketball in the late afternoons, pastrami-on-rye when Julia was home to make it, Torah on the dash of his parents' old Volvo when it rained too hard to play ball. All the missives that were posted now had him behind his Crosby mask, the vocoder he spoke into making him sound like a cross between Darth Vader and the Jerky Boys. The fourth missive was taken up by legions on Facebook, shared dozens and then hundreds and then tens of thousands of times. As soon as it went viral, so did the previous missives, just as Regan suggested they would, the rising tide of viewership floating all diatribular boats. Each time he imagined his own success from outside of himself he imagined it through Cassie's eyes, imagined her impressed, alongside him. Mark watched as the number of views beneath his videos went from the hundreds, into the thousands, and up into high tens of thousands and then hundreds of thousands, caught in a matrix of viral growth. There was an undeniable sense of success, data to back up the quality and importance of his words—it was quantifiable and it was knowable and it was public, confirmed viewership trackable in a way magazines and newspapers, pamphlets and protest had never been trackable.

While he bumped around in different chat rooms over the course of his first weeks, behind the cloak of TOR, most of his chatting took place on a channel in an IRL chat room Regan had suggested called #micromacrohackro. He chatted there, and posted links to his videos. At first he didn't say anything, just posted links and then lurked as he watched others talk about his postings. The chat room itself was ostensibly for talking about issues related to economics, and Mark later learned that it was started by the son of a famous macroeconomic theorist at McGill, a kid who clearly didn't know much about economics at all but pretended to because of his famous father. He was the chat room's moderator. As discussion tended toward one of Isaac's missives—and then toward a discussion of the effect on baby boomer profligacy more broadly—the chats went on unabated and were joined by dozens of users. As Isaac watched he saw that three users kept popping up: Coyote, HHH, and Silence.

After a couple of weeks of choosing not to engage even when addressed directly after he posted a video one afternoon, Mark found himself engaged.

CHAPTER TWENTY-SEVEN

IT WAS A TUESDAY WHEN MARK FIRST ALLOWED himself to chat, and he did so against his better judgment. Silence—who posted so much, and so often in disagreement with himself, that it became clear to Mark over time he was not just one person, but a handle many users used—started talking about how funny Isaac's latest missive was:

> **<silence1>:** holy shit i was lmao at #7
>
> **<hhh>:** fucken a me too
>
> **<hhh>:** i mean #1 was funny as hell and that got me into it to start w but they get better funnier bettier with time
>
> **<boomer1>:** What makes you think they're funny? They're not meant to be. They're dead fucking serious.

As soon as he typed it Mark felt a monumental sense of regret. After weeks of looking and waiting, he'd allowed himself to see how things went in these chats, to hear how people talked and how they talked about him. But more than that, even just less than a month was long enough to settle into a rule-based routine: He could get online after running TOR. He could log on. He could read what people were chatting about. On occasion he could post a link to one of his own videos when it was finished.

But he would not allow himself to engage in unfettered discussion. Users had asked questions of him, addressing him as Isaac or Boomer1, but when they did it felt almost as if they were asking someone else, and he'd followed his own rules, hadn't engaged. His voice was on his videos, and he posted them, but he did not chat as Boomer1.

Now, all in one single contentious line he'd broken his own well-honed rules. It was like after years of being a wallflower finding one-self out on the dance floor, in the middle of the circle, everyone waiting to see your moves.

> **<boomer1>:** I mean funny is all well and good and funny is funny but the missives are dead serious.
>
> **<boomer1>:** fucking
>
> **<boomer1>:** fucken
>
> **<boomer1>:** fucken dead serious

No one typed anything for a second. Mark watched the cursor on his desktop blink and blink and blink for what felt like a whole day until a new line popped up:

> **<hhh>:** is this boomer1 or are you a nark this is all very nark sounding
>
> **<hhh>:** narkish
>
> **<coyote>:** narkiest
>
> **<silence1>:** narktastic
>
> **<silence1>:** maybe boomer1 is a baby boomer himself lurking around looking for some fresh hot milenial ass online
>
> **<boomer1>:** This is Boomer1, Isaac Abramson, and I'm fomenting an open conflict against the Baby Boomers. They've taken our jobs and they've plundered our futures and they've
>
> **<coyote>:** that's the shit right there boomer1
>
> **<coyote>:** thanks for bringing the ruffles bringing it see what I mean fucken hilarious
>
> **<coyote>:** serious serious ruffles
>
> **<hhh>:** you can see its pretty fucken hilarious ruffles boomer1 can't you see the ruffles

\<silence1\>: ruffle it up mofuck

\<boomer1\>: Ruffles?

\<hhh\>: ruffles my brutha it's all about the ruffles

\<silence1\>: oh jesu cristo

\<silence1\>: what I gotta be fucken urban dickshonary for you

\<silence1\>: ruffles = ROTFL = ROTFLs = ruffles

\<boomer1\>: got it that's cool and that's all well and good and I'm as much for a good laugh as the next guy but I'm

\<silence1\>: we gotcha boomer1 and we gotcha and you can have your whatever serious serious blah blah narky narky blow but we're in it for the ruffles so keep it up

Mark came to feel over the course of a month that he had developed almost a friendship with these guys—or women, Mark had no way to know for certain, though in his head between the cursing and the taunting and the general overall trolling, all the bro-ing and brutha-ing, even against all he'd learned in his academic life about not making heteronormative assumptions, he allowed himself to assume they were guys. While he wouldn't have been able to articulate it himself, part of what felt so freeing in those rooms was the sense of being alone in an unerotic, unromantic space—the idea of Cassie or for that matter any woman listening in or even seeing what he was typing was ridiculous. The fact of being alone here, almost like going all the way back to the sausage-fests of parties he and his guy friends had in middle school, while sitting in the basement where he grew up, was part of the sense of safety. Much of it. He'd had a close friend in high school, in the very Baltimore where he now sat, whose nickname was Costco based on an anecdote that had stuck to him and never let go, so the idea of these online kids giving themselves ludicrous online handles didn't seem all that extreme. It did, on the other hand, confirm them as boys.

The main users who cropped up were Coyote and HHH, whose usernames made more sense to Mark once he asked after it, having in a couple of days learned to stop with capitals, and the ending punctuation, and the correct spelling, and the multiple independent clauses, if he was going to fit in. Simplify, simplify, simplify. That was the way to enter their skaz. Type like you were writing the liner notes for a Prince album—it was growing clear that Prince's approach to written language may have been the single greatest linguistic influence on Internet writing, an article Mark might once have wanted to write for *TUT* but which didn't even cross his mind now. In fact, the very idea of publishing in traditional venues seemed silly now that Mark was growing inured to typing on-screen and posting online, the long gestational period for even an e-mail becoming some quaint habit of a former self, a long-surpassed and ancient culture.

It wasn't easy after twenty-two years of school, growing inured to the rules of grammar and typography, and years of magazine editing in between, growing more meticulous than he had known he could be, but there was a wild, addictive freedom in learning never to hit Shift— ever; to unlearn typing commas and periods at the ends of sentences and independent clauses, so as not to sound too stiff—like after years of wearing suits and ties to work, showing up one day in a T-shirt and sweatpants:

> **<boomer1>:** so . . . hhh? why hhh
>
> **<hhh>:** if you have to ask you'll never know
>
> **<hhh>:** funky motherfuckers will not be told to go
>
> **<silence1>:** fuck the chili peppers and fuck you
>
> **<silence1>:** happy harry hardon you db
>
> **<hhh>:** fuck you whatever
>
> **<silence>:** your a baby boomer nark pedifile boomer1 so you should know happy harry hardon shouldnt you
>
> **<boomer1>:** of course I know it I'm not a fool
>
> **<hhh>:** well bring it then mofo
>
> **<hhh>:** unless you're just googling it now
>
> **<hhh>:** or asking jeeves or binging it or whatever you geriatrics do
>
> **<silence1>:** microfeeshing that mutherfuck

\<boomer1\>: I don't need to google Pump Up the Volume it was my favorite movie when I was your age—I mean that soundtrack was the

\<silence1\>: prove it what was the best song on the soundtrack

\<boomer1\>: well if I had to pick I'd say it was a toss up between Henry Rollins' version of "Wave of Mutilation" and that one killer Concrete Blonde cover but I could

\<hhh\>: actually it was rollins singing with bad brains on kick out the jams dumbnuts and they didn't do wave thats the pixies and

\<silence1\>: ok fine he got it wrong but fuck he's clearly not googling the shit he's down we got it I can't listen to any more

\<coyote\>: butt fuck

\<hhh\>: fuck off coyote

\<silence1\>: fuck off coyote

\<hhh\>: fuck off coyote

\<coyote\>: buttfuck off coyote

At his cubicle at the magazine, or even in the library studying for his Ph.D. comps, Mark might have felt infantilized, embarrassed to be engaging with these guys. But back in his parents' basement, back at home, it felt almost a natural consequence of all the moves that had led up to it. Here he was sitting in a space free of encumbrance, free of— he had to admit—Cassie. It didn't mean he loved her or wanted her any less—but it was that he'd found a space where his love for her was held in abeyance. A jewel case for the *Pump Up the Volume* soundtrack was in the CD tower right next to the bureau in the basement where he was sitting at that very moment, filed between *Syncronicity* and Paul Simon's first solo album, records he'd listened to with his closest friends throughout their teens, like the tangible referent to memories of having been seventeen once—and thinking like he was seventeen still, fourteen years collapsed like a browser window on his desktop in the stroke of a key.

It struck Mark that this was the most immediate effect of spending so much time online: he rarely kept track of time, and he even more rarely used his memory. Looking at that backlit screen, making jokes, making his missives even, while he was looking at the computer, he wasn't remembering. He wasn't remembering his old job. He wasn't remembering the glory of a gig with the Willows at Pete's Candy Store on a Tuesday night. He wasn't remembering the feel of Cassie's hand on the back of his neck. He was engaging, engaging, engaging, making new words and thoughts and ideas. It was the inverse of listening to music. With music, you listened, but you also let it wash over you as it evoked memories. You put on the original album version of "Sweet Jane," the seven-minute version complete with the heavenly wine-and-roses bridge, and you heard it. But part of your brain also returned to the last time you heard it, and the first time you heard it. Kissing Cassie became kissing Jill Lebowitz on her parents' bed in ninth grade became kissing Jill Lebowitz's younger sister Lilith on her parents' bed in the eleventh grade. Like the way smelling decaying leaves for the first time in fall might evoke previous falls, childhood falls, a synaptic palimpsest of trick-or-treatings, the collapsing of time across years into the evocation of memory.

But that didn't happen online.

Online, in a chat room, you were online. In a chat room. The world fell away and there was just text on a screen, the muscle memory of QWERTY as you typed. A stream of characters sped out before you, became words and moved toward the top of the screen forever. Lost to time and to memory, too.

The more time Mark spent in IRC chat rooms, learning more of the channels there, the more he found there must have been dozens of people who used the handle Silence, exchanging it as they wished. He did a LexisNexis search on them—even after being out of magazines for almost six years he hadn't broken himself of the habit of doing thorough-going Boolean searches on LexisNexis, had kept his password for the service and it miraculously still worked—and found a piece in *Wired* about it. "Silence" was so broadly used as a handle that it had become a kind of loose anarchic organization, one that had acquired some notoriety after executing DDoS attacks on selected targets over the course of the previous couple of years. They shut down websites, humiliated bank executives they targeted as enemies by revealing private information that led to their firings—they referred to it as doxxing—overwhelming their private servers. In the immediate wake of the whole Too Big to Fail debacle (Mark looked up at his CD tower where Hammer's *2 Legit 2 Quit* sat like the etymological antecedent to global economic catastrophe), they'd shut down the websites of all the biggest banks in the country. They destroyed the personal websites of television reporters they felt had done the most to allow those banks to get away with impunity—Mark had read about organizations like them when he was in grad school, had even considered pitching a story about one to a magazine at one point, but at the time, as Mark Brumfeld, even just interacting with a single member of a group like Silence seemed dangerous enough to consider it twice. If he crossed them, they could destroy him and he knew it.

Now he was chatting with any number of Silence members on IRC chat rooms without giving it a second thought. It wasn't the most reckless thing a revolutionary had ever done—at the time it seemed like it might vie for the *least* reckless thing an American revolutionary had ever done—but it was natural and organic and it gave Mark a sense of purpose in the least purposeful-feeling period of his years since being a teenager. Factions of Silence were looking for a way to capitalize on their growth, had been for months, and the Boomer Boomers could be the right iteration for them. Mark knew it and so did they, he felt. He did not discuss meeting with any of them, didn't know their real names or where they lived or what they did for a living—shit, he didn't know what a single one of them even looked like or what state let alone city or neighborhood they lived in—and he did not conspire in any tangible way. But they chatted with each other on IRC chat rooms every day after his first interaction with them, sometimes five, six, seven hours a day.

Then Mark got into his car and drove to play basketball.

He was living three different lives, separated by fixed borders, and he breathed it all like the air that feeds a flame.

CHAPTER TWENTY-EIGHT

MARK WATCHED WITH BOTH GLEE and dread as the Boomer Boomer attacks began in earnest at the end of the summer. They came in three distinct waves. Not one of these waves was controlled by any entity, after its coming into existence as an attack. Mark continued his own missives unabated throughout. He continued chatting on chat rooms and living his other lives, and all of them stayed boundaried by what he felt confident were their inherent borders.

The first wave came to be called Disturb. It came in the form of DDoS attacks on notable baby boomer icons. The last week in August there was an attack on the AARP website. For an hour the organization's site was down, which would not have occurred to many as odd. In an IRC chat one of Mark's correspondents told everyone to have a look over there. Mark typed the URL into his browser, and watched as, in place of the site, attackers put up a single photograph of Joni Mitchell, onstage, a smile on her face. No audio. Just Joni Mitchell's Canadian face, and underneath it in block capital letters:

I AM AS CONSTANT AS THE NORTHERN STAR.

It was a week before the site was up and running again.

Over the course of that week, Mark read in the *Times* that someone sent a series of blacked-out pages to the AARP office's fax machine, so that the machines ran out of toner over and over—between the website attack and the fax machine attack, all communications out of the organization's D.C. office were shut down. Later that week papers reported that someone had sent thousands of pizzas to the AARP office, called their phones constantly. It all sounded trivial, but when a *Times* story reported that the site's being down alone was costing a million dollars a day, it seemed less inconsequential. The attacks were reported in *The New York Times*, on BuzzFeed and Gawker and RazorWire, on all the major networks.

Silence claimed credit for the attacks. On a single video distributed on an IRC chat room Mark had never visited before—it was impossible to keep up with them all even if you tried, and he did try—called #styxxstyxxstyxx, wearing a David Crosby mask and speaking through a vocoder, with a Jerry Garcia poster hung upside down on the wall behind him, the speaker said, "This looks like a Boomer Missive. But this is not a Boomer Missive. This looks like Isaac Abramson, Boomer1, but it is not Isaac Abramson, Boomer1. It is Boomer2. This is Boomer Action Number One. This country has lived long enough with the hegemony of the baby boomers and their profligacy. The time has come to start hitting back. We have shut down the American Association of Tired People. What will you do? We are Silence and we are myriad and we contain multitudes. Resist much, obey little. Propaganda by the deed. Boom boom."

This Boomer Action was not an Abramson Missive. That week Mark watched as hundreds of new videos showed up on YouTube, none of them his, all of them new Boomer Missives or new calls to Boomer Action, all of them different but also the same: a young man sitting in a basement, wearing a David Crosby mask, with an upside-down Jerry Garcia poster behind him. The Jerry Garcia posters were most of them a little different, the walls different colors, as was the skin on the exposed necks and arms of some of the people posting. Each posting made an attempt to take on a new moniker—the highest Mark saw was Boomer137—but there were some duplicates, as new videos were being posted nearly every hour. They were shared on Facebook, tweeted on Twitter, Instagrammed on Instagram, and soon thereafter, reported in the mainstream press.

When Mark saw the first Boomer Action video, instead of pride, he was overcome by paralyzing anxiety. His tongue felt too big in his mouth.

His eyes felt as dry as the silicate packets they packed into freeze-dried fruit containers. The Boom Boom movement was supposed to be *his* Boom Boom movement. In his previous life as a magazine editor the central aspect of his job was curatorial, and it was near complete—he could take a ten-thousand-word story back from a writer and cut it down to five thousand words, four thousand. Pay a 20 percent kill fee and wash his hands of it if he wanted. He could add sentences of his own into the text and leave it under his writer's byline. Then copy would go on to the fact-checking desk, where if a fact was wrong it was cut or altered. He could lose his job if a single sentence went into print incorrectly. Then the piece went on to the copy desk, where sentences were vetted again. And again. He would give over changes to the rules of grammar or the fact of empirical inaccuracy and otherwise he had total control. If there was any drawback to his job as a writer and as an editor it was that at times he wondered what actual impact he had on people, on politics and events that mattered so much to him. But at least he had control. At least he was meticulous. At least what they put out was factual, empirically sound.

Now here he was starting a grassroots movement and already it was out of his hands. And not only was it out of his hands, it wasn't empirically sound or meticulous. It was defined by its mercurial nature, by the fact of its quantity and chaos, its animosity and its anger. He tried to picture Cassie seeing the videos, what it would make her think of him, but he couldn't even imagine it—and he couldn't write her about it. He knew he had to be more careful than that, even while shielded by TOR. She wasn't writing him, either, and that absence hurt even if he understood why she was ghosting him. Her own communications wouldn't be encrypted like the folks from Silence's were. And he hadn't even heard from them. He'd not heard one thing about the actions, about anyone from Silence planning to launch videos or attacks, before it happened. He loved the actions themselves and he loved the sense of his having inspired so many—there was no question his actions here were inspiring further action—but the corresponding idea that he had no editorial power of any kind made him feel hollowed out, like there was no marrow in his bones. He signed on to TOR and was about to log in to the #hacro channel to ask Coyote or someone what was going on, but he couldn't get his hands to move. He'd been a journalist long enough to understand that the FBI would already have begun to investigate attacks like these.

Even while using TOR he would have to be a lot more careful in the days ahead.

He hadn't posted those new videos. There must have been hundreds, for all he knew thousands, of channels all over IRC he didn't know about, didn't log on to—the Dark Web and even just the kinds of chats he was having were so vast and so evanescent, there was no way he could be on them all, and once a single thread reached bottom, it disappeared: unsearchable, unarchived, uneditable, unfact-checkable.

Gone.

There was no LexisNexis search, no Google cache, that would turn up all he needed to know about what Silence was after, what was happening. There was no independent verification that it existed at all, let alone that any of what was posted online was true. Or grammatical.

As he sat in his parents' basement he began also to think: Wasn't this just what he was after? Real followers, if not adherents. Real action. And he hadn't posted the action video himself, so no real culpability, and the protection of TOR encryption. He logged on to his IRC chat room of choice and instead of inquisitive, instead of nervous, he was, well, just a part of it:

   <boomer1>: this. is. amazing.

No one responded for a minute, for another. Terror started to creep back but this time rather than succumb to it, Mark typed again, and this time:

   <boomer1>: boom boom

   <silence3>: boom boom

   <silence2>: boom boom

   <silence6>: boom boom

<silence1>: boom boom

<silence4>: boom bo

<silence4>: boom boom

<silence8>: b to the mutherfucken b

<silence5>: boom boom

<silence1>: see you in #retirer

CHAPTER TWENTY-NINE

MARK WATCHED AS ATTACKS from the first wave continued unabated throughout the last week in August and into September. *Rolling Stone* magazine's website was DDoSed, Jann Wenner's home address, e-mail address, and cell phone doxxed online. Someone hacked into the Eddie Bauer mainframe and reconfigured all their pricing software so that every item sold in every Eddie Bauer store nationwide was marked "$666.66." A group of Boomer Boomers in David Crosby masks and wearing nothing else, their bodies like a Matthew Barney Cremaster installation glistening with Vaseline, ran through the LL Bean outlet in Freeport, Maine, spraying black spray paint and shouting, through vocoders worn under their masks, "Boom boom!" Police arrested one of them but he wouldn't talk and because he was a minor—Mark saw it reported he was fourteen—his name was never released to the public. On the Comedy Central website, someone hacked into all *The Daily Show with Jon Stewart* video clips one morning and replaced all the thirty-second ad experiences—so, just ads—before all the clips on the site with a GIF of a VW bus driving off the side of a tight turn on PCH somewhere in Northern California.

No one was physically hurt by the attacks, but money was lost—millions of dollars lost and millions more now to be spent on web security as a result—privacy violated, the people who ran businesses and organizations robbed of their autonomy for an hour or a day or a week. Within days attacks were reported on *60 Minutes,* at *The Atlantic* and *The Daily Beast* and RazorWire and *Slate* and Salon.com, in every major newspaper left in the country. The words "domestic generational terrorism" started to roll out of the mouths of newscasters and off the pens of pundits, op-ed writers, and journalists, to fall off the tongues of parents with their kids over dinner like they were pulled down by gravity.

And all of it drove more and more traffic to all the proliferating Boomer Missives, Isaac Abramson's the most but not exclusively—sometime in September Missive #1 hit eight million views—all of which were by now encrypted, every video showing its speaker in a Crosby mask and his voice disguised, originating on an IRC chat room if detected at all, protected by TOR, the signal bouncing from his computer to computers in Europe, Asia, Australia, all over the U.S., before an IP address could be detected.

On social media people posted so many varied Boomer Missives from so many varied Boomer Boomers that in the chat rooms Mark frequented, heated arguments cropped up about what was an authentic missive and what was second-wave Boomerism, even faux Boomerism, poseur Boomerism, so-called Boomerism. People speculated on whether the name Isaac Abramson was the name of a single person or if it was a moniker adopted by Boomer Boomers all over the country, much like Silence. Long articles on the organization—many of them questioning if it *was* even an organization, given that it didn't seem all that organized—ran on the websites of *The New Republic*, *The Unified Theory*, and *The Nation*, *Le Monde* and *The Guardian*. The landscape was changing so fast there wasn't time to wait for the pieces to come out in each magazine's print version.

Though many pundits speculated that it might mark a date for a new directive—and though Mark was careful to do a lot of listening and no posting on chat rooms that day—the anniversary of September 11 passed without further action.

The rest of the month was quiet.

In Baltimore the skies were as window-pane clear and blue as the morning a decade earlier when the attacks themselves happened. Then the first week in October a new Boomer Action was announced. It took Mark almost two days to recognize that he'd been invited to one of the main planning channels, #retirer, at the end of the thread when he got back on with Silence. It wasn't possible to tell how many people were on the channel with him, as everyone just posted as Silence, but much was made there about how exclusive it was, and that only an admin of the channel could invite new users. Against his better judgment—he was a thirty-one-year-old man who'd held a job and an advanced degree, who had a 401(k) and bylines in a national magazine—Mark couldn't help but feel flattered to be included. It felt less like being asked to sit at the cool kids' table than like getting an assignment from a new magazine. He still spent less time chatting on the channel than reading and watching—the speed at which these Silence kids typed was so far beyond his own skills that even when he tried to chime in, he was booted out of central conversation before he could make his points. The group chose another of the Silence collective to make the video this time, and Mark couldn't even make a case for him being the one to do so. Who would've thought that the most useful class he took in high school would have been typing, and that he'd be so far behind even after it, competing against kids who'd been writing code since they were seven.

Again this new action was set off by a video that found its way broadly onto the open web in a matter of hours. Again someone who was not Isaac Abramson, but who called himself Boomer2, posted a video, wearing a David Crosby mask. It wasn't clear even after the chats on #retirer if this Boomer2 was the same person as the first Boomer2, or if they were just using the moniker. This time the person said, "Boomer Action Number Two. *Daily Show* clips on ComedyCentral.com at exactly five P.M. today. View it. Then: Vandalize. Vandalize. Vandalize. Resist much, obey little. Boom boom."

After it went live, the #retirer channel went silent. Mark spent the afternoon reading through all the IRC channels he knew but he didn't see postings by Coyote or HHH or anyone from Silence. They might have gone dark or they may just be elsewhere, he realized at this point, and Mark vacillated between panic and peace, happy not to be leaving any kind of footprint—by now the FBI would be trolling some of these rooms, if not all of them. For all he knew everyone in Silence assumed he *himself* was FBI. That night, as the advertisements before every clip on the Comedy Central website, instead of the VW-bus-going-over-a-cliff ad, someone had hacked in and posted a three-minute video clip that was just a long list of addresses scrolling down the screen like the synopsis at the beginning of each *Star Wars* film, heavily copyrighted John Williams score blaring in the background.

Instead of a synopsis, the text contained the workplaces and home addresses of a series of the most recognizable figures in boomer iconography: Bob Weir's address in Marin County, Garrison Keillor's home address in St. Paul, Paul Simon's summer home in the Hamptons, Oprah's house in Chicago, Philip Roth's home in rural Connecticut, Jorma Kaukonen's ranch in central Ohio, Joni Mitchell's birthplace in Ontario, Levon Helm's address in central New York—dozens of addresses streamed down the screen for three full minutes, the biggest mass doxxing in Internet history. At the bottom it read, in block letters, in *Star Wars* typeface:

VANDALIZE.

What followed were attacks not only on private homes but on a slew of central baby boomer institutions. Mark watched it all stream through his Twitter feed in alternating waves of mirth and horror and ego fulfillment and abject fear as the attacks were flashed again and again down the screen on Twitter and Facebook, on the websites of every newspaper, reported on every news channel:

A group in David Crosby masks approached the WHYY studios in Center City, Philadelphia, and threw a trash can through the windows in front of Terry Gross's production studio. A single Crosby-masked culprit threw a brick through the window of the Moosewood Café at the bottom of the hill in downtown Ithaca, New York. Someone spray-painted the words "Boom Boom" in red on the side of John Cheever's home in suburban New York, where his name still adorned the idle mailbox at front. Someone used a drone to spill pigs' blood all over the roof of Stephen King's Bangor home. Boomer Boomers followed directions to the Cambridge address of the remaining Tappet Brother, Ray Magliozzi, and keyed all the cars on his block. Someone had found Barry Levinson's Baltimore home and had thrown Betamax tapes of *Diner* through his windows.

Someone here in Mark's own town of Baltimore, in Charm City, was participating in this wave.

Newspapers and websites published photographs of all the damage—aesthetic damage, superficial damage, but damage nonetheless, real vandalism terrorizing real humans.

This time the national response was far louder. In the weeks that followed the second wave of attacks, Mark watched as news organizations reported on the vandalism, damage in the United States—and beyond. Parisian news reporters were even at the scene just after someone knocked over Jim Morrison's headstone and slammed it with a sledgehammer.

Not all the addresses that had been posted were accurate, but many were attacked. Every night the news was filled with interviews with the name doppelgangers of boomer heroes whose homes had been vandalized—every Robert Dillon and Jon Erving and Irving Johnson in America suffering for the sins of their homophonic namesakes, for the lack of attention to detail in the millennials who perpetrated them. In Baltimore alone a guy named Jonathan Watters had a series of pink lawn flamingos thrown through the bay window at the front of his house.

Mark watched in awe as Wolf Blitzer came on his television and suggested on a long CNN report that since the Boomer Missives—which were now broadcast in the corner of the screen as the news media reported on the attacks—a kind of tipping point had been reached in the three short years since the Great Recession. He had Malcolm Gladwell himself on the show to discuss it. The next day Malcolm Gladwell's website was DDoSed, his info doxxed, a brick tossed through the window of his house. The same happened at William Bratton's New York residence. Reports of groups wearing David Crosby masks throwing bricks through the windows of homes in Northern California, in East Hampton and Vail, in the Berkshires and throughout the valleys and south beaches of California, dominated news cycles.

In late October, a *New York Times* column by David Brooks went viral. It was entitled "Millennials Gone Wild": "Where Islamist attacks drew our fear and ire." Brooks wrote,

Something new has happened in our beloved country in recent weeks. Kids wearing Gallagher masks have begun to wreak their own variety of havoc in the days since the economic downturn.

While others have begun calling it "generational domestic terrorism," I think it deserves its own psychological diagnosis: let's call it Millennial Sociopathy. MLS.

Perhaps one day we'll read about these hooligans in the DSM. I for one hope that's the next and last time we hear from them. The new generation has finally lost its grip on reality, and we are suffering the consequences as a culture. One thing is for certain above all else: it is very, very dangerous.

Mark had edited a short piece by Brooks back when he was at the magazine and was surprised at the time to find him to be quite a nice guy—Brooks had asked him about his own work, and he was flattered. But now Mark felt outright disdain for the man. He watched as the column was posted and reposted on social media. The *Times* was forced to shut down the comments section under the piece after ten thousand responses were posted in the hour after it went live online. Someone DDoSed the *Times* website and Brooks's own website in so synchronized a fashion that each played a GIF of Gallagher slamming his sledgehammer into a watermelon over and over. Instead of the watermelon someone had edited in a photograph of David Brooks's face.

Both sites were back up and running in a matter of hours.

The afternoon the Brooks piece went up and then came down, two of Mark's contacts popped up on the #hackro chat for the first time in a week under their old handles. He'd been searching all the channels he knew. He wasn't going to start a thread—there was some danger in looking like he was trying to lead an anarchic organization—but the #retirer channel was now completely silent, and in each wave of elation and terror surging over him Mark longed at least to chat with someone about how to consider the success this new action was having, and the violence along with it:

\<coyote\>: its been a long time since we've seen boomer1 around

\<hhh\>: maybe he's out

\<silence1\>: maybe he's a nark and he's narked us out

\<boomer1\>: I've been doing more watching than talking these days

\<hhh\>: and some booming

\<coyote\>: thar he blows

\<silence1\>: he blows alrite

\<boomer1\>: do you guys know where any new coordination is happening? I haven't seen anything and then I see everything

\<silence1\>: nark much nark

\<boomer1\>: I'm not narking! I just might like to have some idea of what's happening next and how we're taking all the violence I don't want to read it on the fucking CNN website.

\<boomer1\>: fucken

\<silence1\>: we

\<silence1\>: welcome to new nark city now leave

\<silence1\>: what you wanna have a say or something we are myriad

\<boomer1\>: I know we are myriad. You are. Myriad. But some of what's been happening is a little, I dunno, chaotic, uncontrolled, don't you think?

\<silence1\>: its a revolution revolution is chaos

\<boomer1\>: I know but that doesn't mean it has to be—it just seems like there could be discussion about it and how to roll it out. Should be

\<coyote\>: you want to walk back a revolution you started

\<boomer1\>: I'm not saying I want to walk back anything! Or that I started anything. I'm just saying that

\<silence1\>: nark

\<silence1\>: banish

\<silence1\>: narc

<boomer1>: not a fucken nark

<boomer1>: I'm not a narc

<boomer1>: I'm not!

And as would be the case so often in the months ahead, that was it for that thread. Mark thought better than to say anything more. He was frankly starting to sound even to *himself* like a narc, like Quentin Compson trying to deny his hatred of the South, that hatred growing clearer with each denial. The more he thought about it, the more he started to wonder . . . Well, why wouldn't he think that *they* were narcs? He'd started to foment a revolution. Of course you couldn't walk back a revolution. Who would want to even if they wanted to. He was all in now. It was full bore ahead.

CHAPTER THIRTY

IT WAS AS IF THERE WERE THREE LIVES Mark Brumfeld was living. The third life he lived was the one anyone could observe outside his house, surveillance or otherwise. While the opposite might have been true, in those days it was the component of his life that least felt in control. He had no choice, so he found a job as a barista at an independent coffee shop, and when he wasn't chained to the screen in his parents' basement began to return to the stores and restaurants he'd frequented when he last lived in Baltimore. The same Barnes & Noble in the same shopping center where Mark had worked at a TCBY when he was a teenager was still open.

One afternoon in mid-October he ventured out into this third life. He'd avoided Starbucks when he lived in the city, where there were fair trade beans at every corner, a Gorilla Coffee at the corner of Fifth Ave. in Park Slope where he would go out of his way to buy beans, websites where you could pick out not only a flavor profile but the country of origin of every bag of coffee you bought, blogs and commentary on every cup, links to conical burr grinders and French presses and cold filtration systems. But that was not one of the three lives he now lived—it was a life he'd left behind, and would continue to put behind him, not returning since that *TUT* party. Now here he was, inside a chain bookstore at a chain coffee shop, buying an iced grande caramel macchiato from a sixteen-year-old barista who'd just finished a long morning at the high school Mark himself had attended in the life before the life he'd put behind him.

It was shameful.

But this was the life he found himself living. He went to the Barnes & Noble and he sat down to read a long feature in *The New Yorker* but found he couldn't concentrate. He was thinking, of all things, about Cassie. The longer he went without being touched by a woman, the longer he went typing in his basement, the more his memories of her overwhelmed the interstices of his life. That time spent chatting online might have pushed her from the forefront of his mind, but that didn't keep her from rushing all the way back in when he came back into the IRL daylight. There were ways you could keep parts of your life discreet, but love smeared itself all over like you were greasing a baking sheet. And it wasn't as if his other lives crossed this public life—here in the Starbucks in the Barnes & Noble, he opened his laptop and opened his browser to see how many hits he had on his latest missive. There were five thousand more than when he last looked.

He opened his e-mail and saw he had no messages from Cassie.

He closed the window.

He closed his laptop.

He browsed the racks. There was a lot of journalism, a lot of information well packaged, well written, and well researched, that didn't pass his purview when he had sat at his computer, waiting for social media to tell him what he should read next. Though he had given his twenties over to editing a magazine, somehow he'd now come to prioritize the speed and impermanence of what he saw on his computer, same as everyone else.

During the years when he worked at a glossy magazine, Mark came to lose all sense of what he was doing. Even though all he wanted was to be a writer, being an editor was something, and going to an office every day gave him the sense that he was doing something even if he wasn't. That was in no small part the effect of having a job: Even if you were hung over and simply did a top-edit on a page on the latest Japanese selvedge denim, you were doing something. Even if you'd identified a great story and were working on a pitch, if you didn't get it finished by the time you left, you'd done something. By sitting in a chair, in front of a computer, fielding calls, you were technically being productive. Every day he was in an office made bright by natural light coming from the plentiful glass-window walls facing Eighth Avenue, he never set foot in a bookstore. He had piles of books all around him.

Now he was home. He had no job. He was doing the same thing he'd often been doing when he did have a job, but he was in a bookstore lit by fluorescent light, standing on the other side of an invisible partition cordoning him off from a chain coffee shop, and there were all these magazines: *Guns & Ammo* and *Southern Living* and *Garden & Gun,* on and on into gun oblivion, these thousands of dollars of paper and pulp he'd once contributed to helping produce, copyedit, and fact-check.

He was about to open his laptop again to e-mail Cassie against his better judgment just to check in when he heard someone say, "Mark? Mark B? Is it possible?" It took him a moment to respond to his own name. For weeks every communication he received was addressed to Isaac Abramson, and he'd grown used to thinking of that as his name. But now here he was, exposed in a way he never was online.

The man standing in front of him was maybe five foot five, with a long black beard and a clear strip of scalp down the center of his head where he had gone almost entirely bald. It took Abramson longer than he would have liked to realize that this was his old friend Christian Long. Chris. Costco.

"Holy shit," Costco said. "Brah, it's been what, like a decade or somewhat?"

"I think it has to have been at least that long."

"Well, what the fuck are you doing back in Charm City, brother? Why didn't you get in touch?"

Pale sodium light shone down. Mark didn't know how he was meant to answer a question pitched to him so directly. For a month he'd chatted online, where no one could see his eyes, where he could interject a thought or not by typing, but where interaction was limited to his fingers and his brain and consideration for his body qua body was nil. His years working at a magazine pushed him to a point of squirming reticence. Each Monday morning his boss came by his desk to ask a question or two about his weekend and then said, "Um, so if you could do a LexisNexis to find everything there is to know about the attack on that school in Grozny, in Chechnya I mean, by, say, the end of the day, that'd be great. Thanks."

"So what've you been up to since then, brah? I feel like you worked in newspaper reporting or something. And then you were in the Big Apple, right? Dude, I remember now, I saw your byline on a story in a magazine I was reading at the airport a while back. Back visiting your folks?"

"Yes, to the former. No, to the latter. I'm back here, I don't know, reassessing my options." He wasn't going to mention the Boomers and didn't have it in him to confess he'd gotten a job working as a barista. It was something of a miracle Costco hadn't happened upon him there in the month since he'd started back to it. Somewhere Mark's brain flashed images of a six-figure number of hits on a YouTube video, an IRC chat with Coyote, the little pleasure punch of seeing a blue super-script number appear below a video on YouTube as another viewer watched. It was a visual and an emotional memory, the memory of pleasure injected in one small, finite, knowable dose.

"Reassessing—oh, shit, you're back in your parents' place, dude. So you lost your job? Oh, man. I get it. Sorry. I mean, sorry, but. You know, me too. In the basement?"

"Just taking a break to reassess, as I say," Mark said. "Found some work here in the meantime." The door to the women's room opened and the sound of a hand dryer wheedled out like a tiny lawnmower, then went silent as the door swung shut. "But yes. Just like the Isaac Babel story. In the basement. What happened with you?"

"Oh, I was killing it, brohim. Got this job at T. Rowe, doing data analysis. Working on 401(k)s mostly, some Roth IRAs here and there, 403(b)s. Man, I learned every fucking thing there was to know about 403(b)s. Distributions of blue-chip stocks against less aggressive funds, yield analysis, mid-cap and large-cap and the whole kit and kabloozle."

"You?" Mark said. "I mean, I just wouldn't have thought you'd be interested in, you . . . you know."

"I know, brother. But what the fuck choice. I was making good money there for a bit. Then, you know, like everybody else—the Great Decession hit and they had redundancies and whether I knew it before they made it official or not, I, my brother, was redundant. Am. *Yo soy redundante.*" Neither of them said anything. "That was more than two years ago."

The sodium lights of the Starbucks inside the Barnes & Noble inside the shopping mall inside the Baltimore Beltway inside the suburb inside the state borders inside the country inside North America where they were sitting lent a flat look to Costco's face. The milk frother blew so loud in its compressed heated burst it was the only sound in the place.

For a moment Mark was self-conscious: He thought of his own face, how it must have changed, given how much Costco's had. The scar over his eye at least had healed, now months since his fight with Finkel. In the wake of the burst from the milk frother he heard a series of layers of sound that were ever-present but which it took such an awkward social silence to note: the clicking and banging of the espresso machine, the whirr of air-conditioning, the smell of coffee and bleach so pungent he could almost taste or touch it. Very faintly, under each of these sounds on the stereo in the store, only the bass of a song it took him a second to place. Costco heard it first, and Mark could see it in his face.

"Holy shit—isn't this Steve Miller Band?" Costco said. "Oh, brah, this was our jam when we were what? Sixteen?"

"Way younger," Mark said. He had a black hole's memory for dates, years. "Thirteen. After Ashley Abramowitz's bat mitzvah."

Though when they first saw each other Mark was considering each way he could avoid the conversation, hoping to fold back into himself and thinking over and over again about his favorite stanza from a Galway Kinnell poem he'd loved, called "When One Has Lived a Long Time Alone"—he'd found the book in his house when he came home and remembered how much he loved it—Costco and Mark found a table in the Starbucks itself, and they hashed out all they remembered of their history together:

Christian Long was the kind of person who didn't believe in anything, and so he was apt to believe in everything. Though his parents were Episcopalian he refused to attend church even on Christmas—"That's just some Pagan bullshit being carried over into Christian theology," he'd say. He read C. S. Lewis and then Gandhi, and in each phase was as into the question of whether Jesus was Lord, Liar, or Lunatic as he was whether we should practice ahimsa, attempting not to disturb even the mites in our eyebrows. He read *Zen and the Art of Motorcycle Maintenance* and was quickly a practicing Buddhist. His girlfriend bought him James Redfield's *The Celestine Prophecy* and for months he talked about the energy aurae he could see around every living panthe-istic thing. He discovered the writings of Malcolm X as a sophomore and then Allen Ginsberg as a junior.

By the time he was a senior he'd run away to live in Eugene for the whole fall semester. He came back in January with the egg-yolk yellow of two black eyes still healing, his nose now twisted to the side, track marks on his arms, and a tattoo of Jerry Garcia's face covering the en-tirety of his lower leg, pastels of the man's face obscured by leg hair. But he and Mark had been inseparable for years. When Mark and Costco were in eighth grade this was the exact song, the exact node upon which their obsession with their parents' baby boomer music be-gan, until it took Costco all the way to Eugene. On a mix tape Costco's sister had given them, filled mostly with NWA, Public Enemy, Boyz II Men, Ice Cube, and a song or two from the Guns N' Roses *Use Your Il-lusion* records was that song. They listened to it over and over, pressing the two backward-facing triangles on Costco's Aiwa compact stereo, complete with three-CD changer. From there Mark and Costco began to peel back the layers of their parents' music. They moved to Van Morrison, not to *Astral Weeks* or *Bang Masters* or even *Tupelo Honey*, as they would later, but to "Brown-Eyed Girl." Then on to *The Doors*: The Oliver Stone biopic was in theaters.

"I remember after you got the soundtrack I went and found each rec-ord each song came from," Mark said, sitting there in that Barnes & Noble, mainly letting Costco do the reminiscing and quietly allowing the layers to silt away in his mind.

"For six months you pretended your girlfriend was Pamela," Mark said. "You were Mr. Mojo Risin, Jim Morrison."

"Dude," Costco said, "I even figured out my own Mojo Risin name, right? It was—okay, I'm embarrassed to admit I remember. Glitch Arinson. I tried to get everyone to call me Glitch for one whole winter."

There was a newfound sense in them, that something strange and rock and roll had been hiding in their very homes, and which sent both Costco and Mark to their parents' record collections and from there it exploded: from the stringy-haired Southern girls on the jacket of the Allman Brothers' *Brothers and Sisters* to the giant flying pig balloon on the cover of Pink Floyd's *Animals*, Mark and Costco both slid right down the slide to *Workingman's Dead* and *American Beauty* and then hundreds of tapes of live Grateful Dead shows. They listened to all the bands affiliated with the Dead: Moby Grape and Traffic, Jefferson Airplane and Spencer Willmont and the Cherub Band, Jorma Kaukonen solo records and the New Riders of the Purple Sage.

Clarity was not up for offer in those days. It did not even occur to Costco and Brumfeld then that they were listening to their parents' music. They were smoking and eating and snorting the same drugs their parents had. They were long past any semblance of feeding off the music of their own generation. They were steeping themselves in the sound of an era their parents had lived in when their parents were the age they were just reaching now. Unlike every other generation in American history, their generation was only too happy to accept as revolutionary the music their parents had handed down. By the time they were high school juniors, and Costco also inherited his parents' bronze Audi, they themselves mail-ordered tickets to four-day runs of Dead shows at RFK Stadium, at Giants Stadium.

Mark was surprised how clearly he remembered that day. Here was one consequence of talking to another human in person: It evoked memory, memory which came unbidden, fragmented, and unpredictable. IRC chats had almost never done so, only impelling themselves forward as text moved in fitful jerks toward the top of the computer screen. Brumfeld found himself remembering that in the days around the time they'd discovered their parents' records, a kind of anger and violence had been building in him. He hadn't thought of it in years. At night he went to sleep so angry at nothing specific that he fantasized running around their house with a baseball bat, smashing in television sets, breaking windows, and smashing drywall. There was no impetus and there was no explanation behind these fantasies.

"Oh man," Mark said. "Remember we saw those kids on the hill at that first RFK show?"

"We'd just sucked all that nitrous," Costco said.

"Some part of me thought I might never go to a show again after that," Mark said. While he knew Costco wasn't, he was thinking about the Boomer Actions now: vandalism, violence. That afternoon when they were teenagers, Costco's lips were still purple after sucking a balloon of nitrous when over the crest of a hill next to the prickly yellow grass where they lounged, they saw a kid with dreadlocks whipping against his back come flying past them. He was about their age, with dark freckles stippling his face, and as the world was returning to them, the nitrous finishing its brain-scrambling, joy-inducing work, another kid came right after him, pulled back a field hockey stick, and slammed the dreaded kid in the head. He got on top of him, punched him in the face over and over while the guys who'd just sold them their balloons ran over and pulled the field-hockey-stick kid off. A rope of blood swung down from the dreadlocked kid's mouth. No one stuck around long enough to see the EMTs show up.

Mark remembered looking up in horror and looking over at Costco and being shocked by what he saw on his face: a look of sheer joy, almost avarice. It was a look that foretold Costco's departure, those black eyes he came back from Oregon with.

Costco Long had never believed in anything, and in not believing he was susceptible to anything.

"Thems was some crazy, crazy times," Costco said. "Rough. Violence. Was some violent times back then. But then, now we live in even crazier fucken times, don't we?" Costco wasn't going to let that conversation drop. A sensation shot up Mark's spine like a human-sized spider crawling up his neck. There were three different lives he was leading now and two of them were crossing, well beyond his control.

He didn't like it.

Costco looked at him.

"I'll just go ahead and say it, this Boomer Boomer shit is the bomb. I mean, not the bomb maybe, but it's some energizing shit. Those speeches Boomer1 gives? I'd follow that guy anywhere."

Costco looked down at his hands like he'd said too much, like he realized he was with another adult he hadn't seen in a decade. But then a sense of recognition passed over his face. This was his old friend Mark Brumfeld after all, the look on his face said, with whom he'd participated in who knows how many felonious drug-based acts. He looked up. Mark was just looking right at him still.

"I mean, how could you miss it? Even if you weren't a journo in your former life. Shit, you must have all kinds of ways of understanding the shit that's happening that the rest of us don't."

"Not exactly," Mark said.

"Close to the actual action," Costco said. "All we ever wanted to be was close to what was going down. Maybe this is it but maybe this is not it. Is an attack on the baby boomers the way to get this shit done? Maybe it seems misguided. Think Gandhi. Think Thoreau. Think Dostoyevsky, man."

"I think Dostoyevsky would've approved," Mark said.

"Right," Costco said.

He looked up and for the first time since they first saw each other he grinned the grin he used to right after they swallowed a tab of acid. "So. Boom boom."

Costco didn't look Mark in the eye and Mark couldn't tell if he meant it ironically. But Jesus, it seemed close to an admission. They'd come of age in the Clinton Era, in a time of such broad and ubiquitous American prosperity that seeing a suburban kid at a Dead show get pounded in the head with a field hockey stick might have been the most violent single act either of them had ever witnessed.

"All I are saying," Costco said, "is give peace a chance. Or whatever."

"Maybe that's what they're going to do," Mark said. He realized after it was out of his mouth he was being dangerously indiscreet. A burst of milk frothing blew in Mark's ears. Clouds fled the sun, ditching its cover, and the space around them heated just barely. "Don't go getting any ideas in your head, Brumfeld. You missed being a millennial by about three birth years, my friend."

"Did I?"

"Did you ever."

"Demographers place millennials as pretty much anyone born between 1980 and 1990 or so. I was born squarely in 1980. As were you."

"I was born in '81, brah. But now? Now I am a prematurely bald, very nearly middle-aged man. You were not present for the course of the hair's disappearance, but you got eyes. Any other generation in human history, and by all rights I should have a wife and seventeen kids by now. Be out hunting or gathering, working as a titular councilor. Now instead I got my parents' lawn to tend to, and a whole lotta sperm wishing they didn't end up at the bottom of an overused tube sock every morning. I am become forever adolescent."

"Yeah," Mark said.

"Well, shit, man," Costco said. "It is *very* good to see you again, brother, but I gotta get back to work. But we will see each other again?"

"We will see each other again," Mark said.

"Give me your cell, brah."

After he gave Costco his number, a sense of peace surging through him when he had reason to take the phone from his pocket and check the message, the green script of a text from Costco easing down his spine, Mark said, "So what are you doing for work, anyway?"

Costco looked down at the shirt he was wearing, then looked up and said, "Oh, right, sorry." He reached into his backpack and pulled out a forest green knit cotton collared shirt and a forest green baseball cap. Both had the Starbucks logo on them. Mark looked down, then back up.

"Right," he said.

"Right-o," Costco said.

Mark was working for an independently owned café. Costco was working for a corporate one. Costco was thirty. Mark was thirty-one. They said good-bye. They would see each other again. And again. And again. And again and again and again, etc., etc., etc., ad infinitum.

PART SIX

JULIA

CHAPTER THIRTY·ONE

THERE WERE TWO DISTINCT WAYS in which Julia Brumfeld had suffered from serious hearing loss in the years just after her first and only son was born—one of them literal, the other not as much. The literal deafness began in earnest in Julia's thirties. It came on so slowly it was almost as if it wasn't happening. During Mark's first year of life Julia would sit in a darkened nursery on the second floor of her and Cal's suburban Baltimore home and rock him, rock him, rock him for so long she felt as if something inside of her was going to break free and drag her to the floor. In the sharp light of day she could look down at his impossibly small pink rabbit face, his impossibly small eyelids shot through with the purple lightning of veins, and smile just to see him there. Existing. Being. Breathing in her arms.

And during those daytime rockings she would return to the most active creative part of her life—she would parse a phrase or a lick she'd played onstage with the Cherubs over and over, taking apart the bass line and the guitar licks and the rhythm chords, figuring out new arrangements for the songs she'd done with Spencer on the road. She would take a bassline and walk it up an octave, change the fingering, all in her head, all while she sat and rocked, rocked, rocked the baby. It did not occur to her that there was a sense of loss and nostalgia in doing so. Here she was, a homeowner, married, rocking a newborn, and her mind was still working over songs that they played on the classic rock station. She would open her eyes and look down at Mark and see that he was at perfect peace, and she'd figured out a new kick to open an old song, and she'd be at peace, too.

Not in the darkness amid sleep. At night, rocking him in hours that were neither night nor morning, rocking and rocking and rocking, felt not like peace and ease but like battleground and strife, like the territory on which some epic duel was being fought, and in the days after his notoriety reached its peak Julia would wonder if some of the groundwork for it hadn't been laid then—a capitulation to her son, to her scion, the decisions parents make every day to get through, to get sleep, to get on with it. This duality had defined her experience of having a kid: her friends would gift her Dr. Spock, old copies of *Our Bodies, Ourselves*, and new-agey book after new-agey book about the beauty of pregnancy, the glory of the early years with a child. To Julia this was bunkum. She loved her husband and she wanted to bring a child into the big bad world and she even longed to be a mother, but since she'd discovered she was pregnant her body felt as if it were being taken over by some inexorably burgeoning cancer—which in some clinical way it was. The foreign cells in her would develop in her womb, under a genetic plan, and one day become another human she was meant to love and nurture. She and Cal went to the theater when Mark was five and watched as a silver-faced alien burst through the abdomen of Sigourney Weaver and all she could think was: That's just what it was like when, somewhere deep in my own gut, Mark was ready to get out.

Every morning of her first trimester and well into her second she would wake with silver swimming minnows squirming before her eyes. She would make it through the shower and down to a bowl of Grape-Nuts and a couple of sips of Tab to try to settle her stomach before she felt it coming—she had just enough time to burst out through the back door and onto their ample Pikesville lawn before she emptied the contents of her stomach, slimy brown granular Grape-Nuts mess, onto the green grass. By the middle of April she'd grown so adept at it that she didn't even need Cal to hold her hair back—she could essentially vomit standing upright, into the bushes, wipe the back of her right hand across her face, and head in to pack Cal's lunch before he left. She was a grown woman, soon to be a mother, who'd learned to boot and rally like a frat boy from morning sickness. He was a grown man, soon to be a father, who still had someone packing his lunch for him for the day. He still hadn't ever boiled a pot of water to make macaroni. It wasn't even clear he knew how to make a PB&J. She barely did herself. Sometimes she snuck a whole handful of Twizzlers in the afternoon instead of eating lunch. She knew how to make Jell-O, and maybe three different casserole recipes she'd clipped from the *Parade* magazine that came with the Sunday paper. They were still just kids. Kids with a kid. They would never, in Julia's estimation, become full-fledged adults. Even pregnancy would only dent it. She'd still be wearing red Chuck Taylors and Velvet Underground T-shirts when they bore her along in her casket, and fuck if she wasn't proud of it.

If she was honest with herself the first signs of her eventual hearing loss were starting even then. She hadn't played fiddle in a band in a decade by the time she discovered she was pregnant—she gave private lessons on weekends, would down the road teach music in an elementary school classroom, but when parents found out she didn't use the Suzuki method they grew indifferent, weren't interested in a teacher who would teach kids to play only by ear—but after a long day she would often come home, pull out her imitation Strad, and saw out a fiddle tune or two. She played in A, all the main fiddle tunes were in A, and there was something about having two flats available to her, that A-flat especially, that left open such an air of possibility, as if having flats in a chord gave it a greater sense of breadth. After playing, the screak and cry of her first finger way up the fingerboard on her E string, a long high tone would continue to ring in her left ear. Sometimes she couldn't shake it from her head for hours. It would still be ringing as she rocked the baby to sleep that night. Or earlier in the evening Cal would come up the back stairs and into the kitchen, his face a rictus of disappointment and anger she couldn't decipher.

"I've been calling you for five minutes to bring me and Irv a beer, hon. What're you, going deaf?"

She wondered a decade later if he remembered saying it, if he suffered guilt for having done so when it turned out that if she wasn't going to be functionally deaf yet, she was, in fact, losing her hearing.

The high end started to go first, stripping itself from her aural range like a snake sloughing skin, but it felt less like a loss than the muddy gaining of a kind of indecipherable low end of the tonal scale: a snake choking down a rodent it couldn't digest. She noticed it most around the time Mark turned three. The first three years of the kid's life felt like thirty, or like a whole new series of lives she didn't know could be lived, nested inside each other like onion skins. The OB made them stay in the hospital for a week with the kid, he was so jaundiced. They went into a room in the NICU where he lay under the Bili lights, black sunglasses over his eyes while the infrared shot through his skin into the syrup of bilirubin accreting yellow in his bloodstream. She loved the kid to the point of aching already. To Julia, the sitting there in her wheelchair peering through the glass, the sitting and waiting amid the hospital hallway that smelled like some weird combination of Aunt Jemima's and iodine, was almost more painful than the constant sharp throbbing she felt from her episiotomy. Which was of course its own kind of pain. When her closest friend from shul, Alice Janowitz, came to visit and meet Mark in the hospital she said, "Oh God, after my first kid I just referred to that whole region as my ver-blah-blah." Cal hadn't laughed much when he heard it so Julia didn't say it again aloud, but that was how she thought of her own nether region for weeks.

But life was measured out in weeks instead of months or years until Mark turned three, three and a half, and it felt like a return to herself she'd not felt since she was last on tour across the country with the Cherubs. She met every morning as if it was a discrete unit, and often the meeting of morning arrived while she was already awake, rocking, rocking, rocking in that nursery with Mark. Perhaps that was the greatest trespass of the endless nights rocking—the sense that at the moment when days came to feel most vibrant, most wholly unique units marked by darkness and then light, there was a needy imp in the nursery next to their room waiting to wake them so often, tugging like a rutting pig at her nipple, as to make days and nights feel indiscriminate, turning time into some brown muddle of unified existence.

Just when that ultimate and overwhelming sleep deprivation had come to feel like it would be the only existence life could offer, the baby started to sleep through the night. The soldiers cleared the field and Julia's capitulation was muddied. Years after she'd laid down her own weapons and given in to the kid, now here the other side had laid down their arms, too. Sometimes he would just go to sleep like a, well, like a human being. He was three and a half and one Saturday morning she found herself meeting the morning sun with indifference, putting the pillow over her head and going back to sleep for an hour, only waking when the ringing in her ears grew bad enough she needed to rise and take an aspirin. Cal even let her sleep, went down to read the *Baltimore Sun* rather than kissing her neck to see if morning sex was in the cards.

Whatever joy that new sleep might have brought, instead it brought Julia to a kind of reconvening with her senses—only to find that one of the five, the one that had in her life brought her the most joy, was failing. Throughout Mark's third year and into his fourth, Julia started to suffer tinnitus so bad she found herself not sleeping not because the kid was waking her up, but because of something inside. They would get a babysitter—finally, they could leave the kid with a babysitter, no matter how he cried when they left—but at parties if more than four or five people in a room were talking at once she couldn't hear half of what a person right next to her was saying. One afternoon she took Mark to daycare at their synagogue on Park Heights Avenue and headed into the city to see an ENT, the ironically/unironically named Dr. Steinway. They did a series of tests for conductivity, cognitive function; she wore headphones like she wouldn't see again until Mark was in college and the kids walked down the street with them on instead of ear buds—lids, they called them. She sat in a room listening for beeps, most of which she didn't hear. Seemed about right. The lid of the world coming down and sealing her from it.

"Is there any family history of hearing loss?" the ENT asked her. The only family history she knew of was her father's nervous breakdown. "Did you attend rock concerts often as a kid?" he said.

An image flashed across Julia's visual field: the darkness of Fillmore West, the motes she could have reached out and swirled like glittering mica in a sunlit pond in the space above the crowd. Behind her a huge wall of amplifiers. Months and months of amps in clubs across the country with the Cherubs, years of amps in basements and garages in Baltimore when she'd given up her hope of getting Spencer Willmont back to the States, knowing the closest she'd come to him again was reading about his death in *Rolling Stone* one day, when in the lat seventies the punk scene was burgeoning and she bought an electric violin, played backing up spiked-haired guys playing Gibson Firebirds slung below their beltlines, SGs strapped so low they almost couldn't find the strings with their picks, until she realized that music couldn't possibly continue to interest her.

Yes, she said. She'd been to quite a lot of live music performances in her days if she was being honest.

"Well, that will do it," Dr. Steinway said. "New research shows that if you've attended as few as a half-dozen rock concerts in your life, you will most likely lose most of your high-end hearing by age fifty. High-end goes first. And then . . . well, it's still too recent to say what will happen—it's only ten years since we started going to concerts where the amplification even *was* loud enough to do such damage to our hearing. It will be years before we know what kind of toll it will take on us ten, twenty, thirty years down the road. In fact, I'm starting to do some of that research with a colleague at Hopkins. I don't suppose you'd be interested in joining a clinical study in acquired hearing loss?"

Julia said she didn't suppose she would be interested in any such thing, no, but thank you for asking. Her father had been in the hospital because he had to and it had ruined him. She wasn't about to come to one voluntarily. In words that she'd just learned, she soon enough might not be able to hear anyway.

Some part of her never would have attended enough shows to have gotten to this point with her hearing to begin with. But after she and Cal got together, he was enthusiastic about her continuing to pursue music. He was a third-year medical student at SUNY Upstate. She had come back to Syracuse after taking the fall off after Spencer left for his France jaunt. He was gone and she was just an undergraduate again. She didn't even tell anyone what had happened out west, and Willie never came back to campus. She and Cal met at a bar in Westcott, far from the noise of the city itself, and when he discovered that she was a fiddler, that she was Julia, that she was beautiful and full of talent, and then she discovered that his own mother had been a classically trained violist, it was a matter of hours before she found herself in his bed. "I want you to play for me," he said. He said it, said it, said it as they moved from Syracuse, to a residency at Johns Hopkins, where he matched, in the city where he'd grown up. Baltimore was close enough to Philadelphia for her to feel comfortable she could see her mother when needed, could come help with her father. Could visit him when he was healthy enough to accept visitation. Somehow the mere fact that Cal was going to be a doctor must have attracted her to him in the first place—there was a sense of authority doctors had played in her life, a control they held over her family with the unfulfilled promise, the unfulfillable promise, that her father may one day again be healthy enough to return home. How could he recover when it wasn't clear just what he was recovering from—catastrophic inability to handle the traumas in one's past?—but being near trained medical professionals outside of a formal setting put Julia at ease.

But being around trained medical professionals, even one who had provided a home and a son and a life easier than it could have been had Julia become a rock star, or had fallen in love with a teacher like herself, wasn't going to restore her hearing. Nothing would. The only thing that could provide help was hearing aids. Dr. Steinway made clear that for now, in her thirties, she shouldn't need them. Not yet. The tinnitus was uncomfortable and could cause anxiety and sleep deprivation, but he could prescribe her five milligrams of Valium if she wanted. She wanted. Until it started to distract her ability to get through daily activity, he suggested she start trying to lip-read if she could.

CHAPTER THIRTY-TWO

BY THE TIME MARK WAS A TEENAGER, Julia had grown far more than adept at lip-reading when talking to him, talking to Cal, or in the classroom as she needed it. The irony of a music teaching job opening at Woodlawn Elementary right as the ringing in her ears wouldn't stop struck her and didn't—it was either irony, or whatever the opposite of irony was—but no matter how inept kids were, she could still clap and find a rhythm and she could teach technique on violin, viola, cello, and bass. Her aural world had grown into a single amorphous blob of watery basslines and rhythm, but the aural world was better succumbed to than fled from. She still put on her old Bill Monroe records from time to time to hear what she could hear, to discover if any of Tater Tate or Kenny Baker's old fiddle lines were still available in her spectrum.

Mostly what she heard was the thumping of the bass, which in blue-grass was as repetitive and boring as music got—one, four, one, four, one, five, one. Monroe had always liked playing in B-flat, no matter how challenging that was for fiddlers, and Julia had learned to play those melodies in closed positions with her left hand, unable to hit any open strings. One day in a book on astrophysics her book club was reading she discovered that when astronomers made actual audio recordings of the sound produced by a black hole, the black hole emitted a B-flat fifty-two octaves below the spectrum the human ear could hear. That seemed right. Her whole aural life was black-hole-bound, waiting to be sucked in for all eternity to a substance made of pure, soul-sucking gravity. That was a fate she'd have preferred to what was ahead.

When Mark was eight he took up piano, and Julia felt beyond grateful he'd not wanted to play the violin as Cal suggested—"But you could teach him everything you know!" he said. She could do no such thing. By that point she couldn't even tell if her own intonation was on unless she was playing in first position on her G string—it was one thing to teach in a huge room full of kids whose faces she could read to see what was happening. But doing so one-on-one with her own son? He needed lessons from a real teacher. From someone who could still hear the upper registers. And besides, she told Cal, it just wasn't possible for her to discipline the kid in the way he needed—the first time he touched the hair on her bow, the first time he unscrewed the bow's frog and let the hairs swing taut and loose, she grew so angry she wouldn't let him near the instrument for a week. The piano—that was the instrument for them. It was tuned every six months by a professional tuner and when you hit a key, it produced a note. Playing piano required precision but it did not require intonational precision. Whatever she needed to do to help Mark when he came home to practice she could do by sight and by feel.

Lip-reading became more of an issue as Mark's friends started to come over when he was in high school. By that point Cal knew something was wrong with her hearing, but there was almost nothing he could do to help—no help she would accept, anyway. "You know, you could go see Steinway again," Cal would tell her. "He's developing all kinds of novel approaches to hearing loss himself, at his clinic."

"Hearing aids," Julia said. "Devices that look like plastic barnacles hanging off the sides of your head. I will not wear fucking plastic barnacles on the sides of my fucking head. I'm fine. I'm a young woman. A young mother. I can hear plenty. I can tell everything you're saying, can't I."

For the most part what she was saying was true, even if she couldn't quite hear herself saying it. Within a matter of weeks in the classroom she knew her students well enough to understand the vast majority of what came out of their mouths. If you could *anticipate* what was being said—if you knew for example that third-graders didn't know a half note from a whole note, couldn't even wrap their right thumb around the frog of a violin bow, didn't know what an arpeggio was or how to identify a G clef—there was still a whole lot you could teach them. And there was the added benefit that the unbearable squeaking of an improperly bowed E string, while it might send a student's classmates squirming in their seats, was for all intents and purposes inaudible for Julia. She appeared to any casual observer a saint gifted with infinite patience as she sat through the sourest notes ever played on a violin and viola, day after day, public performance after public performance. If you knew what you needed to beforehand, if you knew most of what was being said and played, you could understand 80, 90 percent of what you were hearing from context, experience, and prior knowledge.

It occurred to Julia only after the trouble arrived for Mark that this was the very definition of growing conservative: listening for patterns based on what you already knew, comprehending new stimuli based on set assumptions about the world and its context, waiting to hear a version of what you expected to be told and dismissing out of hand any new or contradictory information. She wondered how much it had come to blind her—deafen her—to what was happening in her own basement, trying to match what she saw in her son to what she wanted and expected his behavior to be. It was by necessity that she had no choice but to listen by watching, and wait to hear a version of what she was expecting to hear. Rather than reject it, she came to accept this new information: that there was a good reason people grew conservative as they grew older, as their failures and dysfunction got the best of them and left what it left behind, and she could do worse than to swallow it whole, even if it lodged in her throat like an undigested rodent.

CHAPTER THIRTY-THREE

THE SECOND WAY JULIA lost her ability to hear was more metaphorical—but no less a part of her life: she lost the ability to hear her son. It, too, was a gradual process. She and Cal would never have squelched any desire the kid had, and perhaps that was its own failure—they could have pushed him into medicine like his father, into teaching like his mother, early on. But the longer he persisted in trying to make it as a journalist, as a writer, the less sense it made. Mark had spent his early twenties not receiving validation that he was barking up the right tree. Julia could find no sentence, no melody, no way to communicate this to her son. Maybe it wasn't her job to do so, but she was his mother and she wanted what was best for him, even if it wasn't at all clear what was best for him.

By the time Mark arrived home at the age of thirty-one to return to living in her basement, Cal and Dr. Steinway had found a way to convince Julia that hearing aids weren't "plastic barnacles" anymore—new research allowed people to have cochlear implants, to have the effective functional restoration of their hearing. But Julia Sidler Brumfeld was sixty-three years old and she had grown comfortable in the wash of bass notes that now served as soundtrack to her daily life, a thudding rhythmic life that had come to suit her. She found all kinds of new music to listen to, music whose basslines you could feel even if you couldn't hear them—Brazilian dance music, Afro-Cuban bands, the D.C. funk of the early seventies, even some early hip-hop that she could blare so that the bass vibrated through the house. She could literally feel the music now, the vibrations of the subwoofers she installed in each room, the subtle glottal pop of melody as treble notes burst from the tweeters she put on bookshelves. She owned a pair of hearing aids but refused to put them in, a fact that had not been an issue until Mark returned to the house.

When he'd first told her over e-mail he'd be returning she had a jolt of sheer joy, the idea of having her boy back in the house. The love she felt for him wasn't something she could articulate but it was a fact that every day he was gone from her house, some part of her was hundreds of miles away, with him wherever he was. Some part of her was thrown out into the world with Mark, some insane emotional attempt to guide him along and watch over him and, if she was being honest, to keep him under her watch. There with her, loving her. It's not that she thought about him every minute, but that some part of the middle of her chest was focused toward him out in the world like a Jew facing Jerusalem during prayer, a Muslim toward Mecca. The East to which her heart faced was, of all things, her son Mark.

But as soon as Mark arrived in her house she felt a kind of encroachment on her own routine, the rhythms she'd learned to get through her day, that led her straight into an active and overwhelming depression. She didn't know it but the empty hollow of that basement with its instruments was a foundation below her, and now it was lousy with thirty-year-old son. No matter how capacious, her heart would not suddenly face right down below her feet. Now it was as if she had no direction at all to face during prayer, the Western Wall and the Kabaa having moved into her very own basement. She would be standing in the kitchen, cutting vegetables for a salad, doing the crossword puzzle, and suddenly as if she'd been shocked by a surge of damp electricity Mark's vibration would be rumbling down the stairs and across the foyer and then touching her elbow, or just standing in a doorway waiting to be seen, his sound as omnidirectional as bass. She loved him—but she loved him like the cancer that had issued from her very own body that he was. All the maternal love in the world couldn't make up for the fact that when she was startled by his sudden appearance, or when he forced upon her in the safety of her home that she could not hear anymore, a sense of overwhelming friction rose up in her.

Then one afternoon in early winter, months after Mark's return, she saw, peeking in the high windows of their front door, the face of a middle-aged man. She walked through the soundless air of her front foyer and answered. Standing next to the middle-aged white man was a young black man, younger than Mark. Lip-reading would never allow her to be able to make out someone's last name the first time they said it, but she understood that the middle-aged white man was saying they were from the FBI—a fact confirmed when he took out a badge with a shield on it. She could both hear this man and read his lips enough to get that he was asking to be let into her home.

"May I see your identification?" Julia asked.

She took the badges from both of them. The middle-aged one was Mike Cimber. The younger one was Decius Brutes. She said sure, yes, they could come into her home. What could she have to hide? What else was there to do? She hadn't broken the law in two decades. If there had been an intruder she would have called the police, but even if she felt these men were intruding upon her silence just as Mark was—well, they *were* the police. The federal police. And it all happened fast. When she'd lived in San Francisco from time to time she would be in a house where police would come—back in those days musicians might cross paths with someone from Weatherman or the SLA, but the bands she consorted with sure as shit didn't, so there was nothing to hide. She didn't have that kind of revolutionary fervor herself. It took any paranoia out of the equation, knowing that she knew people who might have met Eldridge Cleaver or H. Rap Brown, but that she didn't hang out with anyone who did.

So now she asked the agents if they'd like a glass of water.

They both demurred.

For the next fifteen minutes they asked her questions about Mark, most of which she could understand by watching their mouths. She didn't catch every word but it seemed they were saying there was some kind of organization he may or may not have belonged to when he lived in Brooklyn, and they wanted to know if he was acting unusually, if she'd seen him with any new acquaintances, if there was anything unusual in his behavior. For a period Agent Brutes seemed to be asking something about the Internet, something called Silent, but she didn't follow the names of some websites they wanted to know about, and she wouldn't have known anything about any websites anyway—she did not spend time looking at or reading websites herself—and so she just shook her head.

"Well, he is my thirty-one-year-old son, now living in my basement again," Julia said.

When she said the word *basement,* Cimber looked at Brutes and Brutes wrote something down in a notebook. "But no. Mark was a journalist. Successful. Enough. Successful enough. He's just home for a period while he readies for his return to his career as a journalist and a writer."

Again she saw one agent look at the other and then Cimber write something in his notebook again, and while she wasn't sure why, she felt she was done with this intrusion in her home. She said so, that she thought it was fine for them to have asked some questions, but that was enough.

"I understand," Agent Brutes said. Julia understood him perfectly. Agent Cimber put his notebook away. "We hope it's okay if we come back to ask you further questions sometime," he said. She said that would probably be okay. She was a sixty-three-year-old woman talking to the FBI for the first time in her life, a life that had included travels with musicians whose fans at least surely included members of SDS, Weatherman, Black Panthers. Who was she to put them off any further. "And of course if you wanted to have a look at what Mark is up to on his laptop, we wouldn't discourage it," Brutes said as they were leaving.

"I'm afraid I still believe in civil rights, even those afforded my own son," Julia said. "Even if the young people seem to have collectively forgotten it, we all have a right to privacy."

"At least until we forfeit that right," Agent Cimber said.

Julia did not respond. She closed the door behind them.

Whatever craziness these men thought was somehow related to

Mark, they had no idea what they were talking about. Right? Right? It occurred to Julia that there was only one way to find out and that she was lucky enough that Mark lived with her now, and he'd be coming back and she could ask him. That night when Mark got home, she was waiting to talk. Her lip-reading skills, combined with the fact that she was talking to her own son, allowed her to understand maybe 80 percent of what was being said. He'd seemed like a bundle of angry nervous energy of late—his hands would worry each other as he talked, his fingers intertwined like he was playing here's-the-church-here's-the-steeple-open-the-doors-see-all-the-people and he talked for maybe four minutes, complaining about the minutiae of his job, until she was able to change the subject and get to it. It somehow alleviated the nerves she had been feeling since the agents left to have so normal a conversation building up to broaching the news. Before she could even tell Mark about what had happened he had launched into three separate diatribes about who-knows-what was bothering him. Conversation with her son had always been this way, overwhelmed by his logorrhea, but conversation with her son didn't often find its way to her having to divulge that she'd been visited by the FBI. Agents who were likely looking for him. So she just broke in and said, "Listen, Marcus, I have to talk to you because this afternoon two agents came by to talk to me. They wanted to know about you."

She told him about the visit. They were asking about him, if he was part of some kind of organization or something. She watched his face very closely as she spoke. He didn't seem to know what she was talking about.

"So you're saying, like, federal agents," Mark said. "Were here. At our house."

"That's right," Julia said. "What did you think I meant?"

"Oh, I thought you must have meant like a literary agent or something." Though after he said it she could tell he wasn't, he just didn't know what she could be talking about.

"No, Marcus. Federal agents. FBI agents. They wanted to know if you were looking at some websites or some such. So . . . have you? Been looking at websites?"

"You're being serious here, Mom? Am I looking at websites? Yes, I look at websites. There's not a single human my age, or many ages above the age of five, that doesn't look at websites. Like, virtually all day. You're going to have to be more specific."

"Something about a site called Silent or something."

Now Mark stopped for a minute. His face went white. Then the color returned.

"Silence is not a website, Julia. Silence is an Internet organization committed to a series of social justice missions that are actually pretty impressive. I mean, not all of it. Sometimes they can get a little out of hand and there are some members who—"

Mark started into some minutiae she could not follow no matter how she concentrated—even if she could hear him, Julia wouldn't have been able to follow whatever technobabble her son was now technobabbling. While he talked, her heart calmed. She looked at this son of hers. Above his left eye there was a long pink scar from where he said he'd taken an elbow at a basketball game just after he got back that summer. He was a man now, this son of Julia Brumfeld's, hair thinning on top, almost gone in the space between his forehead and a third of the way back his head. As with many Jewish men his age he still had thick shocks at the sides of his head, but not much left on top. A couple of times she watched as the flesh below his left eye twitched just the slightest bit, like the fur of a cat jumping away from an unwanted touch.

"—and they don't have a website, anyway." Mark was still talking. "They operate on the Dark Web, chatting on boards that you'd have to know about in order to find."

Julia looked at him.

"What?" Mark said. "I've read a lot about them. We were thinking of profiling one of them when I was still at the magazine. I mean I wasn't going to edit it myself but I would've done a top edit. Well, my boss would've. But I would've helped. But. Fuck. FBI agents were at our house. I'm sorry, Julia. That's crazy."

"It is," Julia said. "It's crazy. But I hear you, honey. Just let's all be careful. Even just being mixed up with whatever an FBI agent could think you were mixed up with would be bad."

"And I'm not," Mark said.

"I know," Julia said. She assured him that she believed him and she heard him and she loved him.

Still, for the next week Julia paced the house, trying to decide if she should go into the basement. She'd respected Mark's privacy since he was a teenager. Even when he came home in high school reeking like a skunk from the expensive pot he was smoking—pot didn't smell like a skunk when she was still smoking it—even when the T-shirts he wore had sticky black resin at their bottoms from where he was clearly cleaning out his glass bowl after smoking, she didn't raid his room to look. Well, except for the one time when she went in and found a bong in his closet. But she put it back and didn't tell him she'd seen it. It eased her worried mind just to know she'd seen it and could talk with him. They talked soon after, and she didn't mention the bong at all, but when she asked if he'd been smoking pot, he looked her right back in the eye and said yes. She and Cal decided that if he was going to be smoking he might as well do it in their backyard, where he wouldn't get arrested. But now here he was, back in her home, and federal agents had been asking questions about him. She felt certain she'd seen their car outside the house again on two occasions since they'd been by to talk to her. Once on her drive to the Giant for groceries she could've sworn a black sedan was tailing her three cars back.

So, four days after their visit, after four days of deliberation and self-flagellation and anxiety, she went down to Mark's basement room and opened up his chrome Apple laptop. It required a password but she knew that this password had always just been the five digits of their street address, so she entered them. It opened. The screen looked like—well, it looked like the screen of a computer. She clicked on the icon for getting on the Internet (Mark had taught her when he was home on vacation from college that it was called "Safari" and then apparently "Firefox" and then for a while "Chrome" but then back to "Firefox"—she couldn't understand why the Internet couldn't settle on one name for itself, it seemed like it was purposefully designed to confuse). When she opened it, it was the Internet. Just like any other Internet. You typed in names and it brought back websites. You "surfed" it. You could even buy clothes and groceries from it now.

As she sat there in front of the computer two things occurred to her: she did not want to be looking into Mark's personal computer, invading his privacy, and she did not know what she would be looking for if she did. So she did not mention it to Cal, she did not call the police, she did not get involved, and she did not mention it again to Mark until it was, by a long shot, too late.

PART SEVEN
MARK

CHAPTER THIRTY-FOUR

THERE WERE TWO LIVES Mark was living back in Baltimore, and the second of his lives was lived in his parents' house as it was lived when he was a teenager—quietly, in desolation, and with extreme reticence. Alone. He talked to Julia when she was home, and when he arrived back to his house after seeing Costco Long for the first time in a decade, his mother was busy at the kitchen counter. There was an air of indifference toward his arrival he wasn't used to—but it was a welcome change so he swallowed it whole. In front of Julia was a large head of iceberg lettuce, a bowl full of homemade ranch dressing, a half-dozen sickly-looking half-white tomatoes, a half-dozen quartered radishes, and a stack of Ziploc bags. She was cutting up individual servings of this salad and putting them, separated into bags, into a large Tupperware container.

"Hey M," she said. "How was your afternoon, honey?" It was verbatim the greeting she'd invited him home with every day of his teenage years. Something elemental had changed in her voice, though—it was lower, muddier than he'd remembered it, almost like she was making fun of the rotund, imprecise way congenitally deaf people talked. And there was a kind of removed tone that he could feel in the balls of his feet. Something seemed off. "You look good. Color in your cheeks. Good day?"

Mark thought to tell her about having run into Costco, but it was a kind of crossing of the discrete parts of his life he wasn't comfortable thinking about, let alone relating to her. When he'd first gotten home his mother had asked him about his relationship with Cassie, nudging around the edges like some hometown yenta. He couldn't take it. He didn't talk to her about it at all. And here now he didn't want to talk to her about seeing Costco. Somewhere in the back of his head he calculated the amount of energy it would take to accept how happy this single reconnection with Costco would make his mother. For years he went to an office where he tried everything he could think of to please his boss, his editor, anything that might improve his chances of moving from his position as an editor to working full-time as a writer, a near impossible move but one perhaps helped by cordiality verging on servility.

Now here he was at home with his own mother and the last thing he could imagine doing was saying even the simplest thing to make her happy. He loved her, but she exerted power over the editorial choices of no national publication. She would let him stay in her house rent-free no matter what he did. There was nothing he could do to change that fact. He knew his mother would love him, would support him, no matter what—she'd probably come visit him in prison if he was in prison, the only Jewish mother sitting on the other side of the glass. He didn't have the stamina to handle the emotional toll of her boundless satisfaction at his own happiness. In principle, there was nothing that would make him happier than to see her happy; if he wasn't around her, in her physical proximity, sitting in her very kitchen, knowing she was happy would make him feel something akin to joy.

But in practice, the emotional effort it took to say the thing that made her happy while he was standing here with her in her kitchen was so fatiguing it felt like it might give him cancer, Crohn's disease, smallpox, Coxsackie, all at once. So he just talked, talked, talked about nothing at all. Since he was a teenager he had developed a singular set of defenses, reflexive and insuperable, based on the very idea of protecting himself from his mother's oppressive emotional support. He was the single remaining white blood cell fighting off the mutation her love could cancer him with. The only person who'd ever broken through that defense system was Cassie, and where had that gotten him? So instead he said, "Oh, and so what was that thing you'd wanted me to help with?"

"Not worried about that right now, to be honest, Marcus." His name wasn't Marcus, it was Mark. Sometimes his mother called him by that full name to signal a seriousness more serious than the situation called for.

"And so what are you worried for?" Mark said.

"What?"

She narrowed her eyes and seemed to be squinting at his mouth.

"I said— Oh, don't worry about it."

"I'm not worried about it," she said. "I have to talk to you about something and that's where I have to start, kind of thing."

"Kind of thing," Mark said.

"What?"

"Half the people these days, when they talk, that's how they end every sentence. 'Kind of thing.' What kind of thing? What's the point of even saying it? It's just like an opportunity to say one more sentence, the nervous tic someone makes when they're not sure what to say next."

"I wasn't nervous before you said all that, Mark, but I kind of am now. What on earth are you talking about?"

"It's somehow worse than the period when in front of sentences it was always 'At the end of the day.' 'Well, at the end of the day I guess you just have to figure some of the banks were too big to fail.' 'At the end of the day, I guess all those credit default swaps were kind of a bad idea.' 'At the end of the day, you just have to get a job and keep it and make money from it.' 'At the end of the day, the day will be over because the day will have ended at the end of the day.' It's as if every human was getting paid two dollars a word for speaking, and they were throwing the extra lexicon in there to pad their paycheck."

Julia sat there looking at him. It appeared as if she'd stopped listening to his rant at some point in the middle, and was now on to thinking of something else. As if she'd grown tired of listening to what was outside of herself and was now focused on something she heard inside. His MacBook Pro never did that.

"If you think about it, I guess that is how people talk a lot of the time, Marcus, sure."

"'If you think about it'!" He said it so loud and clear she couldn't have missed it, no matter what else she was thinking about.

"What, Mark? What's wrong with that!"

"At least 'at the end of the day,' 'kind of thing' are just empty phraseology, filling up the space. But 'if you think about it'! That's actively insidious."

"I hardly think our sitting here having a conversation, mother and son, is 'insipid,' honey."

"Insidious. And it is. It is. The thing is, it's how people talk whether you think about it or not. That one isn't just filler in conversation. It suggests a kind of solipsism that can account for almost anything. People use empty language to fill up conversation if you think about it *or not*. You might as well say its opposite: 'Well, if you *don't* think about it, I guess people do use a lot of empty rhetoric.' But it's not empty rhetoric, that 'if you think about it.' I mean: right here and now, *think about it*. If I were to say to you, 'If you think about it, CTE is a brutal disease killing off dozens of NFL players after they retire,' the sentence literally suggests that the contingency is such that if you *don't* think about it, it isn't true. 'Well, if you don't think about it, CTE doesn't exist. Phew! Now let's go watch some receiver get his head taken off on a crossing rout, then deal with it for fifteen years until he commits suicide. Happy Sunday!'"

"Listen, Marcus—"

"I don't want to listen. I want to finish. I mean, this continues all the way on to the worst acts of the latter half of the twentieth century. 'If you think about it, the Hutus' treatment of the Tutsis was genocide'— 'If you think about it, the U.S.'s plunder of Vietnam, then Korea, then Afghanistan, then Iraq'—only you don't think about it. That's the trouble. You don't think about it. But in our complacency people feel as if it's okay to sit back and say, 'If you think about it at the end of the day kind of thing—bum-dum pah dum.'"

Mark finished talking. His mother sat in front of him. She appeared to have not one thing to say to him.

"You know, lately you really have been doing a lot of what someone who didn't know you as well as I know you, as your mother, might call ranting."

This comment, of all others, did, in fact, stop Mark's rant. He'd come dangerously close in his conversation with Costco earlier that day to feeling like his online and daily lives were crossing.

"Listen, Marcus, I've been trying to say that I have to talk to you because this afternoon two agents came by to talk to me. They wanted to know about you."

The first thought that came to Mark's mind when he heard the word *agent* was the word *literary* preceding it. He'd talked to various agents over the years about story ideas, and it struck him in the moment that one could have read his Emma Goldman piece in *TUT* and might have interest. But then how would they have found him down here in Baltimore? At his parents' house, no less? And why would there be two.

"They were asking about some organization I've never heard about, about things that happen on the Internet, some thing called Silent or something. Do you have any idea what that's about?"

Now it felt as if no saliva had ever been anywhere in Mark's whole body before. He couldn't swallow, and he guessed his face must have looked like it had no blood in it at all.

"So you're saying, like, federal agents," Mark said. "Were here. At our house."

"That's right. What did you think I meant?"

"Oh, I thought you must have meant like a literary agent or something." It was a ridiculous thing to say aloud, a ridiculous mistake, but the sheer audacity of it, Mark could see, helped the situation. He could see the lines on Julia's face ease at this mistake—*Of course,* she must have been thinking. *There's nothing my son is up to that would bring federal agents to our house. There may be, on the other hand, things he's doing to bring literary agents.*

"So you have no idea what these agents were talking about?" Julia said. "About some online organizations? You're not consorting with Internet organizations, are you?"

"No," Mark said.

"You're sure."

"I don't even know what an 'Internet organization' means," Mark said.

"Okay, well . . . phewph. That's a relief." She didn't say anything for a moment. Mark didn't, either. "So are you working on something with a literary agent, then?"

Mark said he couldn't say, and he was so ready just to be out of that kitchen with his mother he headed down to his room without finding out anything further about what the FBI that was there was asking about him.

When he got to the basement he had both a text from Costco, who wanted him to come by his place for a drink that weekend, and of all things an e-mail from Cassie. An e-mail from Cassie. How many times had he opened his e-mail looking for one from Cassie to find nothing? And now Julia was telling him about fucking FBI agents asking if he was affiliated with Silence and here she was. That was just how it went—you could check e-mail a zillion times looking for something to come up, but it only came through when you weren't looking. He didn't write Cassie back at first. He shot Costco a quick "Yup send me your addy" and only then turned to Cassie's e-mail, feeling some relief at the normalcy of it after talking to his mother.

Things were fine for Cassie, the note said; she'd just gotten a new job and she was psyched about it and wanted to tell him all about it; did he think he might be up for having a visitor down in Charm City sometime in the next couple months? She was getting tired, hadn't had a respite from the city in forever, and she knew it might be awkward to find somewhere for her to stay in his parents' house but she'd be up for it if he'd have her there.

He couldn't think of one thing he'd rather have happen. A visit from Cassie. It might have been the only information that could turn his head from his conversation with Julia. He felt grateful for the very existence of e-mail—for the distraction, for the chance to talk to her about what was going on. Had Cassie said this to him in person, he wouldn't have been able to contain himself, might even have seemed so eager to have her come stay that it would turn her off, possibly even lead to her not coming down after all. Even if it had come up on an IRC chat he wouldn't have had the time to think, and to say the right thing, before conversation had moved on, scrolling ever up the page until it had vanished. Poof.

But now he could write a sanguine draft in his e-mail drafts folder saying, Yeah, sure, he figured it'd be fine to have her down there if she wanted to come. He could hold off on sending it until later that evening. He wrote the note, saved it as a draft, reread it, saved it again. He closed his browser and opened up a new video file, feeling that the only other thing that might, might make him feel better about what his mother had just told him would be to make a new video:

"Boom boom," he said. "This is Isaac Abramson, Boomer1."

CHAPTER THIRTY-FIVE

THE THIRD WAVE OF BOOMER attacks started in December. Yet again they weren't set off by Isaac Abramson. Mark had been chastened by the knowledge that actual FBI agents knew where he lived. Had talked to Julia. His mother. Off and on for weeks he found himself invited into channels where planning was taking place, then booted off, then let back in. It wasn't clear he even wanted to be on there right now. But it was also difficult to tell how serious to take all the badgering from the Silence guys—they called him a narc a lot, but they called each other narcs a lot, too. By the beginning of the winter he had come to feel like a single temblor amid a far larger quake—a prime mover, an occasional voice, but the effect of the motion was too great to decipher. Even if he did have to talk to a federal agent there wasn't much to say: he chatted on the Internet. He made untraceable videos he knew were encrypted. He'd done nothing wrong. Political speech was a clearly protected category. When he was at the magazine Mark had worked on a story about the proliferation of small earthquakes all over Oklahoma and Arkansas, regions that had never had earthquakes, but who now had hundreds a month, all caused by fracking companies that were disposing of waste and wastewater by injecting it deep into the ground, where it hit once-stable fault lines. These had to be the first large-scale man-made earthquakes in natural history, and now here he was, causing something of the same himself—and then finding that it set off a greater temblor, shaken by some other force, undetectable, separate. Again it had to have been someone in Silence's myriads who sent out the Boomer Action that led to not only their downfall, but Isaac Abramson's.

Just before the action was called for, the #retirer channel went live again, and there was a wild, chaotic conversation. Mark hadn't been let in on the planning for the call to action itself, but he picked up on the fact that there was a series of targets being considered for attacks. No matter how he searched back up the thread, it wasn't clear what was settled upon as a target. Mark asked a couple times what the plan was, but each time he just got the same response:

\<silence1\>: narc

He couldn't have told any of them about the feds if he tried. Chatting with them with what he knew made it feel like less of a threat—a secret he held, and owned. Meantime Mark could do nothing but watch as the hackers in Silence went after old media. Hijacking the advertising experience ahead of an episode of *The Daily Show* on the Comedy Central website was one thing. But now they went after the centerpiece of the American home: the TV. For years people had been talking about the Golden Age of Television, about how with the advent of shows like *The Wire* and *The Sopranos* and *Breaking Bad* we were living in a moment when TV, once the basest form of entertainment—aspersed by parents and critics and David Foster Wallace alike—had overtaken cinema for artistry, for cultural reach.

So Silence went after it.

They used it.

On NBC, on *Sunday Night Football,* they managed to overtake one full thirty-second advertising slot. It went out to tens of millions of viewers, and then on to tens of millions more the next morning when people who had made videos on their phones of televisions broadcasting their message posted it to social media. After the first quarter of a Patriots–Broncos game, both teams undefeated and starting the two most popular quarterbacks of the era, the first ad that came on after play began featured someone calling himself Boomer1. It was not Boomer1, of course—Mark was Isaac Abramson was Boomer1, and he had nothing close to the knowledge, wherewithal, or desire to hack into a major network television broadcast and put a Boomer Boomer video up for the whole world to see. But it came on-screen, someone sitting in a basement that looked a lot like Mark's parents' basement in Baltimore, with an upside-down Jerry Garcia poster over his right shoulder and wearing a David Crosby mask.

"This is Boomer1," the person on the hijacked ad said, his voice disguised by a vocoder. "We are Silence. We have something to tell you. This is the next and final Boomer Action. It is to be called ROWRY." The person in the video said it so it rhymed with the name Rory, but in big yellow capital letters the word "ROWRY" flashed on-screen like the 800 number in some late-eighties television commercial. Mark had been the first to use the word, on his own video. Now it was being broadcast across the country on network television. "That's ROWRY, as in: Retire Or We'll Retire You. The legal retirement age in the United States of America is sixty-six. There are hundreds of thousands, millions, tens of millions aging adults in this country still working long past that age. They are baby boomers. They have the jobs we want. Those are our jobs, the property of the young. They are taking the jobs we should have. Their grasp is tight, and it must be loosed. We want the jobs. You have them. We are not unreasonable in our demands but we want them met. You have three months to retire. Blah blah blah the Ides of March. After that: boom boom."

The feed cut out. NBC returned its viewers to the advertisements advertisers had paid for, starting with a spot for Chevy trucks.

The real Boomer1, Isaac Abramson, Mark, was not on his computer when it happened. He was not on chat rooms, searching for IRC channels where Silence might be discussing the fallout. He was, of all places, over at Costco's parents' house, watching the game. He'd gone out for drinks with his old friend a couple times since they first ran into each other at that Starbucks. Costco texted and e-mailed, and when he invited Mark over to watch the game it was the first time he'd gone to his friend's basement, the same basement he'd hung out in hundreds of times as a teenager.

When the Silence hack started, Costco said, "What the faaa?" His parents were out of town for the week, and he and Mark were smoking a spliff. Then the ROWRY call came out. "All right, dude, this shit is just blowing up. Hacking an ad on national television? What did we just see. Fucking MNF. Those dudes are killing it."

Mark wasn't sure what to say. It was one thing when he'd seen Silence's videos for the first two waves of attacks, sitting alone in a room waiting to see if Coyote or HHH or any of the multitudinous Silence posters might have a comment. But now here he was with another human. Another human who was stoned out of his gourd and also appeared to be in support of what Silence was doing.

"I . . . don't know," Mark said.

"Dude, are you okay?" Costco said. His eyes spidered with veins from the joint they were smoking. Part of Mark felt like this might be a time to tell Costco he was being surveilled, maybe, by the FBI. But he didn't know how to say it and he didn't know how Costco would take it. That, and Mark had a long history, when they were teenagers, of freaking out a little when he was smoking pot. Once at a party he'd taken a bong hit and then proceeded to grip the edges of the Barcalounger he was sitting in for five hours, earning him the nickname Rodin, which it took him a semester to live down. Now Mark sat there in a different kind of terror.

"Just a little too stoned, I think," Mark said. "You? You fucked up by it?"

"Not fucked up by it," Costco said. "Listen, I just gotta fucken say, I kinda know the guys who did that shit. I mean, in whatever way you can say you know someone on the interweb. I know that seems crazy."

Mark stared at him. He wasn't sure if he was paranoid or if Costco was suggesting what he was suggesting.

"You know I was always into computer shit," Costco went on. "And so you know when I got canned by T. Rowe it was because I was looking at some sicko shit on the net while I was at work. I got real caught up in IMing with people I didn't really know. They showed me all these sites. This one website that had this thing called a sideboard where you could go and Jesus it was just the sickest shit—I mean if you weren't careful you could find yourself surfing child porn or snuff films or scat porn or who knows—stuff that makes *Two Girls One Cup* look like *Fraggle Rock*.

"Anyway, these guys I chat with, a lot of them call themselves part of a thing called Silence now and you can get on it and off of it and they're the ones getting the word out, I think. I mean, dude—you wanna see?"

Mark wasn't sure what to say so he said sure, he'd see. So while Al Michaels and Cris Collinsworth emerged back on-screen after having been upended by the wave of Silence taking over one of their commercials on *Sunday Night Football*, their badinage less energetic for the rest of the game, Costco pulled out his laptop and showed Mark a bunch of things Mark already knew: how to get onto the TOR router, how to open windows on the Dark Web and log on to IRC channels and chat. He explained how it was so deeply encrypted even the feds couldn't track you down on it. Hearing his friend repeat that fact made him feel less paranoid. Not less stoned, but less paranoid.

Costco logged on to a couple of the IRC channels Mark regularly hit, but there was nothing there. Just a blinking cursor.

"Fascinating," Mark said. He said it like he meant it and he was trying to sound like he meant it but Costco said, "Honestly, dude, IDK what the fuck—I figured these boards would be lighting up after that hack. Who knows. They must be somewhere else. Sometimes they say which rooms to head to and sometimes they don't—it's just chance. But I swear. I think these motherfuckers are the guys. They're into some serious shit." Mark didn't say anything. "Well, shit, now you're making me all paranoid. You're being all narky. You're not gonna tell anyone I'm into this shit, right? You're not like researching a journalism story or something, are you?"

"I am not," Mark said. It was the longest sentence he'd uttered since the ROWRY commercial aired. "If I'm being honest, I'm fascinated by what they're up to, too."

"Okay," Costco said. "Okay, word." He let his own grip on his Barcalounger slip. He pulled a big head nug out of a jar and started breaking it up to roll a joint. "Okay. Okay, well, if you have a look at some of those IRC chats, lemme know what you think. If nothing else, those guys are funny as fuck. And, you know, right. Someone's gotta do something."

"I thought you thought Gandhi might be more right," Mark said.

"Even Gandhi has his limits. And you know me, bro! I'm always changing my mind. Out of my mind. Where is my mind."

Costco rolled his joint and they smoked it and Mark headed out.

When he got home he felt emboldened by getting on TOR with Costco, by the tacit sense of consent implied by looking at chat rooms alongside another live human, so he logged on and found that the IRC channels were all silent. Nothing on #retirer, even, where he was somehow sure he'd find someone online. On the surface web—on Twitter, on Facebook—comments sections of articles were blowing up with questions about ROWRY, which was already #ROWRY: how seriously were all those people sitting behind desks at academic institutions, the CEOs of just about every Fortune 500 company, to take this threat? When the second wave of Boomer attacks was spurred on, they went quickly. They were incontrovertible. They had a real, tangible, IRL effect, something the sixty-and-above demographic could understand as a threat. Mark dipped one toe into the #hackro room, though he knew all those threads were dead. Same at #retirer and all the rest. He'd started a revolution, then considered trying to walk it back—and now the main initiative, ROWRY, was back harder than he could ever have imagined. Hoped. Dreaded. He didn't know what the plan was for March, and it wasn't entirely clear if anyone at Silence did, either.

CHAPTER THIRTY-SIX

IN THE WAKE OF THE HUGE WAVE receding after the MNF hack and the ROWRY call, Mark's ex, Cassie Black, the only woman he'd loved in his adult life and if he was honest with himself the woman he loved still, was to get on the Amtrak Northeast Regional to come down a couple weeks before Christmas to Baltimore and stay for a couple days. Mark got into his parents' Volvo wagon to pick her up and turned the key and nothing. Click, click, click. The battery was dead.

Cassie was coming and he didn't want her waiting, didn't want any single thing to go wrong on her trip down, so he did the only thing he could think of and texted Costco, who said he didn't have a shift that day, so sure okay why not he'd be there in a minute.

They arrived just ahead of Cassie's train. When she came walking through the gossamer air of Baltimore's Penn Station, Mark felt a kind of ease in his chest he'd not felt since he first started on the IRC chats. Being berated by Coyote or HHH might have felt like friendship at times, even been a kind of friendship, but if it did bring camaraderie, it didn't bring calm. Even spending time stoned with Costco did not bring him the peace that being around Cassie brought him, no matter how painful it was to think of how he'd been jilted and how unlikely it was he'd ever win her back. That was the trouble with having love smeared all over the inside of you. You could wash all you wanted and your fingers were still bound to be greasy.

They hugged hello, and he took her fiddle case off her shoulder for her. He introduced Costco.

"Oh, Mark's told me a lot about you," Cassie said.

"Dude, you shouldn't tell people things about me," Costco said. Cassie just looked at him. "Kidding, sistah. That's cool. Like what kinda things, though."

"You're the Jerry leg-tattoo guy, right?"

Costco reached down and lifted the leg of his baggy jeans. There on the outside of his right calf was a full-color tattoo of Jerry Garcia's portrait from the cover of a late-period Jerry Garcia Band record. His full gray hair was blowing in the wind, and all around it the scraggly, wiry black hairs from Costco's leg obscured him.

"That is really . . . something," Cassie said.

"It's permanent like a tattoo," Costco said.

Mark said they should get going.

Costco got behind the wheel and Mark sat shotgun and Cassie sat behind him and they drove out past the MICA building, up north out of the city, through five-story renovated brick buildings full of artists, architects, the new businesses of urbanly renewed Charm City. Mark thought of a line from one of his favorite short stories, the opening of one of Harold Brodkey's stories about St. Louis, a lyrical description of brick buildings. When he first read it he thought if you replaced "St. Louis" with "Baltimore" the line might cover his own childhood. But as he drove past the UMBC campus and its collection of redbrick buildings with Cassie now, he thought he'd have to undo that idea. He hadn't thought about the baby boomers in the wash of all the complicated moves in the wake of the latest call to Boomer Action, had grown so focused on the events themselves, but now here with Cassie, downtown, he remembered what it had been about from the first. No more baby boomers. That story was a baby boomer story, and now he had to find a way to unlove it. Open-Apple-Z it. To undo it, upend it, make it his own by washing it away, and replacing the name of one city and giving it the name of another was hardly enough to do so. Their job in those days, as Mark saw it, was not to *stand* on the shoulders of the generation before them. It was to stomp them.

Costco drove up to the highway but it felt wrong for them just to go back to his parents' house. He asked if Cassie and Mark wanted to take a drive. Mark turned back to her and said he figured she might be tired but she said no she was good, sure whatever.

"Just happy to be out of the city for a little while," Cassie said. "Let's go anywhere." There was something inscrutable in her face. He loved her inscrutability and always had. She wasn't looking at Mark or at Costco, but out the window as they drove. He was glad she was here and for some weird reason he was happy Costco was there, too.

"Maybe out through Woodlawn," Costco said. "The long way. And then back."

"Okay?" Cassie said.

"Whatever," Mark said.

"It's like ten minutes from here."

They turned up roads that looked like any roads in the Northeastern United States, uniform double yellow lines between two lanes, well-paved asphalt shaded by deciduous trees in areas where shadows cast a blotchy latticework down below them, houses and strip malls where the sun shone thin through the winter air. Costco reached over into the glove box of his mother's Saab and pulled out a glass bowl and handed it to Mark. It already had a sizable nugget in it, bright green crawling with white-flecked red hairs. Mark hit it and passed it back to Cassie, who hit it and passed it forward to Costco.

They drove on.

Suddenly almost against his will Mark found himself reciting the stanza from the poem he'd thought of when he first saw Costco, the only stanza in all of literature he'd ever memorized. It was the ninth section from that Galway Kinnell poem, including an allusion to Milton: *It is better to reign in hell than to submit on earth*. After he finished reciting neither Cassie nor Costco said anything for a minute until Costco said, "There's a whole eighth in the console if you want." Mark packed another bowl and they smoked it and soon they were coming up though Woodlawn.

"Look at this place," Costco said. "Woodlawn motherfucking Maryland. A suburb like any other suburb." Cassie just said okay. She got quiet sometimes when she was baked. Mark said he knew, he'd been there plenty of times.

"It's also the home of the Social Security Administration's central office," Costco said. "Did you know that?"

Mark said that he did and he didn't—he knew it, he guessed, he didn't *not* know it. But he'd never thought about it. Cassie just said no.

There were three lives Isaac—Boomer1—Mark Brumfeld was living, and Cassie came from a past life, a life that had existed before the three new ones he'd espoused while continuing to exert its emotional traces over all three. Now, here, they'd all crossed. He was slamming Cassie into this other life now, breaking boundaries while maintaining them, at the same time that Costco was slamming his other lives together all at once. They drove straight through Woodlawn and then out a long road into the near-rural side of the Baltimore suburbs west of the city. Out the driver's side of the car, out on the other side of his window, sat a low-lying collection of newly renovated, white stucco and glass and chrome buildings like any other office park in America, only a little cleaner, newer, more expensive. Too expensive, really, to be sitting on the edge of a suburb of an American city the only distinguishing features of which were its murder rate, and a television show that helped the rest of the nation understand the complicated civic and social underpinnings of its murder rate.

"That's the Social Security Administration Building," Costco said. "Where all the records of all the Americans are kept. The place of origin of every Social Security number. Of every single baby boomer about to receive a check."

"You know there's also a Social Security building right down the street from Penn Station, where we just were, right?" Mark said.

"I didn't," Costco said. He thought for a second. "But it's *a* Social Security office. This—this is, like, *the* Social Security Office."

"Okay," Mark said.

"For the whole country," Costco said.

Costco looked at Mark, who didn't react. For the first time since they'd gotten in the car Mark turned and looked Cassie in the eyes. It was like looking into the sun—or better yet like looking at someone and seeing yourself looking back. Whatever it was, it was too much, and he turned his eyes back to the road. He faced forward again. Costco was still distracted. The car jerked a couple feet out of its lane, and he pulled it back straight. Then they were all quiet.

"So I need to tell you both something," Mark said. They were stoned enough that they each continued looking at what they were looking at, Cassie and Costco, but they were listening. "Julia—my mom—told me the other day that some agents came by the house wanting to talk to me."

"What, like, literary agents?" Costco said.

Mark didn't have the heart to say that was the same thing he'd thought when she told him.

"No, like, federal agents. Who wanted to know about my own on-line activity."

"Online activity," Costco said. "Makes me think of like, 'Oh, now we'll do some papier-mâché—online.'"

"They came to see me, too," Cassie said. Now this was something new. "Not the same guys of course. And not about you. I've been work-ing on some pieces at RazorWire about Boom Boom attacks, and Silence, and they wanted to ask questions."

"So did you tell them anything?" Mark said.

"Feebees?" Cassie said. Mark wondered where she'd learned to sound so casual about it. It only made him love her more. Costco looked again at him. Something passed between them, something unspoken—it was clear to Costco, Mark thought, that he was into something. "Fuck no. You just don't tell them anything. After dealing with them in a journalistic capacity you kind of just learn to handle it."

"Dude, you must've learned that, too, at your magazine," Costco said. Mark didn't have the heart to confess he hadn't—Jesus, he'd never worked on a piece that led to him talking to law enforcement—so he just let it pass. "Sounds like I'm the only fucker here who doesn't have that experience. I mean, I'd be paranoid out of my fucking melon right now if it wasn't for you guys. You're big-time, you two." Mark and Cas-sie let the compliment hang there, and let the whole conversation drop.

Their silence continued as they drove past the buildings all the way back to his parents' house in Pikeville, twenty minutes from their destination. Mark had made a reservation at the one good sushi restaurant he'd found since his return—that was one more than had been there when he was growing up—and Cassie said she wanted to get some rest and take a shower before they went. Costco said he had to head home for the evening, which made Mark perfectly happy, given that he didn't want his old friend to join them for dinner anyway.

CHAPTER THIRTY-SEVEN

WHILE CASSIE WAS CLEANING UP, Mark signed on to his computer and got on TOR and then found his way to Google, where he looked up the Social Security Administration. The main Social Security offices had been moved from downtown Baltimore to Woodlawn in the 1960s. Somewhere within those renovated buildings they'd driven by that afternoon was every person employed by the government to oversee the dispersal of Social Security funds; every Social Security number of every American citizen in the country, and all the attendant information on all of America's citizens. There was even a museum dedicated to the history of the New Deal, and the financial safety it had extended to every baby boomer, a safety net that Mark now understood would not be extended to him, to Cassie, to the members of their generation, when the time came.

When Cassie got out of the shower and dressed, Mark tried to take her down to the kitchen to say hello to Julia. Before they did, Cassie grabbed him by the hand and his heart jumped. It could be like a dream, her taking him into a bedroom—he moved toward her but she let go of his hand and moved farther into the room.

"Holy fucking shit," Cassie said. "You didn't tell me about all this."

She was pointing to where all of Julia's instruments were propped up on stands around the room. There was a Lloyd Loar Gibson F-5, and an early-forties Martin D-18. Mark took her by the hand now, and walked her over to a green Calton hard-shell case. He let go, bent down, and flipped the clasps. Inside was a Cremona-colored fiddle.

"That's Julia's old player fiddle," Mark said. "It's an American custom, from the fifties. It sure does have some bark." He thought Cassie might ask to play it, but she turned back out of the room.

"Maybe we could play some later?"

"Maybe."

"Jesus, there must be five hundred thousand dollars' worth of instruments in that room," Cassie said.

"And you," Mark said. Cassie didn't respond. "And no one to play them. They all used to be in the basement but Julia moved them up here when I came back. I bet she spent, like, ten grand just getting them set up as she moved them. It's like all she does now."

"Fuckin' A," Cassie said. "Too bad none of us plays anymore."

They descended the stairs, away from the music. Julia was always in the kitchen in those days. She didn't need to be retired from a job by Silence, or by the Boomer Boomers. She'd long since retired from her job teaching music at the middle school near their house, and other than putting individually wrapped salad bags into a Tupperware container and making him sandwiches when he wanted one, Mark wasn't sure what his mother did to keep occupied.

Today she was in the kitchen. The television was on. It was a show on which a number of boomer-aged women sat around a table heatedly debating current events without bringing up any of the particulars or conveying any empirical facts related to their view. It was like they were in Plato's cave with a stone rolled across the entrance, no trace of the world of forms discernible in their darkened hovel.

When Mark and Cassie got to the kitchen, the women on the show were discussing Silence's hijacking of ad time on the football game days before. Their words were broadcast on closed captioning in big white letters at the bottom of the screen—the TV had broken with closed captioning stuck on years before.

"I think they should all be brought to justice, whatever these millennial scamps think they're doing," an older white woman said. "Let them have the Internet! They can play their Gameboys or whatever. But an advertisement during the football game. That is crossing a line."

The comedian next to her said, "Well, at the end of the day, they do have a point." You could see each of the other women around the table push back just a bit. "I'm not saying they're right! But look at us, ladies. We all still have jobs."

They all laughed. Julia laughed with them and it became clear she wasn't going to notice Mark and Cassie without their announcing themselves.

"Mom, you remember my bandmate—friend—bandmate, Cassie," Mark said.

Julia looked up. Her eyes were heavy-lidded, as if waking from a deep slumber. Cassie walked over and gave her a hug, but Julia didn't have time to stand up, so it was an awkward embrace that looked almost like a tackle. The top of Julia's head nestled against the frog-belly white of the underside of Cassie's chin.

"Oh, what's that," Julia said. She brushed her thumb across a substantial red mark on Cassie's neck. A look of recognition passed Julia's face.

"Fiddle hickey," Cassie said. She put a finger to her neck, letting her index finger sweep across that rough piece of flesh where the chinrest of her fiddle had raised an almost permanent callus. Julia put her fingers to her own neck, where there was no such mark any longer. "It's been fading. Not so much time to play since my new job and all. But. We were looking at all your amazing instruments upstairs. Mark tells me that you used to play."

"Lifetimes ago," Julia said. She did not offer to let Cassie play her fiddle. She put her finger to her left ear and pushed, as if attempting to dislodge a sound or a thought from her head. The television was still blaring in the background, so loud Mark almost couldn't understand why it would need to be so loud, and all three of them turned to look where a still taken from one of Silence's postings showed someone— not Mark—in a David Crosby mask, his face filling almost the entire screen, so you could not see the poster over his shoulder. A wave of heat flushed through Mark's body as he wondered if a video of him had been made into a screen capture, if something from her own basement might catch Julia's eye if she saw it. But on-screen it was a kind of purloined letter. Julia could see a photo of her own son on that television set and not understand she was looking at him; such is the displacement of looking at one's own life on television. It was like the distance between who Isaac was in an IRC chat room and who Mark was here in the room now, an impermeable membrane between.

"Mishigas, what these kids are up to," Julia said.

"Is it?" Cassie said.

"Making videos on the Internet to stir up some misguided attacks. They say they don't advocate violence against people but who knows when it will stop. Or how. What do they think is going to happen in March? Even if it's nothing, to sit through the waiting. C'mon. Don't they know that our generation was the generation that *invented* revolution? That's who they want to have retire—the people who got them to where we are? We marched on Washington. We followed what Weatherman was up to. Patty Hearst. Black Panthers. These kids, they Twitter or whatever, put little movies up on the Internet and call it revolution."

"We," Mark said.

He could feel a different kind of wave washing over him now. This was far from the experience of having his anger broken open by the concentrated flush of a blast from water-fractured shale. This was something nature itself was flushing him with, a wave forced by the tectonic shifts of undersea earthquakes, so out of control, a swelling so large that at first it didn't even look like a wave.

"Wait, what," Julia said. Cassie looked at him, nothing on her face, just looking.

"I mean we're basically millennials, too, Mom," he said.

"No, you're not," Julia said. "You're Generation X. Or Y or Z or whatever they call you. I think I'd know if I'd given birth to a millennial."

"He's kind of right," Cassie said. "I mean, demographics are dumb. There's just humans, people, born at different times, who all think different things at different times and are unpredictable. But they do call us, anyone who was born after 1980, part of the millennials."

Julia stood and walked across the kitchen. She opened the refrigerator, pulled out the Brita with its nearly ice-cold tap water, and put it down on the counter.

"Would either of you like some water?" she said. They both said no. "So you two think that these Silent people, or the people in the masks, have a point?" She was looking at Mark. He was looking down at his feet now.

"Silence," Cassie said.

"What?" Julia said.

Mark exchanged glances with Cassie and before he could say anything more, she said, "Well, they may have a point, but whatever they're after seems dangerous."

"Well. I don't agree and won't. So. That's that. It is what it is kind of thing. What are you two going to do tonight?"

"We're going to dinner. And oh, I forgot, the Volvo wouldn't start. Maybe you could call AAA for me? I think it's the battery. And we could borrow Dad's Audi."

"What am I going to say, no?" Julia said.

Before she could say anything more Mark grabbed Cassie and they headed out, got straight into Julia's car. They were barely out of the driveway before Cassie started talking.

"Okay, so I'm just going to say a bunch of things all at once, and I don't want you to have an opinion on any of it until after I've finished. The first thing is just holy shit that was awkward but I kind of think we both handled it as well as we could, didn't we? You don't have to nod. We did. But that's not the point. The point is that I'm glad to have met your old friend Costco and all, but what on earth was with all that shit he was talking on that drive out through Woodlawn? *And* the feds came to talk to your mom? Jesus. What the fuck. So does this friend know about you and the Boomer stuff?"

"He does not," Mark said. "Or he did not. Based on your and my somehow both now telling him we've been talked to by the FBI I'm sure he's guessing something at this point. That said, *he* showed *me* how to use TOR the other day. For whatever that fact might be worth. But I have kept my mouth shut beyond that—and telling you both about the FBI thing."

"Jesus," Cassie said. "What the fuck."

Now he turned to look at Cassie again, only this time he did not look away. He saw the small hairs that came down from her hairline on her freckled forehead, where his lips had been so many times. He saw that at the edges of her eyes, at their very edges, for the first time the slightest faintest creases of crow's-feet were beginning to etch themselves, marking the passing of time. He saw Cassie, but he saw himself, and he saw his mother, and he saw.

They were just about at the sushi restaurant. It was in a strip mall out Reisterstown Road, in Owings Mills, only a couple miles from the shopping center where he'd worked at a TCBY when he was a teenager, where the Starbucks inside the Barnes & Noble inside the strip mall inside the universe where he'd been meeting Costco was. He didn't have the heart to point out to Cassie, whom he hadn't seen in months and who was his bandmate and who in a different circumstance could've been his wife, him with a wife and a job figuring out how to pay off the taxes on his stocks and still living in New York where he had had zero interest in ever leaving, where it was. They pulled into this other shopping center in this other part of the Baltimore suburbs where he drove with friends and smoked pot in moving cars when he was fourteen, when he was sixteen, when he was twenty-one and home from college to see his parents, where memories overlapped with each other but they were in the end all the same memory of the same traffic lights and the same trees that had been there before he was even born, where even the biggest tsunami that could possibly hit the Eastern Seaboard couldn't create enough wave to soak this suburban dreamscape so in need of being soaked by a wave, and if it wasn't going to be a Chesapeake wave it might as well be another kind of wave, the third wave, a wave that he'd maybe started but that Silence had grown on its own to the size of a tsunami, and all memories were the same memory and so not overlapping at all when you came to think of it. For months now when he wasn't typing in chat rooms he was thinking about Cassie Black, but now here Cassie Black was sitting beside him and he realized there was no chance of his getting her to love him. He just knew it, there in that car. Cassie was looking at him and he was looking at Sushi Palace and he said, "What the fuck indeed."

CHAPTER THIRTY-EIGHT

SO MUCH DEPENDS UPON a black Jansport duffel bag, sitting in a suburban basement, empty as of yet. Cassie had been gone a week when Mark found himself over at Costco's. This time he was in Costco's room, where they were taking bong hits. He was stoned out of his skull as he always seemed to be when he was with his old friend. He'd had the time with Cassie that he'd hoped to have. They talked, they did not kiss, they picked up Julia's prewar D-18 and her old fiddle and they sang a lot of Louvin Brothers songs, Bill Monroe and Ralph Stanley—"Polly, pretty Polly wontcha come along with me/ Polly, pretty Polly won't you come along with me-ee"—and played a lot of fiddle tunes together, and playing music made him happy. He assumed it made his mother happy to hear them playing, too, the first time there'd been music in her house in ages.

Now this was the first time Mark had been in Costco's house since their trip out to Woodlawn. Neither had said anything about the trip, or about his telling about the feds. When he sat down, his old friend handed him the glass bong like he always did. Mark took a rip, sat back on Costco's unmade bed.

"So Cassie's hot," Costco said.

And it was as he said it Mark noticed it in Costco's open closet: a black Jansport duffel bag, zipped up. In the middle of it, a large cylindrical bulge. In the closet next to it an empty Cuisinart box in a Williams-Sonoma bag. Costco saw him looking.

"Dude, remember when we were in high school and we used to go to

Williams-Sonoma for nitrous poppers? Those little pink things? Those were the bomb before I got that tank."

"Your nickname could've been Sonoma instead of Costco," Mark said.

"Costco is better," Costco said. "Fucken hate Sonoma. Just a bunch of rich asshole baby boomers looking for a massage or a mud bath or some such."

They were quiet for a moment.

"You know I went down the coast when I was out in Eugene. Stayed in Bend, then down through Crater Lake, hitched all the way down to Cali." Mark had never heard this story before. Costco had refused to tell stories of his time out there when he got back, just showed his Jerry tattoo and moved on. His face was now blanched like one of Julia's tomatoes. "And there were these old heads in a little town north of Sonoma, way north, north of Eureka even. Called Dewberry. All these old, old heads. Boomer heads who'd dropped out, moved farther and farther north from San Fran. They fed me tons of acid. I think they must've been fucking with me. Doses like they used to drop. Like, a cup of liquid. Must've been like a hundred fucken hits. I flipped my fucken lid. Couldn't put on clothes for a week. They say they found me curled up in a ball in the sand and no one could come near me 'cause I'd just scream if they did."

He was quiet for a moment.

"I don't even fucken remember. My folks flew out. They sent me to Minneapolis for a month to get my shit together. Now I take Zyprexa, but it makes me fat. And it was enough to get through Goucher, get a job. But man—again and always it was the fucking boomers, like you say. They gave us *los drogas, asi.*"

"Well, we *are* smoking weed right now," Mark said.

"That shit ain't *drogas!* The acid. It fucking liquefied my brains, brutha. And they did it. The boomers. And you are right. They need to pay for it. For what they done."

"What was Woodlawn all about," Mark said.

"What do you think Woodlawn was all about."

"You want me to guess?"

"Like you made me guess about the feds, which you didn't mention?"

"I told you."

"Like you've been making me guess about everything else, Abramson?"

Costco looked long and low into Mark's eyes. His hair was receding just like Mark's was, and Mark noticed for the first time since they'd started hanging out that he had crow's-feet developing at the corners of his eyes. Like Cassie had. Cassie, who was now his just-friend and who he would never be with again.

"It seemed like way too big a coincidence at first," Costco said. "I mean I'd been listening to the missives since you started posting them. And I guess in the back of my head I'd thought like, Shit, that kind of looks like my buddy Brumfeld's old basement. But then when I came over the other day and I saw it and I just fucken knew it. And then when you and Cassie both had your stories—icing, cake. Done. What are the chances, you and me both in the same chat rooms?"

"I guess," Mark said, "about the same that you and me would end up back in our parents' basements. Which, as it turns out—well, not so bad. Those chances."

"Well, brah," Costco said. "You're fucken smart. And you're more of a badass than I could've guessed."

"And you?"

"Me what."

"I'm looking at a black duffel bag. With the box for a pressure cooker next to it."

"Don't forget what else is in there, brah."

"Well, I can't forget what I didn't already know," Mark said. "But I can guess."

"If you guessed, I'd guess you'd guess a big old box of matches for the match tips, a bulb from some Christmas lights, and a whole bunch of nails and ball bearings for shrapnel. I am not inspired by *Inspire*, but yup—there are copies of *Inspire*. There is some good information in there. Better than when we used to look at *The Anarchist Cookbook* back in the day."

"And so what is the plan, then?"

"There is no plan, exactly," Costco said. "Anarchists don't make plans.

They're Anarchists. There's just some goods, and a place to bring them. And a lot of fucken anger, old and new. And I know we both know you're not coming with me, whenever it is. It's on me, and that's good. But I just want to hear one thing from you, brah."

"And what's that," Mark said.

Costco said nothing for a second. He pulled the bong up to his lips, lit it, and pulled some smoke into the chamber, pulling it like a cumulonimbus cloud right up to the space in front of his lips. Then he took it from his mouth and he said, so that his old friend could say it back to him:

"Resist much, obey little.

"Propaganda by the deed.

"Boom boom."

PART EIGHT

JULIA

CHAPTER THIRTY-NINE

THERE WERE TWO WAYS she had gone deaf after she had a kid, and the second way Julia Sidler Brumfeld had lost her ability to hear was in her not hearing her son anymore, but much like her actual hearing, she didn't know how she could have stopped it. In November of the fall after he returned to live in their basement, his ex-girlfriend Cassie came to visit them. She saw Mark happier than he'd been since he'd returned home. They'd even picked up her instruments without asking, and she was livid at first but then happy enough, knowing at least *someone* was playing them. Mark had also been hanging out with his old friend Chris Long, who by some chance also happened to be living back in his own parents' basement, and it came as a relief to Julia that Mark had a companion in Baltimore.

Chris had been a troubling kid when Mark was in high school—she knew Mark smoked pot, but she saw all kinds of signs in Chris, times he came to their house with his pupils the size of espresso saucers, talking in clipped Zen koans and obviously tripping face. It was almost comical to Julia that Mark didn't understand she knew what it looked like when someone had eaten acid and was tripping in her own home. He'd grown his hair into dreadlocks and seemed unhinged, it was rumored he'd had some kind of break when he was out West and came back changed, and she was grateful when Mark went off to college and stopped talking about him. But the kid seemed to have gotten it together as an adult, or as together as a thirty-year-old living in his parents' basement could have it together. He'd worked in financial services for a period, and with his hair thinning like Mark's, he at least looked like a grown man, despite the hoodies and sneakers, the hacky sacks and devil's sticks he carried around, the fact he didn't quite seem capable of uttering a coherent sentence to her. And who was she to talk, in her own red Chuck Taylors, her own kid living in the basement.

And when Mark's ex-girlfriend came to visit, Julia was smitten. She was a fiddler herself, full of sarcasm and edge that belied her background growing up in rural central Ohio. Julia could never quite understand what Mark and Cassie's relationship had been—for as progressive as she'd been, playing in rock bands, eating and snorting her way through the late sixties, she'd still been married by twenty-six. The fact that Mark and Cassie seemed to love each other, had lived together and played in bands together but couldn't find a way to make it work, had confused and disappointed her. It didn't help of course that her son was incapable of having a candid conversation about love on the phone with her.

But when Cassie was in her own kitchen all grew clearer: she came in with her hair tight and short to the back of her head, flashing her fiddler's hickey and her brown corduroys, and the way she responded even just when Julia touched the red callus at the base of her chin it was somehow clear that she was attracted to women. In fact it was so clear it was something of a surprise to Julia that anyone would ever have expected her to be attracted to men. Whatever she'd tried to make work with Julia's son seemed fine, but Julia was convinced within minutes of meeting her that there was no way of their relationship ever working. If only her own son had understood it.

Unfortunately those observations were confined to what she could see, what she could touch and smell while Cassie was there. His old bandmate churned through the house like a late-afternoon summer storm. Mark barely gave Julia a moment to turn off her television show or put in her hearing aids—it was basically the first time she'd ever actually *wanted* to put them in—before they were off, and Julia didn't get another chance to talk with Cassie. The closest she came was peeking in while the two of them were playing music together.

With all that was to come she never saw Cassie in person again.

CHAPTER FORTY

THE BIG RESONATING BLACK HOLE of a B-flat note struck slowly, and then all at once. Tuesday morning. Mark was at the coffee shop when Julia saw the images start to play and play and play on her television screen. In the bottom corner of CNN it said, "Social Security Administration Building, Woodlawn, Maryland," and closed captioning in its halting blocky arrhythmic beats spelled out that someone had bombed the Social Security Administration Building just ten miles up the road. Jonathan Weinstock, Harry Block, Wilma Bauer, Hirsch Green, Rivka Goldman—names of Pikesville friends who worked for the government flooded Julia's head, and who she knew could have been in the building that day. The images themselves were nowhere near as dramatic as those that had come out of the World Trade Center or the Pentagon a decade earlier, but a telltale wisp of smoke trailed up out of the glass atrium at the building's front, and it was clear the bomb was substantial.

Before she had a chance even to turn the television off Julia felt a bass rumbling in the soles of her feet and then felt something hard constricting her upper arms and she was slammed up against a wall. Only it wasn't a wall. It was made of linoleum. They did not have linoleum walls. They had linoleum floors. The floor had jumped up and smacked her in the face. Only by thinking about it with words did she understand she'd been thrown down off her chair, down onto her own floor in her own kitchen. She couldn't hear any of what was being said to her and she'd never know for certain if the federal agents had knocked, knocked, knocked at the front door and she never heard it, as they later claimed, or if they'd just knocked down the door and come into the house. Before she knew it she was standing again, she could see that steady line of smoke still lifting from the Social Security building on the television. She saw Agent Cimber and Agent Brutes had her by her arms. They were in their loose-fitting navy blue jackets with "FBI" in yellow block letters, not in the tight-fitting suits they'd worn when they came to question her. They sat her in her living room and while a handful of other agents dashed down the basement stairs— How many? What was happening elsewhere in her own home at those moments?—they yelled at her, barked questions. She wanted to tell them she didn't have her hearing aids in, that she couldn't hear them but if they would just wait she could grab them even though she'd never at any point in her life used them, but the agents didn't have time for that and as disoriented as she was, the question became familiar enough that she didn't need her hearing aids or even a larger sense of context to understand—they were asking her, over and over, if she knew where her son was. Where is Mark, where is Mark, where is Mark.

They stopped talking long enough for her to say that as far as she knew Mark was where they thought he was. He was at his barista job. He'd left for it that morning just like he left for it every morning. It was hard for her to believe they wouldn't know it. Of course they did. Already. Just like when they'd come to talk to her the first time, this was a ruse to get into her house. They were at her house to collect evidence. Mark lived there now. She looked around and saw agents—how many, how many men and women were swarming her house—pulling down books and vases and everything off of shelves, pulling out drawers. She saw one of the two agents turn and put his finger to a bud in his ear and then turn back and bring the other agent away, she saw both of their shoulders relax a bit. She could understand then, as they got her to her feet so they could take her into custody, that they were telling each other they had him, her son.

They had Mark.

CHAPTER FORTY-ONE

JULIA WAS ONLY IN CUSTODY until three in the morning the day of the attack, March 14, straight through the ides. Agents notified Cal they had her and he came down with a lawyer. Julia couldn't understand what they were saying enough to be able to answer any of their questions with any nuance. She'd been in enough apartments with large enough quantities of weed and acid in her twenties to know that if you were asked any real questions by cops after a crime had been committed, you asked for a lawyer before giving any real answers.

The house was ransacked. It looked like another late-afternoon summer storm had hit the place, this one not named Cassie. The stuffing from couches, the dishes from cabinets, papers from shelves were torn from their idyll, scattered across floors. A back door had been left open and was swinging just a bit against its hinge. For the first time in her life Julia was ready to wear the plastic barnacles, to hear what Cal had to say, to hear what they were saying on CNN, NBC, CBS.

But her hearing aids were nowhere to be found.

She didn't remember where she'd put them. Now every possession she'd ever possessed was in a pile somewhere in that house. She walked into the basement, where even the posters from Mark's wall had been ripped down. She'd comprehended enough in interrogation to understand the agents had come in so fast because they knew that if there was anything on Mark's laptop it could be deleted by simply closing the top, this was how hackers worked, booby-trapped their laptops to destroy evidence, so they had to get down into that basement as quickly as they could. She wanted to say that her son was not a "hacker," but she realized she both didn't know if that was true or what it meant. She still believed that Mark hadn't lied to her when they talked after the two agents came to their house that first time but who the fuck knew. Who knew anything about her son anymore.

She came back up to her kitchen, the safest space she knew, where she'd spent more of her days than any other place on Earth. Her chair was lying on its back on the linoleum floor. She picked it up and sat down. She put the television back on. Somehow in the banging and the chaos, the closed captioning had been turned off for the first time in a decade. No matter how much she searched in the days that followed she would never find the remote control—maybe the agents threw it into a bag with the rest of the electronics—and she didn't want to buy a new TV, she wanted to maintain some semblance of her life before it was swallowed by the B-flat of the black hole, so she watched the television in relative silence and without closed captioning.

On-screen now she watched the crawl at the bottom as it reported that a suspected accomplice to the bomber had been taken into custody. A manhunt was on for the second suspect but the FBI had identified him. In the upper right corner of the television was an image of Christian Long. It was an older picture of him, from a period before Mark had come back to Baltimore—he still had a little hair, was wearing a collar and tie and must have been on his way to his job at T. Rowe Price. But under the picture it read "Christian 'Costco' Long" so there was no mistaking her son's old best friend. The explosion had so much force that it took a day for them to realize his body was in the Social Security building itself, killed by his own blast. Only Mark, who hadn't been there when the blast went off, had survived. So now it was Mark's face that appeared on every television station, every newspaper and magazine in the country that week.

Julia had never understood why Mark and all his friends had called Christian "Costco." She'd never find out. It wasn't the kind of thing she was going to ask her son in the days ahead—not given the circumstances, and not given the fact that, domestic terrorist or not, Costco was dead. For those moments, sitting in her ransacked house, her focus on the images coming back to her from the screen, she was thinking of the fact that it appeared her son, Mark Brumfeld, aided in Costco's bombing of the Social Security Administration Building.

CHAPTER FORTY-TWO

THERE WERE TWO MAIN FACTS that Julia learned in the days after the bombing, one harrowing and the other comforting. The first was the worst news imaginable: three people had been killed in the bombing Mark had been arrested for helping to aid. Three people in addition to Costco, that is. All three were low-level administrators. None of them was from Pikesville. But that didn't mean the horror of it didn't land squarely on their community. Not since Herschel Grynszpan killed a German charge d'affair in France had a Jewish man perpetrated such an offense against a Western government, and a certain amount of anti-Semitic backlash was inevitable. Elected officials did their best to downplay the shock of it, but the ugly rhetoric of Fox News, of Stormfront.org, of Breitbart News, of the elected officials of Congress, allowed a certain air of questioning of the religious aspects of terrorism to waft through the airwaves. Then a drone strike took out Anwar al Awlaki and there were two major attacks in Europe and the news soon enough shifted. But it shifted long before any kind of rehabilitation of Mark's reputation had even been hinted at.

It would never come.

It did not shift in the Brumfeld household, the comfort Julia was granted as the FBI continued their investigation into her son. He was held in federal prison awaiting trial but the facts began to look good enough for him. There was evidence of his having participated in chat rooms, of his being a part of conversations about the Boomer Boomers.

But it was also clear that Julia's son Mark, her adult son living under her own roof, had nothing to do directly with the Social Security bombing. There was no evidence of Mark's having been anywhere near the building on that day or any other, no material connection between him and the pressure cooker bomb. No fingerprints on any of the materials Costco used for the bombing. Nothing really.

That didn't mean Mark wouldn't spend years in jail, decades even, for his role in Costco's actions. But it could have been worse. It could have. And amid it, all the legal bills began to pile up. The first week Julia and Cal were planning to go to visit Mark at his medium-security prison down in Virginia, their first lawyer bill was due—it was astronomical. Numbers that, no matter what they had in a Roth IRA or would come in a future paycheck, they didn't have liquid. There were not parents for them to appeal to for a loan. They were the parents.

"How the fuck will we even pay this?" Julia said.

Cal looked down at the table between them. She could see he had some idea already in his head. That he assumed she knew what it was before he even said it.

"That prewar D-18 alone is worth like forty grand now," Cal said. "Who can even imagine what the mandolins are worth."

Julia was about to argue—to say something, to say, And you, what are *you* going to contribute if I do give those instruments up?—but what was there to say? That her nostalgia for a time when she was almost a professional musician, her satisfaction at knowing she had all these vintage instruments upstairs in their guest-room-slash-music-room that no one played anymore, could have a price tag? The last person who had even played that guitar was, of all people, Mark himself—who come to think of it had played it without asking, and along with a woman who wasn't ever going to be his wife, wasn't ever going to bring anyone any happiness.

So the day Cal went down to visit Mark the first time, Julia was in her car driving up to Mandolin Brothers in Staten Island, the best shop she knew for selling instruments. She could have gotten 25, even

30 percent more for the D-45, for the F-5, and for a couple of her old fiddles. But what she needed was the cash today.

"Look," the salesman at the shop said. "We're not a pawn shop. Why don't you just leave them here on consignment? That way you can at least get ninety percent of what they're worth. These are major pieces you've got."

Julia didn't have time for that, and so she took what she could for the D-45 and left the mandolin on consignment for now—with the understanding that if it wasn't gone in a month or two she'd just have to sell it to them outright. As she headed down over the Delaware Memorial Bridge the anger under Julia's skin grew and grew, and for the first time since he was in her womb Mark started to become less a son than an abstraction to her, a need and a necessity and a source not of worry but of anger. She'd go visit him, she knew. But the next time Cal went down to visit Mark, a month later, she had to make another trip up to Staten Island to deal with picking up a certified check they needed after the mandolin sold, and suddenly two months had passed since her son's arrest on felony charges and she hadn't been to visit him. She'd visit him. But for now, with the anger she carried and logistics of lawyers' bills in hand, it would have to wait. And wait and wait and wait.

Other than those trips up I-95, which she dreaded more than anything she'd ever done, Julia watched on television as closed-circuit tapes appeared on CNN of Costco going to Williams-Sonoma to buy the pressure cooker, going to Modell's Sporting Goods to buy the black duffel, going to Home Depot to buy the ball bearings and nails and all the awful malign goods. Mark would be tried as an accessory but not as an accomplice, as a domestic terrorist, for simply being as close to Costco as he was. Of all things, at least Julia could spend the rest of her days knowing her son hadn't killed anyone.

He also hadn't helped force a single baby boomer to retire from a single job.

He hadn't ever let her know what he'd been up to when he was living in her basement, or expressed his intent in communicating with Silence, with Costco. There were two ways in which Julia Sidler Brumfeld had stopped being able to hear in the days leading up to her son's being branded the most notorious domestic terrorist of his generation, and at this point she was willing to take both. She didn't want to hear another word.

PART NINE

CASSIE

CHAPTER FORTY-THREE

THERE MUST'VE BEEN 613 WAYS in which Cassie Black changed in the months after Mark Brumfield and his childhood friend Costco attacked the Social Security Administration Building, but her name wasn't one of them. She was Cassie Black now and she would stay Cassie Black. Claire Stankowitcz was a distant memory never to be returned to. But there were two immediate ways she changed in the weeks and months that followed the attack—one of them professional and the other personal, though over time the two grew to be indistinguishable from each other.

Cassie had been following company policy of posting video alongside the native content she created for RazorWire for months, and while she did long to hold herself aloof of the intricacies of Adobe Premiere, each time she opened it with the intention of correcting a header or a footer someone had created, she found herself understanding how to use it a little better without even meaning to. At first it was basic stuff—in the upper left-hand corner of the application were the source videos, in the lower right-hand corner were lines that represented each video, audio and written lines that came together to make the finished video. Her job was to double-click on the text inserts and edit them.

But over time she found herself editing some video. It was easy enough to see that hitting Enter would return you to the beginning of a video, that the space bar would pause and play. And once she dug in she saw that she basically knew how to use it—the cropping and design tools were more or less the same as PageMaker, which she'd used for her school newspaper. Editing tools for the video itself were almost identical to ProTools, which she'd used for the sound editing when she and Natalia made roughs for the Pollys' first and second records. It wasn't exactly the same, but the keystrokes and the concept were, and it didn't take long for her to see how little it would take for her to master Premiere whether she wanted to use it or not.

One afternoon not a month before the ides of March, she found herself deep into editing on a four-minute documentary about the life of a golden skink that was to be posted the next day. She'd had lizards in her house growing up—mostly geckos; her father would never have let her buy an iguana like Lindsay Henderson down the street had—and for Hanukkah when she was ten her mom had bought her a golden skink. It was long and sleek and glistened under the incandescent lights in her room. She'd loved it more than the family dog until one morning she woke to discover it inert, purple indentations on either side of its body. The new hermit crab in the cage had crushed it. So when she saw that one of their writers had submitted a video of the life of a skink named Golda, Cassie took an interest. She didn't even think to look at what it was native content for.

On the fly she found herself opening video files, cutting and condensing, slash-cutting and perfecting. In that lower right-hand box each video appeared as a four-inch gray rectangle that could be manipulated— she could go in and expand the bar so it represented, say, ten seconds of video, which itself was slow-mo and represented only one second of real time. Or she could expand it to show just one second of video. Or a tenth of a second, bearing in and in and in on the moment when Golda's pink-tongued yawn was first caught on video, slowing time to a near standstill both on-screen and in the world around her. What did it do to her conception of time, to her sense of memory, spending her day manipulating time like this? Did writing, slowing and condensing the world into words, do the same? Cassie wasn't sure. On-screen before her eyes, time had slowed to a literal standstill, the time of the image and audio she was editing represented by a solid gray box. It was as if a unit of the fluidity of a substance with immutable laws—time followed its arrow in one direction, always moving just out of reach—had been encased, caked in some chalky substance, and left to sit inert on-screen. There was an enormous sense of power mixed with an enormous sense of futility in seeing the flow of time interrupted, interrogated, and enhanced this way. All in the interest of making people feel things while watching a caged golden lizard yawn. Cassie had been editing for so long and with such intensity that she was startled into jumping from her seat when Regan's voice woke her from her editing reverie.

"The fuck's that a video for," Regan said.

"I don't even know," Cassie said. "Well, it's a golden skink named Golda. It's a . . . well, it's a biopic about a lizard." She got up from her desk, saved the file, and left it on-screen while the two of them went out for pho.

She didn't give the video another thought until two days later when she got simultaneous e-mails from the videographer and from Mario. The videographer, a thirty-three-year-old divorcee living in Akron named Weary, had written to chew her out.

"Cassie—" his e-mail read. "I've been working on that fking PetSmart lizard spot for a year and you go in and cut a full minute of content? Do you even understand what a slash-cut is? On whose authority r u making these edits? How do we go back to my original cut?" Fuck. Cassie couldn't believe she'd made all those edits live and hadn't consulted anyone—it just seemed obvious that it was at least a minute too long to hold anyone's attention. Before she could write back she saw Mario's e-mail pop up and assumed it was to berate her—even the subject line, "HOLY SHIT," seemed to suggest she was in for a world of conflict. Here she was, director of research, editing native content video.

She opened Mario's note and it wasn't what she'd expected at all. Mario, formalest of all the users of "thusly" she'd ever met, for the first time in all the time she'd known him had sent an e-mail that didn't even start with a formal salutation. It looked more like a text message in its informality and it read, "Have you seen the Google Analytics on your iguana spot? Seventy thousand plus in the first morning! Shit's gone viral. We think we might have a million by end of week. VAF (viral as fuck! I think I just coined that). Come see me."

She didn't go see Mario. She didn't take the time to tell him Golda wasn't an iguana—she was a golden skink and who the fuck would name an iguana Golda when they could go with Juana. She e-mailed Weary in Akron and let him know that she'd have been more than happy to restore the original cut on the site but had he seen the fucking numbers on that piece?

"That shit's going viral AF," she typed.

He wrote her back with complete and total sycophantic contrition.

"I'm just feeling lucky to work with talented folks like you," he wrote. They were e-mailing back and forth so fast they might as well have been IMing in 1998. Without even thinking Cassie typed, "And well look it's not like the creator of some fucking gecko hagiographic PetSmart ad had final cut approval," then double-clicked and deleted it. But before she closed out of Google Chrome she sat back for a second, opened the video, saw that the spot already had almost two hundred thousand views, and said fuck it. She hit Open-Apple-Z and restored the e-mail and sent it.

She waited.

Two new e-mails popped up. The first was from Weary and it just had the text stand-in for a winking-smiley-face emoji. The second was from someone at Atelier. There was no "thusly," no heavy come-on. Just a note that said, "Saw your Golda doc. Have been following your rise for some time. Wanna come work for us? We'll double your salary, whatever the fk Rzr's paying you. Not remote either. We want you here." It was like a combination between an e-mail and a text and in the midst of the total typing freedom Cassie Black was feeling in that moment she wrote back, "triple it," and the guy from Atelier—it turned out it wasn't a guy but a girl—woman—named Sandra—wrote right back:

"Word. Done deal. You know we're in SF, right?"

CHAPTER FORTY-FOUR

THE FIRST WAY CASSIE BLACK'S LIFE changed in the weeks around the time of the Social Security bombing was that she'd taken a new job making hundreds of thousands of dollars a year, but it meant she would have to move to San Francisco. They wanted her to start ASAP and what really would it take for her to make the move? She could fit everything in her apartment into a ten-foot U-Haul and be in the Bay Area in three days. She cut her lease—she just went ahead and ate the rest of the month's rent—packed up, rented a U-Haul from the place down off Atlantic Avenue where the first World Trade Center bombers had rented theirs. She hadn't been in this part of Brooklyn in ages—being in Williamsburg confined her to the L, a quick east-west swoop in and out of Lower Manhattan. She could hardly believe how much downtown Brooklyn had changed. She got off the Q down on Fourth Avenue, a four-lane-and-a-concrete-median expanse that used to house, more or less exclusively, gas stations and garages. The concrete median strip was still there, but now there were bars and coffee shops at every corner, and half the spaces between.

She'd planned to walk up the slope of Park Slope toward the U-Haul when she got down there but she'd ridden the Q one stop too far. She passed the corner of Baltic where a beautiful new public school had been built. Once she hit Atlantic she turned right and there was the Barclays Center, rising out of the concrete like the rusted hull of a beached freighter. The last time she'd been here was to play the back room at Freddie's with the Willows, but it had been closed down to make room for this new center, where the Rolling Stones and the Nets could play on successive nights. They'd played a bunch of gigs at Southpaw when it opened, but there were so many new venues all across Brooklyn that even that one, with its glorious velvet curtain that opened to greet the band like they were a stage act, had closed.

There was a time when witnessing all this growth and change would have raised Cassie's hackles—she'd come down to protest the building of the Atlantic Center project, carrying signs that read "Ratner is a Rat!" and "Intensification not Gentrification" and "Oh no, Hell no, the Brooklyn Nets have gotta go!"—but to be honest, it was just a huge improvement. There were actual yellow and white lines painted on Flatbush Avenue to keep cabs in their lanes. The Barclays Center, for all its distressed-jeans-of-a-rusted-façade artificiality, was only fifteen stories tall, nowhere near as tall as the iconic Key Savings Bank to its west. It was all somehow peaceful, and tasteful, and unobtrusive. After setting up her U-Haul rental Cassie walked up Fifth Ave to O'Connor's, where she'd planned to have a drink with Regan, who was already there when Cassie arrived.

"You know Elliott Smith used to drink here," Cassie said. She put the two Jack-and-gingers she'd bought down in front of Regan. "He'd play in the back sometimes."

"Uh, yeah," Regan said. "*I* was the one who told *you* that."

Cassie was uncertain if that was true but she didn't want to argue. She was the one who was leaving, all at once, the job Regan had put her up for and the city where they both now lived.

"Long-distance," Regan said. "I'm not sure I was ever in favor of long-distance."

"Everyone we know says long-distance isn't that bad these days," Cassie said. "Remember how Hussein and Jill said they used FaceTime that year she was up in Cambridge for her Radcliffe? They said it was more like hanging out than talking on the phone. They could just have it open and talk and even watch movies together and—"

"Netflix and chill, but on FaceTime."

"Right."

"And with auto-chill."

"Right."

"I don't know," Regan said. "I just . . . do . . . not . . . know."

"Well, there is a San Francisco RazorWire office now, right? We haven't even talked to Mario about that yet."

"Mario would say no."

"You don't know that."

"You do. I do. Plus what the fuck kind of Bay Area-er would I be? Riding the Google Bus down to Palo Alto for meetings. Weekends for wine tours in Napa. Would I have to start smoking pot? Pot makes me paranoid. I don't drink wine."

"And you hate tours."

"Right," Regan said.

"Right."

CHAPTER FORTY-FIVE

THERE WERE TWO CENTRAL MOMENTS Cassie focused on along her drive west in a U-Haul containing all of her possessions as she headed for San Francisco. Atelier had offered to buy her a plane ticket and have a moving service move her stuff cross-country, but Cassie liked the idea of three days alone in a truck—and more than that, she liked the idea of pocketing the ten thousand dollars in moving expenses the company had offered as a start-up fund. She owed almost half of it to her current landlord for the rest of the month and the next month's rent since her lease required a month's notice and she was giving zero months' notice. And also since, though she'd believe it when she saw it, word was that SF was even more expensive than New York these days, what with all the Facebook Google Yahoo! Instagram capital out there.

The first moment was mundane enough. It came just east of Columbus, Ohio, on I-70 heading west. She was almost ten hours outside New York by the time she started seeing signs for the turnoff to I-71N. The blue-and-white sign served as a kind of trigger to childhood memory. She was surprised to find herself flooded with ambivalence. It was just two hours up 71 to her parents' house. She'd told them she was moving but hadn't filled them in on any of the details—it wouldn't take much to make a detour, spend the night there.

She just couldn't do it. She'd spent the better part of a year picturing Mark Brumfeld alone in his parents' suburban basement, and if it hadn't been before, that image—a thirty-something alone with his parents in the house where he grew up—had come to be the very metonym of failure, like a road sign heading south. The idea of sitting in the space of failure for even a night seemed too dangerous to test. She had momentum, and if her almost thirty years on the planet had taught her anything it was that you didn't stanch momentum when you had it. When the video was moving ahead in real time you sure as shit didn't hit the space bar. Forward forward forward was the path, the path away even from Regan and Mott Street and refurbished Brooklyn, and far be it from her to stop progress.

She did make a compromise with herself. She exited 70 in Columbus, where she could stop to gas up and get lunch. She and her friends came down to Cbus a couple times a year to see bands when she was in high school. When her friends had first said they were heading to Cbus to see bands she thought they were going to some kind of Sea Bus, a mistake that was dispelled when they arrived on two-dimensional-flat-and-landlocked-as-shit High Street. Around that time there were three punk bands from Cbus that actually got national attention, one of them even covered in *Rolling Stone*.

She drove down High Street past OSU, past the redbrick houses of German Village, and stopped at an Ethiopian place she'd always loved. She wondered if the owners would recognize her from her high school days, but it must have been their son who waited on her, so she ate her lamb curry, wiped up the sauce with the spongy injera under it in silence, alone. For all Manhattan had, it didn't have any good Ethiopian she could find, and here she was in central Ohio, enjoying ethnic food she hadn't had in years.

She ate in silence. She had no one to talk to. She'd forgotten the sheer pleasure of a meal alone. She'd made a deal with herself not to look at her phone, not to read the *Times* or keep up with media, while she was on this cross-country cleanse. When she got into the U-Haul in Brooklyn she swiped her phone to Airplane Mode, bought an atlas, and had it open on the empty shotgun seat next to her. But here in Blue Nile she had her phone on the table—doing so was reflexive—and she kept looking down at its black face. All that looked back up at her was, well, her.

The second moment that would stick with her forever occurred in Colorado. She'd been on the road for two days of long cross-Indiana, cross-Missouri, cross-Kansas driving when the Colorado border came into view. She'd seen on her road atlas—she didn't use Google Maps, unplugged, it was all going to be unplugged and there wasn't a USB cable in the U-Haul anyway—that there was an immense lake in the unironically named Kanorado (why not Coloransas? or Koloransas even? why fucking not?), right on the Kansas-Colorado border. It would be a little before noon when she hit the crossing, still in the low seventies now in mid-fall, and she figured she'd dip a toe in as she gazed west at the Rockies. But the lake was room temperature and furry with algae all the way to the water's bottom, and before her lay the manifest destiny of AutoCAD-flat land as far as the eye could see—not only to the west, but in every direction.

She got back into the truck and found that the entire eastern third of Colorado was more Kansas than it was Montana—flat flat flat Kansasean land all the way to Denver. To her surprise, Cassie had found herself listening to talk radio more than music on the ride crosscountry, but now she put on Nirvana and blasted "Territorial Pissings" at 38 of 40 on the volume on the dashboard.

So it was amid boredom and disappointment compounded by Krist Novoselic's off-tune sardonic blaring of come on people now followed by Kurt Cobain's distorted Fender Jaguar chords blurt blurt blurting that, twenty miles west pre-rush-hour traffic in Denver, with the sun moving toward her line of sight and pink beginning to bleed cut-steak blood across the far horizon, suddenly Cassie found herself driving through the first staggering outcroppings of Rockies.

She reached for the stereo and turned the music off.

Outside of Boulder, 70 cut through convex jagged cliffs looming down onto the highway. Cassie could feel her breath catch in her throat—she rolled down her window and tried to look up but no matter what angle she looked from she couldn't see up to the tops, only every quarter mile or so getting a respite as the sun glinted phosphorous white through a break in the cliffs. It was like nothing she'd ever seen, felt like nothing she'd ever felt—the sheer physical mass of it kept taking her breath from her—and she was at ten thousand feet climbing switch-backs to drive over Independence Pass, over the Continental Divide, before Cassie realized that something new was in her head, crawling up her back, absent from the buzz in her forearms.

She wasn't thinking about Mark.

She wasn't thinking about Regan.

She wasn't thinking about videos or the computer in her pocket.

She wasn't thinking about anything. It made her wish she had a quarter of purple kush, that she had seventeen beers or a guitar in her hands, until she realized that it made her happy to have none of those things. She was at peace in a truck with no music on at all. Time was moving forward, her moving through it in a kind of eternal present. Even the instinct to click on one of Adobe Premiere's gray boxes and edit, slash-cut, manipulate to tell a story, was gone. Images were gone. Sound and melody and harmony disappeared. Words were gone. Here she was, Cassie Black, alone in a U-Haul, free from love, free from sound, free from envelopment, free from her past, flying clear west toward the bright open future. She stopped at a pull-off just as she hit the most dramatic heights of Independence Pass. The air was rarified and icy in her nostrils and cold rang out in her ears and as she looked back east all she could see for miles were bright open valleys amid the Rockies. Even the instinct to take a selfie fled her as she realized that her phone wasn't in her pocket. She didn't even fucking know where her phone was—and if she did have it her instinct now would be to take a video, not a photo, and there wasn't a thing to capture here. It was impossible to imagine that the flatness on the other side of Denver, all that Kansas spreading east all the way to St. Louis, existed at all. She shrank deep inside herself. All at once she was a toddler again. Fuck executive function. Fuck object permanence—if you showed her a penny then put it in your pocket right now, Cassie would assume it was lost to this world for all eternity. She didn't give a shit. What she couldn't see didn't exist. All she wanted was just to breathe this air alone.

And she did.

Then she got back in her car and drove with nothing on the radio and just the sound of her tires whirring on the long flat blacktop until

I-70 hit I-15 South, where she'd hole up for the night before the last leg of her trip across Arizona, Utah, and a long, flat expanse of Nevada tomorrow before she hit, for the first time in her young life, the soil of California.

CHAPTER FORTY-SIX

SO CASSIE WAS SINGLE, in a U-Haul with a couch and a half a ton of books from her bookshelves, pulling into a BP station outside of Baker on I-15W, when she learned of Costco Long's bombing of the Social Security Administration Building and his and Mark's arrests. She'd hit the California border. It didn't have one-one-millionth of a percent of the effect of Independence Pass. After six hours of tearing across the blank Nevada desert west of Vegas, doing eighty-five in a rented truck and having Honda Odyssey minivans pass her doing a hundred, she saw the sign for California and saw it pass in the same desert blankness. Every iota of the freedom she'd felt the day before had disappeared in the grinding push of moving across Western desert. Maybe arriving at the Pacific would feel more exciting.

No matter what she was or wasn't feeling, she had done it, she'd driven across the country alone and without the Internet and now she wanted the Internet again. She opened iTunes and hit the first song she saw, Violent Femmes' first record in a flash blaring on the radio with its everything, everything, everything, everything—she rocked out to it for a second, then turned it down.

She turned the key in the ignition, pulled it out, and pocketed it. She got out of the truck, filled it with gas, bought a Vitamin Water—the one with taurine for the jolt, though it tasted like the spit from someone who'd been eating a pomegranate popsicle—and got back into the truck. She located her phone in her bag and went to Options and slid the Airplane Mode to off, a little sliver of green going white, and then the thing started buzzing buzzing buzzing in her hand. Twenty-seven texts flipping through at rapid pace at the top of the screen, a little red superscript showing thirteen new voice messages, all of them from Regan. Well, and two from Natalia. Natalia? She didn't even have time to look through any of it before she went ahead and called Regan.

"Listen, you don't need to worry," Regan said.

"Worry about what?" Cassie said.

"Uh, about your own safety," Regan said. "I already talked to my lawyer and he said you should call him as soon as you can. I'll text you his number when we get off. They preserved all your e-mail here at the office, so I was able to access it, and clearly you had nothing to do with it."

"What. The. Fuck. Are. You. Talking. About."

"Uh, okay. I guess I should say: Where the fuck have you been? I've been calling for two days." Cassie said that of course she'd been, well, everywhere there was to be between New York and Baker, California. Driving across country. She'd decided to put her phone on Airplane Mode until she got all the way west so she could have some peace.

"And I did," Cassie said. "I had some peace—holy shit, the Colorado Rockies! I've never seen anything like it. I think maybe I had an actual mystical experience or something."

"Airplane Mode is for when you're on an airplane," Regan said. "Because no one is on an airplane for two full fucking days while the world goes crazy while they're gone." Cassie didn't say anything. "Well, whatever. Mark Brumfeld and his friend bombed the Social Security Administration Building. People died. It has totally overwhelmed the news. His friend is dead and Mark is in custody, but listen, you don't need to worry."

"Mark . . . and Costco . . . did what the fuck now? Say again."

Regan kept talking but Cassie wasn't listening. Couldn't. Couldn't bring herself to. Make herself. She took the phone from her ear and hit the big black button at the bottom and opened the *Times* app on her phone. There it was, the first story on Top Stories, or what used to be called The Front Page: Mark's mug shot and a picture of Costco and a picture of smoke trailing up from the white buildings in Woodlawn

Costco had driven them by when she was down in Baltimore just more than a month ago. What. The. Shit. The *Times* story went away and her phone just said "Regan" in that signature Helvetica Neue, and a green button to answer or a red button to tell her to fuck off. There was a weird ringing in Cassie's ears that was different from the ringing she heard from the cold of the Rockies. She could feel a squiggle in her esophagus and she barely opened the door to the U-Haul in time to vomit pomegranate Vitamin Water onto the pavement of the BP station. She spit twice, three times, and called Regan back.

"I had nothing to do with this," Cassie said.

"I know you had nothing to do with it," Regan said. "So does our lawyer."

"Lawyer?" Cassie said. "Our?"

"Yes. I've been in touch with him. He's been in touch with a contact at the Bureau and you don't have anything to worry about. I mean you'll need to go in to make a statement, but beyond that you have nothing to worry about. I've been through your e-mails here like I said, and like I said they look great for you—Mark asking and pining for you but you just giving cold shoulder. Stuff about playing in a band together. And nothing at all about his activities."

"Been through my e-mails?"

"Had no choice, dear Cassius Clay. You've been radio silent— Airplane Mode—for two fucking days, right after your ex-boyfriend committed a domestic terroristic act. You're lucky you have me. And Lucien."

"The lawyer. Lucien the lawyer."

"Yes. He was awfully glad you had your contract from Atelier on your desktop, too. What a godsend that turned out to be. It's all airtight, time-stamped and dated and clear cut. Even with you MIA. But still, call him right now. Don't wait until you get to San Fran. Call him."

So she called Lucien the Lawyer.

"Listen, first and foremost don't worry," Lucien Williams said.

"I'm not worried. Do we know how he is?"

"Who?" Williams said.

"Mark."

"No," Williams said. "Please don't worry about him, either. Whatever trouble he's in now he's made for himself. And he's made plenty."

And so that was it. She drove on to the Bay Area with her head full of Mark Brumfeld all over again. It would be weeks before she could think of anything else. Before anyone could.

CHAPTER FORTY-SEVEN

THE SECOND BIG CHANGE IN CASSIE'S LIFE, which only hit her a month or so after she'd been living in San Francisco, was that she found she didn't need love anymore after all. She needed Regan for the contact with Lucien Williams. But FaceTime and chill was a complete nightmare with Regan, and after a single conversation with a federal officer at an unmarked office near Union Square, all the rest of the dealings to do with Mark, any official word, went through Lucien. Just like Regan said: Cassie's e-mails, the timing and legitimacy of her move to work for Atelier that week, time-stamped documents, cleared Cassie of any final connection with Mark Brumfeld of any kind. She was almost a thousand miles west of Woodlawn when the bomb went off, eating lamb curry and injera in Cbus fucking Ohio of all places at the moment it exploded. Agents had talked to the waiter there and confirmed it. The paper trail of her interactions with Mark showed just what it was—a long history of an increasingly unhinged young man pining for his ex-fiancée and former bandmate, a fact that, true or not, played well into the government's case against him. Terrorists were far more often spurred on by love than they were by hate, and if there was one thing Cassie could confirm for anyone, feebee or non-feebee, it was that Mark for sure did continue to love her. Of course she didn't mention that at one point she may have loved him, too.

Which in its own way confirmed for Cassie that what she did not need in her life, now or ever as far as she was concerned, was love. Love just fucked everything—everything—up. Maybe that was what she'd

learned in that reverie at Independence Pass, a moment that felt
more like the memory of a dream than a memory memory: she'd been
alone, twelve thousand feet above Cbus level, and she'd been the happiest she was in years. She had a huge salary, a new apartment, a new
city. Her conversation in O'Connor's in Park Slope with Regan felt
unreal when it happened, like the bottom line of a video she was editing on Premiere—all you had to do was select it and press Delete
and—click!—it was gone. Whatever she'd felt or not felt for Mark, once
he'd left New York for Baltimore, she had spent some time thinking
about it. Mostly it was because he was e-mailing her all the time, but if
Cassie was being honest, she thought about him, too. It wasn't love but
the residue love leaves, that need to know that care itself was immutable,
that like energy it couldn't be destroyed but could only be transmuted
into new forms. And all forms for Cassie now were alone forms. The only
love she would allow herself to feel would be love for herself, maybe
love for a dog small enough to be crated and left in an apartment while
she was at work all day.

As she unpacked each weekend in her new apartment, she didn't
find herself thinking about Mark—or about Regan. The folks at Atelier had found her a one-bedroom on Mission between Twenty-first
and Twenty-second. It was small but she was used to small. On weekends she sometimes took her new Pomeranian, Polly, for a walk down
to the green bulbous indica-bud hills of Dolores Park where she lay in
the cool San Francisco sun among all the hipsters and start-up employees and weekend hippies, walked down Valencia to the McSwee-
ney's Super Hero Outlet or a place called the Curiosity Shoppe, where
she bought decorations for her apartment. They sold books at both
places, too, but it occurred to Cassie that along with not caring about
love anymore, she couldn't give a living fuck for the written word.
She'd spent a year-plus fact-checking for a website and now she'd
moved into video. Video was so much more satisfying. The sheer number of more views, more hits, you could get for a video than for even the
viralest of viral listicles was undeniable. There was a store in Noe Valley
where you could buy books by the pound, selecting them by the color
of their spines. Cassie bought thirteen pounds of pink-lemonade-pink

books and three pounds of lime-green ones for her main living space a month after she'd arrived.

If there was one thing living in the Mission had showed her after just a month, it was that even with the ginormous new salary she was earning, she would need to make a whole fuckload more money if she was going to live well in California.

CHAPTER FORTY-EIGHT

THE LAST TIME CASSIE heard direct word of Mark in her life came a year after she'd moved to San Francisco to work for Atelier. She was producing and acquiring videos for the company at a crazy pace, and she rose rose rose through the ranks. There was a Mario here at her new job, too, but this new Mario's name was Jason, and in addition to VP for native content video development, he gave her the title of chief of recruitment.

"Dude, you can just spot talent like a motherfucker," Jason said a couple months into her job. The new office had no bocce court, but it did have a bank of Ping-Pong tables at the center of the warehouse space, and Cassie had grown up with a Ping-Pong table in her basement as a kid, so unlike on the bocce court, there was no learning curve. She could kill anyone in the company, and did on breaks. "I think you should just look for folks making the best video out there and bring them on. Make offers. Do it to it." He served from his left to her right and the ball skittered out past them and into the banks of cubes at the middle of the big open loft off Union Square where they worked.

So one day, a year into the job, Cassie went back to her desk and saw that she had an e-mail from one Julia Brumfeld. Mark's mother. Great motherfucking Caesar's ghost. Julia Sidler Brumfeld. She hadn't thought of that name in months. Finally. The terroristic stink of her association with Mark hadn't followed her here—one thing Lucien Williams was good at was keeping information under wraps—and she sure didn't need it. She wasn't going to e-mail Julia Fucking Brumfeld from her work e-mail. She went to take a picture of Julia's e-mail with her phone—she didn't even want to type it with her thumbs—but she had to slide the photo function to the right, off of "Video."

Her camera app was always set to video these days.

Before she could head off to lunch she wanted to get in touch with some new talent she'd been watching at RazorWire. In the beginning she'd handled recruitment a little like Jason had when he first wrote her, super informal, but at times she'd find that she didn't hear back from people at all when she did so. She saw one talented meme developer at a conference that winter and asked him why she hadn't written her back, and the meme developer looked at her funny. "Wait, that was actually fucking you, *the* Cassie Black, writing me? Honestly it was so casual I thought it was a joke. I would've moved out here to work for you. I just work from my parents' basement in Bethesda right now."

So when she wrote to potential major recruits she'd take it far more seriously, as she did now. She didn't know the guy's full name but his screen name was DiceHard.

"Dear Dice Hard," she wrote. "I'm writing as I've recently become a big fan of the work you're doing on screen captures from eighties films. You're use of *Space Balls* footage in and of itself is wildly imaginative. I wonder if you might be interested in sitting down with me and some colleagues about some amazing opportunities we have here at Atelier these day? Are work in Native Content videos, particularly some new ideas we've been developing in the realm of Crowd Sourced Political Video News Clips, are prepped to explode in advance of our upcoming IPO. Please do give me a call hear if this sounds like it could be interest"—Cassie typed in her cell number, her office number, and hit Open-Apple-S to save it to her desktop. In the past she would've almost certainly have printed the letter out and proofread it—there was just so much you could catch when you printed, typos and errors you didn't ever pick up on-screen—but the truth was that Atelier didn't have a printer in their office. Everyone there was twenty-two, and twenty-two-year-olds were the first generation in the history of the world who didn't do their reading on anything but screens. Some of her colleagues there didn't even compose formal documents on laptops or desktops, but did so right on their phones, as if the concept of opposable thumbs had culminated in the ability to type quickly on a tiny touch screen. Thumb thumb thumb thumb thumb. So Cassie didn't save her letter and let it sit for the afternoon so she could see it with fresh eyes as she might have in the past, but just went ahead and attached it and hit Send. Send.

She decided she'd take a walk to clear her head while she waited to hear back from DiceHard. Halfway down Market she pulled out her phone and e-mailed Julia Brumfeld back. What the fuck did she want? Why was she getting in touch at all?

"I was hoping we could talk," Julia wrote. "Maybe I could ask you some questions via e-mail."

No way was Cassie going to create a paper trail with Julia Brumfeld, fully a year after the last time she'd even been in touch with the woman's son. She knew in advance what Lucien the Lawyer would say about her having been in touch even this much. She wrote back—"no-can-do but if you want to call me on my cell I guess we could talk"— and went down to a bodega to buy a pack of Ammy Spears. She needed a cigarette. She paid her thirteen dollars for a pack and looked at her phone again.

"I'm not good on the phone these days," Julia wrote. "I'm sorry. But I would really, really love to be in touch with you, sweetie." Before she could think better of it, Cassie typed, "Well we could FaceTime if you want." Julia wrote back to say that could work. Cassie was in the middle of typing to say she was really busy at work today but that she'd be happy to set up some time to talk this weekend when her phone started buzzing in her hand, and a 410 number popped up in Helvetica Neue. Julia was trying to FaceTime with her *right now*, while she was standing outside on Market Street, amid the din of Japanese tourists, tourists from Milwaukee and Chicago and Phnom Penh lumbering by on streetcars.

Well, what the fuck.

She hit the green button on the phone.

Nothing at all happened for maybe ten seconds. Cassie tried to formulate thoughts, to anticipate what Julia might want, but before she could there was Julia Brumfeld's face on the phone. She looked older, her hair almost entirely gray, strands of bangs falling across her forehead. In the upper right-hand corner of the screen Cassie saw herself. She had aged, too. Her hair was just plain dirty blond now, the memory of blue streaks in it long passed, and she could see where the faint lines of crow's-feet had started to spread back at the corners of her eyes. The resolution of the Retina display on her iPhone was so impressive.

"So," Julia said.

"So," Cassie said. She turned the corner and put her back to a wall on Fulton, far from the madding tourist crowd.

"Can you do me a favor while we talk?" Julia said. "I know it sounds weird, but if you could make sure you're looking into the phone camera, I'd appreciate it. I just need to be able to see your mouth to hear you."

"Sure, whatever," Cassie said. "So this is weird. I don't know if we should be in touch. Why don't you tell me what you wanted to talk about." The FaceTime cut out for a second. Julia's face froze there, unmoving, like she was stuck in time. Watching for her, waiting for Julia to return, the rest of the world fell away from Cassie. Technology was addictive when it *was* working, but when technology *wasn't* working, it was more addictive than heroin. All one's desires and thoughts went to waiting for—hoping for—it to work again. There was no frustration like the frustration of a frozen screen. It was worse even than a blank one. So Cassie was now more focused on Julia Brumfeld than she'd ever been on Mark, and she watched as the image on her phone sped way up and all at once Julia was in the middle of a couple sentences sometime in Cassie's unforeseen future.

"—and so the truth is I didn't go down to talk to Mark much at first. I was busy and a little angry. A lot angry. But now I've been down there monthly and I've come to some peace with him. Not with what he did, but with him. My son. I don't even get out of the house much, and I miss him. I've been piecing back together what those days before— before. Were like. And Mark said it would be okay to contact you. Also this won't make much sense but I thought I saw you in a Dean and Deluca's down in Georgetown. And. And I wondered what you knew."

"I know nothing," Cassie said. "I mean, nothing. We e-mailed around that time, but he didn't tell me anything about what he was doing."

"Well, you did come down to visit that weekend when I saw you."

"I know I did," Cassie said. "But it wasn't like that. Mark had pretty much walled himself off at that point—I mean I knew he was lonely. He was so damn isolated." She saw something change in Julia's face and stopped for a second. "Sorry. I know he was with you so I don't mean it that way. But like without people his age or who he could fall in love with or kiss on or whatever. He told me he was lonely. I knew he wanted to get back together so I avoided conversations about that kind of shit. Do. Still do. Avoid conversations like that."

Cassie looked down into the phone. She could see Julia look away to her left, then back at the screen. The feed cut in and out again so Cassie moved a couple steps away and turned her back to the building behind her. Now the connection was much better but with the sun at her back she could see that the image of her in the upper right-hand corner was alternating between visible and invisible—and just a glaring blot of white sun. It eased something in her not to have to look at herself while she was talking.

"The truth is that when we were together on days like that we just played music. We were working out this Louvin Brothers tune and we spent most of the time just working over the chorus and some harmonies—"

"Which?" Julia said.

"Which what?"

"Which tune."

Cassie hadn't thought of that afternoon since it happened and it did bring her some happiness to think of it—it was the last time she'd touched a fiddle. There was a peace to losing herself in playing and singing, but she did remember that she didn't get the jolt, the joy, she once had out of it, either.

"Well, there were two," Cassie said. "'If I Could Only Win Your Love' and 'You're Running Wild.' We both loved them both."

"Wonder why," Julia said.

"What do you mean?"

"Those songs both have some pretty clear lyrics," Julia said. "Jilted, lonely songs."

"I don't really think that much about lyrics when I'm playing," Cassie said. "Was. Was playing. I don't play anymore. But when I did. I always focused on the notes, the melodies. So that's all I can remember to say about it," Cassie said. "I don't remember a whole lot more." Cassie looked at her face in the upper right-hand corner of her screen and it was just a big white blurt.

"I'm sorry, honey," Julia said. Cassie could see a pained expression on her face, her eyes squinted in and her lips scrunched. "The sun was just blaring over you while you were talking. I didn't get much of that. You said something more about the Louvin Brothers' lyrics?"

Cassie peered into the screen and for the life of her she couldn't bring herself to talk music right now. Music was finally out of her life. She was free from that particular striving. She'd said it once and she wasn't going to try to remember again. A green-and-gray box carrying text popped up on her screen and she saw it was from DiceHard—"Totally into Atelier and super interested to hear all about Native Content political division et al. Have a free minute now can talk." Cassie thumbed the green phone icon again.

"Something like that," Cassie said. "That's all there is to say, Julia. I'm sorry about all of this for you, but I don't know how much I can help you."

"Still having a hard time seeing you," Julia said. "I didn't catch—"

"I know you didn't," Cassie said. "I know. Well, maybe we'll do this again sometime but the truth is I gotta go deal with some business shit right now."

Cassie turned her back to the wall again and though she could now see her own image in the corner of the screen, Julia's face had frozen again. The connection was just awful. Who knows if Julia even heard what she'd said or would hear what she said next, so Cassie said, "I'm sorry for you, Julia, and I know your life ended up a mess because of

Mark, but this shit is out of my life now and I want it gone forever good-bye."

Cassie put her thumb to the red button at the bottom center of the screen and cut off the call. She would never know if Julia heard the last of what she said. She took out an American Spirit, lit it up, and called DiceHard so they could talk about the possibility of him joining her in a lucrative new opportunity at the horizontally integrated content-driven web company where she was now, and where she hoped she would be for many of the years ahead, working.

PART TEN

COUNTERPOINT

CHAPTER FORTY-NINE

THERE WAS ONLY ONE THING Julia Brumfeld wanted in the months and years after her son was branded a domestic terrorist, and that was to be left alone. She was too old to look for a job again, and she was collecting Social Security after all, and selling her instruments had brought in more than she ever could've hoped to earn at a job. She stopped contacting her friends and she stopped calling her old friends from growing up and she stopped making trips to Philadelphia to see her extended family. If Julia Brumfeld wanted one thing beyond being left alone in the days following her son's actions, it was not to have to leave her house at all.

And though the one thing Julia wanted was to be left alone, Cal grew quickly and ardently committed to finding some way to get her out of the house. Months passed, and then more months, and Cal wanted to take Julia to the aquarium, out to dinner downtown. He wanted to get in the car or on Amtrak and head up to Philadelphia, to leave the country (which they couldn't really justify with all the legal bills anyway) or to just go out to a movie. He wanted to get her to go shopping for clothes at the Nordstrom's or go shopping for groceries at the Giant or to go just do something. Anything.

She wouldn't.

Above all Cal wanted to take Julia to see the Baltimore Symphony Orchestra. He'd said it for almost a year and she failed to respond just as long. It was the one thing he was consistent on and persistent about. Still she said no, and without the help of hearing aids, it was easy enough for her just to pretend she hadn't heard him offer. It had taken a full week to clean the house from the FBI raid and in all the cleaning she'd not been able to locate her hearing aids. The last thing she wanted to do was go back to Dr. Steinway to get new ones made. She'd make do without them. No matter how vehemently she did not want to go out, it made leaving the house easier when the time came.

First were the looks she got in the Giant when she did finally go out for groceries. People had been telling her about Fresh Direct for years, a service that would deliver your groceries to your house, but if anything Julia was more intimidated by the idea of going onto the Internet to do anything at all. She could hole up for only so long—she could keep from the rest of her daily activities, but she would have to go to the Giant and pick up groceries. When she was accosted in its famously minuscule parking lot—"What's it feel like to be the mother of a terrorist?" the woman was saying and Julia would never know for how long she'd been saying it, didn't hear the woman until she was right up in front of her—she started driving the twenty minutes to Catonsville where, though she might still be recognized, at least it would take people a minute to place her face. Which had been all over CNN, NBC, ABC, CBS, for months after the bombing. An image of their squat brick Pikesville home was seared into cultural memory like OJ's white Bronco, the house in L.A. where the SLA made their final stand, the swastika at the middle of Manson's head. Agoraphobia, a therapist would've diagnosed, if Julia had had the heart to go to a therapist. Until therapists started making house calls, she wasn't interested in therapists.

"I'm sorry, my love, but you've got to get out of the house," Cal told her again and again. He was her opposite—he could hear everything where she could hear nothing. He could hear the clicks of her tongue when she disagreed with him, the whirr of the air-conditioning mid-fall when he felt it was an unreasonable expense to keep the house so cold. But Cal wouldn't be able to truly hear music if it was blaring in his ear. Julia still caught the rhythms of her day, if not their melody, then the cadence that grew more precise and confined the longer she stayed in the house: the ticking in the soles of her feet as the refrigerator made its ice, the liquid r's and n's of the boiler coming on in the basement all winter, the sibilants of the central air-conditioner out back all summer.

But now the beginning of winter was just about here. It had been a year since she'd been out of the house to run basic errands. Finally one night when Cal said, "Let's just go downtown and see the symphony next week, I want to take you, I will not take no for an answer," after a year of refusing, Julia gave in. She didn't know what had changed. Maybe it was the oiliness of her unwashed hair, the creak of her back as she realized she didn't even leave the house anymore. Mostly it was just that she didn't think she could listen to Cal complain anymore. If it would get him to stop asking, she would go to the BSO.

First order of business was that she would, in fact, have to go to the Nordstrom's to get something to wear. She avoided the Towson Town Center where she was certain to run into people she knew and instead made a day of it down in Georgetown. It was only an hour-plus drive down I-95, and she parked on M Street. In the Laura Ashley she found a turquoise printed dress that looked almost like something Stevie Nicks might have worn in the late seventies. She went into the dressing room, where in the mirror, in that small space, she found two things at once: first, she looked a lot older. Not in any particular way—her hair was just more fully straw-colored, her eyes more puffed with nimbussed skin. She came out into the store wearing the new dress before she realized a salesgirl was asking if she needed any help. She found that in fact she didn't. She didn't need help. She still wanted to be left alone. Her whole body felt the vague pain of being in public. But she was happy enough, in fact, at purchasing a new dress, at being out of her house for an entire afternoon without seeing a single person she knew. If anyone on M Street in Georgetown recognized her, she didn't recognize them.

Before getting back in the car for her ride home to Baltimore she walked down to the Dean and Deluca, where she ordered a prosciutto panini and saw a girl who looked exactly like Mark's girlfriend Cassie. Same brown hair, same confident grin. She almost walked up to her but who was she kidding? This wasn't Cassie. Prickles washed over her body. It was as if she was responding to internal stimuli. It was a phrase she hadn't thought of in years and hadn't thought of in relationship to Mark because she didn't allow herself to think about Mark, just allowed her heart now to face northwest to the prison where he was being held, where she and Cal went to visit him for conversations that neither told her anything new about what had made him do what he did nor gave her a sense of how he was doing now. And now that he was in her head again she saw flashes of images she hadn't seen in years— three red streaks on a white tile floor, her bubbe ironing tinfoil—and a new image, the floor of her living room covered in the stuffing from her sofa.

Julia had had her head down on the table in front of her before she realized anyone was even near her. She felt the hand on her shoulder and she sat bolt upright.

"Just seeing if you were okay, ma'am," the man said. He was store security, wore a baggy white shirt. He was a kid of maybe twenty-five.

Julia told him she was fine, she was fine, and she walked back to her car.

When she returned to her house she decided that if she was going to go to the BSO with Cal, first she wanted to do one thing.

She wanted to talk to that Cassie Black.

She knew from what she'd read about Mark that he'd been in love with her still, that people wanted to believe his unrequited love for Cassie had had something to do with all that happened. She didn't know if that was something she could ask.

It took almost the whole rest of the afternoon for Julia to figure out how to use the Google app on her phone. She typed in "Cassie Black" and there was a huge list of women with that name. She knew Cassie had worked at that website, though, and it didn't take her that long to discover a story from AdWeek that said Cassie Black had left Razor-Wire for some other company called Atelier. These companies all had huge websites with easily discoverable e-mail addresses. All you had to do was press your thumb on the address and suddenly you were writing an e-mail. It was almost too easy. Julia wrote Cassie and Cassie wrote her back and the next thing she knew she was pushing a button that said "FaceTime" and there, like the two of them were characters in the fucking *Jetsons*, was Cassie Black's face and her own face, side by side. Julia couldn't see her that well and her face kept freezing, but there was Cassie in her kitchen again, one last time.

Julia asked Cassie a couple of questions about Mark. Cassie told her, in a way, what she wanted to hear—they just played music together, there wasn't much more to know about it. They'd played Louvin Brothers songs, which made Julia's heart leap up in her chest for a second, but she just felt a new jolt seeing Cassie's face. She couldn't hear much of what Cassie was saying, and the sun kept blotting out her face—just a big sharp white glare on her phone. Julia had to look away.

"Well, look, I don't know what I was even calling for," Julia said. "I just left my house for the first time in ages, and I saw a girl who I thought looked like you down in Georgetown, and I thought I'd call."

She looked down at her phone, but there was nothing to see. Cassie's face had frozen like some weird supernova flash on-screen for ten seconds, twenty, and if she was talking, Julia couldn't hear it. She pressed the button on the side of her phone to turn it off. She took the new dress out of her Laura Ashley bag to clip the tags. She'd left her home for an extended period for the first time in a year for something not related to her son's needs, and she was tired, winded even, but tomorrow night she would do it again.

CHAPTER FIFTY

FRIDAY NIGHT ARRIVED as if it had preceded Friday morning. The last humid afternoons of summer had evaporated into fall, and with a low crack Julia could feel in her elbows the thunder dully snapped and the rains came. The sky cleared and the kitchen brightened like an invisible mouth was blowing into the space. The sun was casting thin pink onto the underside of ever whiter clouds, then causing everything to grow a little thin, grainy, brown. By the time Cal arrived home from work Julia was in her new turquoise dress. It was a size smaller than she wore before all that went down—she hadn't been able to eat a full meal for a year. They got into Cal's Audi TT, a purchase he had made two years before their son had been sentenced and their bank accounts run low by lawyers' fees. They made their way down I-83 into the city, forgoing the prettier drive down York Road so they wouldn't miss the opening. Cal hadn't told her what they would be seeing—Dvorak? Beethoven? Bach partitas or solo piano sonatas? Stephen Reich or Rachmaninoff?—and Julia hadn't had it in her to go onto the Internet to find out what it would be. Searching around for Cassie Black had been about the limit of what she could bring herself to do on Google. The BSO no longer advertised in *The Baltimore Sun,* so the information wouldn't be there, either. *The Baltimore Sun* had never been much of a paper, but a person arriving in their house now directly from 1970 wouldn't even recognize it as a newspaper at all, it was so thin. It was more of a pamphlet, a flyer, almost wholly devoid of any real news.

As they turned down Calvert Street and then up Cathedral, the

Meyerhoff arose out of the city streets before them like an orotund ship arising out of disparate waves, a cone of impenetrable sound arising out of silence, one big vibrating B-flat lifting up above the muted tones of the city.

They parked and walked to the building. Inside Julia felt every look at her as if it were a physical touch, like every person she came in proximity to was too close, their gazes like the literal strike of a needle tip against the skin of her arms. That was one of the strangest things about her loneliness—there was no prickle in her cheeks, her face, though to be sure she blushed. But anxiety itself, the pain of being looked at when you didn't want to be looked at, arose as prickles across the tops of her arms, the skin on her raw, pink knuckles. She knew Mark loved a Galway Kinnell book he kept on his shelf, *When One Has Lived a Long Time Alone*, a book federal agents had confiscated when they tore up his room, but that she found in a bookshop in Fells Point months later, one of her few excursions out of the house in those first months after the bombing. She'd read it maybe two dozen times now, had come to know the impressionistic greens and reds of the Klimt detail on its cover. She guessed that the lines that resonated with her most were not the same lines that struck her son, but hers were the opening lines, about not harming so much as a mosquito or a toad. Its tranquil cadences and sense of pacifism, ahimsa, were so precise Julia couldn't help but wonder if her son had ever even read that stanza himself. When she looked around her in their house, in their lawn, on the way to the Catonsville Giant, Julia saw the world as a series of signs Mark had missed, drawing him away from his actions. She hoped to read them where he had failed.

No matter. As she walked across the red velvety carpets of the Meyerhoff, Cal went to check their coats, and she entered the airy white space of the hall as if walking onto a spaceship for abduction. She wore her new turquoise dress but she noticed what at first seemed like a galling lack of formality in everyone else in the place. The last time she and Cal had gone up to Manhattan to the Met she'd been surprised at how few tuxes she saw, at how men now often wore suits to the opera, but this was different. A man with a huge beard passed her in a tie-dye

Grateful Dead shirt from the Lithuanian Olympic Basketball team. She didn't believe the bromides about the other senses growing stronger when one went deaf or blind—that hadn't been her experience—but now she could detect the skunky smell of weed on him. He brushed past her and she almost jumped to get out of his way.

She made her way all the way down to the front row, where Cal had gotten them seats. Three places to her right was a couple as dressed up as she and Cal were, but she looked down to see the man was wearing Birkenstocks. She hadn't seen those sandals in years. They were just so awful even in the right context. Here in the Meyerhoff they were a direct affront to her sensibilities. Had the entire population of Baltimore lost its mind? She could see the spidery hairs atop his big toes and it turned her stomach. His wife was looking right at Julia now, seeing what she was looking at.

"He insisted on wearing them," she mouthed.

Though she hadn't talked to anyone in person other than Cal in months, Julia could tell every word she said just by looking at her lips. Still she didn't smile fast enough. The woman's face grew pinched, chastened. She looked away.

Cal arrived back at their seats as the house lights flashed, signaling the symphony was about to begin.

"What on earth is everyone in this place wearing," Julia said to him. "Has the whole world gone batshit crazy?"

He whispered into her ear in his lowest bass tone: "You're in for a surprise, and a treat."

Members of the orchestra took their seats onstage. The room filled with the cacophony of strings warming up and being tuned. To Julia it was a mash of sound and the lightest touch projecting onto her skin. But they were sitting so close she could see as the dust of rosin lifted off the bows of the violins. She could feel the low vibrations of the cellos and basses projecting slow and wavy into the crowd on the balls of her feet. The conductor came out onstage. He, too, was wearing a tie-dye T-shirt along with his traditional tuxedo pants. Now it truly felt to Julia as if she was going crazy—in the year she'd been holed up in the house had everyone lost their sartorial minds? She turned to her husband.

"The Dead," Cal whispered. The strings started in, violins and violas bowing slow and wide from their elbows. The upper registers were a thin syrup too far above her range but after thirty long seconds or so Julia heard, felt, the familiar bassline. Bump-dah, bumba-dah-bum-dah-bum. Bump-dah, bumba-dah-bum-dah-bum.

They were playing "Dark Star."

Of all things, Cal had taken her to the Meyerhoff to see the Baltimore Symphony Orchestra play Grateful Dead covers.

Julia drew her right arm in tight to her side so it would not be touching Cal's. This was at once the worst and the best gift she could have been given. The best because she was out of her house on a Friday night in Baltimore, because she was sitting in a room full of people and not out on an errand and not being forced to think about her son, and she was not feeling the agoraphobia she'd always felt. But it was the worst because she could not think of a cultural event she would rather see less. A symphonic adaptation of the Dead! It was the least revolutionary thing she could imagine. Taking the wild sound out of the wild and trapping it in this spaceship, in this cage—one of her favorite novels of the early seventies referred to museums as "centers of art detention." Here she was in a center of sound detention. A place where music went to live out its dying days.

"Dark Star" drew into a crescendo she could feel on her skin, the tenor notes like pinpricks all up and down her skin, and she looked behind her. In rows all the way to the back of the Meyerhoff old people—old people! Not aging parents, not youthful middle-agers but old people, people with liver spots on their arms and far more salt than pepper in their hair and their aging beards—bobbed their heads and turned and smiled at each other. Could she give in to the pleasure of it? Could she let Cal have the ease he needed?

For the next couple of songs she did her best. She looked at the woodwinds as they puffed their cheeks out, watched as the indifferent basses took a moment to turn pages and rest their bulging forearms. She tried to forget that they were Grateful Dead covers being played and just allow it to be elemental. Broken down into their component parts these songs were just notes and chords coming together to make a wall of sounds that projected out from the stage and onto her body and for a moment Julia was feeling it, she was moving in time with it, she was overwhelmed by the bass she felt humming in her feet so that she took off her shoes and let the balls of her bare feet rest on the cool floor of the symphony hall and buzz up into her body, and something quieted in her for the first time in as long as she could remember. There was a peace and even an elation that surpassed anything she'd felt when she was down on M Street earlier that week. She couldn't identify it, couldn't place it until she realized what it was: she was not thinking about Mark. She was not fretting, she was not worrying. She was not thinking she saw Cassie Black in a Dean and DeLuca's. She was in an open space, in public, not thinking about her son. She'd returned to the inexorable flow of time.

She turned to Cal and he was bobbing his head now and he turned to her and he mouthed, "'Scarlet Begonias'!" The song finished and it was quiet in the hall. She could not hear the crinkling of programs and the low hushed chatter of everyone in the room but she gave herself over to it, she awaited the next song.

The violins picked up their bows and the tie-dye-T-shirted conductor lifted his arms, elbows strung up as if marionetted from the ceiling high above them.

The basses and cellos were quiet and the violins bowed their melodies and Julia listened harder than she'd listened in months, in years, and all at once as they played it came over her what they were playing.

She could hear the melody in her head when the chorus hit and the bass started in on its pizzicato and then the words were in her head. Lyrics. She knew them in her heart before they materialized in her mind: a narrator's lamentation at turning twenty-one in prison, serving the start of a life sentence—and acknowledging all along that his mother had pled with him to do better, to get right. "Mama Tried." Of all the hundreds of songs the Dead had covered in their career, here it was. It was symphonic, toothless, and interpreted by the BSO, but undeniably they were playing Merle Haggard's "Mama Tried."

In her head she could hear Bob Weir singing it. She looked at Cal. She could see he didn't know what song it was. He was wholly ignorant of what was happening in her mind, what she knew. He bobbed his head like the rest, all around him, this room full of people who were focused on the music and were not focused on her, this room full of not aging hippies but old people, people who had decades before fought their fights and strove their striving and now were in a position to sit in a concert hall on a Friday night in Baltimore and let the teeth be extracted from the music that mattered to them most, the life be extracted from them. Just like the music, they were all going to die one day and be removed from the inexorable stream of time, and she was, too, they were sitting in that hall, many of them retired, at rest, and she figured while she sat there in the Meyerhoff Hall, at rest, too, her husband next to her and her son having been out of her head if only for a moment, in the time they had left they might as well enjoy it.

ACKNOWLEDGMENTS

How lucky to work with some of the finest people in letters. Brettne Bloom is the best agent in the land. She provided invaluable reads over years. George Witte is the most thoughtful, insightful editor a writer could dream up, along with Dori Weintraub and Sara Thwaite.

My colleagues and brilliant students at Bryn Mawr College have provided support and a fertile environment for writing. The folks at the Jewish Book Council have given and given and given. Laura Farmer, Miciah Bay Gault, Lauren Goodwin Slaughter, and Eric Rosenblum gave me useful reads, as ever. And of course none of it without all the support from my wonderful wife, Erin Torday.